For
Dad & Papa.

Shan Crav
"2017"

NIVEUS

The Wintergrave Chronicles
(Book Three)

A Novel By

Sharon Cramer

Publisher's Note:

This is a work of fiction. All names, characters, places and events are the work of the author's imagination. Any resemblance to real persons, places, or events is entirely coincidental.

Author's Note:

The backdrop for this story is fourteenth century Europe. However, I have interpreted within this period events, timelines, characteristics, and people—both fictional and real—in a loose manner that may not coincide with the actual historical course of events. I have done this solely for literary embellishment. It is my greatest wish that the reader would enjoy simple and gratuitous entertainment of this piece of historic fantasy.

NIVEUS

PROLOGUE

The Wintergrave Dynasty

The girl stood at the edge of the woods.

A mist rolled from the darkness of the forest only a short way into the small meadow before stopping as though deciding this was not the place to be. It paused, folded, and billowed softly back upon itself, gathering around the bare ankles and feet of the silent girl.

She glanced down at her gown. It clung to her thin frame, damp from her walk through the tall grass on the way to the forest. Steam rose softly from her shoulders, the only indication that she was truly human—not a ghost passing through—and the quarter moon gave her figure the faintest of shadows as she paused, still as stone in the last moments of night.

The girl gazed into the woods, her rose-colored eyes large and sleepy. Everything seemed reflected in them; it was the effect they always had on her surroundings. Her hair, white as the snows that would soon come to the realm, hung in knotted tendrils down her back, nearly to her waist.

Pale as a dying star, she moved like one—slow, purposeful, denying inevitability with a fire that raged silently within her heart. No one knew of this fire, for it had never been summoned or released, had never needed to be.

Niveus was...perfectly peculiar.

As the woods beckoned with open maw, begging to swallow her up, she glanced backward over her shoulder at the tiny village and the castle with its walls rising beyond their simple rooftops like a benevolent keeper. A smile tugged gently at her lips but, as it always seemed to be, was never quite born.

Then, Niveus followed that which drew her and slipped, in the earliest hour of dawn, into the reaching arms of the woods and the wild darkness beyond.

CHAPTER ONE

Risen rolled over in bed, drawn from the edge of a happy dream. He had been holding Sylvie in his arms, had kissed her—meant to make love to her—when something stirred him abruptly from his slumber.

As wakefulness pushed into his senses and Sylvie's memory waned, the young man pushed disappointment from his heart and rolled over with a sigh. Pulling the blanket over his hips, he allowed his arousal to die and squinted lazily at his bedroom window.

His beloved wife was gone nearly six years now, long enough that he welcomed her memory without nearly so much of the pain. He was twelve when they married and scarcely thirteen when she died. Now, Risen was eighteen.

The light that fell through the castle window was an uncertain one, cast by a waning quarter moon. Sylvie drifted farther from his thoughts, and he wondered if it was still the middle of the night. Then, he decided morning was indeed on the rise, and a pressing sense of responsibility washed over him.

Ravan and Nicolette were gone from the realm with matters of importance, and their son was left in charge. It was the first time Risen was to govern Wintergrave Dynasty alone.

He swung his bare legs over the edge of the bed and rubbed the sleep from his eyes, stretching liberally before donning his trousers and shift. His long frame was beautiful in the feeble light, black hair hanging freely down his back. Risen looked very much like his father. He *was* very much like his father but also…very much not.

Once dressed, the next thing the young heir to the dynasty reached for was his knife—*Monster-Killer*. The last hand that to rest upon the tragic blade had been that of his long-lost bride. Sylvie had killed a demon with it in a faraway land. Since then, Risen had allowed no other hand to touch the blade.

Out of habit, his palm lingered on the smooth handle of the knife before he holstered it and slipped it into his boot, strapped to his leg. Once it was hidden away, he snatched up his coat and stepped from his room to greet the day.

His personal guard sat just outside, hands resting casually upon the hilt of a battle sword. The man yawned and used his planted sword to push himself lazily to his feet.

"Good day, my lord. You've rested well?" Without waiting for an answer, he added, "I'll see to the fire before I change the watch."

"Good morning." Risen's dark brown eyes shone warmly against his handsome face, and he smiled easily. "Yes, it *is* cold enough for a fire this morning, isn't it?" He rubbed his hands together to chase the chill from them, and slipped into his long-coat.

"And what have you on your schedule today?" the older man wondered aloud.

"A trip to the village to check the silos for next winter. I don't want Father and Mother to worry about it when they return."

The soldier replied, "Lord Ravan will be proud of you as will Lady Nicolette. You've taken great care of the realm in their absence."

Risen rested a hand on the guard's shoulder. "Wintergrave takes good care of me." He patted the man warmly before walking alone down the long hall, taking the staircase two steps at a time as he circled to a floor below— the floor on which his sister slept. Reaching the landing, it was only then that his smile fell from his face.

There, in front of Niveus' room, sat a guard hunched over as though deeply asleep. And it was not the first time a guard had reposed in such a fashion outside of her door.

Risen hurried to the man, knelt, and carefully lifted his chin. He knew instantly that this was no ordinary sleep, and he shook the man earnestly.

"Moulin, Moulin, wake up," Risen called urgently to his old friend, but the man neither spoke nor moved—his slumber was that sound.

Leaving Moulin to his enchantment, Risen flung open Niveus' door, knowing her room would be vacant even before he witnessed it. As he feared, and just as before, there were her shoes, left on the floor beside her bed, and her coat still on the hook.

He charged out and down the long, spiraling flight of stairs to the door that exited the east side of the castle. As he sprinted across the expanse to the stables, frozen leaves cracked and kicked up from under his feet, and his breath blew frosty in the crisp autumn air.

Leon saw his approach and was pulling Alerion from his stall just as Risen arrived. "She's gone again?" His expression betrayed his worry. "How? I don't see how! The sentries are posted at all battlements and...and..." The stablemaster trailed off, unable to offer explanation.

Risen only nodded. There was nothing he could say, for he was at as much of a loss for explanation as Leon was. He helped his friend tack up the stallion and in moments was mounted and off, galloping toward the front castle gates. The guards stationed there exchanged worried looks as he slid the horse to a stop in front of them.

"How?" was all one of them asked.

Risen shook his head. He had no good explanation for how Niveus had once more escaped the castle walls, nor was he prepared to waste time discussing it. Charging through the barely opened portcullis, he turned the steed south toward the nearest bank of forest that was only barely visible through the thick morning fog.

The edge of the woods was still almost a mile away, and he gave the horse its head, allowing it to thunder across the field toward a setting crescent moon. As they approached the edge of the dark forest, Risen slowed, jogging the stallion in a wide zig-zag until he found what he was looking for—the soft trail left by his sister as she had walked along, her nightgown pulling the dew from the tall blades of grass.

Here. Here is where she went in, he thought as he paused, gazing into the dark expanse of the forest. The sun wasn't even on the horizon yet, and night creatures whistled and cawed from beyond the edge of the woodland realm.

Urging the horse forward, he stepped into the forbidding beyond and rode slowly, picking his way carefully. It wasn't long before his sight adjusted somewhat to the darkened interior of the forest, and he glanced overhead, hoping he might see the lightening sky above. It was not to be, however. The canopy forbade it, holding tight to its secrets. Risen could not help but believe she would want it this way.

Onward he searched, nearly three miles, backtracking several times as he repeatedly lost Niveus' trail and struggled to pick it up again. Her footstep was so soft upon the forest floor that he, trained by the best there was, had once accused her of being the most difficult person he had ever tracked.

She had studied him with what he thought was patient disappointment. "Then stop *tracking* me. Find me with your heart instead. You *know* you can." That was Niveus to the core.

"Don't say things like that," he insisted.

"Not to anyone? Or just not to you?" She seemed disappointed in him.

"All right," he admitted. "Say it to me if you will, but remember, it's dangerous to speak of such things to others, except to Mother and Father."

"Because they will think me insane." It was not a question.

This had frustrated Risen completely. It was what everyone said, what the townspeople and even those who lived closest to her in the castle whispered, that Niveus was touched by great forces from the beyond—forces others could not comprehend and some even feared.

For the longest time, he tried to convince himself this was not the case; that his sister was simply a mystery, perhaps difficult to understand but sane as the rest of them. Ultimately, Risen silently admitted this was not the truth after all. He knew his sister was unusual beyond reason, even more so than Nicolette, and though he was closer to Niveus than anyone, on days like today he felt miles removed from truly knowing her.

Riding quietly through the woods, he recalled her gentle advice and struggled to still his mind and open up his heart to the essence of her presence. He *had* once or twice felt that which she spoke of, just briefly enough, pulling at the core of his being like a soft, guiding thread. But the voice had only been a vague whisper, and it simply made him doubt himself more. Frustrated that he had not been able to develop the connection, he ceased trying.

Even so, this morning he could not help but feel there was something else drawing him along, something more than the nearly nonexistent tracks his sister left behind.

Then, he heard it before he saw it...

* * *

Niveus sat in the middle of the small opening, arms around a newborn fawn. It was tiny, not even a day old. The mother doe was nowhere to be seen, and the baby deer lay comfortably on Niveus' lap, its soft chin resting on the thin arm that wrapped around it. It was beauty of another sort, the ethereal girl with the tender creature settled so delicately in her grasp.

Around the lovely pair circled...wolves.

Bare feet tucked beneath her, Niveus hugged the tiny fawn more tightly and spoke to it in whispers, her voice queerly singsong as she murmured into the quivering ear of the infant deer. The baby's eyes were like chocolate orbs, enormous and damp, and its ears flickered back and forth, tracking the encouraging words of its protector.

All the while, the wolves circled with predator stares and lips curled back in wicked anticipation. There was no yipping or snarling. Instead, the sounds that came forth from the advancing pack emerged from deep within, a throaty growl of expectation, a thirst for impending murder.

But the wolves hesitated as they neared, unsure of themselves. Never before had they encountered prey…like this one.

Niveus lifted a pale hand, her muted eyes flashing, looking not at the wolves but at the small, clear opening of sky above. Gazing still at the heavens, she dropped her hand and swept it in a loose arc around the fawn and then toward the nearest pair of advancing wolves.

One of them yowled and leapt back. Its companion flattened its ears and snarled, the growl rumbling forth in short snorts of aggravation. But, neither did this beast advance beyond its sulking comrade.

Niveus' free arm swung first around the fawn again then loosely behind her shoulder. Two more wolves yelped their frustration and retreated back into the darkened cover of the trees.

Before long, a single wolf—the alpha male of the group and bigger than the others—became suddenly bolder as it first slunk and then trotted across the small meadow.

Niveus turned and stared at the beast as it charged, breaking into a gallop as it lunged, leaping through the air…at her. She uttered something quite foreign to the human ear as the wolf soared.

Mid-leap, the creature bellowed—an awful, shrieking sound—and contorted as it crashed to the ground. Whether the wolf cried out from Niveus' words or from the arrow that penetrated it just behind its shoulder would never be known.

The beast fell at her feet…dead.

The fawn kicked weakly, eyes enormous with fear, but calmed just as swiftly beneath the girl's touch. A second wolf fell to the command of another arrow, and the remaining pack, confused and smelling the blood of their fallen leader, gathered farther away. They snapped at each other, their maws dripping with anticipation, but they had lost their resolve and circled weakly. Their heads shot up in alarm when they heard the swiftly advancing horse, and finally they scattered, disappearing into the woods.

Risen rode into the tiny meadow, bow in hand, the stallion prancing and snorting as it eyed the two dead wolves that lay near Niveus' feet.

"Why?" Risen yelled his frustration as he swung from the horse.

Striding over to Niveus, he snatched her up easily by one arm. The fawn struggled weakly in her grasp as she yanked her arm free of Risen, clutching the baby all the while firmly to her chest.

"Do not speak to me with such a tone, brother! You found me because I *allowed* it, and for no other reason. Do you understand?" She fixed her gaze upon him. "Vent your frustrations in such a way to me again, and you will find me nevermore," Niveus cautioned in a low voice, her eyes flashing dark as old blood.

She might appear small and frail alongside her brother—son of the most legendary mercenary ever—but she was more defiant than anyone Risen believed he had ever known. He drew up short, not sure what she meant, and wrapped both arms around her. The fawn hugged snugly between, kicked its thready legs weakly.

"Niveus," he cried, "don't you understand? I *love* you. I cannot bear to lose you." He held her at arm's length, searching her face. "I would fall on a blade for you, but if you do not allow me, I may not always be there to protect you from the wolves."

She pushed away from her brother and cradled the fawn like a baby, glancing calmly from him to the deer and back.

"There are more wolves than you can ever battle, brother. But you will never lose me, not unless you choose to." Risen swallowed deeply when she added, "The day will come when you must let me deal with the wolves as I must...and let me fall if I will."

"That day will *never* come," Risen insisted and moved to lift her onto the horse. As Niveus slid to her spot behind the saddle, her expression was enough to tell him...he was wrong.

* * *

She sat behind Risen, arms wrapped loosely around his waist. In his lap he cradled the fawn as the horse picked its way back through the woods into the growing light of day. Behind them dragged the alpha wolf, a rope entwined through and around its jaws, tying its massive maw shut.

The carcass was enormous and slipped as it dragged along the forest floor behind the horse. Its pelt would be significant and would serve where it might. Risen intended to use it on the floor of his sister's room since she seemed so determined to walk about barefoot even on the coldest of days. *Perhaps*, he thought to himself, *it will also remind her of the perils that lay beyond the castle walls.* Then he thought, *no...it won't.*

"You cannot save every fallen creature of the forest." The echo of Risen's voice in the forest was all he heard in return. "Its mother abandoned it because it was born too late. Winter is nearly upon us, and the fawn will not survive. It is as God wished it to be."

Again, Niveus said nothing, but he felt her gaze pressing softly between his shoulder blades and looked back at her. She rested her chin on his shoulder, their faces but inches apart.

"Very well," he admitted wryly, "it *will* survive, but only because you feed it goat's milk."

He glanced down at the beautiful fawn and knew in reality that it would be the second tame deer to cavort about the castle grounds, rescued from the jaws of death by his sister's nighttime ventures into the forest.

Niveus' pink eyes darkened to nearly rose, and she tipped her head elegantly to the side. "You could help me feed it, brother."

It was as near to teasing him as she would ever come, and his heart lightened for it. Risen chuckled. "I'll help you feed it until it is big enough to feed *us*."

Her expression remained unchanged, but that didn't matter. Risen knew Niveus—knew her queer demeanor better than anyone else did. And...he loved her for it.

CHAPTER TWO

Klarin's Dynasty

The old gelding groaned, buckled, and dropped to its knees, rolling heavily onto its side. Its cataract-ridden eyes glazed over as it contemplated its misery, finally come after twenty-eight years in this world. The dozing stable boy heard the old horse fall and snapped awake, running first to the stall then to the mansion.

Crashing through the front doorway, the boy called, "Master Viktar! Master Viktar! The time has come!"

Viktar appeared at the top of the elegant, grand stairway with two heavy blankets and scaled the steps two at a time, fearless of risk to himself. Dashing to the front door, he snagged an overcoat on his way out, grabbing the lantern from the boy as he ran. Sprinting the distance across the courtyard, he knew exactly where he must go and ran down the long alleyway of the stables, skidding to a stop at the last, biggest box stall.

He heard the groans of the old horse before he even entered. Hanging the lantern outside the stall so that the light would not offend the beast, he eased the stable door open and whispered into the subdued darkness.

"I've come, old boy. I am here."

The horse, upon hearing the man's voice, groaned again and thrashed its legs about as though it intended to stand. Deciding otherwise, it flopped back onto its side, its great head thudding into the straw as it did.

"Ah, there, there, good fellow. Let's just have a rest now, shall we?"

Viktar reached a hand for the animal's shoulder as he knelt, moving up close so he could stroke its big head. With one hand scratching him beneath the mane, just where he liked it best, Viktar stroked the animal's cheek with the other, sweeping his palm over and around the horse's eye.

This was familiar to the beast and, labored as its breathing was, it calmed under Viktar's touch. Next, the young man spread both heavy blankets on the horse and sat again, taking the creature's head into his lap.

"We've been friends for such a long time." Viktar's voice carried a sweet cheerfulness he did not feel. "Father gave you to me as a birthday gift, the day I was born. Remember? You were eight years old. Almost before I could walk, Father would take me for rides on you."

He swept his hand around the old horse's eye again and straightened its forelock, as he had done so many times before. The demeanor of the animal's expression calmed even more and it blinked sleepily.

"Ah, what grand days those were. You and me, flying across the countryside."

His old horse snorted weakly and closed its eyes.

"Remember the wolves? I was ten when they set upon us. Oh, how fast you ran, faster than anything. They couldn't catch us, try as they might...could they? The wind could not have caught us that day—how fleet you were." The soft smile fell from Viktar's mouth, and he bit his lip to stop the sad trembling.

There is courage born of lack of option, and then there is another courage—one born of love. The young man, cradling his best friend in his arms, now summoned that sort of courage as he steeled himself to do what he must.

"Where you go, the sun is always warm on your back," Viktar murmured, the first two fingers of his right hand locating the carotid pulse along his horse's long throat.

"The pastures are always green, and the mares are kind, not standoffish."

He drew the stiletto blade from his jacket's inside pocket.

"And all you must do is romp and play, and..."

He slipped the stiletto blade upward in one swift motion. The horse scarcely moved at all, the fine nick was so precise. "...wait for me there."

The warm spurt of blood ran over the blade, down the horse's neck and onto Viktar's knee before collecting in a slowly expanding, sticky pool on the floor. Eyes still closed, the old beast licked its lips and rested, ears twitching back and forth, content to hear the words its friend wished to share.

Viktar hummed softly, just as he had many times as they had ridden across the fields and streams, through the forests, from sunup to sundown. It had been a wonderful journey as the boy stepped from childhood to manhood. And now they set upon one last journey together, a journey from which only one would return.

The minutes turned into nearly a half-hour as the horse bled out. Finally, the animal gave one last, shallow breath, and its tongue lolled from the side of its mouth.

Quite damp from the blood and stiff from sitting still in the cold for so long, Viktar leaned over his horse, hugging it for another good while as he murmured a final goodbye.

"I will see you there," he whispered. "Just wait for me...on the other side."

Finally, Viktar sadly drew himself from the stall, extinguished the lantern, and walked up the long, darkened aisle of the stable. The other horses were strangely quiet, watching with big, liquid eyes as the man left their dead comrade.

Just outside the large, double doors, the stable boy lingered, head hung as though unable to face his master. "I'm sorry," the boy mumbled. "'Twas a good horse."

Viktar halted, his back to the boy. "He was a *friend*, fine as they come," he said more harshly than he meant to. The cold night drew a shiver from him, and he cleared the thick sorrow from his throat. "Tomorrow, see to it that he is buried...down the meadow, by the black walnut tree. And...mark the grave."

The young man strode back up the hillside and did not see how the boy swiped tears from his eyes.

CHAPTER THREE

Red Robes

Malik's pale eyes betrayed nothing as he stood beside his nervous bride. Only the scarce crease of a smile foretold his grand anticipation for what was to come.

Her gown was red—a vivid, bright red. He had insisted on it, and it stirred in him something very primal. He shifted, aroused by the circumstances of it all, and pressed his threatening erection away with the heel of his hand, turning to his side so that none may notice, for he was never that bold.

It was a sodden day; they were always sodden anymore, and he gazed long overhead, so long that the priest cleared his throat. When Malik's attention was drawn to the small gathering of people, with their cautiously expectant faces, most of them looked away.

He laughed inwardly. If they had been able to see into his heart, if they could see past the mounting excitement that filled every ounce of his being, they would have seen how relieved he was to finally stand upon these hallowed stones.

Perhaps, eventually, they would understand. Today would open a new door. It would be official, and tomorrow would hold wondrous opportunity for him and all of Red Robes! How could they begrudge him that? And yet they did. He could see it—see the judgment on their stupid faces. But that didn't matter, for they weren't like him. They held no *power*.

Now…he looked only at Roza, at her face—at how it betrayed how courageously she intended to step from one existence to the next. This was so like her and why everyone in the realm loved her so.

She was nearly twenty years younger than he. Oh, and she *was* beautiful, her auburn hair pulled so carefully off to one side in anticipation of the day.

Her creamy, ivory skin blushed beautifully in the cool, damp air. She too looked long at the weeping sky, her lovely mouth set grimly, firmly closed.

All the words were spoken, the etiquette followed explicitly. God had been implored, disgrace vanquished, and all that was left to do was consummate the deed. Roza trembled as the moment of ritual arrived. Malik smiled. The others could not see it, but *he* could, and it thrilled him.

The wind moaned, a cold, lonely lament as it swept past the little stone sanctuary and across the frozen land.

"Here." Malik pointed to the flat pavers at his feet and motioned for her.

Roza turned slowly to face him and nodded. Stepping closer, it seemed she might faint, and two men helped her daintily to her knees, directly in front of Malik, her face but inches from his groin.

Malik smiled again, stroking her hair. "You know how much I love you," he murmured to his bride.

She only dropped her head, unable to meet his gaze. He softly, tenderly, rested the palm of his hand on the back of her head and traced a finger along the back of her neck and across her jaw.

All the while, Roza whispered a prayer.

A single muted sob escaped someone's lips in the small crowd.

Finally, Malik drew his hand from her and stepped back. "It is done," he commanded. Then…

…the executioner's blade fell.

* * *

Malik sat on a massive, ornate chair—his imaginary throne—with restless contempt. He was ruler of a sizable realm but king to none, and this thought was too bitter to swallow, so he drank another swig of ale instead. It was no secret he had become lord of his realm through brutal acquisition of the land. There was scarcely a furlong that was not marked with the blood of a good man, and now the realm was called Red Robes.

The name was first given the land by the peasants who lived there, for it was to them as though living beneath a cloak stained of blood. When Malik heard the peasants' appointed name for his dynasty, he was not angry. On the contrary, it fed something within him that thirsted for just that.

Recently, he struggled to gain appointment into the Hanseatic League. It was a maneuver to gain recognition, for Malik had every intention of pursuing a greater power, perhaps even that of Emperor. But he was ill-respected, and had been called to order by the Church. They demanded he bring matters of the realm more to order.

There were several things he truly despised, and this was one—that there should be someone, or something, of greater power than he and that he must yield to that greater power. Malik was impatient. He hated the English, despised the Emperor, and prayed to whatever god might listen to grant him even greater power so that *all* of their blood should stain the robes of his realm. He would not be happy until there was a river of it, and perhaps not happy even then.

But the gods had leant a deaf ear lately, and Malik was convinced the only god that might grant fulfillment of his greatest lust was…himself.

Winter was fast approaching, and his temper shortened along with the days. The Emperor and Throne had both placed him under increasing pressure to produce an heir or…arrange for one. The Church had a nasty way of sticking its fingers where Malik resented them most, and he wanted—more than anything—to sever them.

The servant held up the basin of warm water again, and he dipped the cloth twice before dabbing at the stain on his gown. He had stood too close this time, but he *liked* to stand close and, consequently, Roza's blood had spattered on him. Now, it just seemed too much effort to change before his sister arrived for the audience. Damn her to hell anyway! Inconveniencing him on *this*, of all days, taking nearly all the joy out of it.

Klarin was fast approaching, the sentries had announced, and would be intruding into the great hall and his unhappy world before the afternoon was up. He had been notified of her impending arrival right at the culmination of the beheading, and Malik was in a foul temper because of the poor timing. He would much have preferred to savor the deed and now felt the desire to satisfy *other* needs because of it.

Slurping his ale, he scowled and slopped the soiled rag through the basin one last time. He was not only aging, but was without a son. This was no fault of his, he believed—that he had no heir. It was certainly not for lack of trying or for *them* dying.

But God had been unwilling to extend compassion to his plight. Holy men had prayed for many hours, per his orders. The fools had studied their folded hands for days as they knelt upon the stone floors, and all on his behalf. But the Almighty had never lifted the curse, never heard their pleas. And he *hated* God for it. God be damned. He had no use for the useless.

Neither had Malik's closest advisors been able to identify the cause of the curse. Taking great cares to do exactly as they bid him, he had reverted to pagan rituals to try to solve his dilemma.

First, he anointed himself, hung the herbs where he should, killed in order a kid goat, a calf, and then, out of his own misguided rage…several of his brides—the last one, Roza.

A dog, enormous, boxy, and vulgar, sat at Malik's side. It had soulless eyes, abnormally small ears that pointed stiffly up, and an eternally wicked smile, except when it snarled and snapped, which was often.

The dog lapped up the tepid, pink water in the wash basin. "Leave it!" Malik commanded, suddenly preoccupied with the water. No amount of blood had appeased God…*or* the pagan gods. Nothing would bring fertility to his loins, and the thought of another taking control of his realm infuriated him to the depths of his soul.

And now his sister was coming to see him—she and that miserable son of hers. The Church and King had grown impatient with him and declared it would be so, that his nephew would take his place as head of the realm upon his demise. His region was considered too volatile to risk falling outside the grasp of the Holy Roman Empire.

It was, to the powers that be, a terminal issue, and the pronouncement was sealed with the King's blessing. In preparation, it was determined that Malik was to take his sister's son as his own heir and prepare him for the inevitable—rule of his dynasty. The thought was putrid on his tongue, and he spat it back at the Empire. It further enraged him that, as much as he despised the notion of a *nephew* heir, he feared war with the King even more.

War in itself did not bother him, not at all. With Bora Vachir at his side, there was no conflict he wouldn't enter willfully, even happily, for he loved a good skirmish. But, he feared defeat and knew that, should he go head to head with the crown, he would be trounced thoroughly.

Malik seethed. He could tolerate his sister, barely, even begrudgingly admired her strength at commanding her own realm without a husband. She had refused to remarry after her husband's untimely death, had instead fortified her realm without someone beside her until it was nearly as strong as Malik's. She had done it despite strong opposition, making shrewd calculations along the way.

He resented her power a small bit, but resented greatly that *others* respected her. It made his life…complicated. Furthermore, her son would be heir to her lands, made even stronger when he stood on Malik's grave and took Red Robes as well.

With this thought, Malik's lips separated in a snarl. He held no fondness toward the boy. Viktar was soft-spoken and sincere; weaker, he thought, even than a woman, and these were traits Malik believed to be character flaws.

How was the boy expected to inherit the realm? How would such a gentle heart rule in such treacherous times as these? Would he be capable of putting his own wife to the butcher's block if she failed to produce an heir? Of course he wouldn't!

No—it made no good sense to Malik what the Church and King believed reasonable, and after he was dead and gone, he told himself it would make no difference what chaos might ensue in his stead. And because he hated the idea more than he could bear to admit, he had secretly decided that if he could not live forever, he would rather burn it all to the ground. Let the black ash of war tarnish Red Robes and mark its final chapter. It would be fitting, he thought— a perfect end to his life and legacy.

"Get me Aya! I wish to have her anoint my feet!" He slapped the washcloth back into the basin of water, and a servant scurried from the great hall.

Aya was one of Malik's only true weaknesses. She was beautiful, brown and lithe, and had scarcely aged as the years crept cruelly by. Now in her mid-thirties, she had belonged to him for nearly twenty years, taken in a raid when she was scarcely thirteen by his closest ally and friend, Bora Vachir.

Bora, a Turkish Mongol, was a vicious warrior and had been ruthless during the great Timur's capture of Damascus. Killing many innocents, he also took slaves—amongst them the peasant girl. Bora brought several much-appreciated things to his new friend's esteem—a keen appreciation for good swordsmanship, an appreciation for war, and the slave girl, Aya.

Vachir gave the girl to Malik as a gift, and seeing the surprised expression on his face, had insisted he take the girl in front of him.

"I cannot," Malik refused, intimidated by Bora's insistence.

But his friend would not be denied. He cleverly plied Malik with enough wine that, eventually, the Prussian ruler stumbled to the cell and, with Vachir cheering him on, raped the girl. Aya scarcely cried out as she endured Malik's fumbling efforts. But then...Bora raped her, more brutally, and the last thing Malik heard as they left the cell was the whimpering of the chained girl.

The next day, something drew Malik back to the hollow cell. As the girl lifted her head in sad expectation, there was just something about her. He unchained Aya, dragged her from the dungeon, and commanded she serve him for all time. Malik considered his obsessions very gravely and was comfortable in his cruelty toward her, only...she mustn't die. He also forbade Bora from ever again touching her.

Now, as Malik slouched deeper into the massive throne chair, the scowl on his face lifted when the Syrian slave entered.

Aya was small and meek like a fawn. For many years she had endured this grave ruler, and his joy at casting his unpredictable rage upon her was the greater reason for calling her to his side, even more than his lust.

Aya stared only at her feet as she approached, wearing traditional Turkish clothing—a bell-shaped gown that was cinched tight and plunging through the torso. Her hair was intricately braided and gathered up beneath a silken head-dress. She was adorned with jeweled chokers and rings, not because she wished it so but because *he* did. Across her cheek was a scar, perfectly shaped like a sickle. He had marred her beauty that one day and had at first regretted it. But now he saw it as part of her—the smooth keloid a tawny, grisly grey— a sad crescent moon just below her left eye.

Carrying a small ceramic bowl and a flask of oil, Aya clutched it to her chest, cowering as the terrible dog hit the end of its chain, froth slinging from its awful, gnashing teeth.

"Take Kobal away!" Malik ordered, meaning the dog, and two guards struggled to drag the hell-hound from the room.

Aya, trembling, watched until the beast was gone before bowing deeply at the foot of the Prussian lord. The guards standing on either side of Malik, as though on cue, hastily departed, leaving Malik alone with the girl as she knelt before him, in front of his knees. He groaned as she slipped a shoe and stocking from one foot and passed her warm, brown fingers over his sallow skin.

Pouring the oil into the bowl of steaming water, she dipped both hands beneath the surface to warm and cover them with the floating oil. Malik sighed heavily as she wrapped her hands around a foot, kneading it expertly as she massaged the weariness from it. It was tiresome business—that of beheading wives—and Malik relaxed visibly.

Closing his eyes, he leaned back as Aya massaged first one and then the other foot. His face softened as she worked, and he was suddenly surprised when she appeared to be done, wrapping his feet in warm towels to dry them. She started to rise, but he planted a meaty paw heavily on top of her head.

He chuckled, "No, Aya. You are not finished…yet."

He folded his arms across his chest and spread his knees as he felt his erection swell.

The slave girl's expression held an eternal sorrow, one that she had known longer than she had not, born of many years, but Aya said nothing as she gently lifted the heavy robes to expose her master's groin.

Inching forward on her knees, she loosed his trousers, freeing his ruddy penis as she had done so many times before. He strongly preferred she not touch him with her hands, and so, obediently, she placed her palms on his bare thighs and closed her eyes as she leaned in, mouth open.

Just then, a herald slammed into the great hall and Malik jerked his robes to cover himself. Unlike Bora Vachir, he did not have the courage to satisfy himself while others watched, at least not unless he was drunk.

Aya fell away at the intrusion, scrambling backwards, still on her knees. She hesitated as though uncertain whether to first snatch up the bowl and oil or to replace Malik's stockings and shoes.

He kicked at her with his bare feet and snarled, "Be gone!"

The herald was scarcely in the room, sputtering his apologies, when he was shoved aside by a middle-aged woman dressed in noble finery.

"Stop sulking," Klarin said flatly from the distance. "There is nothing to be accomplished by it, and its effect is lost on me. You know that."

Malik's sister strode confidently down the long entryway into the castle hall. She was correct on this count. Malik knew his foul mood was lost on her, always had been. "I will be ruler," he had once challenged her as a ten-year-old, "and you will bow to me!"

"I will be queen above you, and you will never rule me," the twelve-year-old-girl had replied before shoving him hard to the ground. She was the only one ever possessed of the courage to challenge him, and it appeared today was to be no different.

Malik thought very briefly how his fondness for his sister was at an all-time low and that he might enjoy seeing Bora take his sister apart, piece by piece—something the barbarian particularly excelled at.

Klarin motioned from behind, and her son, Viktar, stepped beyond the door jamb into the hall, taking his rightful place beside his mother. As they approached Malik, Aya continued to clamber out of the way, but Klarin ignored the slave girl, her attention set firmly on her brother.

"You remember your nephew, Viktar? Or perhaps you don't." She scowled. "It has been nearly three years since you've had us to your house."

"Yes, and you were not invited today."

Malik's face fell. Not only had his sister interrupted fellatio from the slave girl, but his nephew was no longer the boy he remembered. He was tall and lithe, with soft brown hair and honey-colored skin, and his eyes seemed so large that they might fall from their sockets. Malik briefly searched those eyes, trying to identify one ounce of malice in them, but there was none.

And the boy seemed to walk with a growing confidence. Immediately, Malik looked for a weakness, a flaw, anything imperfect about the young man, and deplored that he found none.

"Where is Roza?" Klarin asked.

Malik waved the question aside. "She is away."

All the while, he was unable to draw his gaze from Viktar. The Red Robes ruler immediately disliked his nephew, even more so than the last time he had seen him. He despised everything about him: his genuine expression, the warmth in his smile, his coltish charm. No, it was more than growing dislike that Malik felt toward Viktar. In less time than it had taken to separate his wife's head from her shoulders...he *hated* him.

Viktar, as though oblivious to the thoughts that raged between Malik's ears, knelt earnestly upon one knee, received his uncle's hand, and kissed the back of it with soft, warm lips. Malik sneered as the young man swept his cape aside and spoke with a heartfelt baritone that filled the empty hall like a sweet, sad song.

"Uncle, it is such a privilege to see you again."

The sincerity in the young man's voice rang true, but honest as it was, Malik could find no space in his heart to appreciate it. On some wicked, pathetic level he imagined all the ways Viktar must be superior to him. *No doubt the whelp could outlast him in bed, and women would swoon for him like filthy whores, throwing their legs apart for him with abandon. No doubt even Aya would bend over in a moment's notice to let the young man thrust his...*

Malik's sordid thoughts were interrupted as, rising to his feet, Viktar took his uncle's extended hand in both of his and shook generously.

"I so admire you, Uncle. I am truly honored to learn the many things you have to teach." He shook Malik's hand again, a wide smile animating his soft features in a beautiful way, and crossed himself genuinely. "It will be, God willing, a long and blessed time for your good name and this realm, and I wish my presence to only serve you nobly."

"God's will be done." Malik pulled his hand coldly from his nephew's as the lie escaped his lips easily as an icicle might slip from a warm eave.

Klarin's expression belied the generous words spoken between the men, her lips narrow with caution.

* * *

Viktar was to remain with Malik and Bora Vachir while his dear mother returned to her own realm. Before she left, she drew her son into the privacy of her room.

"Learn from Malik what you will, but do not allow your uncle to break that beautiful heart of yours." She leaned up to kiss her son on the cheek. "He is a despot ruler, but your rightful place is in his stead when he passes. The King has ordered it, the Church has blessed it, and the people deserve it. We will persevere. We must, for righteousness' sake."

"Mother, you worry too much." He hugged her, his warm face flush with happiness. "I will learn much, honor my good uncle's name, and send word so that you will see everything is as it should be." Viktar knew the insurmountable odds his mother had endured for her realm to survive, and he wished not to worry her further.

Klarin sighed as she gazed upon the beautiful honesty of her only child's face. She wrapped a lock of his hair behind an ear and forced a smile. "Remember, he is strong, but you are *stronger*. And Malik must bow to the Emperor. He knows this, and it is a weapon you have, should you need it."

Viktar smiled again, innocently, and kissed his mother on the forehead as they bade their farewells.

* * *

Three months later...Viktar, bound, shirtless, and on his knees, was struck again by a guard while Malik looked on, a sneer distorting his wretched face.

"Take her!" Malik commanded of his nephew regarding a slave girl who cowered, terrified, on the stone floor before them.

The girl, forced to watch the brutality, tried to cover her face as though she could no longer bear to endure the cruelty heaped upon the young man.

"I will not." Viktar sagged against his restraints, sputtering blood through his battered lips, eyes defiant through the split bruises. "It is pitiless to her and would insult the woman I shall one day love." What he *thought* was that given the first opportunity, he would gut his uncle and send Red Robes into a new chapter of being.

"Your *love*?" Malik's demeanor darkened with incredulity. "There *is* no love, you impudent fool! You are weak! Weak and hopeless." Malik stepped forward, grabbing and shoving Viktar's head back by the hair as he raised his other fist high above him.

Viktar, still on his knees, looked defiantly up at his uncle, not flinching.

"You insult the integrity of your people, and you defile your family's strong name. Let the girl go." He gasped, his neck bent at a forbidding angle.

Malik's face turned to such sudden rage that he trembled, his hand still suspended in the air.

The younger man did nothing, only kept his stare fixed on Malik. Quite unexpectedly, Malik turned and struck the girl instead, then turned on Viktar. "Take her! I command it, or I will kill her!" he screamed.

"She bears no guilt in this! It is *I* who defy you! Strike *me* instead!"

Malik grasped the girl and pummeled her twice more then turned again to see if his nephew watched.

Viktar's heart ached, not for his own plight but for that of the girl. He believed slavery was an abomination, but even amongst slave owners, Malik was most cruel.

"I will kill her! I swear it!" Malik shrieked.

Viktar closed his eyes for what he knew was to come. "Then *you*...not *I*, will own your inhumanity." It was all he could do as he struggled one last time against his bonds.

Then the young Prussian was knocked nearly senseless by the guard, the cold floor pressing callously into his battered and blackened face. Viktar did not see Malik draw his blade and strike the girl down with it. Neither did he see his uncle straddle her and wrench her head back, drawing his blade across her throat.

A dull thud that was the girl's skull hitting the stone floor nearby drew Viktar from his stupor. He roused enough to see, dimly, the bare feet of the girl as they dragged her close enough that, had he been stronger, he could have reached out and touched them.

Then, all was blackness.

* * *

Several weeks later, Malik, at Bora Vachir's recommendation, commissioned the making of a Damascus steel sword. It would be something that would symbolize the mighty power of Malik's realm and would be deadly, extravagant, and unmatched in its beauty, just as its owner believed *he* was. And, it would be fashioned by one of the greatest artisans to ever take up a forge hammer.

Never was Malik without his guards. Never did he eat without the food tasters eating first. It seemed, with the death of Roza and the new presence of his nephew, that his paranoia was growing day by day. He was becoming swiftly obsessed with the prospect of a legitimate heir and his own mortality.

As for Viktar, he skirted his uncle at every turn. That is not to say he wasn't called into his presence at intervals. There were *lessons* to be taught, and they inevitably resulted in a beating. Viktar quickly discovered that saying nothing at all was the best way to shorten his moments with Malik. It seemed his uncle's attention span was short, even where brutality was concerned.

The terminal event came on the shortest day of the year. Viktar was called to observe his personal horse—the one he rode alongside his mother into the kingdom—as Malik destroyed it. Forbidden to ride any of Malik's mounts, the young Prussian was now not only horseless, but without a friend in the world.

* * *

Through his grim experience beneath the boot of his uncle, Viktar began to change. Fractured were his optimistic outlook and blind, happy trust. He carried upon his being a new cloak, one woven of fear and regret. But there was something else that also wove itself into this mantle—an undying will to live.

Cleverly, he took notice of things. He paid attention to the number of grain silos, or the lack thereof, in the realm. He observed rampant, untreated illness and abundant forced servitude. And, he discovered that Malik's army was not only strong, it was *very* strong. All of the tyrant's reserves seemed to go toward building his military, and when he believed he fell short on that front, the peasants paid dearly. It was a very fine line his uncle walked, countering the risk of tipping his own realm over into revolt against the might of his great army.

Young men of the village were forced into Malik's ranks at the age of thirteen. All girls and women over the age of ten were required to sew hauberk doublets for two soldiers before they were allowed to fashion clothes for their own families. Two-thirds of all shorn sheep's wool went straight to the shops of the empire's tailors.

Yes, there were many things Viktar took notice of, and all the while, he made no effort...to leave. Neither did he send word to his mother that anything was amiss so there would be no suspicion on her part of his plight. Klarin had a sizable army of her own, and it would not do to entangle her in a battle of strength against her brother. Most importantly, Viktar intended to finish what the Emperor had seen fit to request: that he succeed his uncle in power over Red Robes.

Two wretched months later, the despot leader took Gorlik—a mammoth of a man who was his personal bodyguard—and his nephew on a journey to a tiny island in the Mediterranean.

The three set off to retrieve the great sword from the sword-smith, Sayid, of Crete. Viktar was happy for this, not for the journey but for the opportunity it might avail.

It was only because Malik had become quite taken with abusing Viktar that he even wished to travel with him. It became a game for him, to see how much the boy could endure, and the Prussian lord refused to admit how surprised he had been at his nephew's fortitude. And so Viktar sailed under the ruse that his uncle was *enlightening* him—that they were sharing some of the mysterious ways of foreign lands. And this is what Viktar wrote to his mother.

Through all of the cruelty, Viktar held steadfast to what Malik believed was a ridiculous cluster of moral beliefs. That infuriated the ruler most, that he could not tear from the young man a code of righteousness he was sure his sister had bestowed upon her son. Malik believed, however, that given enough time…he would.

The eve before they left, Viktar wrote with an unsteady hand.

My dearest Mother,

I write to you with great love in my heart. I have learned so much of the ways of my uncle and believe that I now know him better than any other ever has…even you.

I've gained so much wisdom, much more than I believed possible, and I ask that you would pray God's will be done at His discretion. That is vital, and I cannot impress upon you enough how many hours I too will spend in prayer asking for his guidance.

It shall ultimately be as you wish. I intend to step with great joy into my uncle's place when the time comes. I promise you this, for I am convinced it is the right thing to do. On that day, I shall accept the burden willingly. Until then, do not worry for me. My uncle and I have quite the understanding. And tomorrow we venture forth to learn more of the great world beyond this realm. I will write when I can. You will be in my heart always.

Your son,

Viktar

CHAPTER FOUR

Twenty-two years earlier

Bora Vachir thirsted for blood. War was a beautiful thing to him, more beautiful than a cowering virgin's cry or a mortal enemy's bended knee. And there would never be enough blood in the world to bathe him sufficiently. It was as though he wore his skin on the wrong side—he yearned for it that much.

He was scarcely twenty years old but had campaigned with the vicious Timur long enough to have developed a grave appreciation, and appetite, for those things that fed his thirst. Stack the heads to the sky; they would not tower high enough for Bora. He would clamber to the peaks of them and scream to the gods, "Higher! Higher!"

This wickedness that infected Bora's soul was neither bred nor created through circumstance. His was an evil that transcended simple heartlessness, and long before his body would be cold in a grave, it would move onward, for evil walked the face of the earth, certain as the wind that swept across the scorched fields he left behind.

This morning, the sky was a bright, commanding blue, and the cliffs rose in chalky white and gray ribbons on either side of the narrow valley. Bora was not in Mongolia, nor was he in Africa. He was not in his beloved east at all. This morning he awoke in Spain, northeast of Calatayud.

Bora had already sampled a taste of this particular war, *The Hundred Years War* they would call it one day. It agreed with him, and he was happily consigned to King of Castile as a free agent, not so much for gold as he was for the precious crimson that he craved. But the gold wasn't entirely without value. It would buy armor and weapons, a stronger horse, and passage to the next battle, or home.

What would be the battlefield today lay rocky, barren, and cold, the canyons crisscrossing the mountains more steeply to the north. Truthfully, Bora cared little for the outcome of the war between Castile and Aragon. He cared only that the fight was a bloody one and that he walked away from it.

Already having fought at the sieges of Moros and Cetina, he anticipated great success in Calatayud. They had thoroughly trounced the King of Aragon's forces in the four previous skirmishes and now anticipated pressing Aragon even farther back into France.

But this time, standing opposite Castile's forces...and Bora, was a new army, freshly consigned to the King of Aragon. The good king had commissioned help and paid dearly for it. Consequently, amongst the ranks stood an extraordinary warrior—a mercenary, twenty-two years old, who fought as a slave soldier for a mercenary king named...Duval.

Bora was restless, but there was nothing to do but wait, for battle could not be waged in the dark. Others lined up around him, talking, boosting their morale as they eagerly awaited what was to come. Finally, the conversation fell to silence. All that could be heard was the snorting and stamping of the horses in anticipation of what was to come.

At the break of dawn, horns sounded—first from one side and then answered by the other. The canyon was narrow, towering up on either side of them, the sky a faint, blue ribbon overhead.

The armies pressed forward until they faced each other, scarcely a hundred meters apart. There would be no scattering from this fray. *This* would be a battle to the death, and Bora approved.

The final battle call signaled, and the fight began.

Bora screamed—a terrible, frightening roar—as he spurred his horse forward. His battle cry was cut short, however, as arrows rained down on them—wave after wave, slicing Bora's ranks in half nearly straightaway. One arrow skirted the shoulder plate of his horse, wedging behind the beast's withers, causing it to stumble.

Down Bora went, smashing onto the ground so hard that it knocked him nearly senseless. The horse clambered to its feet and retreated...riderless. Bora was scarcely able to pull his shield from over his head as the deadly darts continued to fall like piercing sheets of rain. One more lanced his thigh, and he cried out in rage as much as in pain.

As the first aerial wave of battle subsided and the opposing infantry moved steadily in, Bora dropped his shield, broke the arrow off at the fletching, and lifted his sword to fight.

But this was no ordinary army they faced. He had yet to realize these were the dreaded mercenaries of the mercenary king Duval. These men struck, parried, swept, all with great precision, knocking their opposition back step by step—a machine of destruction with only one purpose.

Bora struggled, barely fending off his third opponent when he first glimpsed the wraith. The man appeared nearly inhuman, like no other warrior on the battlefield, and his horse, black as pitch, stomped on the bodies of the fallen without care.

As the dark warrior picked his way through the mayhem, he wielded a sword more expertly than Bora Vachir had ever seen. Left, right, he swung, flaying arms, decapitating heads, pouring the bowels of those unfortunate enough to be marked as opposing ranks. And he did it with such ease!

Bora was overcome. For the first time, he was stricken with terror, for this was death incarnate come to stare him in the face and draw from him his final breath. He was a superstitious man and certain this was the intent of this fiend—to draw the very life-breath of all those around him.

Bora Vachir tripped backwards, trying to kick out of the line of sight, but it seemed the mercenary commanded the entire field, and so the Mongol kicked away again, retreating from what he was convinced was inevitable.

But there would be no escape as two more men fell to the awful blade of the black knight. With a final cry, Bora hurled his lance short of the dreadful warrior. He knew immediately that this error would be his last, for the soldier spun his horse about, his piercing gaze searching intently until he saw…Bora Vachir.

The black stallion bellowed a monstrous scream as it obeyed its master and charged for Bora. In time with the beast's stride, at ten meters away, the mercenary lifted his blade.

Bora fell, mewling in terror as he pulled the carcass of a fallen comrade half against himself for protection. There was nothing more he could do but wait and fall, finally meeting that fiend named Death.

Just then, a giant appeared distantly in the smoky carnage, riding a mammoth steed. The giant called out harshly to the dark mercenary, and the wicked horse skidded to a stop. The savage had Bora fixed in his haunting gaze as…the giant called again—a name Bora would never forget.

Ravan…

The warrior looked down upon the cowering Bora Vachir with an expression cold as anything the Mongol had ever seen. There was no contempt, not pity, no disappointment. Ravan simply ceased doing that which he did better than Bora ever dreamed of doing.

Ravan stopped killing, turned…and rode away.

CHAPTER FIVE

Twenty-two years later: Crete

Ravan unfolded the parchment and read the fine script, neatly penned by an artist's hand.

Lord Wintergrave,

It is with great delight that I see you have accepted my terms. Frankly, I am surprised. And so all that is left now is for us to meet and get on with business.

I look forward to making your acquaintance. Enclosed find a gesture of my earnest intent—passage paid for you and a guest. I assure you, you will not be disappointed by what you discover, but I believe it is I who stands to gain the most.

Until we meet, peace be upon you.

Sayid

The mercenary folded the note and tucked it into his coat. Seconds later, Nicolette's eyes opened. She was like that, never really wakening in the ordinary fashion that most people did. There was no turning over, stretching, or sleepy yawn. She was simply no longer asleep.

The ship rolled in big, galloping swells as she gazed at Ravan and said, "We shall arrive before long."

As though a shipman read her thoughts, it could be heard overhead the call that land was in sight. Ravan smiled softly, leaned over his bride, and kissed her…deeply.

* * *

Stepping from the draw-plank of the ship, Ravan walked down the long pier and contemplated the picturesque village of Candia, Crete, and beyond. Nicolette moved noiselessly, lingering at his side, and laid her hand warmly on his arm. His heart swelled with happiness, or as near to happiness as one like Ravan might feel. She had not intended to come with him on this journey but, on last notice, had announced her desire to travel with her husband, and it thrilled him that she wanted to come.

He clasped his hand over hers and took in a deep breath of the earthen shore. There were many appetites Ravan intended to feed on this trip, and his footstep was light with anticipation as he led Nicolette down the pier.

The mercenary was nearly forty-five years old and determined that his legacy, and everything which it defined, would be solidly in place long before his demise. He, better than most, knew that life was uncertain, and so he was driven to fortify the fragile existence of this world as best he could. This journey to Crete was a link in that mighty chain.

He stopped at the end of the pier and spun about, his black hair sweeping around behind him. "I will be here for at least a month, perhaps two," he explained to Salvatore.

"Better here than Syria," the Spaniard replied wryly.

The ship's captain, one of Ravan's dearest and oldest friends, had followed them onto the dock and announced he had plans of his own for his short stay on Crete. Smiling broadly, he clasped a strong, tan hand on Ravan's shoulder. "I'll be here overnight to resupply and sample the town's...*festivities.*" He grinned, his brilliant smile a beautiful contrast to his tan face. "Then I'm off to Portugal, but I shall await word from you and return immediately at your call." He became more serious. "You know I could be here at a moment's notice if you need..." he glanced at Nicolette, "or *want* for anything."

Ravan nodded and held tightly to the Spaniard's hand. This was someone with whom he had shared much joy and sorrow over the years, and it warmed his heart to have Salvatore at his side.

"This is a journey of great fortune. I will send word when it is done. Until next time, my friend."

Nicolette, dark and ethereal as always, remained silent, looking beyond both men to the distant ocean's horizon. She gathered, as she always seemed to, considerable attention from Salvatore without saying or doing anything at all. There was simply no denying the effect she had on him...and others.

Salvatore stepped directly in front of her line of sight and spoke as though Ravan was not there at all. "My beauty, when will you deny the one who has captured your good senses and come away with me? We could sail the seas together." He embellished with one hand over his head as though painting a picture of what magnificent adventures they would share. "And I would make you queen of many countries and all the waters between them."

He gently grasped her hand and leaned toward her, meaning to kiss her on the lips. When she turned her head softly to the side, he waited as though to see if she would return to him. When she did not, he lifted her hand and planted the kiss, instead, on the back of it, lingering much longer than well he should have.

"The seas will have to be content with only the magnificence of yourself," Nicolette replied coyly, her emerald eyes reflecting the glorious water, which danced laughingly below the pier.

"Yes. Well, until next time, I suppose." Salvatore's eyes flashed and, as much a rogue as ever there was, he glanced at Ravan before releasing her hand and taking his leave.

Ravan sighed and nearly smiled as he watched the Spaniard turn lightly on his heel and stride back down the pier toward the beautiful vessel that was moored at the end—his latest and most extraordinary ship. It was called the White Witch—named, he claimed...after Nicolette.

"If I were not so fond of him, I might be inclined to kill him," Ravan murmured as Salvatore disappeared back up the gangway and onto his ship.

Nicolette said nothing, one eyebrow barely rising as she regarded her husband.

Fleet as the ship was, it would not be long before Salvatore was back to Barcelona—his home—while Ravan was entrenched with business of a curious sort in Candia. It was neither leisure nor the draw of the quaint village that pulled Ravan from his beloved France. It was an extraordinary man who hid himself within the stone city walls of the island—a foreigner amongst the Greeks—a reclusive master artist named Sayid.

* * *

Sayid was not French, nor was he Roman Catholic. He was Muslim and the only survivor of his family when the Turkish Mongols invaded his precious city of Damascus. That was many years ago when the young man, scarcely twelve years old, had watched in horror as his father refused to surrender their Syrian home to the invading Mongol, Timur. To this day, the terror of it haunted Sayid's dreams, crouching in a room of things he longed to forget but never would.

Nothing compared to the barbarism that swept across Damascus on that wicked day. Their beautiful city was sacked by Timur's monster horde. Nearly all of the inhabitants were beheaded, their heads stacked in towering pillars to mark the unrivaled power of the evil that had befallen them. The rotting columns of terror were a grim warning for any who might pass and believe they could stand against one as savage as Timur.

Sayid's father—the great bladesmith Nizar—would ordinarily have been spared because he was an artisan. Timur expressly wanted all artisans sent to his homeland, but Nizar refused to go, fighting magnificently as the extraordinary swordsman that he was.

Timur's ranks suffered more than they anticipated at the hands of the gifted Nizar, and when the bladesmith finally fell to the overwhelming ranks, Sayid watched in frozen horror. The boy's mother was slain next and his sister dragged away in the fresh horde of slaves by the evil Bora Vachir, one of Timur's generals.

Sayid's life was spared only because he was *also* an artisan—a surviving student of his esteemed father. Shackled, he was to be sent to Timur's homeland where he would be forced to craft the rare swords. But Sayid broke free that awful night and fled, leaving everything and *nothing* behind.

All was lost as the young Syrian traded work for passage on an old cargo ship, first sailing to Cyprus and then on to Crete. It was a treacherous time for the boy, and he had nearly starved to death before eventually falling, face down and weeping, upon the white beaches of Crete.

All of it was, to him, beyond Hell. God had forsaken him, and the pain in his heart was begotten from such cruelty that Sayid never again spoke of it. But he vowed, on that day, to *never* forget.

Now Sayid was a goat amongst sheep as he privately lay his prayer rug down in the tiny Christian town of Candia. The only things that remained with him when he fled Syria, besides the dreaded memories, were his faith and his extraordinary knowledge of the Damascus steel. Both were gifts given him by his father, and the prayer he whispered every morning and every night was for a *Malak-ul-Mawt* to come, one that could dispatch...*revenge*.

Time passed. Eventually, in honor of his father, Sayid once more kindled the fire and took up the hammer to forge the rare blades, just as he had been taught. But exquisite skill such as his would not go unnoticed. Before long, men discovered him and his great talent, coming from afar to commission Sayid's magnificent creations.

* * *

Ravan's brow furrowed as he studied the small village. Unlike the others who had come before him, he did not come to commission a blade. No, his journey was of a different slant, for he wished for more. It was the *knowledge* he sought. But it had seemed Ravan's wish would not be granted until the bladesmith reconsidered, offering an unusual proposition.

In France, Ravan's dynasty was becoming fast known for its fine metallurgy. Some of the greatest swords were being crafted from the forges in his realm, and it was he who taught his own smiths the delicate art that had come so naturally to him, so long ago when he was only a boy at an orphanage. The blades were extraordinary but…they could be better.

This was why Ravan stepped with such hope from Salvatore's ship onto the island of Crete—because Sayid was one of the few remaining artisans who knew how to fashion the unequaled Damascus steel. And it was with great humility that the mercenary quested to the Syrian's door.

When the others came, just as intent as Ravan to know Sayid's secrets, he had agreed only to build the blades, for the right price. But, until now he had been unwilling to share the *knowledge* of his craft—had held his secrets near to his heart as a reverent memorial to his father.

There had been no denying, however, that the dark mercenary was different from the rest, and Sayid recognized something uncommon when he first read the hand-scrawled letter, sent by Ravan himself. That night the Syrian ceased praying for the *Malak-ul-Mawt*. The death angel had come— his prayer had been answered.

Ravan would spend several months with Sayid to learn firsthand the rare art of refining Damascus steel. In return for the unusual arrangement, Sayid had asked for just one thing—that the mercenary kill a man named Bora Vachir, the slave owner who had taken Sayid's younger sister…*Aya*. Then he was to bring Aya safely to Candia to live forever, or more likely, he must return with proof of her death.

Agreeing to the grave exchange, Ravan promised to discover the fate of Sayid's sister. And he would execute it with supreme finesse when the time came. He vowed that, if Aya was yet alive, he would find her and bring her home. If she was not, he would kill the men responsible for her death and bring proof of their demise.

The terms of the unusual barter agreed with him, and as Ravan stepped into the cool, humid, late-winter air, he turned and reached for Nicolette's hand to help her from the carriage. A storm was breaking over the island, and dark clouds whipped and rolled across the late autumn, ocean sky. Nicolette's hair flew about her, giving the feeling that a great warrior had arrived with his witch. Truth be known, he had.

Sayid greeted Ravan with eyes wide. Likely no amount of correspondence could have prepared him for what he saw when he opened the door. With a halting half-bow, Sayid swept his hand wide.

"Welcome. My modest home is now yours."

His accent was wonderfully thick and precise as he greeted the couple, and he smiled warmly, his dark complexion striking against the white garments, which hung with a loose humility from his thin frame.

The Syrian's entire demeanor belied the deadly weapons he was known to craft. This was Ravan's first thought as he studied the little man who greeted him.

"Thank you." His deep voice rumbled across Sayid's threshold, his armor and battle leathers an odd contrast to the relative meekness of the one who stood before him. Ravan nodded and indicated his bride. "May I introduce my wife, Nicolette."

Sayid bowed a second time. "Yes, of course." His gaze flitted between the two. "You are both welcome guests in my home, for as long as you care to stay. Please..." He motioned that they should follow. Ravan nearly had to duck to step through the front door of the tiny stone house that sat tucked tightly between two other homes at the obscure end of a darkened, muddied street.

"I trust your journey was good?" their host wondered aloud over his shoulder before introducing his guests to his wife. Without waiting for an answer, he chirped, "And this is Luchina, jewel of my heart!" Luchina's expression lit up, and she smiled broadly, the gap between her front teeth adding an almost virtuous charm. And...Nicolette smiled back.

They were then led through a short maze of tight rooms to a surprisingly open workshop that lay attached to the back of the home. There was no way to see, from the front of the house, the expanse of the studio hidden behind. It was tall and circular, and in the center lay a great forge, chimneyed through the roof.

As Ravan stepped into the workshop, he turned slowly about, taking all of it in with keen appreciation. He could only imagine the great weapons that had been created here, and he was struck with a sense of awe.

Along one bench lay an assortment of blades in various stages of development, each with its own space and element of reverence. These were an unborn army of the most elite warriors, waiting to be called to their ranks.

Ravan's gaze wandered farther. Clay crucibles lined one wall and wooden crates another. The crates contained an assortment of supplies. Chunks of iron, chopped wood, green leaves and branches, and dried cattle and goat dung protruded from them, begging to be a part of the next creation, waiting for their moment to take part in the birth of something dreadfully wondrous.

Tools hung from hooks on the wall—some of them familiar to the mercenary, some not—and more tools lay scattered along several heavy long tables.

Close to the rear door of the studio, a long trough allowed a small creek to run directly into the dwelling, through the trough, and out the other end as it exited the building. Ravan envied the arrangement, knowing this would provide a steady current of water that was continuous and cool, something necessary for the crafting of forged weapons. He intended, upon his return to France, to construct a similar setup and do away with the water vats he currently utilized.

The mercenary was beyond impressed, something that was difficult to accomplish. So it was here, he thought to himself, in this cloistered haven, that Sayid and the only other man he had taught his trade—his partner, Halil—tempered the exquisite steel weapons that were so admired.

Ravan felt a sudden sense of sweet urgency and could scarcely wait to begin training. But the evening was getting late, and the beginning of this journey would have to wait, at least until morning.

* * *

It had been a long day, and Luchina led Nicolette out the rear door of the studio. The smaller woman studied the porcelain beauty who walked as though her feet did not touch the ground.

They wound their way along a narrow path overgrown with foliage to a tiny dwelling behind the shop. The cottage sat nestled in a remote corner of the garden and would be home for Ravan and Nicolette until the mercenary had learned all that he could from the artisan.

Sayid's wife seemed nervous as she bade Nicolette enter first. She pushed open the quaint cottage door to find the interior remarkably comfortable and inviting. There were several large, stuffed chaises, a table with benches for seats, and a small kitchen area with a tiny, ornate, wood kiln stove. Nicolette shed her robes and wondered briefly if it was ever really cold enough in Crete to warrant lighting the stove.

In the corner of the cottage was a shallow, wooden tub. It had next to it a shelf with several pitchers and an assortment of exotic combs, soaps, and oils.

In the center of the one-room house, however, was an item that could not be ignored. It was an enormous bed, the posts carved of Syrian Cedar with inlays of white bone. It was incredibly out of place in the humble little cottage and commanded the attention of any and all who entered.

Nicolette stepped near to it, running her fingers along the soft silk of the lavish spread. Stitched into the fabric were images of men and women, couples entwined with each other in satiny bliss, very risqué. The pattern invited any who slept beneath to join them in their rapture.

Smoothing the spread with the back of her hand, Nicolette glanced over her shoulder at her host. She said nothing, her bemused expression saying more than words ever could.

Luchina shifted uncomfortably, knitting her fingers together as she stared at her feet. "It is from the old country. A gift for services rendered by my husband. I mean..." she added hastily, "for swords. I-I hope you and your husband will be...comfortable with it."

"I'm sure we will be *most comfortable*," Nicolette murmured. "The client who gifted it must have had very particular ideas on what is...priority."

Luchina almost laughed. "That was my thought exactly!" She became more relaxed and animated, indicating the towels on a wall shelf. "I cook, and the stove inside is always tended. There is usually hot water on, and I can heat more whenever you wish to bathe. Please do let me know if you need anything."

"Thank you. It is perfect," Nicolette replied, her expression barely curious. "Will they begin work tonight?"

* * *

Sayid and Ravan sat at a small table in the shop and shared, in tiny clay cups, a sweet, spicy wine. Sayid poured first, and his guest observed with keen awareness the ritual—hold the cup palm up before pouring his own.

The mercenary poured next, and Sayid's expression was of warm appreciation, his head bobbing as he accepted the wine from Ravan in the same manner.

In those first few moments, the two men discovered a great deal about each other. They talked about the vanishing tradition of fine bladesmanship, about what gave courage to a rare sword, and of the dismal lack of worthy men who could wield them with the honor they deserved. They spoke of these weapons as good friends might speak of one another.

Sayid could not know that a very special weapon, *Pig-Killer*, fashioned when the mercenary was only a boy, lay within his boot at that very moment. The knife possessed a legend all its own, and Ravan was still, years later, never without it.

It would have been unusual if they could have seen themselves sitting across from each other—the small, dark-skinned man in the linen robes with his hair chopped nearly to the skin and the grave mercenary, long hair and beard, dressed as always in his battle leathers.

As the evening waned, their dialogue invited the mutual fascination and respect they held, not just for the art of fine bladesmanship but for each other, and their demeanors…were nearly the same. It was destiny in its purest form.

Their kinship was almost immediate, and for Ravan the conversation flowed more easily than was normal for him. He delighted in his new companion and indulged freely of the wine.

When Ravan finally bade Sayid goodnight, his spirits soared, and he nearly swayed as he made his way to the cottage. Humming quietly to himself, he could not remember the last time he had allowed spirits to affect him so. Ah, yes…Salvatore had been responsible.

Ravan hummed contentedly as he ambled along, but when he discovered the massive bed that waited for him in the cottage, and the beauty who lay upon it, he was as happy as he had ever been.

Happy complacency, however, was as unwelcome to Ravan's destiny as a wolf was to sheep. And right on schedule—the next morning—destiny of another sort thrust itself into his world…

CHAPTER SIX

✝

Ravan awoke before anyone else and left Nicolette sleeping as he slipped from the cottage and walked, making his way through the silent town. His stride was long, his footstep light, and he moved as a ghost, disturbing no one as he made his way through Candia.

Breathing the scent of the tiny coastal city, he briefly remembered another village, one to which someone very dear to him had been taken long ago, one where he had nearly lost *Risen*, his only son. For this memory alone, he was reminded that coastal towns were not his favorite. His heart drew him more to the woodland forests and mountains of the mainland.

But last evening had been good, *very* good, and this was a journey of another sort. When all was said and done, he would bring home a vast knowledge that would help build the Wintergrave Dynasty even greater than it already was, and it would secure the legacy for his son and daughter forever.

This warmed his heart. His greatest wish—to provide for Risen and Niveus where his own father and mother had been unable to do the same for him—would be fulfilled. As his children slipped into his passing thoughts, Ravan's determination settled even more. He walked happily onward through the quiet, waning night until the sky began to lighten and the sounds of a wakening city began to murmur their gracious good mornings.

By the time he made his way back to the Syrian's home, the gray overcast of the night before was clearing to a bright, blue sky. He paused on the doorstep of his new friend's home, daring to feel at ease in this unfamiliar world.

Laying a hand on the rough-hewn jamb of the door, he murmured a vow to Sayid. "I will find her, my friend. I will find Aya and bring her to her rightful home. Or, for you, I will kill the one who has forbidden her return."

Then he drew from his boot another old friend. Pressing the tip of his knife *Pig-Killer* against the palm of his hand, he twisted it until a small pool of blood welled. Dipping his thumb into the deep crimson, he stamped a tiny mark over the doorway, something anyone other than he would scarcely notice. It was a promise for which Ravan would die, if need be.

Stepping quietly through the door into the small parlor, Ravan was surprised to find Sayid, lips to the ground in prayer. The mercenary begged forgiveness for the intrusion, but Sayid rose from where he knelt and rolled the small carpet under his arm.

"Won't you please join me for breakfast?" Sayid said, smiling.

Making their way to the studio, Ravan sat opposite Sayid. Nicolette emerged just then, and Ravan observed how the Syrian's face brightened at seeing her.

"I trust you slept well?"

She glanced briefly at Ravan. "Splendidly."

Luchina served a breakfast of yogurt, fish, and vinegar preserved vegetables. She snuggled against Sayid, and they all sipped chamomile tea laced heavily with honey. Nicolette spoke softly to Luchina, asking her about her life on Crete. As fate would have it, she had come from Portugal, met Sayid, had fallen in love, and stayed.

Ravan was happy for them, especially knowing something of the bitter history Sayid had endured. He noticed how much Nicolette seemed to enjoy Luchina's quiet company and wondered if his bride's role at home—Lady of the Wintergrave Dynasty—prevented her the happy anonymity she seemed to enjoy today.

He made a mental note to pay greater attention to this, perhaps taking Nicolette traveling more. Maybe that was why she sometimes walked in the orchard in the dark of the night—because it freed her of her daily obligation to the realm.

Taking another swallow of the marvelous, sweet tea, Ravan studied his bride. He knew Nicolette better than anyone, but she was still a fathomless mystery to him on even his best day. As though reading his mind, she glanced his way, their eyes locked on each other for a good, long while.

Ravan chewed slowly, savoring the fish almost as much as the moment. The early morning sun shone brightly, sending a happy, slanting light through the nearly translucent calfskins that were stretched over several octagonal windows, fashioned into the high, domelike roof of the workshop. The effect cast a warm, pleasing aura about the studio, inviting creativity. Ravan breathed deeply. He very much looked forward to this first day with Sayid.

Breakfast done, he watched as Nicolette helped Luchina clear it away and was taken completely by surprise when Sayid asked suddenly, "Your weapons, may I see them?"

Ravan drew up short at the request. The memory of an event from long ago—another request—invaded his thoughts. It was the night in a frosty meadow where he made love to Nicolette for the first time. She had knelt naked before him, fearless and confident. He was clothed, armored, and with his sword at his side, and yet he had trembled with vulnerability.

To have such a master of weapons as Sayid ask to inspect that which was so intimate to him—his battle sword—was a very personal request, and it drew an uncertainty from Ravan not unlike what he felt that night long ago.

A flush drew across his face. He could feel Nicolette's gaze fixed strongly on him. *She* knew where his thoughts had taken him—he was sure of it—and the hint of a smile swept across her lips as she disappeared through the door to the kitchen.

Clearing his throat, Ravan slowly drew from his scabbard...his battle sword. It revealed itself as an extension of the mercenary, as much a part of him as his own hand.

Sayid's eyes widened as the great sword was freed. The weapon made a satisfying ring as it escaped the scabbard, and Ravan held the monster blade straight up, appreciating with great respect the silent warrior for what it was. The light flashed, running along the edge of it as Ravan deftly swung it about. The sword seemed to dance of its own accord as it flipped, now lying across both of the mercenary's palms.

In this fashion, Ravan presented the blade to Sayid.

The Syrian took the weapon with a reverent dip of his head, humbly bowing upon one knee. The weight of the blade was evidently more than the man anticipated for his hands dropped briefly, and his eyes widened further. "Heavy...at least five pounds and then some."

Ravan nodded as the bladesmith stood up and ran his thin, dark fingers along the riser of the sword before focusing on the hilt.

"The grip...it is two-handed," Sayid offered.

"It can be," Ravan answered mildly and was met with a look of surprise.

"It cannot be wielded with only one, not for long." Sayid frowned.

"It can..." the warrior politely disagreed.

Sayid's look of surprise grew, and he declined to hand the weapon back, running his hand instead along the immense horn grip.

The gesture was, to Ravan, almost unbearably personal. There were etchings in the antler, deep and primal—a pattern familiar only to him.

They were cut in such a way as to provide a strong handhold even when the grip was slick with blood.

"What is the beast that gave it such a helve?" Sayid asked without interrupting his study of the weapon.

"It is a Hart of twelve."

When a look of confusion clouded Sayid's face, Ravan explained further. "A Red Deer...*Hart*, with twelve tines, six on either side." He nodded toward his blade. "The grip is an eye guard from that deer."

"M-mm." Sayid ran his hand over the hilt again. "Must have been an immense creature," he admitted with obvious appreciation.

"Yes, a noble beast to be sure. But you..." Ravan extended a polite hand toward Sayid, "...you hail from the land of lions."

Sayid laughed softly. "Syria? Yes...perhaps so, but not for a long time now." His face grew more serious. "And there was never an antler to be had, for such a fine grip as this, that has ever come from a lion."

Ravan appreciated very much the warm personality of the small man, and he relaxed visibly, intent only on the craftsman's keen observations.

Sayid murmured as he walked slowly about the studio, speaking as though to the sword itself. "A curious taper to the tip, slice...*and* pierce." Flipping the blade over in his hands, he held it up so that the light riveted the length of it and back. "The fuller is deep, but not so much that it could not kill..." his voice faded away without finishing what he believed to be the providence of Ravan's blade.

Next, he held the sword, one hand on the hilt, the other lifting it so he might look down the length of it. "You carry the scars of many," he spoke softly, clearly seeing the multitude of nicks and dings that lay deeper within the steel—memories of armor and bone, which could never be honed away without destroying its function. These were the tributes of those men who fell to the great weapon, most to never rise again.

Sayid swung the sword, double-fisted, in a gentle arc. It was immense in the hands of the small man, but he was greatly skilled. Even so, the move was peculiar to Ravan, to see another man wield that which he alone knew so intimately.

The Syrian continued, speaking still to himself. "Cross guard with a thumb hole, I see...yes...yes, and the ricasso is significant, would fit your entire hand easily, if you needed to...to..." His expression darkened as though he remembered an instance of exactly what he spoke. But with a shake of his head, his brow softened, and his attention returned from his lost memories to Ravan's sword.

Flipping it up, he swept one hand over the other and flat palmed it level as though laying a baby to rest. Balancing the blade across only one hand, he allowed it to find its heart.

"Pommel is heavy, but it sets the balance center...quite *well*."

He finally ceased with his musings and faced Ravan full on. "You are a warrior," he said with finality, head bowed as he returned the weapon with great dignity to its rightful owner.

"I am."

Ravan resheathed the weapon with such precision that the Syrian nearly smiled. Sayid stood very correct, hands laced almost prayerfully in front of him.

"It is a magnificent sword. I have never seen one such as this." He extended one hand and shook his head respectfully. "But there are few who can wield such a weapon."

"There are some," Ravan replied, his deep voice a striking contrast to the warm timbre of the Damascus artisan.

"There is only one that *I* know of..." Sayid's eyes danced and remained fixed on Ravan as he walked slowly, thoughtfully, back and forth. He rubbed his beard stubble with his thumb and forefinger. "What if I told you we could build your sword...sixteen...perhaps eighteen ounces lighter?"

Ravan paused. "It cannot be done," he quietly insisted.

Sayid approached his new friend. "Ah, but it *can* be done, with the steel I will teach you to temper. And with it, you shall have a sword like no other, and any would be a fool to challenge you."

The mercenary could not hide his appreciation of what the bladesmith implied. "If such a thing could be done, a warrior would have a considerable advantage over his enemy."

"Yes, especially a warrior such as yourself." Sayid became more serious. "And if you are to retrieve Aya from Bora Vachir...you will *need* it."

There was a polite, almost reverent silence as both men considered gravely what Sayid had just revealed. His words did not make Ravan flinch. In fact, they extracted no reaction at all from the mercenary. There were few things in life most men understood perfectly. Even the face of a lover was hard to exact if one was called upon to recall it—could scarcely be recounted to every minute feature. But *combat* was something Ravan knew implicitly. It was to him as familiar as his own heartbeat. He would, when the time came, face Bora Vachir fearlessly.

Nicolette returned to the room just then, and all were equally surprised when the other door flew open and Sayid's partner, Halil, entered.

He was a man in his mid-forties, very near the age of the two other men who greeted him. Behind Halil, in the doorway, another man lingered.

Halil strode up to Ravan, slowing as he seemed to appreciate the size and countenance of the warrior who stood before him. He bowed. "I am Halil, Sayid's partner." He smiled broadly. "And it is my greatest pleasure to make your acquaintance. I have heard many wondrous tales of you."

"They are certainly only that—tales," Ravan replied modestly.

The man's darker features danced, and Ravan wondered if Halil was also Syrian.

Then the man's attention fell to Nicolette. "And who might this lovely creature be?"

"Allow me to introduce Nicolette, my wife." Ravan lifted a hand as she stepped forward, silently greeting Halil with a dip of her head.

As the stranger who loitered in the doorway edged forward, Halil seemed suddenly aware of the man's presence and gestured for the advantage of all present. As he did, his expression was just a bit less civil.

"May I introduce *Malik*." Halil said. "He is from Prussia and a…a *patron* of ours."

The man was unusual in that his skin was dark but his hair was not. His brown eyes were peculiarly light—a strange color, like rancid lemon—and narrow up and down as though he squinted. He perhaps would have been attractive except for a demeanor that presented itself not well, and he made no effort to improve upon it.

Behind Malik stood two more men, one younger, perhaps twenty. The youth was taller but slighter, with soft, brown eyes both curious and apprehensive. One had to look closely to appreciate the beauty of the young man's face, for it appeared to be healing from a recent beating.

The third man, one of great proportion, held loose and in both hands two immense, curved swords. They appeared to be his personal weapons, and he seemed disinclined to sheathe them in the company of Sayid and his guests. Ravan noticed this first.

Malik moved slowly to the center of the room, his gaze darting about as though he looked for something no one but he could see. His searching stare shifted uneasily until they landed heavily on Nicolette. Then, clearly ignoring everyone else, he focused only on her, unabashedly devouring the length of her. He strode purposefully near, but Nicolette said nothing, and only stared coldly back at the man.

Ravan was accustomed to the effect Nicolette had on most men. Even so, this stranger's liberties extended to the point that Ravan's mistrust of him was complete within moments. Furthermore, in nearly as short an amount of time, he decided he greatly disliked this man.

"Your name, it is not Prussian," Ravan stated outright as he stepped closer to Malik.

Staring only at Nicolette, Malik approached, towering over her, and mumbled, "I'm Prussian by land right, Arabic by lineage."

Sayid, obviously intensely uncomfortable with Malik's poor manners, stepped swiftly between Malik and Nicolette. She edged effortlessly away.

"Malik has come for a sword—a noble weapon to represent the title of his realm," Sayid said hastily, gesturing with both hands to all present. "Perhaps everyone would like to see the blade?" He glanced around the room.

Halil agreed. "Yes, yes! Let us see the blade! It is nearly finished."

Nicolette turned and excused herself. "I will be in the garden."

"Stay," Malik insisted, his stare boring into her.

Nicolette hesitated, not looking back. "I will not." Then she slipped from the room easily as a soft breeze.

Malik frowned, and as though just noticing all else present, he looked blankly about before exclaiming, "I should like to stay the night...*here*. And I've not eaten yet. Food and drink first."

Halil hedged. "There is room at the Inn for you and your companions, sir." He glanced at the two still standing in the doorway. "It is close by. Perhaps you would allow me to make arrangements for you? Then after you've eaten, we can present the sword."

"No. I will stay here." Malik glanced again to the empty doorway through which Nicolette had vanished before settling back on his host. "Perhaps you are unprepared to receive me? Perhaps compensation may be an issue?"

The temper of the room had gone in a matter of minutes from warm and inviting to instantly inhospitable. Ravan's hand went casually to the hilt of his blade, a gesture not unnoticed by Sayid. The Syrian glanced from Ravan to Malik.

"Please," Sayid nodded humbly, "let us retire to the dining room. I will see that you are made comfortable in my home and fed breakfast before we continue."

"I will eat here, in this room and—"

"You will not," Ravan interrupted him with cold authority.

Malik jerked about and stared coldly at Ravan. "Who do you think you are," Malik spat, "...that you would tell me what I shall or shall not do?"

The behemoth moved at once into the room, towering a good three hands over Ravan.

At this point, Ravan thoroughly disliked the stranger enough that he believed he would very much enjoy what he was about to do next. He turned so his right shoulder and hip presented forward and focused his gaze coldly on Malik.

The Prussian reminded him of another tyrant he had crossed paths with, a long time ago. Nicolette had done away with that one, and the thought briefly crossed Ravan's mind that perhaps she could happily do away with this one before all was said and done. The visual fantasy of it gave him brief satisfaction, and his eyes danced with anticipation.

Ravan replied with the ease of someone discussing the weather, "I am the Master's…" he hesitated, glancing warmly at Sayid, "apprentice, and I've work to do that requires you leave." He directed his stare at Malik. "You will dismiss yourself as you were so kindly requested, or I shall be inclined to remove you."

Malik sputtered, "You don't look like an appr—" but stopped mid-sentence when Ravan drew, without hesitation, his sword. It rang with the promise of truth as it escaped the scabbard in a split instant.

Ravan pointed the weapon directly at the face of the ill-mannered guest. The behemoth with two blades moved forward but halted when Ravan shot him a look of *do so at your master's risk.*

"Do you like this sword?" Ravan asked Malik wryly, his voice dropping to a timbre that bespoke impending bloodshed. The stranger seemed only confused, and Ravan explained further, "I am refining the capacity of this blade so that it might do what *it* does best…*better.*"

He flipped the sword effortlessly in his hand. It appeared to take on a life of its own when he held it now flat side up, the tip still pointed at the Prussian's face. Ravan spoke with grave authority but felt as much delight as he had felt for some time as he addressed the rude visitor.

The young stranger pressed himself farther into the room, his eyes quite the largest of anyone present. Malik sputtered, glaring, and finally spun on his heel and left the room, followed by his guard. The younger man, however— the one with the battered face and soulful eyes—held his ground.

"You'll excuse me," Halil apologized to Ravan. He shot an appreciative glance at the mercenary before following the men from the room.

Ravan spied the young man just then. "You will not follow your master?"

"I am Viktar." There was a youthful optimism about the young man, but also a sense of caution. As he stepped full into the room, his energy denied his obvious bad circumstance. "I am his nephew." Viktar shrugged to somewhere behind himself, a look of shame flashing briefly across his face. "I regret that he is my master." Then he brightened. "I am traveling to learn a nobleman's ways, so that I might one day do honor to my uncle's realm and…" He stared at the ground, not finishing his thought.

This gathered from Ravan a peculiar feeling of regret. "My apology if I have insulted you. My quarrel was with your uncle, not with you."

"No, not at all. But…" he glanced at Sayid, "might I stay? I'll not be in your way, I promise."

Sayid appraised the younger man carefully. "Perhaps, but I would ask you to join us this afternoon. For now, please allow me the privacy I require to work with my…*apprentice.*"

Viktar forced a grim smile. "Thank you." He bowed. "Then I shall look forward to this afternoon."

Ravan watched with mild curiosity as Viktar left. There was something about the young man that reminded him of someone else, someone…he just could not place.

Sayid watched thoughtfully as the mercenary resheathed the awful blade. "I am no warrior…" he began.

Ravan unbuckled his belt and laid his sword aside. "You are an artist of the most deadly kind, and a warrior." He leaned his head back as he contemplated his new friend. "I know, just by how you carry yourself."

Sayid nodded. "Yes…I am an artist, and an artist must know his craft. Consequently, though not a warrior, I am not unfamiliar with the art of swordsmanship and do not require you to defend me or my honor."

"I was not defending you. I was…entertaining myself at the expense of a pig."

"He is my patron."

Ravan shrugged. "Perhaps you should not patronize pigs."

Sayid laughed softly. "Perhaps diamonds grow on trees and will fall into my lap."

Ravan brightened. "I would, however, like to see the tyrant's sword."

The bladesmith walked to a heavy chest on a far table and flipped the latch, slowly lifting the lid. From the chest he pulled a blade of such exquisite dimension Ravan drew a silent breath.

The scabbard was lined in gold and stones, the ornamentation so perfect as to be almost shameful. But it was not the scabbard that drew Ravan's attention so completely. It was the estoc blade he drew from it.

The weapon was like nothing Ravan had ever seen. The knuckle guard, pommel, and cross-guard were all delicately ornamented, the stones set with perfect precision. But the incredible steel was what commanded his gaze.

Sayid offered the weapon to him for his appraisal. "Would you like to hold it?"

Ravan silently accepted the weapon and studied the length of it. The longsword was rhomboid in shape, and there was no true edge to the weapon. The tip, however, tapered to razor proportion. This sword was never meant to see battle, but should one wish to impale someone with it, it would pierce armor easily.

Looking more closely, Ravan could see the signature wave and swirl of the Damascus steel. He would never own such a weapon as this one, but he envied Malik for it all the same. It was magnificent, and Ravan handed the weapon back to his host with great care and respect.

"I've never seen anything like it," he admitted. "Your patron is unworthy of it."

The Syrian laughed gently. "Yes, well, it is a token, a relic of noble proportion, but little else." He shrugged. "It was what he desired and will represent his realm nobly."

Sayid laid the bejeweled blade carefully back into the box. When he turned to face Ravan, his expression lifted.

"But *your* blade, Ravan, when we are finished…it will be a blade the *gods* will fear."

* * *

That afternoon, Ravan was surprised when the young man returned to the studio. Viktar entered with nearly silent footsteps. It was his soft breathing that drew the mercenary and Sayid from their appraisal of the magnificent longsword.

"'Tis afternoon." Viktar motioned humbly with both hands about himself. "I've returned so that I might observe, as you said I could." He moved like a caged animal, skirting the perimeter of the wall as he approached.

Ravan's first reaction was one of distracted frustration. He was unwilling to interrupt what occurred between him, Sayid, and their work. The Syrian, however, seemed to feel differently as he lay a hand on Ravan's arm.

"Come in. Sit here and observe." He motioned to Viktar, pointing to a short stool nearby.

Viktar moved swiftly to the stool, sat, and crossed his arms, anticipation gracing his young features.

Ravan scowled and struggled to return his thoughts to where they were moments before. He had been imagining the force it took, on a good day, to sever a man's head with one blow of his longsword. Sayid had claimed to be able to reduce the force by at least a third. That was significant, much more significant than the prattling interruptions of someone scarcely a man.

But Ravan would not be allowed to return to where he had been, for Sayid lifted the longsword—Ravan's longsword—from the bench and approached Viktar.

"You see. It is a warrior's weapon."

Viktar found his feet immediately. "Yes, yes it is."

As Sayid held the blade out to the young man, Viktar brightened. With both hands he allowed Sayid to lay the legendary sword across them and held it out reverently in front of himself as though it were to be worshiped.

"It's…magnificent," the young Prussian murmured.

Wonderful, Ravan thought to himself. In respect for Sayid, however, he said nothing, only crossed his arms to silently observe. It occurred to him just then that Risen and Viktar must be very close in age. How different the two were, but also…*h-mmm.*

"And it's heavy." Viktar said then shook his head, "I mean, of course it is."

He went to right the blade, to grasp it by the helve, and the awkward motion left him with a cut on his hand. He fumbled with the sword, finally righting it.

"I'm so sorry. I seem to have bled upon your blade."

"You would certainly not be the first," Ravan replied in a low voice.

Sayid cast the mercenary an amused glance before focusing once more on Viktar. "What do you feel when you hold the sword?" he asked as he walked around him.

He showed Viktar how to grasp the sword, his dominant hand close to the cross-guard and with a space between his grips. He then grasped him by the shoulders and turned him to face the room center and had him lift the legendary blade to a battle-stance position.

"It…" Viktar spun slowly as he studied the astonishing blade.

Briefly Ravan thought he saw something oddly familiar about the way he moved.

"It asks to…" The young man's eyebrows knit in obvious frustration.

Ravan had by then enough frustration of his own and strode across the short distance to remove the blade roughly from Viktar's hands. The young Prussian stumbled backward and watched in amazement as Ravan swept the sword in a technical, three-stroke maneuver before stabbing it expertly into a chopping block and releasing it, allowing it to remain upright.

"It asks to kill," Ravan said coldly, his back remaining to Viktar.

"Yes.... It would be good to kill...someone...with such a great sword," Viktar agreed.

This brought expressions of surprise to the faces of both Ravan and Sayid. Ravan glanced over his shoulder at the peculiar young man.

Then, in a blinding instant, before Viktar could say anything more, Ravan spun and charged, sweeping as he did the longsword from the chopping block and spinning it so swiftly overhead that it appeared it would surely cleave its victim in two.

Ravan halted, the sword mere inches from Viktar's face, his breathing deep and slow, eyes locked on the younger man.

What Viktar did next was something Ravan was not fully able to categorize, for as the blade begged to do what it would, the young stranger did not...*flinch*, not at all. Instead, lifting the finger of one hand to touch the edge of the blade, Viktar then drew it back and peered closely as he observed the sliver cut—the second time the weapon had drawn his blood.

"Yes," Viktar's whisper escaped him. "I would like very much to *kill* a man with such a weapon."

CHAPTER SEVEN

Niveus' pale eyes snapped open. She lay on her back with her hands folded across her chest, staring straight overhead into the darkness. She did not stir, only…listened.

It was not the sounds of the night that awakened her. Nor was it the wind that moaned outside the windows of her castle bedroom or the call of night creatures to each other. No, she listened to something entirely different, something that whispered to her first from between her ears, slipping next to her heart before perching deep within her soul as it beckoned.

It was a sound Niveus could not deny, the call of a human soul reaching desperately for her, speaking not with words but with groans of pain. And…it belonged to a child.

Sitting upright, Niveus did not grab a cloak. Nor did she don daytime clothes or shoes. She simply walked, dressed in her nightgown and barefoot, to her bedroom door and opened it.

Her guard startled and leapt up from where he sat. He stopped her gently with a gloved hand upon her shoulder. "No, my lady. There is nowhere tonight that you must be but in your bed."

"I must speak to Velecent," she insisted and remained in the doorway, her crimson gaze fixed on the guard.

The man shifted uneasily and glanced about as though others might suddenly appear to help him with his cause. There were many who could not tolerate the gaze of this particular young woman for Niveus was beautiful, in the sense that she was rare, but unusual to the point of causing unease.

"Please," she asked sincerely, her voice light as air as it echoed in the stagnant hallway of the castle, "just get Velecent for me. It is all that I ask."

The guard sighed. It was difficult to deny the girl. That was why he was chosen for the watch, because he was normally impervious to her requests.

But tonight he could no more resist her pleas than he could his next breath.

"Back inside with you, and stay here. I'll wake him and return straightaway."

She nodded, stepping backwards into her room. The guard shut the door and was away for scarcely a minute. When he returned with Velecent, Niveus was gone.

"How? I don't understand!" the guard stammered.

"Never mind!" Velecent ran for the stairs leading to Risen's room. "She moves like a spirit. I think you can no more catch her than you can catch the wind, and that girl will be our undoing!"

* * *

Risen leapt from his bed and pulled his trousers and boots on as he stumbled toward the door, long, black hair flying tangled behind him. Shirtless, he grabbed only his coat.

"Check with the gate guards," he ordered, "then sweep the fields. We have a half moon. If she goes to the forest again, the dew should show her path. If not, we will search the village."

"And?" Velecent did not finish his question.

"We will do what we must." Risen paused long enough to notice the stricken expression of his father's best friend. "You are not responsible. None of us are. Why my sister's taken to such behavior is beyond me, but I intend to see the end of it."

* * *

The child, scarcely five years old, writhed in pain as the fever consumed him. He was flush and delirious, his skin burning to the touch.

Sitting at his bedside, his mother prayed desperately as she sponged the boy's face and chest. All the while the boy's father paced, his slippered feet padding back and forth across the dirt floor of their cottage.

A soft tap on the door drew both their attentions at once. The father eased the door open only a crack to see who might be there. Surprisingly, it was a girl of scarcely seventeen years, dressed only in her night shift and barefoot, even though there was frost on the ground. All would know instantly who she was. Niveus could never be mistaken for anyone else...*ever*.

"My lady." He pulled the door open and dropped briefly to one knee. "What...what brings you out on such a night?" He glanced over her shoulder as though expecting there to be others accompanying her.

"Let me see your son," she said simply. Red eyes, nearly black in the dim light, gave no indication of emotion, and cold as the night was, she trembled not at all.

"I-I…" the man hesitated.

"Let her in," the boy's mother begged in a whisper, her tear-streaked face pleading and exhausted as she glanced over her shoulder.

The father paused before opening the door wide, revealing the humility of their home and the sad scene that played out within. There, in the corner of the room on a tiny thatched bed, lay their only child. The boy writhed, taken by a terrible fever.

Niveus walked noiselessly across the floor to stand behind the boy's mother. The woman clutched her son's wrists tightly, holding the boy so he would not fall from the bed, and Niveus lifted one thin hand and rested it softly on the woman's shoulder. It was a gesture so profoundly sincere, and it brought a gentle sob from the father who remained at a distance behind them both, hands clasped to his chest.

The mother of the boy sat as though frozen. Niveus' hand slipped from her shoulder and, taking the woman's hands in her own, she gently plied her fingers from their desperate grip of her son. With a sob, the woman arose to make room for the albino girl.

Saying nothing, Niveus only gazed down at the very ill child. She did this for what must have appeared a maddening length of time before finally tipping her head to one side. Then, she passed her hand through the stagnant air above the sick bed.

"I don't understand—" the father began, but the mother silenced him.

"Shh…let her do what she can."

The two of them remained at a respectful distance, the father with his arms wrapped around his wife.

Niveus dropped to her knees and leaned forward over the boy. With the back of both hands, she drew an arc along the edge of the boy's bed as though she were spreading wings about his face. Then she pulled her hands back together over him, palms meeting center on his chest.

She reached gingerly for one of the boy's arms. The boy's eyes flashed open, dazed and staring, as Niveus touched his arm with her fingertips, drawing them slowly from his elbow down all the way to the center of his palm where she pressed gently with one finger.

Niveus could not know it was the first time the boy had opened his eyes in nearly two days.

He looked briefly at the girl before his lids fluttered closed again, and he rested much more quietly than before.

"He lives!" the father exclaimed.

"He dies," Niveus replied softly, immediately, without turning to look at them.

The mother sobbed as the father cried out, "*What*? Why do you say this? How can you know this?" He pushed his clinging wife from him and rushed forward as though he would cast the girl aside.

Niveus, still kneeling beside the bed, craned her head about so she could look over her shoulder at the couple. In the gentle light of the candle, her peculiarity was clearly evident, and it seemed enough to stop the father from approaching any further.

"He is ill of a sort that cannot be mended," Niveus said calmly, "but he will live until morning."

She pushed up until she sat on the edge of the bed, next to the child, and rested one hand, palm down, on the boy's heart while she placed the other hand on the boy's cheek. As she did this, she glanced again at the parents.

"I can arrest his pain until such time as he passes to the beyond." She said it nearly matter-of-factly as though not at all moved by her own summation.

"What kind of sorcery is this? I will not allow—" the father began, but the boy's mother stopped him, her voice broken with grief.

"Let her, Luc. *Please*…let her give our son comfort when we cannot."

Niveus was scarcely aware of the tragic debate that ran its course behind her, for her focus was entirely on the boy. Leaning her thin frame over the child, she kept one hand over the boy's heart while the other remained on his cheek. She stayed like this for some time, still as could be.

The child, silent at first, seemed to calm even more beneath her touch. Before long the fire left him, and his skin no longer burned. Presently, Niveus' hand slipped from his cheek, the other remaining on the boy's chest.

His parents crept closer, kneeling at his bedside, his mother touching her son's forehead as tenderly as only a mother can.

"He no longer burns," she said in gracious amazement.

His eyes flickered open again.

"Jori, you're awake," his mother murmured softly as she took his hand.

"Mother, Father…" he said, searching. "I can see you now." He smiled weakly.

His father glanced at Niveus, poised on the side of the bed, her pale hand still touching his son. She neither looked up nor spoke as the small family connected in the dear quiet of this last night.

"I'll die tonight," Jori said calmly.

A soft sob escaped the mother's lips, and speechless, she held her son's young hand to her lips and fought back tears.

"It's all right, Mother. I am not afraid."

The boy looked almost quizzically at Niveus as though noticing her for the first time. She did not stir but glanced sideways, away from the child.

"You helped me," Jori said.

Niveus nodded.

"I'll have no more pain," he added.

"Yes, that is correct," she said simply.

"Thank you."

Niveus continued to quietly minister to the boy as the parents spoke, held, cried, and spent precious last moments with their dying child. The hours wore on, and just as the first rays of morning threaded their way beneath the front door and between the window slats, the boy's breathing deepened and his eyes flitted closed one last time.

Only the cawing of a distant rooster in the wakening town broke the quiet passage of the child. Then the boy's mother cast herself across the body of her son and wept as she cradled him in her arms.

"Thank you." The child's father took Niveus' hands in both of his as she stood to leave, his face drawn with sorrow.

Niveus dropped her gaze to the floor, aware that sometimes her face made others less than comfortable. "I wish there was more that I could have done."

He held firmly onto her hands. "You gave our son solace when there was none to be had. There can be no greater gift than that."

Niveus moved to the front door, the one she had come through nearly seven hours before.

"Wait," the man begged before Niveus could leave. He tore himself away from the sad room and disappeared into another room, returning shortly with a sturdy pair of slippers.

"Please. I made them, and I want you to have them."

Niveus, strangely moved by the gesture, looked from the gift to the man.

The cobbler reached suddenly out and hugged the thin girl as though she was all the strength he had left. All the while, Niveus scarcely moved.

As he sobbed, she began to feel his sorrow and was possessed of it. She tried to shut it away, but it enshrouded her as surely as it did him. It was then that she began to reach a hand up and toward his head.

I can relieve your grief, just a small bit, she thought. She hesitated, not touching him but stopping barely short.

At long last, she allowed her hand to fall softly to her side.

Presently, he released her, and his son's pain now belonged to him.

Niveus slipped the shoes on as the mother pulled herself from her son's deathbed long enough to take a shawl from a coat hook by the front door.

Wrapping the shawl around Niveus' shoulders, she said, "You are an angel sent from God. Never believe those who would ever say otherwise."

Niveus' pale brow creased. "I would not believe anything other than that which I choose," she said simply.

Then, the grieving couple bade her safe journey, and the girl stepped from the small cottage into the barely rousing village. As Niveus made her way home, a few paused and pointed, whispering in hushed voices as she passed. *Look, it is our master's daughter—someone has been ill—someone has died—such a strange child, that one.*

When one of the castle soldiers eventually spied Niveus moving silently along the edge of the village, he scooped her up, sat her on the horse in front of him, and brought her home.

Risen was immediately notified, and he, Velecent, Moira, and Moulin met her straightaway.

"You can't just leave the castle like that!" Risen charged. "It isn't safe! What if someone saw you? What if they take you and..." He did not speak the unthinkable.

"I am no prisoner in my own home," she shot back at him, her strong opinion a contrast to her appearance.

Risen took her hands in his, begging her to listen to reason. "No, sister, you are not. But there are dangers that you expose yourself to without knowing. You—"

"I *do* know," Niveus said flatly. "But there are those who suffer."

He sighed.

"Niveus," Velecent tried, "your mother and father have trusted us with your care in their absence. If something happens to you, it would be devastating for them...for the entire realm. You are their only daughter. It is important that you remain safe. Surely you understand this."

Niveus hung her head. She did understand...everything. Only they...*didn't.*

* * *

Couriers were sent to spread the word.

Nearly everyone gathered at the town square for a general assembly.

As Risen took the stage, a hush fell over the crowd. All knew Lord Ravan's realm held stability in very precarious times, and he and Lady Nicolette were intensely respected because of it. All were also aware Risen was ruling in his father's absence, and most were happy to help in any way possible.

The subject of the meeting was, of course, Niveus.

"She is an angel!" The cobbler's wife spoke up from near the stage, yelling over the crowd. "Yes, the child is...*unusual*, but it is part of who she is, perhaps why she is so..." her voice wavered, "gifted."

Some murmured agreement. Others did not. No matter. Risen cleared his throat loudly. "You are all aware, or have heard, that my sister answers... callings. Perhaps you have been privy to this. Maybe you know someone who has been comforted by her presence. But...I don't believe it is safe for her."

Risen very much struggled as the murmurs from the crowd became louder, more mixed. He stepped closer to the edge of the stage, looking so much like his father that a hush fell across the crowd.

A baby cried in the distance as Risen spoke. "Should my sister," he swallowed thickly, "should Niveus visit a sick family member or friend, I must be notified at once." The murmurs grew in strength as he added, "Just of her whereabouts. There would be no issue, no invasion of your privacy if you wish for her to stay, but I must know, for her safety."

Some nodded. Others scowled.

Risen's voice boomed. "I am your Lord in my father's absence! Should I fall, Niveus becomes your Lady! Until my father's return, we must protect her, for her good, for the good of the realm!"

There were more murmurs of agreement and nods throughout the crowd.

"Once I know where she is and that she is safe, a guard will be secured at the door of the afflicted until my sister is done with her ministering."

The meeting was adjourned, and Risen pushed his way through the crowd. As they rode back toward the castle, he admitted to Velecent, "I think the townspeople understand."

Velecent nodded thoughtfully. "Your sister appears to have some of the same gifts as her mother—as a healer, I mean. No one can be certain when they might need her. It is something even a halfwit would not risk depriving themselves, or their loved ones, of."

When Risen's uncertain expression was all Velecent received in return, the soldier added, "'Tis the best you can do. Much as you hate to admit it, your sister's fate rests in her own hands."

To that, Risen pushed his horse to a gallop.

But no matter how the wind whipped the tears from his eyes, he could not outrun the trepidation in his heart.

* * *

"We must be careful," Moira cautioned softly. "Our sweet girl can be mistaken for…for…"

"For a *witch*?" Risen, face downcast, paced the castle's reception hall floor.

During the short ride home, he had been gradually overcome with a feeling of being trapped, as though his skin were suddenly too tight.

Risen loved his sister in a way no one understood. She knew things about him—things nobody else, not even his parents, knew. And he had no worries she would ever disclose his secrets to anyone. That was how generous her heart and…how stubborn…she was.

His natural inclination was to deny that Niveus was different from anybody else, but he knew he was only lying to himself. He wrestled greatly with this, especially when someone else tried to place a label on her.

He defended himself. "My offense is not toward you, Moira. I know without exception what Niveus is not and what she is, that she is God-given and that I love her. I care not what a few might call her; only that she might fall into the hands of someone unkind."

Velecent said, "Niveus is blessed, but she is also cursed. We cannot know the extent of her gifts or how others will see her, but if we consider Lady Nicolette…" He looked away when Risen planted his stare firmly on him.

Moulin tried. "Our Lord and Lady are gracious and strong, both of them, but there is no denying they are both unique, in ways. It only stands to reason that Niveus, born of them, would be more…*singular*."

Risen turned on them. "*I* am born of them. Can you share what is it you believe of *me*? How do you see me? Velecent…Moira?"

"Yes, you are of them," Velecent conceded, stepping near enough to rest a hand on Risen's shoulder. "But your sister, my lord, she is more mysterious even than Lady Nicolette. You know it is only the truth we speak. She baffles even you at times. I know she does."

There was nothing more to be said, and they agreed that the best they could do was done. Extra guards would be posted, and the town had appeared compassionate to their cause. Ravan's children were beloved, even the mysterious one so seldom seen.

CHAPTER EIGHT

Today, Ravan observed for the first time the steps of how malleable iron would be turned from crucible to Damascus steel. The process was tedious and exceedingly particular. There were many fine factors to be considered. Everything, from the breaking of the raw iron, the water level in the clay crucibles, and the flux material, to the type of wood they burned, would be meticulously metered out. Even the bellows must perform just so to bring forth the quality of Damascus steel they desired.

Several times over, Sayid halted the process and tossed out the raw beginnings only to start again. "It must be perfect. Your life, or the life of the man at your side, may depend on it."

Very swiftly Ravan realized the skill he sought was not a simple demonstration, and he would not grasp it in a single day, week, or even month. What he sought was truly an art form to be mastered.

No more could someone command sword-fighting in a single lesson than they could produce the knowledge he craved. And so, entrenched in the first day of many, Ravan was occupied with learning a great many things.

Nicolette, however, was occupied in quite another way....

* * *

The garden erupted directly from out the back door of Sayid's modest home with uncommon surprise. In contrast to the simple dwelling, it was smothered in beauty at every turn. An arbor of olive trees allowed Nicolette entrance into the sanctuary, an elegant iron gate the only obstacle to the welcoming world beyond. She released the catch and, drawing a breath in as though she could taste the splendor of what awaited, stepped into the hidden garden. It was to her perfection.

Smooth, white stones paved a maze of elegance, sometimes rising in pristine columns and archways, sometimes disappearing beneath the lovely foliage underfoot.

Olives, grapes, avocados, and figs burst from their respective shrubs and trees in dazzling display, enticing any passerby with their dripping fruit. It denied the poverty that screamed at humanity elsewhere in the world.

A small stream trickled and wound its way through the garden, feeding the chestnut, oak, and palm so perfectly that a leafy canopy stretched overhead. Even when the stream was hidden from view, its sound could always be heard nearby.

It was the rainy season, but today was sunny and glorious, and Nicolette's eyes shone brightly as she dragged her fingers softly across the thyme, rockrose, and poppy plants. Tulips, orchids, and iris decorated everything, and Nicolette believed that she could stay for a long while here before her heart called her home to France.

She thought of Luchina. Such a master gardener she was to create something so perfect, hidden so elegantly behind their small home. As she looked about herself, in as close to wonder as Nicolette could be, she believed that of the two, while Sayid made weapons, Luchina forged life. She was the greater artist, but men would likely never see it as Nicolette did.

Nicolette wandered through the tiny jungle maze, finally pausing at a stone bench nestled amongst cyclamen. Billowy white clouds were forming overhead and offered her shade, something she appreciated very much.

Sitting on the bench, she folded her hands in her lap and closed her eyes. If she had been able to see herself, perched as still as the stone upon which she sat, she would have perhaps thought herself just another ornamentation of the garden. The only indication she was not just another statue was the soft lift and fall of her hair in the gentle breeze.

Time became irrelevant, and all the while, she did not stir. Even the singing of the birds and the whisper of the breeze faded from her mind, eventually replaced by the intense silence of another place.

The happy activity of the garden gave way to a chamber of sorts, and Nicolette became enshrouded in a hallowed, dark nothingness. She waited. At last, beyond the silence of where she was now immersed, an element of something more arose. Where she dwelled—*this* place—was *sacred*.

Her consciousness moved to the center of the chamber as she permitted the space to fold around her. Within it rested that which allowed the absence of deliberation. The effect was that Nicolette's mind was clouded with absolutely nothing—not the feeling of air moving in and out as she breathed, not the warmth of her closed eyelids, not even the beating of her own heart.

Then, with scarcely the impression of a thought, she summoned that which she sought—the life thread of her children. Nearly as fast as the thought was born, there they were, both of them—the sparks of light burning brightly. Curiously, Risen's was blue and Niveus' was white. It had always been that way, every time she had ever summoned their essence, ever since their birth.

It was all Nicolette could see or know. She could tell how her children were currently occupied, but it was wholly what she desired. And, it would be what she would tell Ravan later—that their children were *alive*.

Just as swiftly as Nicolette entered the chamber of life, she was ripped from it. Her eyes flashed open, and she glanced about in mild surprise to discover the sun had passed a palm's breadth overhead. She had sat on the stone bench amongst the cyclamen for nearly an hour. But it wasn't the passage of time that had pulled her from her sanctuary. It was the presence…of another.

"Why do you follow me here?" she asked flatly, without looking behind into the dark shade of the trees.

Stepping from between a cluster of young palms, Malik held his hands out. He approached Nicolette casually, wide to her right.

"You are mistaken, my love. I've not followed you. I'm simply enjoying the splendor of the garden, much as you are. It is simply fate which has brought us together." His smile was unnaturally wide, and his voice was smooth and lilting as though an untruth, if sung, should be enough to convince her it was so.

Nicolette frowned at his broad assumptions. "You lie very comfortably," she murmured, not at all disturbed by his presence, only making a cool observation.

Malik's swagger faltered a small bit, but he maintained his cordial approach. "Tell me…Nicolette, is it? What is it that draws you to the barbarian you call *husband*?"

"Why should you presume to know what I call Ravan in the privacy of our moments together?" she shot back effortlessly as she rose from the bench.

He looked her up and down, making no effort to hide the lust in his expression. "You are beautiful. You know that you are." There appeared to be little that inhibited this man as he raised a hand, intending to touch her cheek.

"Touch me at your peril, Malik."

Perhaps it was the threat, perhaps it was the way she spoke his name, but he hesitated, instead dropping his hand to his side.

His expression passed from one of sport to something entirely more serious. Close enough so that he towered over Nicolette, his frame obscured what was left of the sun.

Nicolette did not step away, even when his breath washed warm and too-sweet across her face, "Come with me, my beauty. I leave tomorrow. Come with me to Prussia, and become my queen. You will live as you've never lived before—see things you have never seen. I know now that destiny has drawn me here. You are meant for *me*."

"You would likely cower before the things I have *seen*." Nicolette tipped her head to one side. "It is unfortunate that you have allowed yourself to be smitten of a force you will regret," she advised cautiously. "Know this, Malik. There is nothing you have, nor could ever hope to have, that could draw me from Ravan's side. He has always been meant to be with me."

Malik seemed done with cajoling her, and his lips creased tightly together as the good temper drained from his face like fat from spoiled milk.

"I have killed wives for less than the disrespect you show me now," he snarled.

"But I am no wife of yours," she said gravely. "Shall we press your...*destiny* and see how the lot would be cast should you mean to harm me in such a way as you have your wives?"

Malik stepped dangerously close to her. "You think that barbarian could save you?"

As though summoned, Ravan turned the corner just then, walking up the path.

Malik stepped swiftly away from Nicolette and greeted him hastily. "Your bride was just enjoying the surprise of running into me in the garden." He sneered as though enjoying some mythical victory that only he felt. He began to push past Ravan, but the mercenary caught him firmly by the arm, pulling him harshly to him as he spoke in a low voice.

"Lust for my wife all you wish, Malik. I know what it is you feel in your loins, but lay a hand on her, and I *will* kill you."

Malik jerked his arm free of Ravan's grasp. "How dare you speak to me that way? You have no idea who I am!"

"I have every idea who you will cease to be if you presume to touch my wife," Ravan warned coldly.

Speechless, Malik snorted and took his leave in no small hurry.

Watching until he was gone, Ravan turned to Nicolette. Slipping an arm around her waist, he tipped her chin gently up so that he could brush his lips against hers.

"You feel you must protect me?" Nicolette murmured warmly as Ravan's mouth found hers.

He kissed her deeply, pulling her closer to him as he ignored her question. When she returned his passion to the point that the garden might soon become their bed, Ravan broke free.

"Sayid asks that we join them for a midday meal," he said huskily.

"And give up the meal you would have here?" she teased, inviting him to stay in the garden.

He kissed her again, finally extricating himself only with great difficulty. "Aaagh! Let us feast upon each other later, perhaps on the shores of this island."

"No one will come for us here," she promised and took his hand in hers, laying it on her breast.

His eyes searched hers hungrily. "You know this?"

Nicolette nodded very deliberately, and he allowed her to lead him a short distance away. A covered arbor revealed itself, nestled so remotely as though its solitary purpose was to invite clandestine behaviors.

Reaching for her husband, Nicolette unlaced Ravan's trousers and directed him to sit on the bench. His eyes widened as she lifted her gowns and climbed onto his lap. Then she wrapped her arms around his neck, her warm lips finding his once more.

It was rare that the pair ever had such a sultry, inviting backdrop for their love, and both were immediately inclined to take perfect advantage of it.

Nicolette eased herself wordlessly onto her lover, and Ravan pulled her close, entwining one hand in her long hair as he rested the other on the small of her back. They devoured each other as though to be parted would be the end of all being. The only sound was their breathing and the occasional happy call of a songbird.

In due time, Ravan casually laced up his trousers, his face flush with happiness. He was startled when their host walked cheerfully around the corner of the secluded gazebo.

Sayid appeared, in order, surprised, enlightened, and embarrassed. Averting his gaze, he pointed over his shoulder and explained dumbly, "Dinner is served if you wish to join us," then hastily took his leave.

Ravan shot a look at Nicolette, his expression one of stunned surprise. "You said no one would come!" he exclaimed. "You said you *knew*!"

She smiled demurely, shrugged, and straightened her gowns as she walked past her husband, having had her way in superb fashion.

"I lied."

* * *

Malik masturbated, swiftly and violently. He told himself that he hated them, both of them. He called Nicolette "foul wench…God's whore…Satan's bitch" and said he would not piss on her to put out a fire if she burned. Then he imagined chopping the head from the barbarian and posting it opposite himself at his supper table and forcing Nicolette to dine at the same table.

All the while, however, what he saw in his mind was Nicolette, and what he imagined was her gossamer body, free of gowns, pressed against him.

The *tap-tap-tap* on his door came at a most inopportune moment.

"*Whaaat…do…you…waaant?*" he snarled, grunting and hunched over as he yanked his climax from himself.

Beyond the door, Gorlik's deep voice rumbled, "Supper is served, master. You requested I inform you."

Grasping a towel from the washstand, Malik relieved himself of his indiscretion and tossed the soiled rag on the floor. Opening the door, he shoved at the big man's shoulder with the heel of his hand as he passed, stomping from the room.

"I wish to kill something…"

* * *

It was mid-evening, and dinner was served in the front room of the small cottage. All gathered around the table, everyone…including Malik. The food was simple and magnificent.

Nicolette helped carry platters to the table. Sayid's wife was happily animated, clearly enjoying the company of the mercenary's unusual bride. Delighted that she seemed to enjoy the gardens so much, Luchina recounted how they had discovered the ancient garden in disrepair when they first acquired the property. Setting a pitcher of water on the table, she sat down next to Sayid.

The conversation was light; Luchina asked Nicolette where she was from and how they came by the Wintergrave Dynasty. "It is a realm of familial descent. I was married into it." She appraised Ravan warmly, offering few other details than the general whereabouts of their home.

Ravan was also in exceptional spirits, still basking in Nicolette's afternoon trickery. Acutely aware of how Malik lusted for her, he couldn't care less what disturbed the Prussian on this fine day. On the contrary, he nearly enjoyed flaunting in Malik's face his wife and the liberties he alone enjoyed with her. Juvenile, perhaps, but male to the core, and the mercenary smiled broadly across the table at Malik.

About Nicolette's demeanor, however, was something altogether cautious, and it seemed to settle over her even more as dinner commenced and the conversation turned to Risen and...Niveus.

"You have children?" Sayid asked innocently enough.

Malik's expression became one of intense interest as Ravan answered.

"Yes, a son." Taking another bite. "And a daughter. Both, fortunately, take greatly after their mother." He turned to regard Nicolette warmly.

"You are blessed. We have none of our own." Luchina's smile was bittersweet.

Sayid took her hand in his, his expression speaking of a loss no one else at the table comprehended.

"A *daughter*." Malik repeated with lascivious enthusiasm, ignoring the exchange. "You say she is fair as her mother?" He played casually with his eating utensil, his eyes locked on Nicolette.

Viktar looked all at once uncomfortable. He stared only at his plate, shifting the food about as though he knew well something of the conversation that no one else did.

"Beauty of another sort," Ravan answered easily, "and one even more difficult to define." He smiled through a mouth full of food as he glanced sideways at his bride. To his surprise, he saw not amusement but heedfulness in Nicolette's eyes. Ravan stopped chewing.

There was something about her expression that belied the here and now. He had learned long ago to read such expressions and to trust them implicitly. It had served him well before, and this was one of those moments. His smile faded as he swallowed heavily and took stock of everything in much greater detail.

Time seemed to slow to a dreadful pace as he glanced first at Viktar. The young man had a freshly opened wound above the eye. Next, Ravan regarded Malik, but the Prussian ignored him, his attention cast only on Nicolette as he leered.

"Such grace the world must enjoy that your daughter—one of such beauty as yourself—walks upon it. How *old* did you say she is?"

Viktar cleared his throat as silence settled over the dinner like a bad fog.

Ravan was immediately caught up in the odd exchange and answered with finality, "I did *not*."

Seeing for the first time the truth amidst the lies, he excused himself, hastily thanked Sayid and Luchina for dinner, and joined Nicolette as she arose to take her leave.

"Is the dinner not acceptable?" Luchina worried.

"It is perfect, thank you," Ravan replied graciously. "But I'm not as hungry as I first believed I was."

Nicolette said nothing, only led the way as the mercenary steered her from the room.

That night, Ravan decided he would no longer allow Malik's presence around either himself or Nicolette. He believed there was something about the Prussian that reeked of contagious malignancy, and he intended to stay as far away from the man as possible.

"What was it at supper?" he asked Nicolette, his back to her as he undressed. "You saw something…something I did not."

"His fate. It is…" She sighed, something Nicolette rarely did. "It is, perhaps, entwined with someone we know."

"Malik's? Or his nephew?" Ravan looked over his shoulder to observe Nicolette drawing a finger peculiarly about a candle flame, the fire almost dancing as it tracked her.

"Both…" she murmured.

Ravan crossed his arms on his chest and leaned against the bed.

"We know many of grave importance—kings, noblemen, warriors. Malik rules a significant realm in Prussia. Of course the destiny of his domain may overlap with someone we know. There is no great surprise at the possibility."

Nicolette said nothing, only drew her finger from the flame as she gazed out the open window into the darkness of the garden.

Ravan ceased trying to downplay what had unsettled her at dinner. Instead, he thought of Velecent, Salvatore, Moulin, and others, wondering in what vague way Malik's destiny had become a thread into someone he might know.

Why had he been so careless at dinner? he asked himself. His instincts were normally better than that. Perhaps he had become complacent in the warmth of his host and the island.

He walked over to Nicolette and rested his hand on her shoulder. She laid her hand on top of his. Ravan felt threatened by Malik no more than any other posturing tyrant, but he recalled another man from long ago, one very much like Malik. He frowned. He had underestimated Adorno and told himself he would never make that mistake again.

Now, perhaps he had…

* * *

That night, Malik and Gorlik walked through the coastal town together; Gorlik in front, his beastly gaze sweeping in a wide arc.

Along the midnight wharves were men and women who traded in those things that might be sold in the depravity of the night, and it was not long before a maiden knelt in front of Malik, between the shanty walls that separated the stalls of a sleeping fish market.

Gorlik stifled a yawn as he watched guard, scarcely engaged by what transpired behind him. He had stood guard for occasions such as this many times before and knew it would not take long, but he was forbidden to watch.

In the shadows, the whore did as instructed, undoing the catch of Malik's trousers before lifting his flaccid penis to her mouth.

"That's it," he grunted. "No hands, yes...*yes*..."

She closed her eyes as whores are wont to do unless commanded to watch.

As Malik's passion mounted, he pulled from beneath his vest a fine, sickle-shaped blade, hiding it behind his back. "You like this, *don't* you."

Waiting until just the right moment—when the girl's eyes flashed upward to acknowledge his words—he slipped the blade down, below her throat, and drew it long, from side to side.

* * *

Malik climaxed, and his world washed in sweet red as the surprised eyes of the prostitute flashed wide. Blood ran out her still-open mouth as she slipped from him and fell with a soft thud to the ground. He groaned and grasped his penis, finishing the deed himself. All the while, he imagined what Nicolette's daughter must be like.

Finally, he kicked at the body. When no sound was returned, the Prussian walked hastily from the alley, pushing roughly past his guard.

"Get her out of here."

* * *

Gorlik hoisted the girl as though she were merely a dead sack of worthlessness—a throwaway human being. It was a hateful image of exquisite proportion and drove home the notion that humanity was far from enlightened.

Away from the village, Gorlik waded chest-deep into the salty waters of the choppy shore.

The sea lapped roughly against the frame of the big man—God chastising him for covering Malik's wickedness—as he struggled against his growing buoyancy. Finally, he stopped, prepared to release his burden.

The corpse floated, eyes half-open. Frowning, Gorlik stared at the gaping hole at the neck, skin chalky-white in the moonlight. The wound, curiously clean from the salt water, opened and closed, speaking to him in a cruel way. He regretted...that he had not been allowed to defile the corpse.

Finally, Gorlik released the body of the girl, weighted by a stone, into the sad, shallow depths. Someone's daughter was then left to be fed upon by whatever creature might last have use for her. Gorlik only grunted, struggled to shift his large frame from the water, and returned to his master's side.

* * *

Malik's sword was finished the next morning. Sayid silently blessed it with an Islamic prayer for peace as he drew two fingers gently along the length of it. Then he seated the weapon in a silk-lined case before handing it over to the Prussian ruler. Humbly, the Syrian accepted payment in gold and was not at all sorry to say goodbye to the foreigner.

That day the Prussian, followed by his guard and nephew, sailed from Crete with a beautiful sword and an agenda.

Malik was happy to be finally gone from the island and the witch who had obsessed nearly every waking thought...and much of his sleep. But he would not be heading straight back to Prussia. There were suddenly more pressing needs, and so Malik altered his plan. His primary intention, now, was to go first...to *France*.

CHAPTER NINE

✝

Moira sighed as she impatiently dragged the brush through Niveus' tangled mane of hair.

"You can't let it go for so long!" She stabbed in the air with the brush. After a few more sweeps, she exclaimed further, "That's *it*...you are no longer in charge of your hair. Every morning and evening I will care for it." She yanked, perhaps too hard before summing it all up. "It looks as though rats live there! Is that what you want, Niveus? Rat hair?"

Niveus blinked slowly as she ran her finger slowly along the frame of a round hand mirror, tracing the edge of it. After circling it three times, she paused and pressed the pad of her index finger softly into the middle of the mirror, peering intently at the glass as she did.

No one but she could see what happened just then—how the surface of the mirror rippled, sending a few small waves to the edge of the frame as though someone had touched the still surface of water. It was a portal, and Niveus' gaze was fixed firmly upon it and...what lay beyond.

"Niveus, are you hearing me?" Moira yanked on her hair as she brushed.

It was enough to draw Niveus' attention back from the liquid glass, and her brow furrowed with soft frustration. She glanced sideways at Moira, instantly compelled to say, "Let's just cut it off...*all* of it. Then you would worry no more for it, and I would be worried no more by you about it."

She reached for a delicate pair of scissors, which lay alongside an ivory comb on the vanity, and went to grasp a lock of her own snow-white hair. Niveus hair was not the only thing that was white. So were her eyelashes and eyebrows, and they were so delicate they appeared almost as frosty, lace canopies above her most unusual eyes.

She snipped a lock of her hair, allowing it to fall to the ground, and was reaching for another when Moira slapped her hand away.

"No! Niveus, no!" Moira knelt in front of her. "You must not do such a thing!"

"Why?"

"Because it is displeasing."

"To whom?" Niveus wondered, not at all convinced.

Moira gently slipped the tiny pair of scissors from the girl's hand and dropped them into her own pocket instead of replacing them on the dresser. "To everyone, everyone but you."

"And what everyone thinks of me is important..." the girl said as though from rote memory.

"Good, Niveus. Yes, exactly. It matters what others think of you."

"But, I matter. You tell me this every day." She laid the tip of her finger on the mirror again, but the mirror held its secrets. "Should it not be important what I think of me? Because...I think I should cut my hair off. Just now, it seems significant to me," Niveus appealed to one of her only true friends.

Moira sighed and stood up to resume brushing the tangles from the silken and still terribly knotted hair. "*No*, Niveus. Some things are to be endured for the sake of the greater good."

"I don't see where my having hair or not affects a greater good."

"You insult your public and your family when you behave so...so..." Moira evidently had no words to describe further what she meant or simply chose not to say them.

"So *peculiar*?" Niveus finished for her.

"No! Yes..." She added swiftly, "I don't mean to say that you're...uhmm..." Again, Moira allowed silence to fill in the obvious.

"Because someone might find me ugly and not care for that." Niveus tried again, woefully sincere.

Moira rested her hand on the girl's shoulder and sighed. "Is it so awful that someone might be attracted to you? You never know."

"Like Moulin is attracted to you?" Niveus did not smile, but a smile tugged at her lips as she glanced sideways.

Moira appeared at first astonished, her mouth hanging open, then laughed outright. "*That* is simply none of your concern, now is it?"

"I know you love him. And he loves you, just if you were wondering."

Niveus could not see the soft smile that swept across Moira's lips, but she knew it was there all the same. Her handmaid went back to working the brush through the tangles, and they both lapsed into a long, sweet silence.

Just as Moira finished, Niveus turned and stopped her, resting a slender hand on hers. "Moira. I do understand, about what you said. And I promise, I will brush my hair from now on…if I can only remember that I should."

Moira smiled sadly and took Niveus' chin in her hand. "*If* you can remember…"

* * *

In the small village, which sat nestled between the Wintergrave Dynasty castle and the vast forest beyond, a foreigner slithered through a tavern door followed by two other men. Only a few patrons glanced at them as the strangers threaded their way to a solitary table in the far corner of the room.

The obvious leader made no effort to acknowledge anyone else, but he clearly stood out, skin dark like ale and cropped, coarse hair, faintly blond. His traveler's clothes were musty but not cheap—silken, and ornately embellished—and not of the fashion that was common to this area.

And there was something else about him, about the way he carried himself with his narrow stare and tight set to his mouth. It bespoke a wicked refinement. There was no doubt that the man was not from here.

The two who followed him were unusual in their own right and, most curious, did not behave as friends to one another. It was obvious that the younger man was somehow indebted to the leader. Reticent in every move, he waited until the other took his seat before seating himself. All the while, his expression was dull, much like a beaten horse, and he kept his head bowed. The sense was that, if it were possible, he would have wished himself long gone but had no way to exact such a thing.

The third and largest of the three was clearly there as protection. Despite his monstrous size, the beast was moderately oaf-like. He carried, girded at his waist, unusually curved, matching blades and declined to remove them when he took his seat. It was a gesture crude enough that no one else in the inn would dare engage them.

When the servant girl came around, placing a cautious distance between herself and Gorlik, Malik was quick to speak first. "I come from afar." His accent supported his claim. "What is the name of this realm?" The Prussian's normally tight-lipped expression burst into a warm smile as he lavished his intention entirely on the girl.

She relaxed as her gaze flitted appreciably from Malik to the young man with the soulful eyes and bruised face. Viktar looked away as she hastily explained, "It is the Wintergrave Dynasty, finest in all of North France."

Malik laughed warmly. "How delightful. Of course it is. And the master—is it hard to gain an audience with him?"

With a smoldering twig, the girl lit the small cluster of candles that sat nestled in a wooden bowl before shaking the stick dead and gesturing with the smoky tip of it. "Wouldn't be, except that the Lord is traveling. His son commands the realm in his absence." She glanced happily at Viktar again. He only looked at his hands.

"Son? Ah, I see. And this Lord...*Ravan*, is it? He must be very proud of his son?"

A flush crossed the girl's cheeks. "Risen? Oh, he's so much like his father, only..." she furrowed her brow, "more charming." It was fairly obvious the girl thought highly of the heir to the Wintergrave Dynasty.

Malik played shrewdly into the conversation, directing her as easily as he would an overfed pig. "I think I've heard that before, charming young man to be sure. Too bad he has no siblings."

Viktar shrank away, obviously uncomfortable with the direction the conversation had taken.

"You have heard wrong, sir," the maiden replied eagerly. "He has a sister—Lady Niveus. She's a strange one, though. Never understood people's fascination with her, but I suppose people are drawn to a...an oddity."

The girl covered her mouth with her hand when Viktar's pleading eyes met hers, and tittered, "I mean, she's lovely and all, just...*queer*. But that's no great surprise. She is Lady Nicolette's daughter."

Malik could not be more delighted at hearing that name. "I see...cast from the same mold?" Malik prodded, urging her to betray Niveus further.

"Yes. She's so much like her mother, only...more, I suppose."

From across the room, the Innkeeper shot the maiden an admonishing glance.

The girl blurted loud enough for others to hear, "May I get ale for you and your companions? Perhaps dinner?"

"Yes, all around, and I should like a room at the Inn. One...for them," Malik gestured toward Viktar and Gorlik. "But I must have a cottage." He glared at Viktar. "Just can't seem to sleep with the prying eyes of others all about me. Can you?"

"For tonight?" the girl asked.

"For...the week, I think." Malik glanced about, supremely satisfied, and leaned back in his chair, lacing his fingers across his chest. "I think I fancy this village, and I should like to stay for a while; that is, if you can find the lodging for me?"

The girl allowed her gaze to fall again on the youngest one of the three, and her face brightened. "The stableman's cottage is vacant. It is old but nice—been fixed up for traveling nobles. But we've not leased it for some time. It is the off-season, after all. But I can ask?"

When Malik pulled from his pocket a solid gold coin and pressed it earnestly into her hand, the girl's mouth opened in an astonished, silent, "Oh." Then she became considerably more animated, allowing her hip to brush up against Malik's arm.

"That would be outstanding," he said. "And...do you suppose you could arrange to have me visit Lord Risen and...Lady Niveus?"

"*No*. No, of course not," she said hastily. "It's not like that. Lady Niveus sees no one, ever. But..." She pulled from her waist a cloth, hastily drawing it across the table.

"But?" Malik urged her gently, his smile dancing, dangerous as a swaying viper.

The girl leaned closer, her exposed bosom plainly revealed, and dropped her voice. "Surely you have heard the news."

"*News*?" He spread his hands in appeal. "No, I'm afraid I have not. We have only just arrived today. We are on a sojourn, so to speak. Can you enlighten me?"

"The announcement this morning...about Lady Niveus."

Malik leaned forward with greedy anticipation. "Yes?"

"No one knows how she does it, only that she does. Some say she's..." The girl fidgeted.

"What?" Malik's smile faded, and he took hold of the girl's wrist, pulling the girl down so that her breasts threatened to spill into his face.

Viktar rested his elbows on the table and folded his hands together, dropping his forehead into them so that he looked as though he prayed.

Malik released the girl, and she tucked the rag into the waist of her skirt before saying in a low breath, "Lady Niveus...she leaves the castle, and they don't know how. I think it's magic."

"But...*why*?" Malik pulled out another gold coin, pressing it firmly onto the table's wooden surface with his index finger.

The maiden bit her lip, edging her hand close to his. She tried to pry the coin from under his finger, but Malik held it fast.

"What? What was that you said?"

Chortling nervously, she leaned in again, her lips close to his ear, giving him another look at her barely contained breasts. "To help, of course—when people suffer. But it makes Lord Risen frightfully nervous. He asks that we let him know if she is ever about the village. News makes its way here first, generally."

The girl righted herself and glanced nervously toward the Innkeeper.

"What do you mean, *when people suffer?*"

"The girl, she just knows. They fall ill and she appears at their doorstep." The girl shrugged. "She has the gift, like her mother, they say."

"*Like her mother...*" Malik could not see how his expression was at once very far away. He said hastily, "That's kind of her, don't you think? And very attentive of her brother to worry so for her."

He allowed the maiden to pry uncertainly at the coin with her fingers, his smile widening as she did, his other hand slipping to cup and squeeze the back of her thigh through her skirts. "You're such a good little servant now, aren't you?"

"I am, your lord. Best there is." She flounced nearer.

Tolerating the grope, the maiden finally had the coin in her grasp. She cast a guilty glance at the handsome young man, head still hidden in his hands, dropped the coin between her breasts, and left to fetch their orders.

When she was gone, Viktar insisted softly, "You *lie*, uncle. You know Lord Wintergrave has a daughter. He said so when we were in Crete."

"'Twas not a lie. It was just a way of sorting out the truth," Malik snorted. "You mustn't underestimate a foe. For all we know, it was Ravan who lied."

"About having a daughter? And what foe is he? Red Robes is so distant from this realm, and his allegiances—"

"Why do you argue with me?" Malik slammed his fist onto the table. When several about the room looked their way, Malik took a deep breath and leaned forward, hissing under his breath. "My sister insisted I groom you to the degree required for you to rule my domain! And you challenge me at every turn?" He snorted, "Would you have me beat you again?"

Gorlik peered from beneath mammoth brows. Viktar gritted his teeth and fell silent.

"You know *nothing* of the world and the opportunities that can be so easily overlooked," Malik shot between clenched teeth. "Your purpose is only to watch and learn, not question my every move!"

No more was said as the maiden arrived with venison and porridge. She returned at intervals, overly attentive with the needs of the three. When the men finally retired for the night, Viktar and Gorlik took the room while Malik sauntered, following the maiden down the stone pathway to the cottage, which was hidden in a small thatch of trees not too far behind the Inn. He carried with himself more wine and the Damascus sword.

The maiden, considerably richer for her short interaction with Malik, smiled coyly over her shoulder as she unlocked the door. Turning to give him the key, she curtsied and chortled brightly, "Thank you, my lord," then went to sweep around him.

"Wait," Malik said soberly, grasping her by the arm. "There is still the matter of the gold coins."

"But...but you said—" Her dumb eyes widened in foolish surprise.

"You thought your blathering on and the feel of your arse through your skirts was worth *two* gold coins?"

"But—"

"I only said what a good servant you were. You agreed. Then...you took my second coin. Now it is time for you to *serve*."

When the girl looked nervously over Malik's shoulder, back down the path toward the Inn, he added, "Perhaps the Innkeeper would help us sort this...*misunderstanding* out."

"Oh, no..."

"No? Then, might we sort it out ourselves?" He shoved the door farther open and swept his hand invitingly inside.

"But I've never..."

He glowered at her, disbelieving.

She added, "M-mm, never for coin."

"I predict...you will excel at it."

* * *

Once inside the cottage, the maiden stripped, blushing as she attempted to cover herself with her hands. Her skin was white, doughy, and dimpled, the kind that showed welts easily. She stalled and circled closer to the bed, tittering and batting her lashes as she watched Malik's face transform to something altogether carnal.

"My lord!" she exclaimed when he loosened his belt.

"The bed." He pointed.

"I'm flattered you find me so attractive." She said and began to recline the bed.

"No...*kneeling*," he insisted, and she obeyed, kneeling on the bed, legs splayed vulgar and wide. Malik stepped behind, yanking his penis from his trousers.

"Maybe we should—" She was silenced when he seized her fleshy buttocks, one in each hand, pulled them wide apart, and impaled her. She squealed when he slapped her arse hard.

"My lord!" she cried, bracing herself. "I-I—"

"Cover your face!" he ordered.

"Yes, my lord," she mewled and pulled the sheeting over her head, whimpering submissively as he pounded himself into her. Sniveling little grunts escaped her in cadence to his thrusts, her ample breasts slapping urgently in time.

His fingernails cut into her fleshy hips as he sacked her for what seemed an eternity until, finally, Malik climaxed. Throwing his head back, he groaned a long, guttural snarl and whispered one word…

…*Niveus*.

* * *

Malik girded his trousers, leaned back against the bed, and crossed his arms, watching the maiden scramble about, the greasing he had given her dripping down her legs.

Flush with gold and the rutting she had just endured, the girl teetered for the door. Before she left, his voice snapped her back to attention.

"Wait…now, tell me again, before you leave. *Say* it."

The girl dropped her head, her hand resting on the door latch. "I will come straightaway with any news of Lady Niveus or Lord Risen, especially of their whereabouts, and I will speak of our acquaintance to no one."

"And?"

The girl blushed. "Here, tomorrow night…again."

"There's a good little bitch. You see? You *are* trainable," Malik snorted.

She glanced over her shoulder, clutching the two coins and her clothes to her chest. "But…there will be more gold, won't there?"

Malik's grin fell to a lecherous snarl. "Of course…mmm, what did you say your name was?"

"Modest. My name is Modest."

Surprise flashed across his face, and he laughed outright. "Of *course* it is. And yes, *Modest*, there will be more gold. After all, whores must be compensated." He meant for the betrayal of Niveus that the girl was ready to serve up without hesitation; not the abuse from Malik she would endure for evenings to come.

"Now…get out."

The maiden tripped naked into the night, having thrown propriety to the wolves.

Malik reclined on the bed. His complacency, however, turned swiftly to restlessness, and he tossed, tangling himself in the bedclothes.

Sleep chooses nights like these to elude those without a conscience, and so, slumber would not invite even the slightest dream to interrogate Malik's black soul.

Exasperated, he finally arose, drank the rest of the wine, and paced the cottage floor...like a wolf circling prey.

* * *

Upstairs at the Inn, Viktar steadied himself on a rickety stool in the corner of the small room. Resting his elbows on the ramshackle desk, the only furniture besides the single bed, he frowned and paused from composing yet another letter to his mother. It had become easier to lie to her, but he knew she was clever—probably read the truth in the words he *didn't* write.

Gorlik snored, splayed across the bed, clutching both swords across his chest as he always did. Viktar wondered briefly if he might extract one of the swords from the brute but decided he could not. He wished he had Malik's sword—the beautiful blade the Syrian had made. It was the most incredible weapon Viktar had ever seen, not because of its beauty but because of what it could so easily do.

But his uncle was never without the sword. Neither did Malik allow him any resources. Even Viktar's clothes carried an unwelcome stench as he had no coin to exact laundering.

How do I come by a weapon with no gold? he wondered briefly before returning to his letter.

Shortly, he nodded off to sleep, quill still in his hand. Then, the younger Prussian dreamed of an angel...

* * *

"Who are you?"

The figure did not speak, only remained as though frozen behind a crystal gate.

"You're Niveus, aren't you?"

She said nothing, but beyond her shone a light like Viktar had never seen. Then the porcelain angel beckoned for him, her hand outstretched.

He reached for her, his fingertips almost touching hers.

It unnerved him that her eyes...were on fire.

CHAPTER TEN

The next morning, Viktar was up at dawn and was soon joined by Malik and Gorlik. They left the carriage and departed on horseback. The vision of the fiery-eyed angel weighed heavily in the back of Viktar's thoughts as they loped through the foggy woods and across the countryside of the Wintergrave Dynasty. It was a beautiful ride, but the growing seed of urgency had planted itself in his belly, ever since he had held the mercenary's sword and especially because of last night's dream.

Viktar now believed beyond anything that he must kill his uncle, but executing the act was more difficult than he had estimated. The margin of opportunity was always dangerously narrow, for Malik always exercised great caution. Viktar decided it was something his uncle must have adopted over many years, for hated men of power could never be too careful. Consequently, Gorlik was always somewhere nearby, dreadful blades close at hand.

At a loss at how to best negotiate the wicked waters he felt he scarcely tread, Viktar realized that if he killed one...he must kill the other. But he needed a better plan. Murder on foreign soil might not be workable.

No matter. He could wait until they were back at Red Robes. Then Gorlik would be less occupied with his master's whereabouts, and Viktar could press forward with the...murder. His breath caught in his throat with this thought. He believed he had now scaled the precipice of iniquity and fallen off the other side into the pit of immorality, for...he was prepared to destroy another.

He felt shame this morning at sending the letter out to his mother with such happy words of optimism and hope. He wanted to let her know— yearned to share his dark secret—that her *son* intended to kill her *brother*.

These were Viktar's heavy thoughts as the magnificent castle came into view. Breathing deeply of the frigid air, he recalled again last night's dream.

It had rattled him thoroughly and given him a queer sense that they were intruding upon something forbidden, approaching Ravan's dwelling as they were.

It was a truly splendid castle, its fine spires thrusting high above the immense walls. The tip of one elegant spire almost seemed to snag the overhead clouds; the castle seemed too decadent for the mercenary he had met in Crete—the one whose sword he had coveted. Viktar could not know the castle had long ago belonged to another.

Onward they rode, along the edge of the forest, and even Malik fell silent. Viktar noticed how his uncle *always* peered in the direction of the castle, his stare fixed as though magnetized by it. What was it that the wretched man saw? Viktar wondered briefly of the young man left in charge of the dynasty. Risen, wasn't it? Unusual name for a boy...

The day dragged on, and this was all they accomplished. *Ride, ride, ride,* back and forth, watching the distant fortress. At day's end, when they returned to the inn, Modest was much more subdued than the night before. She seemed distracted, as though she had other business that needed tending to, but she did whisper at intervals into Malik's ear. He only nodded, saying nothing about it. His face, however, brightened.

At night's end, Viktar noticed his uncle slip the maiden yet another gold coin. What he didn't see was how shortly, in the cottage, Modest stripped for the second time. Only tonight, the Prussian lord would not have his turn at pounding the wench. No, something about her had annoyed him today, so instead, Malik reclined by the fire and watched, thoroughly entertained as Gorlik spitted the girl backwards and forwards like a prize pig.

And she squealed like one, more so than last night, scarcely able to swallow what the brute thrust upon her.

Finally, nearly an hour later, Modest tottered from the cottage after the giant filled her to overflowing.

"Same time, tomorrow!" Malik called to her back.

"Yes, m'lord," the naked tart mumbled beyond the slamming door.

* * *

It went on like this for just over a week—up for an early breakfast before scouring the lands surrounding the castle. There was no sense of adventure in the insanity of it, and on this particular afternoon, when they pulled their mounts up for a rest, it was just as before. Malik only wished to watch the castle.

As always, Viktar saw nothing remarkable. They observed supply carts come and go from the front gates, but the drawbridge was always kept drawn and the portcullis closed. All entries were closely guarded from the ground as well as from the surrounding towers and battlements.

"Uncle, why do we not ask for an audience?" Viktar pressured his uncle. He knew Ravan had intimidated Malik splendidly, so an audience with Risen would likely be out of the question. Perhaps then, more importantly, Malik might decide to leave Niveus alone. For some reason, it was *her* Viktar worried most about.

He tried again. "We've ridden nearly the entire perimeter several times over. If you truly wish to meet Lord Risen and Lady Niveus, then—"

"Not yet!" Malik spat. "I want to know the surroundings first." He swept with two fingers then stabbed them toward Viktar. "It is always good to have a feel of the land before you meet a strong man. You never know; Ravan, or his bastard son, could be an ally but just as easily a foe."

"Bastard *son*? I, uh...*foe*?" Viktar blinked. "But, if you are not seeking his allegiance...I don't understand—"

"What do you know about Ravan?" Malik spun his horse about, his face suddenly twisted. "What do you know about true *power*?" He spat the words as though spitting the plague from his mouth.

The young man frowned and drew his horse up short. "I know you carry great power, and the Emperor believes you loyal. But you know as well as I that this long diversion to France was unreasonable. Now I wish to send word to my mother, to explain why we've been gone so long."

Malik could scarcely draw his attention from the distant castle.

"Enough of your squalling! I sent word two weeks ago," he lied. "Your *mother* will be adequately pacified, and...I have changed my mind. I wish to be gone before the week is done."

This surprised Viktar, but at least he had an answer. Whatever it was that drove Malik here would be on a distant horizon before long. He sighed, but scarcely had time to consider his good fortune when a scout emerged from the trees and rode straight up to them, hand resting loosely on his sword. Viktar could not help but notice how well the soldier was outfitted, how fine the horse and armor.

"We are just passing through, visitors come to experience your land," Malik said in a thick accent. "I've heard the realm is stable, where many around here are not, and that the hunting is good." He gestured toward Viktar. "I've brought my nephew from afar to taste of your resources, but good fortune doesn't seem to travel with us today."

He held out empty hands for the scout's sake.

"The realm is stable," the soldier confirmed before asking, "Your name?"

"Lord Vedlund of Poland. I've come to meet with your master but—"

"And you hunt without bows?" The scout crossed his arms casually on the saddle pommel.

Viktar noticed Malik struggle to suppress his sneer. But suppress it he did as he replied sweetly, "'Tis only a scouting ride, to determine where the beasts may dwell. But as I was saying, I was so disappointed to discover Lord Wintergrave is gone. Obviously our correspondences were misdated."

Viktar was about to interject something when Malik cast a warning glance his direction, and Gorlik moved nearer, pressing Viktar's horse aside.

The soldier studied them suspiciously, finally saying, "Please allow me to prepare an audience with Lord Risen in our master's absence. He would be honored to make your acquaintance, and you must stay at the castle. The accommodations are excellent, and you would be most welcome."

"Uh-mm, no...no, I'm afraid that is out of the question." Malik hastily dismissed the proposition. "But thank you for the invitation. We will be leaving this afternoon. Your village, however..." Malik waved in the general direction of the town, "has been warmly hospitable. My regards to Lord Ravan and Lady Nicolette. Good evening."

Malik gave the sentry no time to think further about the logistics of the lie. He tipped his head farewell and spurred his horse about, heading back in the direction of the town.

Viktar could feel the weight of the soldier's scrutiny between his shoulder blades as they rode away. He scarcely believed Malik had told the truth but prayed they would indeed be leaving that afternoon.

That evening, the three sat in the same corner of the Inn, just as they had for nearly two weeks, all morosely silent as they picked at their dinners.

"Gorlik, do you think I waste my time?" Malik asked suddenly.

It was unusual for him to speak to his bodyguard other than to give him commands, and the big man only shrugged.

"Then *you*, nephew, do you believe I am mad for bringing us here?"

At that moment, Viktar was gravely preoccupied with how he might dispatch his uncle's death if Malik changed his mind about leaving, and the question snapped him to attention. He hesitated and leaned forward.

"Uncle, you were offered an audience with Lord Risen and refused. Now you shall never meet the girl." When Malik said nothing, he added, "That *is* why we are here, isn't it? It is what drives you, is it not?"

"You know nothing!" Malik protested weakly, but Viktar persisted.

"I have learned much from you, Uncle, more than you realize. I believe it is time you went home, as you told the sentry you would."

Malik scoffed and drank deeper of his ale, but did not argue the point.

Viktar sighed and resigned himself from his efforts. What he could not know was that after seeing absolutely nothing of Niveus for their entire stay—something which gave the young Prussian a sense of relief but also regret—Malik would make a very bold decision…tonight.

* * *

As the evening hours waned and the patrons took their leave in small batches, Malik downed the stale remains of his ale, slamming the mug decisively on the table.

"We are done!" he announced jovially and pushed his way up from his chair, stumbling toward the back entry. "Come, we shall drink more together! Celebrate our…" he staggered, "…exodus." He motioned sloppily for Viktar to join him.

Viktar hesitated, and Gorlik moved to accompany them.

"No. Not you," the man waved his guard away. "Tonight…I simply wish for more spirits and someone to share them with. Viktar can see to my needs. Besides," his gaze fell heavily on Viktar, "I should like to spend some private time with my nephew, before…we journey home."

The big man grunted and took his leave. A few remaining patrons moved aside as the monster lumbered toward the tavern stairs. Viktar, however, followed as Malik led the way out the back door of the Inn. As they threaded their way to the cloistered little cottage, nestled amongst the firs, Viktar reconsidered his master plan. Perhaps this would present the murderous moment—he, alone with his uncle, at last. But then, Malik had ceased to beat him this last week. Could he be coming around?

Once in the cottage, Viktar sat obediently opposite his uncle, and they shared quaint conversation. The younger man did not notice how minimally Malik sipped his drink. What he did notice was the sword propped casually against his uncle's thigh.

"It is good to see you in such good spirits tonight," Viktar offered brightly.

"Yes. The evening has all the promise of a new day. And…I wish to leave tomorrow."

This surprised Viktar, and he blurted cheerily, "I think that is the right decision, Uncle! It has been nearly two months since we have been gone.

Mother will be so delighted to see us finally home."

"Of course." Malik waved his hand loosely about as though done with all of it. "What care I of this girl, anyway."

Suspicion clouded Viktar's mood. Happy as he was to be gone, it seemed unreasonable to have Malik so suddenly willing to leave unsatisfied. He had seen the way his uncle had coveted Nicolette and knew it was why Malik was possessed of his fantasies of her daughter.

Indeed, the effect Nicolette had, even on himself, was undeniable. And, on some level, he had also been curious to see Niveus—to see if she was anything like her mother. Even to meet Lord Risen would have been a great honor—to stand before the son of a warrior as great as Lord Ravan.

Malik suddenly slammed the brandy bottle on the table. "Empty! Well, now this is simply not acceptable! Off with you, and bring a draft back," Malik snorted.

Hesitating, Viktar finally disappeared back to the Inn and returned shortly with a fresh bottle. He approached the tiny cottage with a growing plan—if he could get his uncle to drink the rest of the brandy, if he could get the sword, *if....*

Viktar stepped into the cottage to discover Malik gone. Thinking he must have stepped outside to piss, he scanned the small space again before stepping farther inside.

Lost in his thoughts, he did not see Malik step from behind the heavy door and move silently...behind him. Then, before Viktar knew what had happened, Malik had a cord about his neck.

* * *

Malik pulled the cord tight, surprised by the strength of the boy as Viktar kicked up and backward. Both crashed to the floor, kicking and thrashing, their feet scattering coals from the fire.

Viktar clawed at his own throat. All the while, the monster held tight, choking his nephew not quite to the point of death.

No. Not death. Not...*yet.*

Something primitive, almost sensual, washed over Malik, burning strong within his belly as Viktar weakened, finally laying limp on the rough plank floor. He was supremely gratified by the stupid expression on Viktar's face, and rolled the unconscious man onto his back, dragging him roughly across the floor to the bed.

Laying his nephew onto the bed, he bound his hands and feet to the posts.

Then, whenever Viktar regained consciousness, Malik choked the life nearly from him again…and again, inviting him to the edge of that precipice called *Death*.

"Yes, you will die," Malik whispered greedily into the ear of the younger man, "and it is I who will rip you from this world and send your pathetic carcass to the next. And your mother shall know it was I who killed you. But not yet…."

In this fashion, Viktar suffered for nearly two hours on the edge of his own mortality before there came a soft rap on the door….

CHAPTER ELEVEN

†

Niveus' eyes flashed open.

She stared vacantly overhead, but what she saw was not dimensional. There was no element to it, no area or proportion that could be defined. It was, instead, darkness of another sort, a pain—pain rent of unkindness—and it was unfamiliar to her. This was the first time she had been awakened to suffering of this sort, and it slowed her breathing a great deal to consider the nature of it.

Reaching a hand up, she moved it slowly back and forth across the nothingness as she lay in her bed. To a stranger it would appear insanity, but to Niveus it was a black doorway, and she was struggling to open it as best she could, to see inside.

Beyond the door was the soul of the man who had awakened her, and his suffering called to her, but at the same time...it did not. For Niveus, the potential of the man to live was what she now sought, or else she would not go.

Then, quite abruptly, she pulled her hand from the air and swept her legs to the side of the bed. Pushing up, she padded across the wolf skin, across the stone floor, but hesitated at the door. This, she had not done before. Glancing over her shoulder, she searched the room before spying what she sought.

Returning to the foot of her bed, she snugged her feet into the slippers. It wasn't that Niveus had no other shoes. She had many, fine as could be made, but they were largely insignificant to her. The boy's father, however, made these slippers: *that*, to her, was very significant. Likewise she grasped the shawl given her by the dead boy's mother. This was also significant, and on some level it appealed to her that Moira would approve.

Moira is right. I should try to appear more ordinary for the sake of the people.

And so, dressed only in her nightgown, slippers, and shawl, she was satisfied that she had met her obligation to be "ordinary," having no idea how extraordinary she truly was.

Slipping once more to the door, she rested her hand on the rough-hewn jamb and leaned her head gently against it. Closing her eyes, she paused, searching for the heartbeat of the man who sat guard on the other side.

There it was, slow and sweet, supremely at rest. She knew this man well and cared much for him, for he loved Moira. And it was because she knew him so well that it would be his undoing. It would not take much to persuade him to do that which he believed he should not.

She planted the suggestion, softly, kindly, that Moulin should look the other way, occupied by something else that wasn't really there—an owl perhaps—sitting on the stone window ledge. Yes, how unusual that would be, and quite deserving of his attention.

Then, just as Moulin glanced away, she slipped silently from the room and drifted the other way, down the long hall to the stairs. Not once did she look back. Neither did she hurry along for fear that he might turn and see her. It was simply not a concern.

Nearly to the main floor, Niveus paused on the last of the circular stairs. Sweeping her long hair up with one hand and tossing it onto her back, she leaned her cheek against the stone wall and peeked, gazing slowly about to see if anyone stirred in the great, front room of the castle.

There were guards posted at either side of the entryway as was normal. She studied them, calculating how effectively she might get past them. One was familiar, but the other was not. Back up the stairs she went and descended a different, much narrower flight of stairs to a service door on the south side of the castle.

Ordinarily, there was no one posted here, and it was barred heavily from the inside. She presumed that, given her recent behaviors, which seemed to distress everyone so much more than she believed it should, there would certainly be someone outside the door.

She leaned her head softly against the timber and sighed so gently she could scarcely hear her own question. "Are you there?"

Like an echo in a narrow canyon, the question was returned, light as a whisper on a breeze. *Yes, I am here.*

So there was another on the other side of the door, and yes, it was also someone she knew. That was good, so she shared the same thought with him as she did with Moulin—the notion that something else deserved the young man's attention. Then, she struggled to slip the heavy crossbeam from its rest.

Niveus could not see on the other side of the door, could not see the soldier peer as though he had seen something move in the nearby orchard. She could not see the soldier walk twenty paces away to see if he could again spy the great stag he was sure had stomped its forefoot, challenging him from beneath the walnut trees.

Likewise, the soldier did not see the waif-like girl in white linen slip from the open door behind him. She disappeared into the darkness, along the edge of the castle, and made her way toward the front gate.

Standing in the shadows cast by a nearly full moon, she peered at the doubly posted guards at the front gate—extra vigilance at her brother's request. Calmly, she switched her path, making her way slowly to a service gate nearby. There she approached the solitary guard.

"Niveus?" The soldier appeared entirely surprised and stepped forward, both hands reaching for her. "Why are you out so late?" His hand went ridiculously to his sword, and he peered about into the darkness as though danger would rear its head at any moment to threaten her.

"I need something," she said simply.

"Of course, my lady, but let us go back to the castle. Your needs can be better met there. It's cold, and I'll walk with you." He went to remove his coat and wrap it about her shoulders.

"I need you to hold my hand," she insisted, gently stopping him.

"Certainly. I-I…" he stuttered and paused.

"You will understand. Just take my hand. Then, if you choose to return me to the castle, I will allow you to walk back with me."

Hesitantly, he reached his hand out to receive her already outstretched one. In the moonlight, hers was terribly small, her fingers thin and pale against his battle glove. She slipped the gauntlet from him so that her skin rested against his. His eyes opened wide as she closed hers…

* * *

A crashing sense of urgency washed over the soldier.

Touching him directly as she was, she clearly transferred to him a calling that he could neither understand nor deny. All he could know was that Niveus must be allowed to do as she wished this night.

Saying nothing more, he only shook his head in agreement as tears threatened. He swept at them with his other gloved hand.

"I am sorry you are so tired," she murmured and leaned toward him. Standing on her tiptoes, her lips nearly brushing his cheek, she whispered,

"But you are a good man and have done the right thing tonight. You and I alone know this to be true."

He nodded dumbly, unable to meet her gaze.

"And I am sorry for your friend." She meant, of course, the dog.

Again, he said nothing, only sat down, leaning heavily against the massive stones of the battlement. Then the young soldier dozed for a while, awakening shortly. The shame he would ordinarily burden, that he had allowed himself to drift off while at his post, was absent.

He pushed himself up and remained at attention for the rest of his shift with no recollection whatsoever that Niveus had even been there. Curiously, he would cease to worry for his old mongrel pet, finally content to allow the gentle beast to die when it would.

Meanwhile, Niveus slipped farther beyond the castle walls and made her way steadily toward the distant edge of the sleeping village, to the one whose soul still beckoned.

* * *

Malik swiftly sliced free the bonds of the unconscious man and stashed them beneath the bed. Moving quickly to the front door, he rested his hand upon it for a gracious moment, allowing something within his being to stir erotically with his vague memory of Nicolette.

Finally! The time has come, he told himself, reveling in his victory.

Finally he would have Niveus and would kill Viktar on the same night. He smiled weakly, his knees unsteady as he savored the moment. Then, he drew the latch free and eased the door open for the one he anticipated would be standing beyond.

CHAPTER TWELVE

Niveus saw first a dimly lit room and a stranger at the door.

"Yes? Yes, may I help you?" The stranger's voice seemed earnest as the man, shrouded in darkness, peeked from behind the door jamb.

She looked past the figure to where a young man lay very still upon a bed, the firelight dancing ominously in furtive fingers across his body.

"I've come to see your friend," Niveus said from the shadows. "He is ill."

When the man opened the door wider, his face flashed with such surprise Niveus believed he would slam it closed again.

"Please," she glanced away, holding her hand in front of her face, "look not at me, if you so choose, but let me tend to your friend, or…he will die."

* * *

Malik swallowed thickly and only stared, dumbfounded. Unable to draw his scrutiny from the disheveled waif who remained at his door, a growing wave of insult washed over him, and he felt his outrage mount.

This was no Nicolette! This was no woman fashioned from the gods! There was nothing about this girl that remotely resembled the ebony-haired beauty he had lusted so long for!

But his indignation ebbed as curiosity drove him to peer a bit closer at the creature who had come in the night, just as they had claimed she would.

Maybe…yes, perhaps there *was* something about the girl that would not be denied, he finally decided, and gestured weakly for Niveus to enter. His demeanor paled when he noticed that, except for a decent pair of slippers and a tattered shawl, the girl wore nothing but a threadbare nightshift on such a cold night. And it was scarcely enough to hide from any onlooker what liberties their imagination might take of her!

Hardly the daughter of a great lord such as Ravan! So that was it! The girl was insane. That's why they worked so hard to shelter her behind the castle walls. That was why no one was allowed an audience with the girl. She was an embarrassment to the realm!

Malik watched, bewildered, as Niveus stepped gingerly into the small cottage and walked straightaway to the edge of the bed. There was an unusual feel to the stagnant air as the girl seemed to falter. His dismay grew as she slowly, deliberately, passed her gaze along the length of the dying young man then, just as curiously, about the edges of the ceiling of the room before settling…on him.

Malik eased the cottage door closed, and the latch fell heavily into place just as Niveus' expression revealed what she knew—not only was she in a room with a dying man, she was in a room with…a *murderer*.

* * *

Niveus' red eyes flashed, her lips drawn tightly together. Malik studied her, oblivious of the fate of his nephew, reposed as though dead behind her.

The Prussian challenged her openly, "*You…*you are Nicolette's *daughter?*"

She remained as though frozen. The only indication she was alive was her slow blink and the way the heat from the nearby fireplace wafted a thin strand of her long hair about her in a peculiar way.

Malik was strangely compelled to stare at her—such an extraordinarily bizarre creature. He was at once drawn to and in the same instant repulsed by her. It was as though he wanted to kill her then…*consume* her.

"You would allow this man to die?" Niveus asked flatly, hand extended with palm open toward Viktar.

"*Him?* You worry for him?" he snorted. "He is no one! Should it not be your own fate you concern yourself with?"

Malik's face contorted into an expression of immense triumph. In that moment, he believed he would finally have his revenge against Ravan, even if it were not with the gratification he so anticipated. No, his intent shifted swiftly to a new direction, to one of murder. Yes! He would destroy Ravan's daughter, would rip her existence from this world…tonight!

He sneered as he lied, "I know your mother and father. Your mother bedded me while I forced your father to watch. And she craved more!"

Malik's vile cruelty seemed not to affect Niveus at all. On the contrary, he was immediately baffled by what he observed next.

She broke her gaze from him as easily as though he was not even there, and moved to sit softly on the edge of the dying man's bed. Passing a hand over Viktar's throat, her fingers caressed the ligature marks that encircled it. The deep purple cuts ran nearly all the way around with claw marks, born of desperation, transecting them. The young man's eyes were swollen and barely open through slits, his breathing ragged and dreadfully shallow.

"*Bisah mis fintlah*," Niveus murmured, her red eyes darkening to nearly black as she ministered swiftly to the young man.

She hummed softly, a strange string of unlinked notes, as she leaned her body over his, sweeping both hands over his head, palms together before pushing softly away from each other as though she pushed something from him. She allowed her fingertips to caress his forehead before falling to the sides of his face and repeated this several times over. All the while, the peculiar words fell from her lips.

Something moved in the core of the evil one who waited impotently near the door. It was, to Malik, almost erotic—what she did to the boy—and he made no effort to intervene; couldn't even bring himself to object. More than anything, he simply *must* watch—a twisted voyeur standing in the shadows.

"*Levliah ent bisah*," Niveus whispered as she drew the fingers of one hand from the forehead of the struggling man down his face, between his brows, down, down, all the way to over his heart. There her touch lingered, her face devoid of expression—frosty white lashes resting quietly upon her cheeks.

Niveus traced a slow circle about the man's heart before slipping her hand between the lacings of his tunic and resting it flat upon his bare chest. Her other hand reached for Viktar's head. Resting her palm gently over his eyes, she sat silent and unmoving.

Malik was beyond fascinated. All the while, he could do nothing but stand as though nailed to the floor. The girl's hair hung down about her, and it frustrated him that he could not see her face. Eventually, Malik shook himself free and crept nearer, taking a silent seat to further watch the display. Still, he could not see the fire that danced in Niveus' being—the connection of life to feeble life as the girl tried desperately to save his dying nephew.

Viktar gurgled and sputtered, his spittle spraying blood onto Niveus' throat and across the bodice of her nightgown. She reacted to this not at all. Where Malik flinched, she did not but only kept her hands pressed softly on Viktar.

His face and throat were still terribly swollen, but his eyes were becoming clearer, not quite so bulging, and his dazed stare passed.

Blinking, he struggled to see and focused on Niveus' face with a dawning look of terror.

"Lea…" he began, choked violently, and collapsed.

He drifted away again, and Niveus murmured something so faint that Malik could not hear. He squinted and leaned forward, prying into the bizarre ritual, and jumped a second time when she turned without notice toward him, focusing her burning, black stare on him.

Her *eyes*—they seemed almost to be on fire! And Malik believed for an instant that she could read his mind, see all the way into the dirty recesses of his vulgar being. This troubled him a great deal, not that she could see into him but for what she might find lying there. Then…it surprised him that he cared at all.

"Your companion will live, but it will be some time before he is recovered," Niveus said.

"What have you done? And what do you *mean* by that?" Malik asked hurriedly.

"He is injured…here." Niveus tapped first the side of her temple and then between her breasts gently with two fingers. "He will be who he was before, but not for a while. It is as much as I can do, but Viktar will live."

Malik had not for an instant believed what the villagers had whispered was true! He shook his head. Niveus was no freak-show. She was a wondrous phenomenon, more so than what any of them could have even begun to describe, if what she was saying was true. And it must have been, for…she knew Viktar's name.

His mind raced. That bitch, *Modest*, was nothing more than a prattling, jealous wench! Suddenly, he felt the urge to kill the tavern maiden on the spot, just for the unkind words she had dared utter about Niveus.

Then, strangely, something happened to Malik—something that could not be opposed. As he watched Niveus, with her strange mannerisms and the fluid way she moved, her translucent skin and snow-white hair, he was inexplicably drawn to her. It was not in a sexual way, not entirely, not yet, but there was no denying he was becoming swiftly obsessed with her.

Suddenly he was constrained with a need to capture her—as though she were a rare bird who could fly through the window at any second. And if she did, he would never again have his chance.

He glanced about the small room, his desperation growing by bounds as the seconds ticked by. All recollection of revenge was fading, growing into something even more malignant. He must, beyond anything else, possess Niveus—*have* her…for eternity.

Viktar roused just then, his attention locked on the phantom that had ministered so kindly to him. His pain appeared nearly gone even if the swelling in his face was not. He peeked through slitted eyes, struggling to more clearly see the girl—the angel who had saved him.

Glancing sideways, Viktar strove to see if another was still there in the room with them. First fixing his gaze on Malik, he hastily returned it to Niveus and reached a trembling hand up, struggling to take hers—the one that rested over his heart—in his own.

The angel's eyes widened as he whispered, "*Leave...*"

* * *

Niveus jolted backward as a blade plunged between the third and fourth fingertips of her hand—the one that had rested above Viktar's heart. She fell away from the bed and spun about on her knee. There the young man lay with a wickedly beautiful sword—one with a jeweled handle—piercing his left shoulder through and through, spitting him to the bed.

From where she knelt, Niveus could see how the fierce tip of the blade protruded beneath the bed, stabbed into the wood planks of the floor. A smooth river of blood ran down the sword and began to pool obscenely below the bed, onto the very bindings with which Malik had used to strangle and tie Viktar. Jumping to her feet, Niveus spun away but was stopped short by something entangled in her hair.

Malik heaved her backwards hard, flinging the girl across the room to just in front of the fireplace. A stray ash burned cruelly into her palm, and Niveus' immediate thought was that she knew precisely why she had so earnestly wanted to cut her hair off yesterday morning.

"Stay where you are!" Malik screamed at her.

Ignoring him, Niveus pushed herself up to her feet.

He lunged for her, striking her down hard with his fist. "I said stay where you are!"

Her head hit the floor hard, and she lay still. Gathering herself, Niveus pushed up once more, even as Malik towered over her, fists raised as though he would strike her down again.

* * *

She staggered to her feet and said, calmly, "I will stay." Niveus could not see the blood that ran from her broken lip down the snow white of her chin.

It was more crimson than anything Malik had ever seen, and he stared at her, at her blood, at the splinter fragments lodged into her chin, and was uncertain what emotion it was that commanded him so completely.

"Sit…there." He pointed a trembling finger at one of the two chairs. "You cannot escape me now. I've captured you, and you should not even try."

Niveus disobeyed…again. Pushing past him, she hurried to the far side of the bed where Viktar sputtered weakly, blood pouring from his lips and nose as it ran down both sides of his face, growing into an awful pool behind his neck and around his shoulders.

Grasping the table's edge to steady himself, Malik watched in amazement at what happened next. Niveus struggled to withdraw the terrible blade from his nephew's shoulder. With both hands, she finally wrenched it free and tossed it aside, across the bed, where it clattered to the floor.

Viktar's agony-stricken eyes flashed open but closed again, his head lolling to the side. Swiftly, she rolled him just enough onto his side to press one hand against the exit wound on the back of his shoulder. Letting his body fall back, she pressed her other hand over his chest, covering the terrible slice just below his collarbone. The sword had missed the heart but speared and collapsed the lung. Niveus' hands against the wounds sealed them, and the awful sucking sound Viktar took with each breath ceased.

She leaned her body against Viktar and murmured in quick succession words Malik was unfamiliar with—words *everyone* would be unfamiliar with. It was bizarre, the starkly white figure, the scarlet red blood seemingly everywhere, the young man lying so torturously still in her arms.

"Get away from him!" Malik commanded, furious and desperate at the same time. "There is nothing you can do for him!"

He could not know that Niveus did not, at that moment, *choose* to ignore him. She was simply so occupied with Viktar that, for her…Malik ceased to exist.

* * *

All at once, Niveus was no longer in the small cottage behind the Inn. She was submerged in a river of darkness, swimming…searching. And, it was so intensely quiet, in a very bad way. Onward she plunged, deeper into the dreadful silence, pawing her way through the gelatinous pool. All the while she listened, stretching one hand after another forward as she swam farther into the black abyss.

Finally, there…there it was—the thready beat of a heart, fast and frail as a dying bird's. She reached for it, seeing within the darkness the faintest glimmer of light. The flicker was so weak, so sadly alone, and as she neared it, she became aware that the blackness was not black at all but an awful red, muted only by darkness.

Catching carefully onto the fragile spark that was all that was left of Viktar's life, she folded her fingers softly around it, cupping it gently in her hands, and drew it to her face.

I have you. Come to me now.

Niveus wanted, more than was reasonable, for this one to live, and these feelings confused her somewhat.

You are so beautiful. Leave me, please. Save yourself.

She was instantly dismayed, for it was the first time a soul had spoken to her in such a way. Concentrating hard, she remained fixated on the dying ember.

I will not.

The soul said nothing more.

Next, she had the sensation that she floated, and all of her energy remained directed toward the trace of light that she grasped desperately in both hands.

Finally, the water thinned and became shallower as though of its own accord, and the black-red river receded, dripping in coagulated globs from her until Niveus stood once more in the cottage, thin arms wrapped around the critically wounded man she so desperately wished to save.

* * *

Behind her, Malik stared, dumbfounded. The words he heard fall from her lips were, *"Bisah mal reapinon."*

"A witch," he murmured to himself, although he had never really seen a witch before. Until tonight, he doubted such a creature existed. "Yes! She is a *sorceress*. Of course!"

He said it as though there was someone else present, watching the fantastic events unfold just as he was, regarding the extraordinary creature as she bestowed the strange gift of life upon his nephew. It was, he decided, impossible.

Malik sat down heavily and followed the girl—every small move she made, every breath that she drew. It surprised him when, quite suddenly, in the arms of Ravan's daughter, Viktar gasped weakly, his eyes opening blindly.

Finally, glancing over her shoulder at the horrid man with the beautiful, bloodied sword at his feet, Niveus said in a low voice, "He may survive. I cannot know."

As though in response to her words, Viktar lifted a hand and rested it on top of hers. His breathing remained terribly shallow, and he did not stir again.

"What do you mean, he will survive? He cannot!" Malik spewed venomously. He leapt to his feet. "What kind of foolish thing is that for you to say? He is a dead man!"

"He is not your friend." Niveus appraised Malik curiously. "He is your family, but you hurt him to bring me here. Why?"

There was such an astonishing amount of Viktar's blood on Niveus gown that it looked as though she was the one who should succumb at any moment. But, even drenched as she was, she remained alarmingly calm.

Malik wiped his lips with his sleeve and ran his fingers desperately through his short hair. Pacing back and forth, he finally pulled the chair around to face Niveus from across the bed and sat again, grasping the back of the chair with whitened knuckles.

"Explain to me what twist of nature you are? You are Nicolette's daughter, are you not?" Malik demanded one answer after another as desperation seated itself heavily between his shoulder blades.

She gave him none. Instead, she seemed instantly preoccupied with something behind Malik—something which crawled on the wall. Her stare became intent as she followed it. "I *see* you," she murmured as though only to herself. "I *know* what you are."

Her behavior was bizarre enough that Malik glanced over his shoulder at the bare wall. Seeing nothing only infuriated him more, and he slammed his hand down hard on the table. "Answer me! Are you not Nicolette's daughter?"

"I am," Niveus said calmly, still looking beyond him, her lovely rose eyes now so pale that they appeared almost entirely white. Her cheek was smeared liberally with Viktar's blood, and from her broken lip her own blood had dried to an ebony-crimson.

She finally cast her stare once more on Malik. "Why is that important to you?"

Malik only drummed his fingers maniacally on the back of the chair, at a pure loss for what he should say or do next. So he just watched, studying her for a good long while as she remained with her hands clasped about his nephew.

"There is nothing more that can be done," Niveus said and began to stand.

Malik reached for her. "No! No...sit." He reached for the sword.

Niveus brow creased in confusion as she eased herself back onto the bed.

The Prussian seethed for a bit longer before interrogating her further. "Your father, Ravan, he rules this realm? Is that not so?"

"My brother rules in his absence. My father has gone to Crete."

Malik rubbed his short beard with the back of his hand. "You speak the truth."

To this, Niveus' puzzled expression intensified. "You would be a murderer, and yet you preoccupy yourself with that I might be a *liar*? Your enemies are poorly defined if you fear me that much."

"I don't fear you!" he snarled. "I fear no one, least of all one such as yourself! Look at you, scarcely dressed as you are and nearly starved. I find it impossible that Nicolette is your mother!"

Niveus gazed down at her blood-soaked nightgown as though just noticing it was, in fact, all that she wore. She raised her chin and fixed her attention on the evil that sat across the bed from her.

"You are a fool to fear no one." Her voice carried a fire all its own, and her head slanted to the side. "Know this, Malik—demon of the land of red— you will not die warm in your own bed."

The way she spoke and the way her stare seemed to penetrate his very soul unnerved him a great deal...that and the fact that she also knew *his* name.

"And what of you?" His voice rose again. "Do you not fear me? As you say, I am a murderer! I could kill you as you sit. Truly, it would give me a great deal of pleasure to destroy Ravan's only daughter!"

Niveus' head tipped to the other side. "I am *not* my father's only daughter. And you will not kill me, not tonight at least, and not tomorrow."

This confused Malik. He shook his head and insisted again, "You cannot leave.

"I can."

"I would slay you before you reach the door," he shot back. Raising the blade, he drew the elegant tip toward her chest. His hand and voice trembled. "I could run you through right now! You and that louse you've so poorly attached yourself to!"

The trembling in Malik's hand extended up his arm and into his being, for her face did not appear human. It was too white—brilliant and cold at the same time. Surely a statue of alabaster had come to life and vexed him sorely. Watching, incredulous, he allowed her to raise a single, blood-drenched finger and touch the tip of the murderous sword.

The Damascus blade cut her as she gently pushed it aside.

She did not flinch, and she said nothing, but her expression told him she knew full well the lie of it all. She *knew*. Without a doubt, she knew he would not kill her, not tonight at least, and she chose not to throw it in his face. This he could in no way comprehend, and he stumbled over his words.

"Just…just tonight then. I will let you live, for now. But tomorrow I might not be so charitable!" He slashed at nothing with the sword as he spewed venom toward the mute vision. Then, he dragged the chair to the door and dropped into it, the magnificent sword level across his lap. Niveus returned all her attentions to Viktar, who slept perched upon the threshold of death.

There was no other exit from the cottage and, believing he had Niveus trapped, Malik eventually dozed, sleeping the sleep of fools.

A few short hours later, with the first glimpse of morning, he snapped awake, spittle dried in crusty flakes on his creased lips. Niveus sat just as before, her hand still resting softly over Viktar's heart, only now she stared, unwavering, at the awful man as he struggled to right himself.

The sword had long ago fallen to the floor and lay at his feet. He dragged a sleeve heavily across his dry lips as he realized she could have retrieved it in the night and run him through as he slept. He snatched up the sword and pointed it ridiculously at her.

Just then there was a *rap* on the door. Gorlik, grunted from somewhere outside, "Your nephew never came to bed."

The beast pressed through the door into the room. Occupying a great deal more space than his lord did, and with only a small repertoire of expression on any given day, he fixed his attention dully on Niveus. Then he scanned Viktar before turning to face his master as though not at all surprised by the unthinkably grisly scene.

"You found her," was all he said.

"She found me, as you can see, at the tragic expense of my nephew," Malik quipped. "We will be departing today. Saddle the horses. We are taking the girl."

"I will not go," Niveus shot flatly and insisted before Malik could reply, "he is not well enough to ride."

"We leave him. Or, he rides—live or die."

The elegant sword gave a satisfying whoosh as Malik swept it back and forth in front of her face, and his voice rose to a commanding timbre.

"You have no choice in the matter." Then, to Gorlik, "Bring rope, and tie him to his horse."

"I have more choice than you believe, and I will not leave him," Niveus looked at Viktar, "not while he is so ill. He cannot sit a horse."

"Why do you care what happens to him? You know nothing of him! He is nobody! I could leave him to the wolves for all that it would matter!" Malik ranted.

Niveus spoke slowly as though the men were both simple and she must compel them to understand. "You may very well force me to leave without him, but it will not go well for you." She dropped her gaze to Viktar. "I am attached to him, and he must stay with me. There is no other way."

Malik in no way believed she could prevent him from just taking her, but there was something about her, something about her strange way of putting her intent to words, that made him uncomfortable. He paused, finally snorting, "What do I care! Let him die on the road. Horse or carriage, it does not matter."

Swinging an arm overhead, Malik gestured at Gorlik.

"Very well! Let us accommodate the princess! Our carriage, then. It suits me better anyway and can carry a dying man as well. But drape the windows—black, I think. Suits the occasion." He stabbed his sword into the floorboards for effect.

Shortly, Gorlik retrieved the carriage. It was large, by contemporary standards, covered, and curtained just as Malik demanded, ready to harbor them in their flight. Viktar was carried roughly from the cottage on a board slab and laid within, still deathly ill and unconscious. Niveus was the last to leave the cottage, ushered beneath a cloak into the waiting vehicle.

Then, the carriage drew silently from the town, and the unlikely group escaped just about sunrise, well before anyone even knew Ravan's daughter…was gone.

CHAPTER THIRTEEN

†

Moulin yawned and stretched. It had been a good night, but he was tired and wanted nothing more than to crawl beneath the blankets and sleep the snowy morning away. Queer, though, the owl that had beckoned to him long about midnight.

The next guard, fresh and at the ready, appeared at the top of the stairs and saluted a hello. "How is our lady?"

"Not a sound, as always." Moulin begrudgingly relinquished the watch to his replacement; it just seemed wrong to have to patrol Niveus' door. He sighed deeply. He needed rest. Besides, he believed Lord Risen was right. It was for the best.

The new soldier exchanged a few words of greeting before settling himself at the watch. It would be an easy shift. The man had only to occupy his mind enough to keep from falling asleep. As Moulin took his leave, he glanced back one last time at the door.

Before long, Moulin was fast asleep, and Moira appeared at Niveus' door around mid-morning. Everyone knew the girl kept odd hours, and it was sometimes a struggle to have her rise early, so when Moira tapped on the door it was nothing out of the ordinary.

No one was worried. The sense of urgency had waned, for the guards had been doubled and tripled, and it had been nearly two weeks since Niveus had ventured off into the night.

Easing the girl's door open, however, Moira found Niveus' bed empty and the blankets cold. She cried a stricken whisper, "*No.*"

* * *

Risen was no longer a boy, no longer the gangly youth who had suffered a wicked abduction at the tender age of twelve. Having lost his one true love at the heartbreaking age of thirteen, the heir to the Wintergrave Dynasty had gained, through cruelty's fate, a generous share of his father's dark mantle. And he had lived through the abduction only because his father had schooled him supremely in the art of survival and battle.

But Risen was also gifted with a generous measure of the exceptional savvy his mother possessed. Now, graced with the best of both, either side of his blessed affliction was likely to surface at any given moment, and that was a good thing.

Now, at eighteen, Risen was tall, with broad shoulders like his father. He bore Ravan's dark features, but there was also something warmly inviting about his expression that drew people to him. Beloved by nearly everyone who knew him, he was respected by the entire realm. And because Risen quite enjoyed humanity in its most fundamental condition—more so than his father did—he connected easily with its people.

But the person with whom the young heir most identified was the one hardly anyone else identified with at all—*Niveus*.

When Sylvie slipped from Risen's grasp and died, he lay, broken as though beyond repair on the precipice of hopelessness. But Niveus' steadfast presence, crouching silently in the shadows of his despair, hooking her lifeline onto his, drew him from the ledge back into the waiting current of life.

He truly believed he might have fallen from this world to the next had she not been there—a mortal anchor to his being. And…no one else knew.

Many wondered about the mystery between them, intensely curious of their young master and his commitment to his peculiar sister. Some even went so far as to speculate on their intimacy, but Risen ignored these rumors, and Niveus was oblivious of them.

This morning, when Risen awoke to find his sister gone again, it was not Niveus whom he blamed. It was himself.

"How?" He paced long strides back and forth in the great hall, past his advisors and closest friends, his battle armor clinking softly as he spun. "How has she done this to me again?"

He knew as well as any of them, however, that it was not something Niveus had *done* to anyone. It was simply who she was and the way she stepped from this world to the next—to whichever one she seemed to prefer at any given moment.

"It is a question we could ask for eternity," Moulin replied, shaking his head as Moira clutched his arm. "Niveus defies explanation. We can only accept that."

Moira's face was stricken with worry. "He's right. We all know Niveus, but none of us really *know* her."

"*I* know her!" Risen whirled on the one-handed woman, refusing to admit otherwise. "She is my sister. My...my..." He caught himself, ashamed that he had allowed himself to become angry with Moira. The woman, rescued from a world of abuse before Niveus was born, had been his sister's caregiver since the day she was born. Surely Moira loved her as deeply as any of them.

Moira stifled a sob, and Risen said, "I'm sorry. It's just that..." He spun away, continuing his pacing. "How does she disappear without someone seeing? Without even a trace?"

Risen asked this more of himself than anyone else. It wounded him on a deeply personal level that Niveus would wander into the night without taking him with her. He would gladly have stood guard outside any door or in any forested meadow, if only she would allow him to step into her world. Then he could protect her—make certain that she was safe...forever.

Velecent shifted and shrugged. "I've tried to fortify the posts to stop her from leaving, but she moves as though a ghost. I believe she doesn't want to be followed; that we might intrude upon what...she *does* out there." He seemed embarrassed to continue and gestured to nowhere in particular, his expression turning to one of regret. "Ask me to guard any of you against the very demons of Hell, and I would. But bid me keep your sister contained, and you may as well ask that I capture the wind."

There were general murmurs of appreciation from the lot of them. Risen scanned their faces again, witnessing the concern they all held for Niveus.

"Then we search again. She has either gone to the forest or is ministering to someone in the village. Surely it cannot be this impossible to find her. Someone must have seen something."

"Our Lord's army is scouring the woods as we speak. If she is there, we will find her," Velecent said with grim determination.

"And we are searching the village," Moulin added. "Surely, if she is with someone, they will answer the knock."

None of them could know...how dreadfully wrong Moulin was.

* * *

By the time Moira found Niveus' bed empty, the black carriage was long gone from the village and headed southwest. The horses were fresh, and Gorlik beat them mercilessly, driving them hard, spelling first one and then another with the two spare horses tethered to the back of the carriage.

Theirs was a striking image—the heavily curtained coach with the towering Gorlik atop, whipping the animals along at breakneck speed. They only slowed when the terrain became too rutted or uneven to prevent them from moving faster.

Staying mostly to the road, the strange group pressed precariously on. And the icy rain, set in as though it was a veil of wicked obscurity, drove their flight along. The conditions deteriorated, becoming so wretched that there were scarcely any travelers out today. Nevertheless, Malik demanded Gorlik not incite attention, and so they stopped for no one, leaving the road when possible to take cover in the trees. It was as though they were a black phantom, vanishing from Ravan's realm.

And so, with all the elements of foul design aligned like a bad constellation, their flight marked Niveus' nearly-perfect disappearance from the realm. And, there would be no trace of her at all had there not been something left behind, something found...within the cottage.

* * *

When Modest cleaned the little house, she knew the three men were not traveling with a woman. That is not to say travelers did not take the company of whores on occasion. Who knew better than she the truth of that! But, *no!* She was no whore! She had simply availed herself of an opportunity and helped the charming strangers in the process—a *business* arrangement.

So, when Modest lifted the shawl, which lay crumpled on the floor, she frowned. It miffed her that the lord had engaged another girl here instead of her—*bitch. And damn the whore that stole some of my money from me!*

The maid possessed terribly mixed feelings regarding the "arrangement," she had held with Lord Vedlund, never fully identifying herself as a prostitute. Certainly the duration of their meetings had not been without its trials.

She flushed visibly as she recalled how the lord had hog-tied her, whipped her, and penetrated her in every possible way. The louder she squealed...or gagged, the more he seemed to enjoy it and the rougher he became. Once, he even choked her, nearly to the point of passing out, but then playfully slapped her round cheeks to rouse her about. *All in fun*, he said, and she had agreed...and taken more gold.

Sneakily concealing her extracurricular activities from the Innkeeper, Modest decided the risk had been well worth it. She was richer than she had ever imagined she could be. But still...

She lifted the garment and examined it in the dim light. This was no prostitute's shawl, and it had a strange familiarity to it. It smelled...*young.*

Too dull to think more of it, Modest went back to cleaning, shortly discovering the coarse rope bindings and...the blood. Stagnant beneath the bed, it seemed to be everywhere!

Retrieving the last two gold coins from her pocket, she held them up in the lamplight. How lovely they were, shining with a light all their own. When Lord Vedlund gave these last two to her, he bade her respect his privacy at any cost. He said something about her peril if she told, and she promised on her life never to breathe a word of any of it.

She looked again at the blood-stained mattress and bindings, and bit her lip. Then, she shrugged. Whores died all the time. *Better that one than me,* she thought, for certainly Malik had had every opportunity to satisfy his bloodlust with her. But, no! He had not, Modest ventured, for only one reason. *It was because I was better!*

She tossed the bloody ropes onto the ruined mattress and dragged it from the bed, grateful the body was nowhere to be seen. It had probably been discarded in the woods on one of their hunting trips. By now it was surely wolf fodder and long gone.

After scrubbing the blood from the floor, Modest burned the mattress and linens behind the fowl house but...kept the shawl.

Five days later, the cobbler's wife, passing by with clean linens, noticed the familiar shawl on the shoulders of the maiden. She hurried over to the wench, snatched the shawl from her and held it out, her hand trembling.

"Where did you get this?" she demanded in a harsh whisper, shaking the garment in the girl's face.

Modest, who had been kneeling by the fireplace, shoveling ashes into a wooden bucket, glanced nervously from the woman to the Innkeeper. The man scarcely looked their way, returning instead to his perpetual polishing of the worn, wooden surface of the bar.

The cobbler's wife knelt beside the maiden, pulling her around by the shoulder. "The shawl—I must know. Where did you get it?"

"The cottage," the girl gestured rudely with her chin. "It was left in the cottage nearly a week ago. It was gratuity for me. So it's mine."

"It is not yours. It is our lady's—Niveus'. I *gave* it to her."

The girl gasped, "No!" Then whispered to herself, "But...but how can that be? 'Twas a whore's shawl! I know it was." She reached with an ash-covered hand and touched the tattered edge of the worn garment.

As though still unbelieving, the maiden's voice broke into a hushed wail.

"And why would Niveus have this? It is so common! And why would she visit the gentleman and leave it in his room, and…"

Modest's whining trailed off as pieces of a crooked puzzle began to fall into place in her small brain. She glanced away as a sickening guilt settled about her like a smothering cloud.

"I gave it to her!" the cobbler's wife insisted again, flinging it at her before taking the girl by both shoulders and shaking her hard. "*Why* was it there? Tell me! What have you done?"

The girl broke free, glancing nervously about before pushing her round frame to her feet. Motioning for the cobbler's wife to follow, she led the woman out the back door of the Inn. A short trek into the nearby forest, and the maiden opened the cottage door, holding it ajar to allow the woman inside. Lighting two candles, Modest unbarred the high, narrow shutters and drew the window treatments aside.

Grey light washed into the room, and dust floated on the stagnant air in an ominous way, like ash after a killing burn. But through it all, there was something else. Something…generous.

The cobbler's wife shuddered and pulled her own shawl more tightly about her shoulders, turning slowly in the silent vacancy of the awful, yet beautiful, space. Where the bed should have been stood only the frame, foreboding as a kneeling skeleton, and she was naturally drawn to it…in a bad way. She could not know what horror and wonder had manifested itself here, scarcely a week before.

"I wondered about the blood," the maiden said forlornly. "Thought it was just a whore. You don't think Lady Niveus was, u-mm…"

"*What?* What blood? What do you mean?"

"The linens, the bed—they were soaked. But the men, they were so noble. Said they came on holiday, a hunting trip, and…to meet master Ravan. Only our lord wasn't here, so I suppose they only hunted."

Modest pouted. "I thought the blood was from an injury. Hunting or…or maybe a *whore*." She shuddered in false disgust. "But it doesn't matter. They paid for the damages, so I thought no more about it." Modest stuck her too-small nose in the air.

"*Who?* Who paid?" the cobbler's wife insisted as she whirled on the maiden.

"The foreigners—Lord Vedlund and…and his handsome nephew, though *he* stayed in the Inn. The lord stayed here." Modest didn't mention Gorlik. "And they kept mostly to themselves. True gentlemen, they were. I'm sorry they are gone."

"And you said nothing of this to the Innkeeper?" The cobbler's wife's voice rose in alarm.

Modest replied hastily, "*No!* Why should I? I've kept no secrets from him, except..." The maiden halted, suddenly overcome as she sank onto the edge of the bed frame, nearly the same spot that Niveus had sat that long night seven days ago.

"What? *Tell* me!" The cobbler's wife took the maiden's hands in her own. "I must know!"

"Niveus. They wanted to know so much about her...at least the master did. He asked questions. All the time, question after question, about Lord Ravan, Lord Risen, and Lady Nicolette. But mostly he wanted to know about...*Niveus.*" She spoke her name as though the girl was a hated brat sister and let go a self-pitying sob.

"He said he only meant to catch a glimpse of her. I thought he was just curious about how queer she is. You know it's true! But Lord Vedlund insisted on knowing everything I could tell him about her. It was maddening, really! He forced me to tell things I shouldn't have."

She pouted and broke into false tears, casting her hands about herself, swimming in the flood of her own deceit. "How could I have not seen it? Why do these things always happen to *me*?"

The cobbler's wife watched in mute horror as the maiden blurted, "It only stands to reason she must have come to help with the injury! That's how she must have left the shawl behind. That's it! But...but..." Modest looked desperately around as though at any moment she would see Niveus step from the shadows to cast blame on her. "Why didn't she just go home? Like she's always done before?"

The cobbler's wife swept from the small cottage, dragging the bewildered girl behind. Before long, they waited in the grand entry hall of the Dynasty's castle. Both jerked about when Risen came crashing through the doors. He was soaked from the heavy rains, and his eyes burned from the sleeplessness he had endured for nearly a week.

"You gave that to her. I remember." Risen took the shawl from the cobbler's wife, adding regretfully, "It was the night she came to see you, to...help your son."

The woman nodded solemnly, head bowed. "She did, my lord, when no one else could." Off to her side, Modest fidgeted.

Risen laid a hand gently on the older woman's shoulder. "I am sorry for your loss. I cannot imagine...I...I..."

He turned away, clutching the shawl as though it were a lifeline.

"Niveus insisted on wearing this, since the night she came to your home." He smiled sadly at no one. "Her wardrobe holds cloaks gifted from kings, jeweled and lined with fur, and yet she insisted on wearing this...and the slippers."

The woman nodded in grave understanding as Risen said what everyone present was thinking.

"Niveus would never leave this behind." He demanded of the maiden, speaking more harshly than perhaps intended, "Tell me of the men who stayed there. Tell me everything you know of them, every last respect."

Modest fawned, faking a near-swoon as she batted her lashes and blurted out, "It wasn't my fault! He made me tell him things. I swear it!"

In this fashion she recounted the tale of the three strange men who had come to the Inn with their foreign accents and peculiar mannerisms, all the while inserting herself as the humble victim.

She described the men in detail—the obvious leader; the handsome, troubled, younger one; and the frightfully large one. She thought to herself, *with the frightfully huge....* She also admitted to the significant amount of gold they carried. Curiously, she did *not* speak of the many evenings she had spent on her knees, servicing the Prussian lord.

"That is all I know," she finished, hands wide in absolution.

One of the realm's scouts stepped forward. "She speaks the truth, my lord. I ran across them, hunting in the forest one afternoon. They spun the same tale, said they were traveling and wished to see our lord."

"See! I told you!" Modest defended her guilt in swift fashion, her dumb eyes open too wide.

The soldier continued, "I told them Lord Ravan and Lady Nicolette were gone and offered them an audience with you. They declined to see you, my lord." He bowed slightly, his face flush with regret. "I should have told you. It was an oversight."

"The gold. You said he paid you." Risen turned his attention back to the tavern maid.

Modest hedged, finally drawing a single gold coin from her pocket, and exclaimed, "This is all he gave me! It was nothing, really, and I worked so very hard for it! Besides—"

The guard silenced the girl with a raised hand.

Risen peered closely at the coin. The rough inscription was unfamiliar, perhaps Turkish, and there was a square hole punched through it. He rubbed the coin between thumb and forefinger. It was thick and foretold wealth...and resources. He frowned.

Modest bleated weakly, reaching past the guard for her coin, but Risen pocketed it, ignoring her entirely.

"It has been six days, and this is the first word we have." He sighed and rubbed a filthy hand across his brow, dismissed the women, and stepped away from everyone, speaking in a low voice only to Velecent. "We have no choice. We must send scouts in all directions; get word to the nearby towns. Surely someone has seen them pass."

Modest volunteered another scrap of information in a high-pitched voice, clutching at the door jamb as she was escorted from the hall. "The carriage they left in, my lord, it was black! Now, about the gold…"

But the doors closed her out.

* * *

Back at the Inn, Modest scarcely felt the sting of her lies. She went sullenly back to work, delivering ale and slinging porridge, and pondered repeating her venture into prostitution. After all, opportunity was not to be denied.

Deciding the debasement she had suffered with Malik well worth the pay after all, she foolishly assumed it was her harlotry that had merited the generous installments of gold, not the information Lord Vedlund coerced from her daily. Consequently, she assumed others would pay just as much for the privilege to ride her however they saw fit.

Setting two ales in front of a pair of strangers, she smiled smugly at one, leaning across the table farther than was necessary. Swinging her arse about as she left the table, she smiled coyly over her shoulder as she left.

That night, complacent with happy musings of her blood money and how she intended to spend it, except for the unhappy coin she had lost to Lord Risen—such an unfortunate turn of events—Modest retired from her late shift. Humming to herself, she made her way to her private quarters at the rear of the Inn.

Once inside her simple room, she barred the door and leaned against it, listening, unreasonably believing it mattered. And when it seemed everything was suitably quiet, she tossed the small, faded rug aside and knelt on the floor. Then, she dug a hole in the earth and dropped the small pouch of gold coins within, burying it where no one would find it for a very, very long time.

With a sigh, she crawled into bed, her fingers falling idly to between her legs. How rough that Prussian lord and his fiendish pet had been with her! She pouted, but her indignation was swiftly replaced with dreamy visions of

Lord Risen and the young Prussian. They vied for her favors, their nakedness swimming erotically in her head as she moaned and drifted off to sleep.

Then…Modest bled.

A slow, steady trickle, for the bastard seed planted in her womb by the vile giant, set the girl into a slumber from which she would never awaken. Nearly half an hour later, her hand fell limply to her side, and her jaw went slack.

Curiously, as she dwindled away her soul called for help, but she was visited and saved…

…by *no one*.

CHAPTER FOURTEEN

✝

Risen knelt before Niveus' bedroom window. In his hands he held the small mirror, the one Niveus claimed helped her to sometimes see through into the beyond. He had never seen it but had no doubt that she did.

His head rested wearily upon his hands, and remaining like that for a precious long while, he struggled to clear his mind—to focus on only her. Consequently, he did not hear the soft *tap-tap* on the door.

Velecent crept slowly behind Risen. "My lord..." When there was no response, he rested a hand gently on the young man's shoulder. "My lord, you pray, but do you wish to ride? The horses are ready. I've saddled Alerion myself."

Risen dragged his head from his hands.

"I do not pray. I seek her. I cannot *lose* her, Velecent. Not again. Not like..." His voice trailed off, and he lay the mirror aside. "She told me I must only clear my mind, that if I try I would know where she was."

Velecent dropped to one knee, eye-level with his dearest friend's son.

"I cannot say that I understand the girl, or her motivation. But...your sister, she can no more be denied than a storm can. If she said it could be so, I believe her."

Nodding softly, Risen replied, "Yes, I believe it as well."

"And?"

"It is so faint. I think I sense her, but then I doubt myself." Risen shrugged in misery. "There is nothing more that can be done. It is all that I have to go on."

"Then it is good enough for me." Velecent clasped Risen's hand and pulled him to his feet. "I will ride with you, my lord. Let us be gone from here, gone to bring her home. And fear not. I will follow you to the edge of the earth, and beyond, if you say Niveus is there."

It was everything the young man needed to hear.

Then, they were on their way.

* * *

The black carriage covered nearly twenty miles a day. Three miserable days into the journey, Malik replaced the exhausted horses with fresh ones, and onward they pressed. Viktar barely held on. His blood had long since dried to a dull, rusty stain on Niveus' threadbare gown, and she trembled with cold but all the while sat at the suffering man's side, her hand on his chest.

Gorlik paused the carriage only long enough for them to rest and re-gather supplies. They ate mostly of the modest provisions they packed and spoke to no one along the way. As Niveus' attention was cast entirely on Viktar, Malik said very little, only watched with increasing fascination her ministerings to his nephew—a man who should be dead. All the while, his obsession with her continued to grow.

Eight days later, the haggard group careened into the muddied streets of La Rochelle on the western coast of France. Gorlik sat silent guard of the locked carriage as his master sojourned on foot into town to make arrangements.

* * *

Viktar blinked heavily. His vision was still blurry, so he could not see where he lay and that the carriage curtains were drawn. And it was dark, especially in the waning hours of the winter day. Glancing about, he wondered if he had been unworthy to pass Heaven's threshold and simply lay waiting to slip into Hell.

Squinting, he focused hard on a sudden movement. The pale hand reached up, sliding the heavy brocade curtain aside just enough so that a glimmer of light lit the inside of the carriage.

Viktar's gaze settled on the shabby figure of the girl, still sitting fast at his side, and he gasped. She was covered in his dried blood, her broken lip mending, and her eyes were so large they commanded nearly all of his attention. Her blood-matted hair hung all about her in such a way that Viktar was stricken in a very profound way, for she was, he believed, more beautiful than anything he had ever seen.

Grasping her weakly by the wrist, he implored, "Tell me you are a vision; that we have gone to the other side together."

"I am Niveus," was all she said in reply.

He grimaced. "I live…because of you. It is true, isn't it?"

"You live because your heart is kind and your soul is not yet ready to depart. But…yes. I have been by your side for eight nights."

After the wave of shock swept over him, Viktar groaned and pushed himself onto his side. Pain shot through his left shoulder but, determined to see her better, he reached a quivering hand toward the curtain and drew it more open. Then, he saw Niveus clearly for the first time.

"You are a phantom—a blessed angel." Fear shot through him, and his lip trembled as he touched her cheek with an unsteady hand. "I told…I told you to leave."

"If I had left, you would have died."

He thought she said it not as though boasting, only that she told the truth. Viktar swallowed heavily, the regret clearly evident in his voice. "Malik means to kill you."

"I know."

"But *why*? Why are we not dead? Why did he let you live?" Viktar struggled to sit, his face nearly as ashen as the girl's.

Niveus' face was lit beautifully by the late winter's setting sun peeking through a slit in the clouds. "He means to cause suffering. It is what inspires him more than anything."

Viktar knew exactly what she meant and grit his teeth, commanding himself not to faint. "I will not let him destroy you."

She glanced to somewhere outside the window. "It will be what it will. Fate can only be so affected before destiny will have its hand in the matter."

"You cannot believe that." He forced a soft smile when she turned to look at him. "I've met your mother, and your father. They would not believe destiny could not be controlled."

She only looked at him, neither denying nor validating his statement.

Viktar groaned as he splinted himself and looked about the carriage. His face was no longer swollen but that the horrid ligature marks about his neck remained. The Damascus sword was nowhere to be seen.

"Tell me. Why did you not let me die, back at the cottage?"

"It is a question you already have the answer to, for you were there, surely as I was."

She scanned the length of him, and he had the sensation that she could see into his soul. He wondered, briefly, uncomfortably, what it was she saw.

At that moment, Viktar could not help but believe she was, somehow, connected to him. He said suddenly, "You're cold. You must be exhausted."

He looked about the carriage and grasped a blanket—the thick one Malik preferred to keep across his legs on the journey—and struggled to wrap it about her shoulders.

Niveus had eaten poorly on the journey, and she was even thinner than before, but to Viktar, even as he straightened her blood-matted hair, she was beauty unmatched. Every curve of her face, the brilliance of her pale skin and hair, her ashen lips, and the alarming pink of her eyes—all of it was grace of a sort that he had never known possible.

She had saved him, and in doing so had touched his being in a profound way. Never was there a gesture as intimate to him as that. Even lying with a woman would never be as personal as what Niveus had done for him back at the cottage; of this he was certain.

"You could have left. I know you could have."

"I could not," she murmured.

"You lie," he said but knew emphatically that she did not.

She frowned. "I could not leave, not because I was incapable, but because I could not bring myself to do so. Search your heart. You will see it is true."

This surprised him a great deal. Viktar could not be sure what she was saying, but he believed in that very instant…that he loved her.

Just then, the carriage door swung open. Malik, a cloak draped across his arm, laughed at seeing the two sitting up together.

"Ah! The prodigal son survives! Very good, but we have work to do, and very little time to do it." He clapped his hands together and embellished, "The ship leaves at the break of dawn, and we, my blessed children, shall be aboard! Grace be with us, we'll be in our dear Prussia before the month's end. And…" his gaze fell heavily upon Niveus, "it will be a *splendid* homecoming."

With that, he snatched Niveus by the wrist and dragged her from the carriage, draping a hooded cloak over her head.

"Cover your face unless you wish to be burned as a witch!" he demanded through gritted teeth, twisting her arm only because he could. "There is little tolerance for one such as yourself in this town. I am the only one who can suffer what you truly are."

Gorlik, with eternal blades in hand, followed Malik. Behind them, Viktar struggled to extricate himself from the carriage. Yet too weak to orchestrate any interference on Niveus' behalf, it demanded everything from him just to follow as he staggered to a flight of stairs attached to the rear of a building.

Up to the second floor of the inn the troop climbed, Viktar lagging behind, trying to keep Niveus in sight.

Twice, he nearly fell, dropping to his knees as he crawled. Dragging himself back to his feet, he stopped every few steps to rest, clutching the handrail with both hands.

Ahead of him, at the top of the stairs, a maiden opened the door as though expecting them. Viktar watched as she glanced suspiciously at the cloaked girl before gesturing for the others to follow her. He was left behind as down a long, lamp-lit hall the others disappeared.

* * *

Feeding a key into a door lock, the maiden held a hand out, saying nothing as the strange travelers filed past her into the room. Malik turned, harrumphed, and nodded at Gorlik. The giant grunted and returned to the hall to find Viktar crawling along, barely inside the building. He lifted the young man roughly, hoisting him onto his shoulders. Viktar groaned as the giant carried him the rest of the way to the room.

Safely hidden within a luxurious flat at one of the oldest hotels in La Rochelle, the four took in their surroundings. The lavish furnishings were in odd contrast to the outside world. Nowhere was there any sign of poverty or illness within the lush confines of the suite. It was a world of splendor quite removed; one Malik had paid dearly for with coin Klarin had intended for Viktar.

Malik turned to the maiden who still lingered at the door. "It will be as we agreed?"

She hesitated, casting her uncertain gaze first upon the cloaked figure standing alone in the middle of the room and then to the nearly unconscious man the giant had dropped to the floor.

"Yes, my lord. She will be here momentarily," the maiden murmured, averting her gaze as she backed from the room and eased the door closed.

"Excellent!" Malik discarded his long jacket on the back of a tapestried chair. "Make yourselves comfortable, everyone! And you..." he pointed at Viktar, "...*you* will guard the door."

Even Gorlik's face was swept with surprise.

"He is not well enough to stand," Niveus said.

"Silence!" Malik thrust his hand up and back as though he would strike her down, but she remained unflinching. "Dispute me in any way, and I will kill him outright. Do you understand?" Malik nearly roared.

Gorlik, obedient as a beaten ox, dragged Viktar to a post near the door and leaned him heavily against the wall. The young man gasped and pressed his hand into his shoulder—the one that had received the sword wound eight days before—and tried to shake his head without Malik noticing. He thought to Niveus, *Do not try to protect me,* and prayed she heard his plea. *Malik will hurt you if you do.*

Then his knees buckled, and he slid down the wall, which seemed a good enough spot from which to guard as Malik said nothing more of it. In a crumpled heap, the young Prussian could only watch as Niveus took a seat on a cushioned bench, hands resting demurely on her knees. Her hood fell away, and with that, his powerlessness to do anything to affect her survival weighed more heavily on him than anything ever had.

Vowing he would allow no harm to come to her, his mind spun with the impossibility of how he might honor that vow. It was a terrible thing—to wish to draw a breath—when he was drowning.

Malik and Gorlik immediately availed themselves of the luxuries of the room. Shortly, they were washed up and enjoying wine. Laughing at their new good fortune, they were an odd contrast to the girl, still in the bloodied gown, who sat as though carved in stone.

Niveus blinked sleepily and regarded them not at all, focusing entirely on Viktar. This seemed to invite Malik's sudden displeasure a great deal.

"Look at me! Look upon the one who now controls your fate!" he boomed, considerably more confident than he had been the night Niveus had come to the cottage.

She said nothing.

Malik became more serious, wine sloshing from his chalice with each gesture. "You don't believe it, *do* you? You think I cannot hurt you?" Suddenly, he pulled from his waist a wicked, hooked dagger and briefly admired his reflection in the blade. Spinning it awkwardly, he edged nearer to Niveus, circling her. "You're wrong, you know. You cannot spare yourself from my intentions. Not now, not...*ever.*"

He reached out with his free hand, tipping her chin up so that she must look at him, but there was no reaction from her. Niveus seemed solemnly prepared to receive whatever harm he intended.

Tracing the fine bone of the girl's cheek, Malik ran his finger leisurely down her throat until his grip settled around it, his meaty paw encircling it easily. Then, as though he could not stop himself, his grip tightened.

Viktar crawled, dragging himself feebly from the doorway, but Gorlik grasped him up in a hug before the young Prussian could intervene. Viktar pleaded, his feet dangling off the floor, "Uncle, please. *Please...*don't hurt her. You've sacrificed so much to bring her this far to destroy her."

Malik laughed, a great, belly guffaw that reeked of scorn.

"Well, well! What have we here?" His gaze traveled slowly, suggestively from Viktar to Niveus and back. "You have feelings for her now, do you? Why? Because she saved you?" He laughed even more boldly. "Well, *that* makes this all very interesting."

Releasing his hold on Niveus' throat, his hand slid over her breast, and he motioned with his other, swinging the knife in a lazy circle. "Yes, very interesting indeed! This journey has suddenly become so much more...*compelling*." His broad grin faded as there came a rap upon the door.

Gorlik dropped his hold of Viktar and tossed him aside. The younger man tumbled toward a nearby bench and collapsed. Malik smoothed his hair back with both hands and straightened his tunic as he approached the door.

He shook a threatening finger at Viktar and Niveus. "Do anything to compromise us and I will kill you both!" Opening the door, Malik gestured for the woman beyond to enter. "Come in! Come in! We are so excited you could meet with the girl!"

The woman, perhaps in her forties, stepped from the shadows into the more brilliant light of the room. She was followed by two attendants, one male, one female—both seeming ready to leap at her slightest command.

Impeccably dressed, painted, and coifed to extreme, the woman glared warily at Malik as she stepped wide around him, fanning her nose with her hand. Purveying the room skeptically, she snapped her fingers. The attendants dashed immediately to the hall and returned, towing between themselves several splendid racks of clothes and a chest of sorts, which they placed with a heavy thud on the table.

The woman waited until all was set up before introducing herself, turning in a wide semicircle as though for the appreciation of everyone present. Viktar thought her accent was French and something else, which could not be identified.

"I am Paulette. I understand—"

It was just then that Paulette caught sight of the waif perched upon the chaise. She let forth a small cry of astonishment and crossed herself before spitting dryly over her shoulder. "By God's cruel mystery, what has afflicted this child?"

"She is a witch," Malik stated simply, gesturing dramatically as he re-sheathed the knife. "Therein lies the challenge. I need her to look...ordinary, as much as you can dress a pig and call it a queen, I suppose." He laughed heartily at his own jest, and when no one gave notice, he became, again, more interested in his chalice of wine.

Paulette ignored everyone as she approached Niveus, inching carefully closer as though she was approaching a plague victim. Drawing a hand up, she covered her mouth and nose. When it seemed she had adequately assessed the situation, she bent over before the girl.

"Child, what is wrong with your *eyes*?"

Niveus studied the woman curiously, almost sadly, before replying in a low, secretive voice only she and the woman could hear, "It is unfortunate about your mother."

"Pardon?" the woman gasped and drew up short.

"The fire, you have regret for the fire. But...you shouldn't."

Paulette, entirely taken aback by the statement, seemed immediately prepared to leave when Malik jumped in. "Pay no attention to her, whatever deranged prattle it is that she says to you. She is a sensationalist of the worst kind. It's nothing more than a trick."

"But...how could she *know* such things?" Paulette was clearly astounded.

"Heard something about whatever it was from the staff, no doubt. Then she capitalized on it. It is what she does best," he lied brilliantly.

"But..."

"Nothing at all...parlor magic," Malik added swiftly and took Paulette gently by the elbow, guiding her back toward Niveus. "Pay no mind to anything she says. I am deeply sorry, but the girl is truly insane. Alas, I am burdened with my, u-mm, *niece*. And it is her own stupid recklessness that has landed her in such disrepair. That is why I am desperately in need of your expertise." He shot Niveus a murderous look, his jaw clenching and unclenching. "Should she alarm you further, please bring it to my attention."

Meanwhile, Viktar struggled. The horrid string of lies Malik was willing to fabricate shook him completely. Even more, the heavy realization hit him that instead of acting on his plan to kill his uncle, it had been his uncle who had tried to murder him first. He sagged on the chaise lounge.

Why have I been so naïve? To underestimate him so?

Ironically, Viktar was becoming much more worldly traveling with his uncle than he ever would have been in the safety of his own realm. Feeble as he was, in certain ways he was stronger than ever.

The young man swayed, a grisly grey set to his lips, and leaned heavily on the armrest, his head swimming as he fought to stay conscious and observe. All the while, he told himself that when the time came, he would never again underestimate Malik or...lose an opportunity.

* * *

Paulette sat gingerly on the cushioned bench, far as she could from Niveus, and wrung her hands in her lap. "Child, what fearful event has turned your hair so white?" She reached, hesitating before lifting with pinched fingers a filthy, bloodstained strand. She rolled the lock, fine as silk, between her fingertips.

"I was born this way."

"Oh. I see…of course you were." Paulette's smile trembled as she cleared her throat and turned to face Malik again. She jumped to her feet, straightened her skirts roughly, and held her chin high in the air.

"The girl needs a bath. There is nothing more that can be done for her until she is cleaned, head to foot. And make no mistake," she warned, shaking a finger at him, "I can see there has been foul play afoot here. But there will be no more of it as long as I am present. Is that clear?" She rested both hands on her hips and tapped a toe, waiting.

An appreciative smile tugged at Malik's lips. "Agreed. Anything…as long as you can do as you *say* you can. And," he added more gravely, "maintain discretion at all costs."

Paulette glanced with regret at the girl and sighed. "I can."

"Excellent! Repair the girl, and I will…" he glanced about for the wine decanter, "drink!"

Paulette ignored Malik and clapped her hands again. Once more, both attendants disappeared, returning shortly on the first of several trips to fill a small, elegant tub in the back of the hotel room with hot water. Finally half full, the steam rose invitingly, swirling on the surface of the water.

"Come," Paulette motioned to Niveus and drew a room partition so that there was privacy. Then she helped Niveus from her clothes and into the bath. Finally alone with the girl, Paulette trickled a pitcher of warm water down Niveus' back and whispered into her ear as she leaned over, "You go willingly with this man?"

"I do."

The water ran in rivulets, following Niveus' ribs, and Paulette's brow furrowed. "I don't understand. From what I can see, you are mistreated, and the young man with you is already a step into the grave."

"That is why I do this. It is for him—for Viktar."

The woman's expression softened, and her voice lowered even more. "Will you tell me? How did you know…about the fire? Please?" She rested her hand and the washcloth on the edge of the tub as she leaned in closer.

Niveus took Paulette's hand and traced the back of it slowly, lightly, finally running her finger down until it touched the tip of the woman's.

Gazing up at her, she whispered as though it was the greatest secret of all, "I can see it, when I look into your eyes. The fire you witnessed is there...inside of them."

The woman's face was stricken with such sadness that she was compelled to look away, and a single tear ran down her cheek. Finally, she said, "I see it too, just as though it happened yesterday. The flames—that is what I see, all I see, sometimes."

Paulette looked away. When she looked back, Niveus asked gently, "Would you like me to take it away? I can, but only if you wish for me to. You will remember your mother, but you will forget the fire, other than that was how she died."

"You could do that?" Paulette asked with painful expectation.

Niveus nodded.

The woman smiled and said in a low voice, "Yes, yes I would like that very much."

Then, as simple as nothing, Niveus reached for her.

"Wait," Paulette halted. "Tell me. Why do you not do such a thing to the one who holds you—change his memory of you so that you are freed of him? You know he has no good plans for what he intends for you and the young man."

"I can only affect one who is willing." Niveus shrugged then softly touché the woman's cheek. "It is only for the kind of heart, and he...has none."

Paulette had scarcely any time to consider what Niveus said. For an instant she felt nothing. Then she saw the flames, one last time, in *Niveus'* eyes. Shortly, the memory of the awful fire was gone, vanished forever. The girl, shivering in the chilling water, finally drew her palm from the woman's cheek.

"Child, how long have we been at this!" Paulette said happily and helped raise Niveus from the tepid water.

"Your mother, she was a very special woman," Niveus remarked kindly.

"Why, yes," Paulette chirped happily. "I lost her, you know. Terrible thing, but she was a wonderful mother...just as you say."

For a moment Paulette thought she must say something more about it, but then whatever it was had gone. She smiled brightly. "Now come, child. We must get you dry and dressed. You have a long voyage ahead of you, and you must look *beautiful*."

* * *

On the other side of the partition, Viktar languished on the chaise, his eyelids dull and heavy, arms folded and limp. All the while, he kept his watch on the partition.

Greatly occupied with the wine, it wasn't long before Malik and Gorlik slipped from the room to find dinner. It was becoming more difficult for Viktar to stay awake, and just as he thought he might doze off, there she was, stepping from behind the partition, wrapped only in a large towel. Gone was the blood from her face and arms, her hair hanging in clean, damp tendrils down her back.

"Quickly now," Paulette instructed the attendants. "We must get her dressed before the master returns!" Hastily she drew a measuring string from her pocket. One of the attendants, the female, lifted Niveus' arms and held them out to either side while Paulette twined the string around her waist, along shoulder to shoulder, and from her waist to the base of her neck, knotting the string at intervals to mark her measurements. Meanwhile, the other attendant unveiled and displayed the racks.

Finally, Paulette moved to the first rack and drew from it several gowns as she dismissed the attendants. "I can handle it from here. Disturb us no more, but be back on the half hour."

Both nodded, bowed, and left the room. Now Viktar was alone with Paulette and Niveus.

"You are a hard one to fit, girl, but I think we have a few." Paulette scarcely noticed the young man reclined on the chaise behind her. Reaching for Niveus, she instructed, "The towel, give it to me."

Without hesitation, Niveus dropped the towel, handing it to Paulette, and stood naked in the middle of the room, skin nearly pale as her ivory hair.

Viktar drew in a sharp breath, which sent pain coursing from his chest up into his throat. He could not drag his gaze from her; she looked inhuman, as though she were carved of snow.

Even compromised as he was, Viktar felt a stirring within his belly he had not felt for a long time. He could not see how his pupils dilated as he consumed her with his stare. Niveus tipped her head to the side and met his scrutiny straight on. Ashamedly, he averted his gaze just as Paulette held the towel up as a curtain.

"That one," Paulette indicated with a nod of her head. "Try that one first."

Reaching for the dark red gown hanging near the end of the rack, Niveus obeyed, stepping into it as she pulled it up over her arms and shoulders. When Paulette drew the towel aside, and before the gown was even properly laced, Viktar could no longer look away.

Pushing himself onto one elbow, he was entranced. He believed there was no creature as beautiful as Niveus was at that moment. He struggled to sit and, mesmerized, watched as the woman tucked, laced, and threaded this and that, fitting the gown perfectly to Ravan's daughter.

All the while, he was intensely and superbly uncomfortable in his own skin, taken with Niveus in a way that was much more than the growing passion he felt. She had touched his soul eight nights ago—had saved his life. He yearned for her to connect with him again—felt he would give anything, even his life, to have her know him as intimately as she had the night she saved him.

Besides the gown, Paulette had Niveus shortly outfitted in satin slippers, gloves, and a cap with veil. "...just to cover the eyes," she explained. "Hmm...no good can come of someone seeing those eyes." She shrugged, "Perhaps if we were not such conventional creatures."

Then Paulette opened the box that sat on the table. From it she pulled a dark-red rouge and tinted Niveus' cheeks, lips and décolletage, giving her a less-pallid complexion.

The effect on the otherwise striking girl was remarkable. Niveus was like a creature hovering on the edge of extinction. Indeed, that was *precisely* what she was.

Viktar didn't find her more beautiful because of what the older woman did. He found it somewhat akin to polishing an already perfect gemstone. All the while, Niveus tolerated the transformation with aplomb.

"There." Paulette rested her hands on her hips. "What do you think?" She looked over her shoulder, directing the question to the ailing young man.

Nearly mute with awe, he whispered, "She's...she's more beautiful than anything I have ever seen."

This brought a look of surprise to Paulette's face, and she murmured to Niveus, "Why, only someone truly in love could say such a thing, peculiar as you are, child."

She glanced at Viktar again, perhaps seeing something in him she had not noticed before, and said to Niveus in a low voice, "That boy loves you. Were you aware?"

"We've...shared something few others have."

Viktar flushed and looked away, embarrassed to have been so forthright about his feelings for her. He swayed again, not at all certain whether it was from his lingering ill health or for what he felt for Niveus.

Just then the door swung open with a bang. Malik and Gorlik, followed by the attendants, poured into the room.

"Sweet mother of God!" Malik swore. "The shrew looks nearly presentable!"

He laughed heartily and pulled from his jacket a small sack of coin. "Here," he said, tossing one gold piece to Paulette, "for doing the nearly impossible!"

"There are two more gowns that would fit the girl," the woman explained. "But they are not with me. I can bring them in the morning before you sail. And some jewelry—simple but exquisite quality—if you wish."

"That would serve immensely well." Malik, in obvious fine spirits, approached Niveus and ran his finger along her jaw. "Almost as well as she will serve me," he muttered in a throaty voice, obscene enough that it made the older woman look away.

"'Tis strange enough language for an uncle to have of his niece," Paulette chided.

Malik ignored her as the attendants gathered the clothes racks and prepared to leave. As they filed from the room, Paulette stepped close to Viktar and said soft enough that only he could hear, "She is rare. How you managed to capture such a creature is a mystery to me, but consider yourself charmed beyond an ordinary man."

"I-I...no, she is not with me," he stammered.

The older woman glanced slyly over her shoulder at the uncommon girl standing across the room. "Then you are a fool not to see what *I* do."

Then Paulette whisked herself out the door and was gone. She spent the rest of the day wondering about the unusual girl at the Hotel de La Rochelle and basking in the happy, warm memory of her mother.

* * *

After Paulette was gone, Malik boasted, "Come! Let us see if the whore's efforts will do the trick on our girl. Downstairs we go, and let the public decide!"

He grabbed Niveus by the arm and pulled her roughly to her feet, shoving her toward the door. When Viktar made an effort to stand, Malik thrust him backwards.

"No, not *you*, imbecile! Stay where you are...*nephew*."

He ordered the giant, "Guard him. I don't want his interference."

Then Malik dragged Niveus from the room and pushed her in front of him, toward the stairwell to the great room of the hotel. As they descended the stairs, Malik's fingernails bit cruelly into her arm.

"I intend for you to sail with me tomorrow. If, however, you cannot pass as acceptable tonight, I will kill you and be done with it. Be on your best conduct."

Niveus stepped softly from the bottom step into the great room. There were many gathered there, enjoying the early evening's revelry. The tables were full, candles were generous, and several men strummed an unfamiliar tune on lyres from a small stage in the distant corner.

Niveus looked exceedingly out of place amongst the patrons, not so much for her appearance but in the way she carried herself. Risen had once commented that his sister did not walk as others did.

"She floats as though the universe slips past her," he had exclaimed.

Even so, of the few who glanced in their direction, none did so for more than a moment before returning to whatever occupied their evening.

Peering out at them through the shroud of her veil, Niveus was curious about the strange energy that consumed the room. She had never been in such a place, had scarcely ever been away from the castle. Her father had forbidden it, saying, "The common world is not for Niveus." He had been adamant about it, and no one had thought of disputing him. He was, after all, right on the mark.

Sidling to a nearby table, Malik grasped her by the shoulder and steered her into a chair. "Sit. You will act as my...*bride*, should anyone ask."

"It is a lie," she said simply. "I cannot agree to such a thing."

Malik leaned in close to her, the alcohol on his breath sickly thick in the stagnant air of the congested room. "Let us make one thing perfectly clear. For whatever reason, you've given me scarcely an ounce of fight in just over a week. I would never have expected such a thing from you, having met your mother and father. And much as I despise the latter, I know he is no coward."

Nearly snarling, he caught himself, replacing it with a disingenuous smile. "And so, I must conclude you have another reason for being so compliant. Let us stop pretending we don't know why."

He glanced in the direction of the stairs. "I realize it is my nephew who tames the shrew. But disobey me, fair Niveus..." he reached a hand lovingly across the table and took the delicate point of her chin fiercely in his grasp, "...and it will not be you I first kill. Viktar will die, and you shall watch."

To this, Niveus' soul stirred, and that surprised her a small bit. Malik could not see behind her veil; he did not notice how her expression changed. All the while, she scarcely breathed.

When a bar matron approached, cheerfully wiping wet hands on her apron as she asked, "What can I serve the two of you?"

Niveus looked calmly at her and said almost sweetly, "My husband and I would like porridge and ale. I would take mine in a basket for I wish to retire."

Malik was pleasantly surprised. Having already eaten, he agreed wholeheartedly, "Yes, two ales, make that four, and porridge to travel." When the matron left, he devoured Niveus with his gaze. "See, my pretty. How hard was *that*? I've made a liar of you in scarcely under a minute. Now let us see if I can make a whore of you before the night is over."

Niveus was occupied neither with Malik nor his threats. Instead, she was searching for the life thread of someone languishing in a hotel room. Her expression was almost sublime as she found it, connecting with Viktar. It was not strong, but neither was it dire as it had been that night in the cottage.

You live, and you will be stronger. Her thought reached for him.

Surprise reached back to her, from the short distance. The young man likely sensed but could not explain the fleeting thought that had suddenly invaded his own, but his reply, *I will, and you will be free,* was returned.

Malik became suddenly suspicious. "What are you thinking?" he demanded under his breath, but she said nothing in reply. "I said, *what are you thinking?*"

Never in all her years had Niveus manipulated the scope of her gifts for nefarious reasons. Not once had she ever even considered it. But tonight she felt compelled to do just such a thing. She wavered on that precipice as she considered the possibilities, but instead of tapping the potential, she answered with complete honesty, "I was thinking that it would be good if you died."

His breath caught. "What audacity compels you," he snarled, "to think you can say such a thing to me!"

She regarded him thoroughly, slipped her hand up to her ear and pulled loose a pin, which held her cap and veil on one side. Then she reached to the other side, freeing the other pin. As she slipped the cap from her head, her eyes, blood-red, bore into him. Two more pins and her hair cascaded silver about her shoulders and down her back.

Immediately, many within the room stopped what they were doing and stared, unable to pull their gaze from the rare creature that sat amongst them. Gradually, even the music stopped.

"Ask what you will of me, Malik..." Niveus said in a strong voice, ignoring all others, "that I should live a lie on your behalf, but never assume that my feelings won't be made clearly known to you as you do. Of that, I am incapable."

The smirk he so easily wore slipped from his face, and before he could reply, the bar matron approached with a wide smile and was about to set two drinks down on the table.

"There's a bit of joy for a handsome couple to start their evening and—" She gasped and stopped short, nearly toppling the drinks from the tray.

"*Mother* of…" she whispered, a hand going to her mouth. Spying shiftily first at Niveus and then Malik, she added as she stepped back from the table, "'Tis witchcraft afoot!"

"I'm sorry," Niveus murmured, slipping her cap and veil once more over her eyes. "I did not mean to alarm you. I have been ill," she lied, almost easily, and peered through the veil at Malik.

The woman stammered an apology, placed the porridge bucket on the table, and abruptly left. The room slipped back to its previous atmosphere.

Niveus leaned closer and said to the Prussian, "To be clear, I go with you because of *him*—because of Viktar. There is nothing more to say about it, but harm him again, and things will become very complicated for both of us."

He stared in shocked surprise, and she added, sweetly as though she was whispering to a lover, "It is obvious that I am the only one at this table completely comfortable with the prospect of death."

Malik downed his drink with one slug and wiped his thick lips with the back of his forearm before hauling Niveus up from her chair. Then, he ushered her roughly through the dining room.

Patrons stopped their conversations and continued to stare as the strange couple scurried past. Several women gasped and covered their mouths as Niveus pulled her cap and veil once more from her head and met their scrutiny with a blank stare of her own.

As the two disappeared up the stairs, those who remained shook their heads and went on with their evening. Whatever the issue of the strange pair, cruelty was a fact of life. Who knew…the girl may very well have invited whatever bad luck attached itself to her this night.

* * *

Moments later, Malik opened the door and shoved Niveus through. Gorlik, stretched out on the couch like a beached leviathan, pushed his large frame up and watched dumbly as his master dragged the girl past them to the sleeping alcove in the back of the suite.

Viktar drifted between sleep and catatonia, his breathing rapid and shallow, like an injured animal. He did not stir from, only remained as though dead to the world as Niveus passed, her hand stretched toward him.

"He needs me," she said and pulled back from Malik, reaching again for the wounded man.

"*I* need you," Malik snarled and wrung her wrist as he dragged her along. Into the master suite he shoved her, closing the doors behind. "Get undressed," he ordered as he grabbed his crotch, fumbling with himself.

She only stared at him, her eyes darkening to nearly black. "You will not want to do this," she cautioned. "It will be of no good for either of us."

"Get undressed or I will rip the rags from you!" he bellowed as he kicked off his boots and ungirded his trousers.

Niveus said nothing more. Standing as a statue, she regarded him with an expression more peculiar than he had ever seen, and it was enough to give him pause and yet excite him further. His rage mounted along with his arousal, simply because of the way she just stood there, and he struggled, finally kicking his trousers aside in a heap.

Then, he advanced swiftly toward her and shoved her hard, backwards, onto the bed. When he pushed her, however, he had the strange feeling that he pushed something else, something not entirely...*normal.*

Back she fell, flat and stiff like a plank onto the bed, her hands falling loosely at her sides. Her gaze was no longer on him. Alarmingly, it was quite suddenly on nothing at all, and a pink tear dripped and ran slowly down the side of her face.

"Undress, I said!" he shouted at her as he grasped one of her slippers and yanked it roughly from her foot.

Still nothing. Niveus only lay staring so intently at the ceiling that he was compelled to glance there as well. Squinting, he searched to see what it was that had her so transfixed, but Malik could never—*would* never—know what it was she saw.

Nearly beside himself, he moved nearer and held his hand high over her. It swayed there for a long moment as he watched, looking for some indication that she would anticipate and flinch from what cruelty was to come. When there was none, he struck her very hard, even more so than he intended.

Her head jerked stiffly to one side and lay just as it rested, her body arcing in an awful way from the shattering blow. Immediately, a terrible bruise erupted on the delicate cheek, grisly and black in comparison to the pale of her flesh, the orbital edge of her eye socket fractured.

"Look at me!" Malik bellowed.

Not a sound escaped her lips. Not a single cry, no words of pleading, not a whimper of pain. Where Malik wished for her to be, she simply was not, and even as he tore the lovely gown from her body, she neither spoke nor responded to him in any way. Niveus was simply not *there*. She was not his—never would be—and this was his desperate thought as he stared dumbly at her naked body, her hair ghastly white and streaming about her like the frozen branches of a dying winter tree.

"Say something!" he commanded. "Speak and I will spare you this!"

He clutched at his penis, furiously trying to yank it awake, but it had likewise abandoned his intentions and was not to be. Desperation replaced rage as he snatched her jaw in his hand and turned her head to face him, but within her eyes he saw no spark of her presence. What he did see, in the black redness of her vacant stare, was the ghastly reflection of himself, his face a contortion of hatred and fury. Suddenly, for no reason he could truly identify, he released his groin and instead reached for her, slipping his hands about her neck.

As his fingers laced behind her nape and slowly began to tighten, his voice dropped dreadfully low, "I'll *kill* you, Niveus. Right now, right here, I will snuff the light from you forever."

He saw his terrible reflection in those enormous, red eyes.

Surprisingly, he felt tears of fear sting his own eyes as he choked aloud, "I will, Niveus! I will kill you…if you say nothing to save yourself, you will cease to be on this night!"

His hands tightened even more. He could feel her trachea, the fragile rings of it, delicate as eggshell in his palms.

"Speak! Say something and live!" he screamed.

Niveus gulped and gasped, an involuntary response to the choking. Her eyes no longer stared fixed in front of her but rolled back in a terrible way, a stream of pink tears staining the sheets as they slipped from the sides of her face.

All at once, Malik noticed how ashen her complexion had suddenly gone and how terrible was the grisly bruise on the side of her face.

Terror gripped him as he felt he could not stop himself. He wanted to, but he was overcome, and as though his fists had their own design, they only squeezed more.

It was not until her body began to stiffen that he panicked, wrenching his hands from around Niveus' neck as he stumbled back and fell hard onto the floor. Holding his murderous hands in front of his face, he trembled as he kicked farther from the bed.

His hands were unfamiliar to him tonight. But why? He had choked the life from creatures before, man and animal, but never had this happened to him! It horrified him that he was foreign, even unto himself.

Never before had he felt as though he had killed part of himself. Tonight, he feared he had.

Frantic, Malik scrambled to his knees. Reaching for Niveus' head, he gently straightened it so she faced him. She gasped weakly, a convulsive response. Soft, rose-tinged bubbles frothed tiny from her mouth and nose. All the while, she remained as though comatose. Malik took her gently by the shoulders and shook her.

"Niveus, Niveus, breathe!" he begged.

She took an even weaker breath but remained terribly gray and still.

"Breathe! Or I will strike you again!" he demanded, raising his hand again but letting it fall just as swiftly. Then he begged, "Live! I command you!"

She did not breathe.

In awful distress, he was quickly taken with another idea. Without thought of his nakedness, or hers, he charged from the room and went straight to Viktar. Grasping the young man by the wrists, he pulled him from his deep repose and dragged him across the plank floor into the master room.

Confused and terribly feeble, Viktar thrashed weakly against his uncle. "Wha…" he gasped.

"Touch her!" Malik demanded.

"Who? Why do you—" The young man struggled to find his knees beneath himself.

"Take her hand! Press it onto your heart! Hurry!"

Malik simulated the act he had seen Niveus perform that first night. Shoving his nephew toward the bed, he took the frail hand of the now entirely ashen girl and, ripping Viktar's shirt open, pressed it flat over his heart.

Just then, Viktar appeared to all at once comprehend Niveus' terrible state. "No! What have you done?" he cried, and pushed himself desperately onto the bed, taking Niveus' naked body carefully onto his lap.

Then, without realizing it, he did exactly as Malik commanded, pressing Niveus' hand against his heart as his lips touched her battered cheek, his tears welling and falling onto her beautiful, tragic face.

"*No*," he whispered…and wept.

* * *

There it was, just as before—that beautiful, tragically intimate light. She was there, perfect as ever, but also broken, speaking in those words he did not know but understood so implicitly.

Niveus' soul reached a feeble hand toward him and…he took it.

* * *

She drew a long, critical breath. Then she drew another, and another. All the while, Viktar cradled her head, his lips against her battered cheek, her hand clutched in his and pressed desperately against his heart.

Malik watched—relieved, amazed, and…infuriated. So compelled was he to regard the two that he remained without trousers and unmoving, his fixed stare leaping from one to the other.

There was no denying something was happening, something so extraordinary that it denied death, and it was passing between the two of them. Whether it had anything to do with his nephew was debatable, but he was certain the greatest gift lay within the girl.

And right there, in the presence of the miraculous incident, jealousy crept over him, for he *envied* it greatly—coveted it in a way he could not explain, more than he had ever coveted anything.

If Malik thought he could accomplish it without losing Niveus, he would have killed Viktar, for at that moment, he *hated* his nephew—hated what the young man shared with Ravan's daughter. Yes, more than anything he had ever hated before.

CHAPTER FIFTEEN

Risen halted on the hillside, overlooking the sleeping town. The horse stood, head hung low, nostrils flaring from the great effort of their final dash to the sea. La Rochelle was a port city, and the town, a bit farther inland, remained very still. The harbor, however, already bustled with pre-dawn activity.

He frowned as he scanned the vista from one end to the other. Risen possessed a grim set to his whole outlook. The last time he was in a port city was many years before, when he and Sylvie were stolen and taken to Turkey. A terrible trip on a slave ship had removed any romance he might ever hold for where the land met the sea, and the fleeting memory of that harrowing time picked unwelcome in the recesses of his thoughts.

Risen gained brief satisfaction as he remembered burning the slave ship. He was only twelve. His father had helped him, and they launched fiery arrows at it together. Then they watched, side by side, as the Virgin Wolf became a fiery tomb, sinking the wicked men who had captured him into black oblivion. Since that day, Risen had been content to spend his years in the rolling, forested, hill country of the Wintergrave Dynasty where Sylvie now lay at rest.

But tonight he stood where land meets the sea once again, only because he had been drawn here. And what pressed him to journey so relentlessly to the port town was not a fast connection; it was not one he even entirely understood. He had simply been compelled to follow a particular path, and it was to La Rochelle that it had taken him.

Closing his eyes, Risen allowed his breathing to steady and his heart to slow. Alerion stood wearily, only his ears asking if this was to be their final task for the day—to just stand on this hillside overlooking the harbor town.

Where are you? Risen thought. The only reply was the lonely wind sweeping up the hillside to blast, unwelcome, at him.

Velecent sat gravely beside him, waiting patiently for Risen to do what he must. He had admitted not understanding the connection the younger man claimed to share with his sister, but it did not matter. Velecent was more than familiar with Niveus and had witnessed firsthand the mystifying gifts that Nicolette possessed. He had no reason to doubt Risen and was content to follow his dearest friend's son across a great deal of France to this western coastal village.

The soldier lifted his nose into the wind. "Smells like fish rot."

When Risen did not respond, he said nothing more. Both men knew there was no good reason why a foreigner would have taken Niveus to this place unless it was to take her farther *from* here. And that is what Risen feared more than anything.

Alerion stamped a hoof on the frozen earth, jarring Risen from his trance. The human nodded to nearly the center of the town.

"There," Risen murmured and urged the horse forward.

"She is there?" Velecent seemed surprised as he spurred his horse to follow.

"No…but she *was*."

* * *

Nicolette's head snapped up, and her expression went suddenly very dark and vacant, even in the considerable light of the workshop. She had been so absorbed in her reading—a study of Sayid's native language—that she had allowed a sunbeam to slant through the ceiling window across her shoulder and onto her lap.

Normally, Nicolette sought the shadowed recesses, enjoying more the misty mornings before sunrise than the direct light of day. She had always been like this, even back in their beloved France. Her favorite times to walk through the castle orchard were always on a moonlit night, and in recent years Ravan had taken to occasionally walking there alongside her. He was happy she allowed this, and when he accompanied her he was careful to say nothing, for she seemed less aware of his presence than he.

They had been in Crete for just over a month, and Ravan had proved a quick study. Sayid was an excellent mentor, and his student both amazed and delighted him. Consequently, the core basics of forging Damascus steel were nearly complete. Sayid was now helping Ravan learn the delicate, final steps of refinement—setting the steel, drawing from it the arc of the blade, and coaxing from it the edge that would defy all reason, causing it to stand up to a blow when other weapons failed.

All had gone so splendidly that Ravan had already sent word to Salvatore. The Spaniard could return to Crete at his leisure, for Ravan would be finished before the month's end.

This morning, while Sayid paused to feed the fire, the mercenary took the moment to gaze upon his wife and appreciate how deeply he loved her. His love for her smoldered as he watched her carefully turn the pages of her book, lost in her studies. If one knew not how strong Nicolette truly was, she might appear frail.

The sunbeam, which lit her ebony hair like an inky halo, told Ravan that her mind was very far away, for she allowed it, and his mouth nearly softened into a smile.

Sayid looked up from where he methodically pressed the bellows and glanced from Ravan to Nicolette. He had quite a knowing expression on his face, which indicated he recognized these two were meant for each other, just as the fine Damascus steel was meant for the raging heat of the fire. A smile *did* crease the Syrian's lips.

Because Ravan was so focused on Nicolette, he immediately noticed her head jerk about and saw firsthand how her eyes darkened in a way he had not seen in a very, very long while. The last time he had seen her like this was many years ago…in Turkey. And now, just as then, it inspired something in him he seldom felt—dread.

Ravan's expression fell from contentment to fear in one swift moment, and he was across the studio like a great cat in only a few strides. Kneeling before Nicolette, he took her hands in his, easing the book from them before laying it gently aside.

She only stared, her head remaining turned at an odd angle as she focused on seemingly nothing over his shoulder.

"My love," Ravan murmured as he reached up and touched her chin, directing her gaze back toward him. "Nicolette, *look* at me."

The blackness in her expression faded as she pulled away from that far, far place to focus on her husband's worried face. Ravan dreaded what he saw and shook his head involuntarily.

"What is it?" he asked. "Nicolette…*tell* me."

Her damp, clear eyes locked onto her husband's, and she uttered only one word…

…*Niveus.*

CHAPTER SIXTEEN

✝

Viktar slept. For three days, he scarcely moved, lying on his back like a corpse. Time rolled over him like a liar causing him to believe it had been only a day...only an hour...scarcely a minute. Vaporous images of the snow-white angel with the burning eyes came and went, and still...he did not die.

When thirst roused Viktar enough that he reached for the pitcher of water, he tried to say her name, but his throat was too dry for him to speak. With trembling hands, he brought the cup to his cracked lips, drank deeply, and lay back again.

"Where am I?" he murmured and imagined everything had been a dream. Then, the twinge in his lung brought his hand to the scar and he knew—it was no dream.

The swaying of the boat threatened to drag him back to sleep, but he forced himself to stay awake.

"The ship. We're on a ship," he said to himself, "and Niveus...*he* has Niveus." Viktar forced himself to his feet and staggered for the door.

* * *

The great ship pitched and roiled in the oceans off the coast of France. Malik swore loudly as he was forced to steady his walk back to his room with two hands along the bulkhead of the corridor, causing him to slosh his ale...again. He believed the ship would come apart, as wickedly as it lurched, but the vessel was sturdy and had traveled the giant swells of these particular waters many times before.

Admittedly, other than the dismal sea conditions, the great ship was comfortable enough, for it was designed not only for commerce but as a passenger vessel.

Even so, Malik craved his home, tucked pristinely along the Vistula River in Thorn. He yearned for the luxuries, and the improprieties, that waited for him there. And, he missed the way the vast, thick forests, which rolled on forever, veiled Red Robes from prying eyes.

Briefly, he thought of Aya and what he would make her do to him on his return. But then, in barely an instant, Aya's memory slipped from his thoughts. He was again occupied with the strange girl he had abducted, and no amount of ocean torment could draw from him the confidence he felt because of it. For the first time in a long while, Malik had a much stronger sense of purpose.

Ever since three nights before, when he had nearly strangled Niveus, he was consumed with thoughts of what could be. If the girl was all he believed she was—the bizarrely gifted prodigy of Ravan and Nicolette—his destiny was now entirely changed, having run a perfectly wicked course. He thought back to the chain of events that had landed him such good fortune. It was divine destiny, he told himself. It was meant to be.

First, so taken with Nicolette as he was, he had meant to *have* Niveus, simply anticipating that she would be like her mother. When this was not the case, not in *that* way, he had toyed with the idea of simply killing the girl, for it would have gratified him greatly to smite Ravan in such a way.

Malik's stomach lurched. He resented Ravan, begrudging the mercenary his stoic confidence and strength, but mostly he despised him because he possessed Nicolette. Almost immediately, these thoughts fell by the wayside.

It was a great new day, and Malik was even more obsessed with the prospect of owning Niveus—of controlling all the power he believed the girl capable of. And she was yet in her teens! Who knew what gifts the girl would grow into; what dominion he might spawn from her!

Malik believed that, with Niveus at his side, he would never again suffer illness and would live a great long time, perhaps even outlive Viktar. Even Ravan was far from Malik's thoughts, for he intended to take the girl back to Prussia and claim her…as his bride. What power she could give him; perhaps they would even produce an heir! She would reign over Red Robes beside him, a queen like no other!

His footsteps became even lighter as he approached his stateroom. He felt invincible, giving no consideration to the nature of the peculiar girl quartered in the small room down the hall. No, Malik cared not at all what Niveus might think of his master plan. Not once did he believe the circumstances of her gifts had any provisions attached to them. He only looked at the girl and her abilities as a commodity, something to command and control.

He paused. There were still several complicating factors. It would be a delicate situation to marry the girl. Great care must be taken to hide from everyone who she really was. If anyone were to discover from what great dynasty she had been taken, no doubt word would be out, and Ravan would hunt him down. He smiled wickedly. Prussia was very far away, and he had been careful to hide his identity all along.

It would be simple enough, he assured himself. He would change the girl's name and fabricate a tale that would support her sudden appearance into his realm. Likewise, he must find the power to coerce Niveus into accepting her fate. No problem there. He was a master at intimidation, and there was always something of importance that could be held over someone's head. He would just have to discover what that was for the girl.

Finally, he must negotiate Viktar's fate, for his nephew was the only one besides Gorlik who knew the truth of the whole matter. Ultimately, this meant just one thing. Again, he smiled...

Details! All of it—just stupid details—and Malik shoved the sniveling young man from his thoughts, for it annoyed him greatly to consider him at all. How terribly inconvenient it had been that Viktar had survived that night in the cottage behind the Inn. How careless of him to miss his nephew's heart with the deadly blade.

Malik snorted. His nephew had shown considerable resolve these last months, but after his near-murder, he had been left weak. For now, he would keep him alive because it was what Niveus requested. He would see the boy back, but only long enough to banish him and his meddling mother from Red Robes.

He pushed all of these thoughts from his mind as he passed his stateroom and approached Niveus' instead. Resting his hand against the door, he paused and dropped his head, steeling himself. He would command her, he swore to himself, but lately...he wished that she would comply of her own accord.

Rapping gently on the door, he announced himself. "It is I, your master. Open the door."

Nothing was all the reply he received.

"Do not make me break the door down, Niveus. I will have my way, and you know it."

Still, nothing.

He slammed his fist against the door. "Niveus! I said, open this door!"

When he was greeted by neither an open door nor a response, he tried the latch, but it was locked fast. His first inclination was to force the door open, but that was an idea he swiftly passed on. Large as he was, he did not possess the brawn necessary for such a task, for the stateroom doors were solid wood and well-installed. Instead, he wondered if Gorlik could break the door down. Only then he would be left explaining the damages to the captain.

Smacking his palm against the flat of his brow, he cursed himself silently. The *key*…the quartermaster would have the key, and access would be his at any time he wished. Shortly, he stood in front of the quartermaster below deck.

"I don't understand." The quartermaster seemed reluctant. "Is the lady in need of something? If she doesn't come to the door, perhaps she requires rest and does not wish to be disturbed."

"My…*niece*…has needs. She does not always open the door for me, or anyone for that matter, and I wish only to check on her," Malik said hastily and forced desperation from his voice.

The quartermaster did not seem entirely convinced. "I will open the door for you, but I will not leave the key with you." Rifling through the ships roster, he stabbed at it with a finger. "The lady is three years of age—seventeen it says here—and unless I witness her inabilities myself, I will not give you unlimited access to her room. It would simply not be right, even if you are her guardian. I can assure you, the girl is going nowhere soon," he added wryly.

"I have paid her passage."

To this the quartermaster's face darkened, and he stood taller than before. "Indeed? And how kind of you, but the young lady remains a guest on the King's vessel. We do not harbor slaves."

Scowling, Malik nodded dumb acceptance. This was as good as he was going to have it, and he had no choice but to follow behind the sturdy sailor as they threaded their way through the passages back to Niveus' door. The quartermaster was agile on his feet and moved as though the ship tossed not at all. Once, when Malik had to catch himself on the wall, slapping his hands against it to keep from falling, the man glared over his shoulder at him.

Finally outside her door, the man inquired kindly, "Madame?" He rapped gently on the door. "Madame, I've come to check on your well-being. Your…" he glanced over his shoulder, "…*uncle* assures me that you have needs, which must be met."

When there was no answer, he asked, "Are you ill?" and tapped again on the door.

Still…no answer. Finally, as though with some curiosity of his own, the quartermaster slid the key into the lock and, releasing the catch, eased the heavy door slowly open.

There on the bed knelt Niveus, ghastly thin and shining as gossamer as a new moon, her long hair hanging unkempt and tangled to her waist. She sat with her back to both of them, still in the blood-red dress she had been outfitted in La Rochelle. Her hand was extended up into the air as she passed her palm slowly back and forth between seemingly nothing.

From the angle of the door, she appeared a frail old woman perched on her knees in the middle of the bed.

The quartermaster drew himself up short, immediately intrigued by the sight of her. He could not know she had not left the room since they boarded three days before, and that there was no more water in her bedside pitcher. He glanced briefly at Malik as though he might have misread the man's true intentions.

"See? It is as I told you," Malik snipped.

"Miss, are you all right?" the sailor began, signaling the Prussian to remain at the door.

"You may leave us now." Malik grasped the man on his shoulder from behind, but the quartermaster shook him roughly off.

"Unhand me, sir." The man shot a look of distinct command over his shoulder. "I am responsible for the safety of all as long as they are on this ship, and I will know the circumstances of the lady's ailment and needs before I will leave her to your care."

"She is...unstable. Must you pry? Her parents are deceased, and I am bringing her home to care for her. Only the best treatment, of course," Malik lied.

Just then, Niveus ceased the peculiar behavior, dropping her hand softly into her lap. She turned, peering solemnly over her shoulder at the two of them. Her beautiful, battered face was immediately visible, and the quartermaster nearly gasped. Before he had a chance to say anything more, they were interrupted by a voice coming from out in the hall.

"Is she awake? Is she all right?" someone asked urgently.

Then, there was Viktar leaning shakily against the heavy door jamb, hands clasped earnestly together. The quartermaster glanced between the young man and Niveus as though not at all certain which one appeared more wretched.

"Excuse me, sir. You know the girl as well?"

"Viktar! This is no business of yours!" Malik boomed. "Back to your room. You look as though you could die any minute, boy!"

"I will not, not until I've seen her," Viktar demanded, standing his ground with a fierceness of eye that his body did not entirely possess.

It seemed the argument was about to escalate right there, between the three men, when the soft voice of Niveus silenced them all.

"Viktar," was all she said, and she turned about and arose from the bed, swaying at the edge of it.

The young man pushed weakly between Malik and the quartermaster and hobbled to her side, guiding her to sitting again.

"Niveus, you look frightfully ill. Please, sit down." He shot a glare at his uncle. "Has she had nothing to eat since we've boarded? And her clothes..." He looked her up and down. "And she needs something to sleep in."

Malik, unaccustomed to not getting his way, swallowed his rage long enough to appear civil in front of everyone. "Yes, yes of course she does. That is why I sought him," he gestured at the sailor, "because I was worried for the girl."

He appealed to the quartermaster with hands spread.

"I only wish to see more to the child's well-being. She refuses to answer her door and, as you can see, is hardly capable of tending to her own needs. And her mother..." He let the sentence fall short as though to leave the fate of the poor girl's *mother* up to the quartermaster's imagination.

Niveus, all the while, was ignoring everyone except Viktar. She stepped nearer him and took his hand gently in hers.

"I would like you to sit with me for a while," she said softly.

The quartermaster cast a suspicious expression toward Malik, forcing him to respond.

"Uh...u-mm, of course he can," Malik begrudged.

"And *you* will pay for food and water for them," the quartermaster announced before indicating an unopened trunk on the other side of the small room. "And she has clothes?"

"She does, but only four gowns. Nothing to sleep in," Viktar explained. "We left on very short notice."

This seemed only to confuse the quartermaster more, and he shook his head.

"I'll see to it that her needs are met. In the meantime, both of you will leave." He looked first at Viktar. "You will be invited to sit with her while she dines as it appears she wishes your presence. I will alert you when she is ready to receive guests."

Then, scowling at Malik, he added, "But as this child appears to be suffering from the voyage, and there is no woman traveling with her, I will be taking responsibility for her cares into my own hands and, by proviso, the captain's."

It was a stalemate, and Malik could do nothing about it. He seethed. "Of course," he agreed, forcing a thin smile. "It is all I ever intended for her when I came to you for assistance."

Viktar said to Niveus, "I'll be back soon."

She nodded but said nothing. Releasing her grasp, he followed as the quartermaster indicated they must all exit.

Once the door was securely locked, the sailor pocketed the key. "I'm not sure what business it is that the two of you are taken with, but this is a righteous ship and owned by his grace, the King. Whatever fate you intend for the girl is your own business, but there will be no foul play toward any of our passengers, not during our sail. If you have issue with that, we have a tribunal within the ranks. Justice could be served swiftly long before we make land."

"I'm offended you would consider me possible of foul play." Malik feigned righteous indignation.

The quartermaster inspected Viktar, looking him up and down. "I will bring double portions when I return. Looks as though you've not eaten in days either. If you wish, you can wait for me here." With one last dubious glance toward Malik, the shipman turned on his heel and was gone.

Malik waited until the sailor was gone before spinning in a rage on Viktar, shoving him hard against the wall, his hands about his throat.

"I will kill you now," he hissed, "and be done with my sister's bastard once and for all!"

Clawing at the hands that tightened about his neck, Viktar was barely able to gasp, "Kill me, and you will lose her. You know...you...*will*."

It was enough to jar Malik to his senses, and he finally released his nephew, threatening openly as he stabbed a finger into his chest.

"I will play this game, for now. But you are a fool if you believe I won't finish what has come between us!" Then, he whirled and stomped, staggering with the pitch of the ship, down the hall the other direction.

Viktar slid down the wall, collapsing on the hallway floor, and waited, his lips pressed softly to where his hand had touched hers.

* * *

It was nearly an hour before the quartermaster returned, carrying a loaded tray. Even though he suggested Viktar could wait there, he still seemed surprised to find Viktar sitting on the floor outside of Niveus' door.

"Come, boy," he motioned as he fetched Niveus' room key from his pocket. "I think you will benefit from this, even more so than the girl."

When it was fairly obvious Viktar might not rise of his own accord, he slipped an arm under the younger man's armpit and helped hoist him to his feet.

"Thank you, sir. I've not been well lately," the young Prussian said sincerely, a weak smile creasing his lips.

"No…good health does not seem to attach itself to any who stray too near your uncle," the quartermaster replied wryly as he slipped the key into the door lock.

When he opened the door, he was further surprised to find Niveus sitting exactly as before, in exactly the same spot, only her hands were lying on her knees, palms upward. She could not see how vacant her gaze appeared, for her being was somewhere else altogether. Additionally, the entrance of the two men was scarcely enough to disturb her.

As Viktar moved urgently to her side, the quartermaster unhinged the wall table and placed the tray on it, all the while watching the strange girl from the corner of his eye.

"I'm here," Viktar murmured as he knelt before her. "Everything will be all right."

Niveus raised an eyebrow. *What a peculiar thing to say*, she thought.

The sailor gave the odd pair a look of skepticism before saying, "I have broth for you both—chicken and fish—and plenty of bread and butter to fill you up." He indicated the meal with a sweep of his hand. "And I've refilled the pitcher. Your uncle has paid for nothing other than passage, for the two of you at least; he spends enough on himself. So I wish I could have brought more. Regardless, you will not starve while you are aboard."

"Thank you, sir, most sincerely, for your compassion," Viktar replied. "It has been a hard journey for both of us. But I am from a good family and you will be doubly rewarded for any sacrifice you make now."

"Hmm…well, I don't know your circumstances, but I know a rotted fish when I smell one." He nodded at Niveus. "But your cousin seems fond enough of you."

The sailor set a parcel on the floor next to Niveus' bed. "Something for you to sleep in, m'lady, and I will see that your buckets are emptied."

Niveus glanced curiously from the bucket to the quartermaster, then asked quite suddenly, "Where is the ship going?"

He hesitated. "Are you *certain* that you are all right, child? Surely you know his majesty's ship, the *Reis Espada*, sails north to Denmark and then east to Prussia, to your home; rather, your uncle's."

He gestured around the small room.

"It will be a long journey, and sometimes we have treacherous seas, as is normal this time of year, but travel by ship is much faster than you could ever make Prussia by horse or carriage." He chewed his lip thoughtfully. "Perhaps you took a greater blow to the head than you first thought?"

"It is not my home," Niveus corrected him.

"I...I don't understand," the sailor began and looked to Viktar for explanation.

"What is your name?" Niveus asked.

"Quin, my lady, at your service."

"You are from Portugal."

He started mildly at her observation. "Yes, but I am at a loss how you knew that," he replied with obvious suspicion. "Other than my accent, but my mother was Spanish."

"And you have a family there. Have you seen them recently?" she asked.

Quin glanced again at Viktar and shifted nervously. "I...I have, just a week ago." His face lit up in the candlelight of the small room. "My son is just turned ten. We celebrated."

Niveus nodded softly. "That is good, that you were with them." She glanced away. "It is a memory you should hold very dear."

It was such a strange thing to say, and when Niveus said nothing else, Quin only shrugged. "Very well, then. Is there anything else that you require this evening?"

"I assure you I am quite well." She folded her hands and laid them in her lap.

"You may say that, but your condition says otherwise." Quin scowled.

Niveus' hand went to her cheek, touching gently the grisly green bruise she could not see. "Oh, yes...Malik hit me. It was broken, but it is fast healing."

The quartermaster spoke suddenly harshly to Viktar. "It is not my place to question the dynamics of your family, but I will not tolerate such a thing on this ship. Just so you know, I intend to lock the door behind me." He gave a look of stern warning at the man who knelt at the girl's bedside. "Not that I think you capable, but I gather anything that might happen between the two of you would be consensual on the part of the lady?"

Viktar, suddenly embarrassed, nodded graciously. "I would do nothing to dishonor or hurt her, sir. She is safe with me, and I will allow no further harm to come to her." He grasped her hand.

"Very well. I will leave you to your dinner."

He gathered the water bucket and tray and paused at the door.

"Take care of the girl. She should be protected, as something...*rare*...I believe."

"I will," Viktar said.

"And so a pup guards a kitten," Quin mused, shaking his head sadly, and left the room.

* * *

Niveus pulled Viktar's hand. "Rise," she said. "Here, sit on the bed, beside me."

"I'm so sorry for all of this." He reached a hand up as though he might touch her battered face, but instead, he took a strand of her hair and tucked it gently behind her ear.

"I don't understand," she wondered aloud. "Why would you think any of this is your fault?" She tipped her head, truly mystified.

He struggled to push himself up beside her. "Certainly you must realize. At first it seemed only unusual—my uncle's obsession with your father's realm. But then I think even Gorlik found it unreasonable, not that the brute cares." He snorted and shook his head. "My uncle covets you. No, it is even more than that. He is consumed with all of it as though it is a challenge for him...a wicked crusade. And he won't stop until he has had his way."

Obviously committed to sharing the truth, Viktar pressed on. "He met your mother in Crete, and she had such an immediate appeal about her, one that even I must confess could scarcely be denied." He swallowed hard and paused. "But I would never think to act on such a thing. My uncle, however..."

"I understand," Niveus murmured. "You should not be apologetic. People are drawn to my mother in such a way. It has always been like that." She believed it should explain everything and shrugged. "But my mother is unaffected by it."

"No, it was more than that. It was not only his obsession with your mother, it was your father. He did exactly what my uncle could not tolerate. *He* was the better man about everything, and he did it so effortlessly."

Viktar waved his hand at nothing.

"My uncle was diminished by it, as he should have been. But then he blamed his humiliation on Lord Ravan, and it was evident to everyone else how pathetic he was. That was, to him, the worst insult of all."

Niveus said nothing, only listened, polite and unmoving as the young Prussian spoke.

"As a consequence, my uncle made it his mission. At first I told myself otherwise, when he decided that we must come to France—to the Wintergrave Dynasty—before returning home. I told myself it was innocent enough."

Viktar leaned heavily on his knees, head in his hands.

"I was weak. I waited, stalling, believing he might come to his senses. But then he waited for you, for nearly two weeks after we arrived. I think I refused to acknowledge the insanity of it all at first. But that is what it was...*is*. It's insanity."

Niveus only watched as Viktar sadly studied the candle flame and continued. "He made excuses, drew it out in such a way as to make it seem almost reasonable. We sported, took in the sights. He claimed to only wish to catch a glimpse of you, to see the daughter of the great and legendary Ravan."

Viktar seemed so intently embarrassed that his voice now dropped to a whisper. "When he refused an audience with your brother, and when it was apparent that you were truly beyond his grasp, he became desperate. He fabricated a plan. I didn't know, but we had all heard the stories about you."

"Stories?"

"Yes, the tales, from the townspeople." Viktar could not meet her gaze. "The wonderful things you did, the kind ministerings, the *magic*."

He laced his fingers together between his knees, his face a map of misery.

"I never thought for an instant he would be so treacherous as to hurt you; that he would trick you by..." His voice faded away.

"By nearly killing you," she finished his thought.

"Yes. That is the all of it. He meant to draw me to death's door to lure you to the cottage. Brilliant, really, but now I know him for what he is—more than a murderer. He is insane. And what grieves me most is not that he meant to kill me, but that he meant to kill you.

"And that is his greatest abomination. And so, I've decided to...to..." Viktar studied his hands. "But I am not strong, at least not yet." He struggled to face her, confirming the truth of it.

"It doesn't matter," she replied.

"How can you *say* that? It does matter! He has taken you against your will. He means to have you go to Prussia, with *him*, forever, and God only knows if your dear family will ever be able to find you."

"Not against my will."

This halted him where he sat, sparking a look of genuine surprise on Viktar's face. "I don't understand. Niveus, I—"

"I have not been taken against my will. I agreed to come with him, so that I could help you. If I had not, you would be dead."

"Yes…yes, I understand. But *why*? You had no obligation to help me. And he's my uncle! I am of the same blood. How could you have known I was not every bit as wicked as he?"

Just then, the edges of her lips curled up into the faintest of smiles. She could not know how beautiful her smile appeared to him, even gracing her battered face.

"I knew immediately, when I first touched you," she said almost sweetly.

"You mean beyond my injury? You gained a sense of who I *am*?"

She nodded and turned toward the candle. Lifting her hand, she slowly unfurled her fingers toward it. The flame danced happily in response to the gesture as though it wished to leap into her palm.

Viktar waited patiently, saying nothing, so mesmerized by it that he startled when she added, "Sometimes it is painful, because the one I minister to—the suffering one—has so much broken within them, but mostly I can block that away."

"You mean with their heart, don't you; not with their body. Broken bits of their heart."

She turned her gaze upon him again, eyes exquisite as a transparent pearl might be.

"But your heart, it was…*is*…beautiful, Viktar." She said it as sincerely as though she was describing a sunrise to a blind child.

He stared, awe-stricken.

"You should not be so surprised," she said. "You should know your own heart better than any other."

"But I do not," he admitted.

"No, you do not. But I think you shall…before this journey is done."

CHAPTER SEVENTEEN

†

Risen stood on the end of a long dock. He squinted into the night fog at the vacant slip which he could not know had moored the great passenger ship, the *Reis Espada*, scarcely a day before. What he did know was that Niveus had been in that space, and then…was gone.

"There." He motioned to Velecent with two fingers toward the pier.

The shack on the end of the pier had a solitary candle lit in the window, an indication business was still open despite the late hour.

Shortly, the two men stood across from a portly man who sat at a table with a collection of wine-stained maps laid out before him. Glancing around the dull room, Risen asked the harbormaster, "You say there were four of them, one of them a girl with hair white as snow?"

"I never saw the girl's face, but her hair was unkempt and white as the ocean is tonight." The fat man nodded somewhere toward where the open sea churned with whitecaps, beyond the haven of the cove.

"Names." Velecent tapped his gauntleted hand on the rough-hewn table.

"There were four of them, as I said, but only two names were listed." The harbormaster scanned the journal with a salty finger. "Lord Balfeur and his nephew, Napoleon. But the girl…" He shook his head. "No, her name is not listed here."

The man seemed to sincerely wish to help them. Even so, Risen struggled to remain patient. "Describe the men."

"Dark skin, fair hair—the lord, that is." The fellow glanced up from the journal.

"I only remember because, even amongst what we see at port, he was unusual. And the younger one, a handsome boy, maybe twenty years old. It was difficult to tell. He looked as though he was failing the good fight…and then there was the brute."

The man shook his head and closed the ledger, holding his finger to mark the spot and shrugged apologetically. "You already know what I know of the girl. There is nothing more I can tell you."

It was all Risen needed to hear and as he feared. Niveus was aboard the ship. And the three who had taken her were just as they had been described back at the Inn—the ones who had secured the cottage for those few weeks. There was blood dried on the floor of the cottage when they left, beneath the bed, and the stab mark of a sword in the floorboards. Risen had wondered at first if the blood had been his sister's. But now he wondered if it wasn't the younger man the harbormaster spoke of, the one *failing the good fight.*

Unfolding a piece of parchment, he held it closer to the candle to read the names scrawled there. It was the manifest from the Inn. They were different from those listed for passage on the boat, but the signature was of the same hand. And this didn't surprise Risen at all. Except for his unusual connection to Niveus, the strangers would be long gone with scarcely a way to find them.

He knew, without doubt, that the moment would come when he would face his sister's captors. Briefly, peculiarly...he thought of Sylvie. Blinking, he swept the cobwebs of his past away.

"Where is the ship bound?" Risen asked as he folded the parchment and stuffed it into his jacket.

"The usual route. 'Tis a sturdy vessel, and comfortable enough, with a good captain and crew. It will head due north to Denmark then across to Prussia before she returns to Portugal."

"And how far did they book passage?" Velecent leaned closer, eyes narrowing as he inspected the chart map.

As though mildly bothered by the barrage of questions, the harbormaster reopened the ledger with a flourish and dragged his finger dreadfully slow down the log.

"Let us see, gentlemen." He thumped the ledger. "Prussia, it seems. All the way to...*Danzig.*" The man flipped the ledger shut with finality. "It is as far as the ship goes."

"When do you have another vessel sailing there?" Risen's face was hopeful.

"To Denmark?" the man snorted. "Next week, perhaps. But...Prussia?" He shook his head regretfully. "It is farther than most are willing to sail this time of year. It will be another month at least before one sails there again. But I can secure passage in advance if you wish."

Risen crossed his arms and stalked the short distance of the harbormaster's shack and back. "And sail time?"

The man shrugged. "Depends on the number of stops. I should think two weeks, m-mm, twelve days...minimally."

Risen said urgently to Velecent. "Forty days...it will be forty, minimally, if we wait to sail. But if we ride..." His forehead furrowed as he ran the mental calculations.

Velecent appeared skeptical. "Thirty, thirty-five, perhaps. And only if we push at least that many miles each day. It would be a ride from hell, but I've ridden worse..." he smiled wryly, "with your father."

It was all Risen needed to hear, and he was flooded with gratitude. Without a farewell to the harbormaster, he spun on his heel and left the dock shack, back to the livery to fetch his horse. Half an hour later, they were mounted once more and charging northwest...to Prussia.

CHAPTER EIGHTEEN

✝

Quin was quite taken with the girl. They were not feelings of intimacy; more that he was strangely protective of and captivated by her. And this was unusual for Quin, for he was, first and foremost, a sailor and a sensible man by nature—very loyal to his post. It wasn't like him to spend precious extra time tending to the needs of a particular passenger.

But, there had first been something about the girl's condition that raised the hackles on the back of his neck. Quin feared for her fate at the hands of the scheming Prussian lord, and now his heart was simply compelled to know she was all right—that it would in some way make his a better life for it.

Tapping on her door, he was not surprised to hear no answer come from within. She *never* answered. Gorlik, standing his post, held a massive paw up to him.

"My lord has her occupied. You are not to enter tonight."

Quin was stricken with alarm. "Not possible! He has no key."

Gorlik only stared dumbly down at the sailor and shrugged. To this. Quin snarled and stepped two paces back, drawing from his side his crewman's dagger.

"Step aside, brute, or you and your master will be cast to the depths before the evening is upon us, I swear it!" said Quin.

The towering thug seemed scarcely concerned and moved as though he would draw his sword, but Quin had him cut across the hand so swiftly it halted him before he had hold of the weapon. Few men were as swift with a knife as sailors were, and this one was swifter than most, for the fate of a good ship might depend upon immediate release of rope.

"My argument is not with you," the quartermaster warned again, wielding the bloodied blade. "If you wish to lay your life down for your master today, that will be your fate if you try to hinder me."

A cruel monster to be sure, Gorlik was best at following simple and immediate commands. He looked first at his wounded hand, then at Quin, and doing just as he was told, stepped aside. Moments later, Quin had the key in the lock and entry to the room as he shoved the door open with a crash.

There was Malik, his hands upon Niveus' shoulders, her gown loosened down the front as though he would draw it from her. With a look of keen surprise, he glanced over his shoulder, spun about, and lunged aside, both hands up in the air.

"What? Wait! You aren't allowed in here!" Malik exclaimed, moving out of reach of Quin's blade.

"How did you come by the key?" Quin demanded, his weapon leveled at Malik's face. He pressed him away from Niveus, across the tiny cabin, and back against the wall.

Malik sputtered, "It was mine by right. The captain—he gave it to me."

"And you would rape your *niece*?"

"I am not his niece," Niveus said bluntly, to everyone's surprise.

Malik shifted a leering glance from her to Quin, finally exclaiming, "The girl speaks the truth. She is not my niece. She is my…*fiancée*."

"I am *not* his fiancée," Niveus added for any who might be interested.

"Not my fiancée…*yet*," Malik wheedled.

Quin, disgusted with all of it, dropped his blade from Malik's face to his chest. "Why? The lie, why were you—"

"She is…uncomely," Malik blurted out, "to look at, I mean. You must admit! The ruse, that she was my niece—it seemed to draw less need for explanation during our travels."

Unwilling to allow the story to stand as it was, Quin motioned at Malik with the blade. "Leave. See to it your guard finds the steward for repair of his hand. I will secure the door."

"You can't! She is mine, and—"

"I will kill you, sir. And, I shall enjoy it." Quin's hand, and the dagger, never wavered.

Malik finally edged along the wall before retreating through the door.

"Wait," Quin commanded. "Your key."

"It is mine!" Malik exclaimed. "The captain issued it to me."

"However you have come by it, I forbade any to enter here." Having nothing but eternal mistrust for this wretched man, he added, "We shall see what the captain wishes after I speak with him. Until then…" He held his hand out and motioned for the key.

Malik hedged but finally drew the key from his pocket and turned it over.

After he was gone, Quin locked the door, sat down heavily, and glanced away as Niveus regathered her gown.

Finally, he asked her, "I must know, are you truly his fiancée?"

"I told you I am not, though he claims that I am."

Quin's face fell with relief but also frustration. It always seemed such a task to talk to Niveus, and yet he was eternally compelled to hear what she might say next. It was a beautiful addiction, he felt, and he tried again, "And what do you claim? Are you to be his betrothed?"

"I do not want to marry him, but I will have no say in the matter. Yes, I will eventually stand at the altar with him."

Quin could not know Niveus was speaking of a premonition, but her gaze affected his heart very much with the sincerity of her reply. It was nearly frightening in its candor.

Waving it aside, Quin asked her more pointedly, "Your father, has *he* given consent for your union?"

"No. My father does not know where I am or who I am with."

"But...but you left your home *willingly*. You told me so!"

Niveus nodded as the fingers of her hand traced the pleat of her skirt.

Quin stopped her, taking her hand up in his. "Child, you are a mystery to me, one I cannot define. It seems you care for the other, the younger one. Please tell me what it is you desire, so that I may help you. I fear this is a dreadful situation, and I have not enough details to help you."

"I desire nothing you could give me," Niveus said with honesty.

Her entire being was to Quin undeniably truthful even though he could scarcely believe her. He sighed and tried again. "If you could be anywhere else, where would you choose to be...right *now*?"

"I can be wherever I wish," she replied, her eyebrows knotting in curiosity. "Quin, I cannot know what it is you seek if you are not asking the right questions."

It shook him to hear her call him by name for the first time.

When he said nothing, only stared at her, she clasped his hand. "Quin," she mentioned his name again, "you mustn't grieve fate. Destiny is nothing more than a door. Death is not as most believe it to be."

"You are not going to die," he insisted heavily and shook his head.

"We must all pass through that door," she nearly whispered this time. "The time will come. All of us will die. It is only a step on an eternal path, only a portal. But, it does not have to be unwelcome."

"Niveus...are you saying...you believe you will *die* on this journey?" He could feel his trepidation rising.

She shook her head, reaching to take his into both of hers.

"No. I will not. But a time will come when you will question what I have told you tonight. Do not be afraid. You will be with *me,* when the moment arises, and your courage will honor me. I promise this to you." She lifted both his hands, planting upon the back of them a cool kiss—sincere, like a child's.

Quin was sincerely confused by now, and the gesture was to him something much more than a simple touch. He felt altogether calmed and almost saddened by it and pulled his hand away, standing so hastily that he nearly toppled the chair.

"You talk circles about me as though you expect to…" He could not utter the words, how he thought Niveus appeared resigned to her own demise, and he shook his head with finality. "Whatever that man is to you—uncle, fiancée—" he nodded at the door, "I don't believe you wish for him to take with you the liberties he obviously intends."

"He can never have me," Niveus said softly, her face glowing with untroubled certainty.

Quin thought her expression was more ancient than any sea he had ever sailed. "He will not be visiting you *here* again. Of that I promise," he said hoarsely, turning his back to Niveus. "See your cousin if you wish; he seems to agree with you. But with our next landfall I intend to send word to your father—to find out his opinion on the matter. He must be notified."

"If it pleases you," Niveus said calmly.

Quin then gathered enough details to fashion the note he intended to send when they stopped to reprovision at a port in northern France the next day.

Lord Wintergrave,

I am in attendance of your daughter aboard his majesty's ship, the Reis Espada, (King's Blade). She is in the custody of a Prussian. Your daughter calls him Malik, but I believe the man travels with an alias. He calls himself Balfeur, and his intentions, I fear, are ignoble.

I must inform you that we are set for final mooring at Danzig before returning to Portugal. From there I do not know where the man will take Niveus but shall try my best to discover this and get word.

Your daughter is rare. You most certainly know this already, but I grieve that she is gone from your gracious care. Godspeed to you, that you may find her soon. I am at your eternal service,

Quin Pereira—servant to his majesty's fleet.

The next day, Quin placed the note in the care of a courier.

"Sir…" the courier stared with dismay at the simple note, folded twice and sealed crudely with a wax stamp, "it is a small fortune to send this, perhaps a month's wage of a sailor's pay."

"Go," Quin instructed, paying the better part of nearly two months' salary for it. The courier nodded dumbly and hid the letter and money in his coat. As he left the pier, Quin prayed the message would find its way swiftly south to the Wintergrave Dynasty and to the father of the pale angel held captive in the hold.

But the courier fell, later that day, to a brute on the edge of town, long before the letter could make post in Stavoren. The letter and the two months of Quin's pay were then given…to Malik.

* * *

Quin was preoccupied. Normally he was joyously happy to be on the ocean and feel the roll of the ship beneath his feet. It was, to him, as close to flying as a human would ever get. And tonight the deck dropped beautifully into each swell, the boat nearly matching the wind as it came alive with the magic that was a great body of water beneath God's eternal sky.

But, ever since the Prussian and his clan had come aboard—most specifically, the strange girl with the white hair and paralyzing eyes— something had tormented him, stabbing deep into his heart and soul.

And there was something else. Because of Niveus, he believed, he had been thinking almost constantly of his son and wife. It was the things the girl said to him, or perhaps it was more the way she said it, that had pushed the tender boy—his blessed son—to the forefront of his mind for the better part of the past week at sea.

Niveus, by saying very little at all, had compelled him to dwell about those things that simply meant the most to him. And he was surprised to discover how those things were, in fact, *people*—his beautiful wife, his son, good sailors who had come and gone, his captain and dearest friend, Xavier.

But he wasn't thinking about Niveus right now. He was coiling the foredeck ropes for the third time, unwilling to pull himself away from the beauty of this night, and remembering how scarcely a month ago he had been sitting at a table with his lovely Selena and their ten-year-old son, Tiago. What a wonderful time it had been—his bride's chocolate-brown eyes dancing with delight as they ate fish and danced before the fire pit, well into the night.

Tiago had laughed and accused his parents of planning a sibling for him if they continued farther down the path they were on that evening. It was a perfect, treasured moment and was etched sweetly into Quin's memory as though it was yesterday.

These were his thoughts as he coiled the rope about his thumb and elbow before laying it upon the stack of others on the foredeck. This was what occupied his mind as the moon peeked above a kinder ocean this night, and...

...it was the last thought he took to his watery grave as the blade slipped between his ribs and his body was heaved by a monster over the railing.

As Quin hit the water and began to sink, the wind ceased all at once, and the sails dropped strangely, their sheets hanging forlornly as though in sorrow for a lost brother.

The immense, wooden body of the great ship lurched, nearly halting against the big wave that lifted its bow, and brushed against Quin, against his hand as he drifted farther into the depths. The last thing he saw as he gazed overhead was the moon, hanging full above the tide. The last thought to capture him was without fear and directed to Niveus...

...thank you.

* * *

Niveus' eyes snapped open. Her cabin was pitch-dark, for it had no window and the candle was not lit. She lay in her bed, and all that could be heard was the gentle slap of the ocean from the other side of the soggy, wooden wall. But this was not what she heard. Something else whispered to her from the inky, black depths.

Turning her head to the side, as though she could see through the wall to that beauty which lingered beyond, she rested her hand against the dense skin of the ship. At exactly that spot, on the other side of the planks, Quin's hand brushed against the sodden wall of the craft and lingered there.

Then...he slipped beyond.

Niveus did not rise from her bed, only remained where she lay in the darkness, the swell and fall of the ship rocking her thin body gently from side to side. For nearly a quarter hour she remained like this, one hand folded across her heart as the other pressed against the wall, gazing into the blackness of nothing, seeing...Quin.

By and by, her eyes closed and her hand slipped from the wall.

Her last thought was for him.

Until we next meet, farewell...friend.

CHAPTER NINETEEN

"Is she hurt?" Ravan appealed to Nicolette.

He, Nicolette, Sayid, and Luchina sat together in the studio, the urgency of the situation causing them to speak in hushed tones.

"How can she answer that?" Sayid wondered, mystified by the strange turn of events.

Luchina rested a hand on her husband's knee. "Not all gifts manifest as fearfully as the destiny of a great weapon."

Ravan immediately thought the comment ironic, for if they only knew the extent of Nicolette's gifts, Luchina might think otherwise.

Nicolette explained, "I have the capacity to connect with the presence of others, especially with my children."

"Then you can tell if they are hurt, from this far away?" Sayid wondered.

Nicolette shook her head. "Not exactly. I sense foreboding," her brow furrowed, "rather I can tell when their mortality is at risk." Her explanation was met with blank expressions.

Ravan tried to help. "It is, she has explained to me before, not unlike having an empty hand and suddenly burdening it with a stone."

Nicolette nodded. "Very much so."

"Ah, I see. And what a gift to have!" Sayid clasped his hands together. "But what can be done of it with the feeling being so general? Perhaps the girl has tripped and injured herself, or maybe her constitution is out of sorts?"

"No. That is not it," Nicolette explained. "Something so ordinary to her well-being—something obviously survivable—would not interject itself upon me."

When she was met again with blank stares, she glanced at Ravan. "What I feel when one of my children is…in harm's way, is more of a sense of malignancy, of impending affliction."

Ravan said hopefully, "But Risen is with her. They are *all* with her. The realm has been stable for some time. Certainly if it were war to come, you would sense the same in Risen?"

Nicolette's brow furrowed again. "It is not war. It is something else, something much more...personal."

"You must go to her," Luchina blurted out.

"Yes." Nicolette said, her expression as miserable as Ravan had ever seen it.

"Salvatore will be here soon, perhaps by two days' end." Ravan slipped his arm around Nicolette and said to Sayid, "I will return to the dynasty with my wife, and we will sort all of this out."

"No," Nicolette objected softly. "I can manage anything wrong at home. There is still a pressing obligation you must tend to." She gestured with one hand toward Sayid, speaking of the promise to find Sayid's sister or the sad discovery of her fate.

Sayid shook his head. "I cannot force this obligation upon you at such a time. I have lost my sister for many years. A few months will make no difference now."

"It is so much to ask of you. We have an agreement." Ravan shook his head.

The Syrian softened. "I have an obligation from you, but more so, I have your friendship...and trust. Do as you must. Then you can repay the debt. I have no concern that you will not."

Ravan's heart lifted. "I promise...I will find what affects my daughter and be then straightaway to discover the fate of your sister. I will not rest until I know where Aya is, alive or dead. And those responsible will suffer for it."

Sayid smiled warmly. "Let it be so." He released his friend's grasp. "For now, we shall have you aboard that ship as soon as possible. Until then...we have a battle sword to finish."

* * *

The *White Witch* dropped sails as it glided into the port of Candia. But there was a grimness that overtook Salvatore's smile when he noticed the expression on Ravan's face. He stalked down the gangway and took his friend's hand before pulling Ravan, chest to chest, into a hug. Speaking into the mercenary's ear, his voice was husky and low.

"Tell me..."

"Niveus—something is wrong," was all Ravan said.

"Let someone have put our Niveus to harm, and I will help you send his soul to bloody Hell. I promise on my life," Salvatore swore.

Ravan appreciated the warm reception more than the Spaniard could know and held his friend at arm's length.

"We don't know the circumstance, only that Nicolette believes..." At a loss for words, he swallowed deeply.

Behind him Nicolette folded her hands solemnly in front of her. Releasing Ravan straightaway, Salvatore went to her, bowing deeply before taking her by both arms and kissing her first on one cheek then the other. He did not do as he usually did—try to kiss her outright—and Ravan noticed how the Spaniard's face was stricken with worry.

With a certain graveness about his normally dancing eyes, Salvatore said to Nicolette, "I will go with you and your husband. We will find out what is afoot with our dear Niveus. I promise. She will be all right."

"You cannot know for certain," Nicolette replied softly.

The gulls cawed overhead as though Salvatore's wishful thinking had been discovered. Shooting a glare at them first, he said, "Sometimes you must have more than instinct, my beauty. Sometimes you must have *faith*."

Nicolette pressed the first two fingers of one hand over the heart of her husband's dearest friend. What she said next shook Ravan to his very core.

"No one, in all the lands, understands the providence of faith better than my daughter does. But Niveus might not choose to interfere with destiny as much as *I* would want her to. We all know that about her, and it is exactly there that the worry lies."

To this, Ravan's heart fell, and the smile left Salvatore's face. He swung about to include Ravan in the conversation. "Then let us be gone from here—straight to France—and let us interfere with whatever is afoot in grand style."

Nicolette and Ravan were shortly aboard Salvatore's ship and bound for southern France. Ravan very much appreciated his friend's dearest infatuation—the sea—and Salvatore's desire to romp upon her at breakneck speed was legendary. The ship was, technically, a merchant vessel, but most often it carried very particular cargo. And, designed and fashioned by Salvatore himself, it was faster than nearly any other ship of its time.

True to his nature, Salvatore pressed the elegant craft to her limits, and it leaned, keeled over against the waves, sails full, and bow cutting as easily as would the new blade that hung at Ravan's side.

"Can you know her whereabouts?" Ravan asked Nicolette as the three of them leaned against the taffrail and watched the island of Crete disappear on the distant horizon.

"I cannot," Nicolette admitted. "I must affect the ritual to determine where she is, and I have none of her hair. It was an...oversight." She looked away.

Ravan wrapped an arm around her shoulders and pulled her nearer. "It is all right, my love. We will be home before long and sort this out. Risen will take care of her until we are there."

"Yes! Risen is capable of destroying anyone who would mean to harm Niveus or the realm. I know this boy as if he were my own!" Salvatore insisted. "Risen will hold the wolves at bay."

"Risen...is affected too," Nicolette said solemnly, staring at the black waters as they receded beneath a rising moon.

This caused Ravan's heart to falter further. "In what way do you sense this?"

"Risen is affected because *she* is. Niveus is primary, and he is lost because of it."

"That is not possible. He knows the stars, and how to map the lay of the land. My son would not allow himself to be lost!"

Nicolette turned to her husband, hiding her face in his chest. "It is his soul that is lost."

There was nothing more that could be done, and so onward they sailed.

To Ravan, Crete did not disappear fast enough...

* * *

Nearly two weeks later, Risen rode Alerion into the small town of Clairvaux. The beautiful stallion was gaunt and greatly weakened by the trek but moved forward willingly beneath his master's leg. Behind them, Velecent's mount—also a worthy steed—was even worse for wear. Both horses were spent and appeared as wretched nags on this black.

Risen, also exhausted, felt guilt at pressing the steeds so hard, for they had covered nearly five hundred miles on them. He slid from Alerion and handed a rein to Velecent, who likewise dismounted to relieve his mount of his weight.

Walking to the cathedral door, Risen lifted the knocker and pounded three times. Briefly glancing behind him, he hardly recognized Alerion, until he noticed the spark in the stallion's eye as it lifted its head, willingness in its noble heart.

Risen spun about when the door slot slammed open, surprised to have so swift an answer so late at night.

A monk peeked through the door slot before throwing the door wide and exclaiming happily, "Lord *Ravan!*"

Risen only smiled as the monk stammered, halted, and caught himself. "Blessed God above. You must be his son, but the very image of him if ever there was one!"

Nodding, Risen replied, "It is I."

The man motioned for him to come in.

"I need your help," Risen declared quickly, sweeping a hand to indicate Velecent and the two spent horses. Velecent looked nearly about to drop as well.

"We need rest for tonight, food, and two fresh horses," Risen explained.

The monk took only a moment to take it all in. "Dire wishes, indeed. And if your father is not here to help, can you tell me what is it that troubles the son of Ravan? I would know so that I might pray about it?"

"My sister. She is taken, and I am in pursuit. My father is away, overseas."

The monk nodded solemnly. "A *daughter*.... I pity the man who would be so foolish as to take a child of Ravan's, especially a daughter." The monk's eyes, even as old as they were, sparkled at the thought. "When your father gets word..." A shake of his shaven head was all the more he had to say about it.

Then, more cheerily, the monk added, "This way. The stables are behind the abbey. I will have Brother Simon tend the animals and secure fresh mounts for you. Meanwhile, you will eat well and sleep in warm beds. Any child of Lord Ravan is welcome to anything I have to give."

Risen followed as the monk led the way to the stables. "Thank you. I am eternally indebted to you."

"You owe nothing, child. Your father has paid any debt you could ever owe several times over...long ago. This church would not stand were it not for him."

Risen wondered at this chapter in his father's history, and intended to ask him about it if.... He stopped himself from thinking the unthinkable.

Alerion and the other horse were watered, fed, and happily bedded in the quiet abbey stables. In this manner, they were left to recover in whatever way a horse might. It was salve on Risen's wounded heart that at least Alerion would know some peace, even if he could not.

That night, Risen and Velecent ate and slept at the abbey, catching precious rest before leaving just at daybreak on fresh mounts.

"I'll come for you, and if I do not, my father will," Risen murmured the promise into Alerion's quivering ear as he said goodbye. "You have taken me as far as you can."

The stallion rested its great head against the thigh of his master. Even with the night's respite, the animal trembled, but when Risen stepped from the stall, the horse tried to follow.

The Cistercian monk assured Risen, "We'll take good care of him. He is safe here. As I said last eve, I know your father. He is a good man. His son...or his son's horse, are always welcome here."

He crossed himself.

Risen was thankful for his family name and gave Alerion one last pat through the rails before swinging onto a fresh horse and resuming his flight northeast, Velecent at his side. It would be nearly two more weeks before they would make the edge of the town called Thorn...in the land of Red Robes.

CHAPTER TWENTY

Xavier Siago captained the noble vessel. With hair the color of sea salt, he was leathery and tall, standing straight as the masts of his ship. Generally, he spoke only the fewest words necessary to command, but his crew knew, just from his expression, whether or not their labors were satisfactory.

His title was earned by years of loyal work in the name of King John of Portugal, and he was highly esteemed, both on and off the sea. When word reached him of Quin's disappearance, he was first mournful then infuriated.

"All hands to deck!" he demanded harshly of his first mate, and swallowed thickly, dismissing even his boatswain. "Leave me now. I will be above on the half hour."

When the first mate and boy left, Xavier shoved his maps harshly aside with both hands. They cascaded about his quarters, falling into the darkened recesses along with the fragments of his broken heart. He planted his elbows on the heavy desk, rubbing the grime from his weather-worn face with the heels of his hands, and poured a draft of wine, and then another. Sailors did not disappear. They went…overboard.

Quin was not only a good sailor—one of the best he had ever captained—he was a good man and dear friend. They had stood together on the swaying decks of the *Reis Espada* for nearly fifteen years and had shared much together—many triumphs, some tragedies, noble tales, and…sworn secrets. To lose Quin was to lose a brother.

Xavier cleared the thickness from his throat and swept a rare tear aside. Taking a deep breath, he stood and straightened his uniform. Then, he marched the forty-one steps that would take him above deck to face his crew.

"What happened?" he demanded as he strode up and down the line of sailors. "Surely someone has seen something?"

He was answered with a gauntlet of puzzled, unhappy looks.

One man spoke up, "He was off-duty, sir. I saw him at supper. He spoke of the *girl*—said he intended to catch the rising moon before retiring."

"And that was the last anyone heard? Anyone?"

A few confused murmurs ran through the sad-faced crowd, but there was nothing else to come of it. All suspected it was just as the captain had been told; Quin was long fallen overboard.

Xavier charged down the ranks. "Quin would not just fall from the ship! There must be something more to it!" Then the captain charged the other way, stopping to stab his finger into the chest of the unhappy man who had just spoken up.

"The girl you speak of, who is she?" the good captain demanded.

"A passenger, sir. Quin tended her needs," the broad-faced, shorter man replied hastily. "He was taken with her, I believe."

Quin? A decent and married man? Taken with another girl? Not possible! He had stood at his side at their wedding, had shed tears of joy with the birth of his son! The captain's ire swelled at the preposterousness of what the man implied. "He would not! He was a good husband and father."

"No, sir, not at all. I mean…" The sailor licked his lips and looked about himself as though intending to gain support from the rest. There were nods from a few. "More like, uh…a daughter? Yes, that's it. He seemed concerned for her well-being. 'Twas all I meant."

"Who *is* she?" Xavier repeated, frowning as details of the mysterious girl began to emerge.

"Niveus," a voice could be heard saying. Another said, "I too heard Quin call her Niveus. And he sent word to her father just yesterday, said he needed wages in advance to pay for the courier."

"What foolhardiness do you speak of?" Xavier picked the man out of the lineup.

"I-I don't know. It was just, well, he requested a courier at our last port, to send something to the Wintergrave Dynasty in Bourbon. Said it was of the greatest importance."

Xavier thought briefly how unusual it was that Quin had not come to him about the girl, especially if there was something of such import that it commanded a letter be sent so urgently.

"Where is she?" Xavier glanced about as though he might see her.

"Don't know, sir. She never comes out from her chamber."

The man dropped his gaze to his feet.

"We jested she is a water phantom, come to steal Quin's heart—that the sea finally had her way with him, as all sailors hope."

He barked a short, nervous laugh, provoking a smattering of dim smiles on the faces of a few of the men, all of them fading just as swiftly.

There was no disrespect amongst these men. All were as sorrowfully stunned as the captain at Quin's disappearance.

More murmurs from the crowd, and finally the ship's chief-officer revealed the ship's roster. The crew stood dutifully and patiently as he and the captain scrutinized the passenger list.

"I don't see her name." Xavier scanned the list further. "There are four aboard who are traveling with unlisted females: Leirinha, Doigner, Malmberg, and Balfeur…who is also with his nephew, Napoleon."

"That's him!" the first sailor exclaimed. "It was the *nephew!*" The man stepped forward and snapped his fingers before pressing them into his forehead. "The boy's smitten with the girl, Quin said. But he called him something else…Verner, Vik-Viktar…u-mmm."

It was enough for the captain, and before long he had Malik and Viktar pulled to his quarters, guards posted on either side of them.

"What seems to be the problem?" Malik spluttered, ruddy-faced, the epitome of unrighteous inconvenience.

"I've lost a man," Xavier said straight-up, studying the expressions of the two men closely.

Malik feigned insincere surprise, but Viktar gasped and nearly staggered. Xavier chose to press the younger man.

"Son, did you know Quin?"

Viktar nodded sadly. "I did, sir. A righteous and kind man. He extended every generosity to me and…"

"Yes?" the captain urged.

Viktar seemed about to say something else, but only offered, "My party, sir. The four of us."

"Four of you?"

"Yes sir. My uncle, his servant, me, and…Niveus."

Xavier caught glimpses of Malik as Viktar spoke, much more interested in the behavior of the defiantly unsympathetic man who fidgeted restlessly. He maintained his study of him as he asked Viktar, "And you are listed as Napoleon, but you call yourself…"

"Viktar, sir," he answered with honesty.

"Napoleon is his surname, Captain—my sister's wedded name," Malik lied before Viktar could say anything more.

"And you, Lord…*Balfeur*…" Xavier ran his finger down the ship's roster, "from where do you hail?"

"Hungary. We are returning after holiday." He bowed insignificantly.

"*Where?*"

Malik seemed somewhat uncomfortable but invented another lie swift as a shot bird falls from flight. "Transylvania, sir. But might I ask what this has to do with your man?"

Xavier ignored the question. "I would like to speak to Niveus."

Malik instantly stood a bit taller and became more rigid. "I'm sorry, but it's simply out of the question."

"*Why?*"

"She is not well. I cannot allow her to entertain guests."

"Quin seemed *quite* entertained by her," the captain shot back easily.

Malik nodded slowly, like a viper following a heat source. "Yes...yes, he was, poor fellow—became immediately smitten with her as I feared he would. I tried to forbid his attentions and post my man nearby." He gestured plaintively. "He harmed my guard, cut him in his desperation. I meant to bring it to your attention but chose not to...muddy the waters, shall we say?"

"Bring her to me," Xavier said flatly to his chief mate.

Taking a step forward, Malik spewed through gritted teeth. "I said I would not allow it."

Swords rang simultaneously as the three cabin guardsmen drew them, caging Malik and Viktar between. Xavier, believing Quin truly was gone to the watery deeps and that the Prussian had some grave responsibility in it all, said in a harrowing voice, "I will have my way, and we will be to the bottom of this before we make port."

Then, to his guard he ordered, "Take them. Lock them up, all except the girl, and—"

"Sir," Viktar blurted, "Quin was the only one with the key to Niveus' quarters. He thought it would be safest for her, and now it is lost."

"I told you your man was smitten with her!" Malik exclaimed.

As convicting as Xavier was forced to admit it all sounded, he was not ready to condemn the memory of his dear friend. He pulled his personal keys from his coat pocket. "I have the only master. Keep them in the brig. I will visit the girl, and then we shall see what will come of it all."

Malik began to object once more but was silenced by the guard's blade pressing between his shoulder blades. "I'll keep them," the sailor assured Xavier, "nice and tidy until you wish to question them."

* * *

Xavier walked through the darkened halls of the great passenger ship, his boatswain tagging along behind, and was mildly annoyed to find Gorlik standing post at the girl's door. All appeared to be as the Prussian claimed it was.

"Stand aside," Xavier ordered.

Gorlik looked dumbly beyond to see if Malik followed them.

"I am ship's captain, and I command you to stand aside, or you will spend the rest of the trip in custody," Xavier repeated.

He took a step back when the lumbering beast's hand went for his short sword, but just as fast the man seemed to resign himself. Shifting his huge frame aside, he allowed the captain access to Niveus' door.

"She never answers," Gorlik mumbled when Xavier tapped on the door. "I wish she would answer the door."

The captain glared briefly up at the monstrous oaf, clearing his throat before announcing himself. "Lady Niveus, it is I, the ship's captain. I must speak with you."

There was no reply, and short on patience, the captain inserted the key and shoved the door open.

There, standing in the middle of the room, facing away, was Niveus, barefoot and in the nightgown Quin had procured for her. It was a strange enough sight to cause the captain to pause.

"Niveus, I-uh…hello? I am the captain," he repeated. "Are you hurt?"

Niveus spun slowly about upon hearing her name. "No, I am not."

This set Xavier back a full step, to see for the first time the girl with whom Quin was said to be so possessed. As frequently happened when people first saw her face, he caught himself looking everywhere but at her. She, however, seemed very comfortable to gaze only at him.

Finally, Xavier gestured to one of the two small chairs at the cabin's solitary table. "Would you care to sit? Do you have a cloak?"

Niveus shook her head.

Whether she meant she did not care to sit or had no cloak was unclear to Xavier. "Please…this may take some time. Will you sit while we speak? I would be more comfortable."

Niveus complied, perching on the edge of her bed, bare feet white as death and dangling just above the floor. She blinked, Xavier thought, too slowly, as though it was all that must be comprehended in this one moment.

He was surprised at how thoroughly unnerved he was by the peculiar girl, and remembered another time, at sea, when he had come across a free, floating ship.

The vessel, a decent size, had no sails set and no rigging secured. Everything was in place, like a corpse in a coffin, but it was far adrift at sea. Even stranger was how the vessel was devoid of crew. Not a single man aboard, nor any indication that there ever had been—no personal items, no ledgers, logs, or manifests. Most critically, however, was that the ship was not named. It was, in a word, *terrifying*, as though a greater power ran it.

The strange circumstances of the phantom ship were never determined, and Xavier ordered it left adrift, just as it was found. He heard nothing more of the strange vessel—no mention of it came from any other sea captain—but the feeling he was left with was very much the same feeling he had as he stood before Niveus.

Xavier looked about the room and noticed a blanket lying crumpled on the floor at the end of the bed. He lifted it and went to lay it in the girl's hands. "There is a chill as we sail farther into the North Sea," he said.

When she failed to respond to this, he draped the blanket carefully across her shoulders and began to fold it across her chest but, instead, thought better of it, letting the corners fall loose. He could not be certain what injustices the girl may have suffered and was careful not to touch her.

She glanced from side to side, clearly uncertain why he had done such a thing.

Xavier pulled up one of the chairs, excused his boatswain, and locked the door. "For your safety," he made clear then sat down opposite her. "Niveus, I must ask you some questions."

Her gaze bore into him in such a way that the captain believed she could see every wrong or sullied thing he had ever done in his life, modest as they might be. He endeavored to be a good man, but all men carry dishonorable chapters, no matter how noble the book. Else they were not human. Immaculate blamelessness was for the gods alone, and even of this the captain was not convinced.

To break the moment, he cleared his throat. "Do you know Quin?"

"No."

"I-uh…" He halted, stuttering, and glanced behind him, not at all certain what he was looking for—perhaps Quin himself to step through the wall and exclaim otherwise. "Are you sure? Because he said—"

"He's dead. I no longer know him. I *knew* him." Niveus pressed a finger against the wooden bed frame, allowing her fingernail to find the worn groove of the plank that it had traced most of the night.

"*Dead?* Child, how do you know this?" Xavier could scarcely remain seated. He leaned toward her, their faces very close as she did not move away.

"In the night," she murmured. "I felt it. He was hurt…and fell. There was nothing I could do. The water has him now."

"How can you…you say you *felt* it?"

Niveus nodded. "Yes, as he died."

Xavier paused, his elbows on his knees, chin in one hand. Finally he asked, "Where were you, Niveus, when Quin fell into the water?"

Niveus turned her head and glanced behind her at the bed but said nothing.

Trying a different tactic, the captain asked, "Did you come willingly onto this ship?"

"*Yes.*"

This also surprised the captain a great deal. He had been so confident it would be otherwise. "Are you certain, Niveus? You can tell me the truth. No one will hurt you now, I promise. Quin thought you were—"

"Yes, I came willingly onto the ship. And someone *will* hurt me; you cannot control that."

Xavier was becoming swiftly exasperated with the girl's bizarre incongruities. "I don't understand. I can see you've been hurt before, and there's been talk about how…" He did not know how to delicately approach what liberties he suspected Malik may have taken with her. "Do you wish to have your uncle visit you, or shall I keep him at bay?" he asked gently.

To this, Niveus gave him the queerest look. "My uncle is dead…and buried by my father's hand long before I was born. If he chooses to visit me, there is little you could do about it." Then, Niveus sat with a look of supreme patience on her face as though it should finally explain everything.

There was no way Xavier could know she spoke of *D'ata*, her one and only *true* uncle—Ravan's brother—the twin who had sacrificed everything to save him.

The captain, at a loss how to proceed, sighed heavily, deciding there was nothing to be discovered from the obviously insane girl whom Quin had been compelled to try to protect. Pushing himself to his feet, he paused at the door.

"I'm sorry, Niveus—sorry that I bothered you. Quin will no longer be here to help with your needs." He slipped his hand into his pocket, disappointment weighing thickly in his voice as he murmured aloud, "'Twas an accident after all, I suppose." Before exiting the cabin, he said lastly to Niveus, "I will assign someone new to your cares, at least until we make port. It is all that I can do."

As he left, he said with a heavy heart, "I only wish I knew why Quin fell."

Then, out the door the captain went, locking it, his footsteps thudding softly as he retreated down the hall.

Behind, still perched on the edge of the bed, Niveus, replied, "Malik killed him…of course." Then she tipped her head gently to the side and wondered to herself why people were so compelled to "*wish*" for things.

* * *

Viktar lay in his bed, fingers laced across his bare chest. His hand slipped idly to his left shoulder and passed over the ragged remnant of the wound. The Damascus sword had nearly taken his life, and his fingertips lingered, tracing the angry, immature scar. Here was where she had pressed her hand against him—he could *feel* it.

He wanted more than anything to see Niveus. This thought consumed him, gnawing at him like a kindred wolf, and the wave of beautiful preoccupation gave him an unfamiliar pull to his belly, one he was not entirely unhappy about. Just as swiftly, shame swept over him that he could be aroused just thinking about her, especially given Quin's recent disappearance.

Quin had been kind to her, had tried to shelter her, and Viktar vowed to avenge his murder, for to him there was no mystery of what had happened to Quin. Malik had surely done his worst, likely had the beast, Gorlik, do it, and he briefly considered telling the captain what he suspected. But he had no proof, and Malik would kill him for the betrayal. Then, there would be no guessing what fate would hold for Niveus.

So for now, silence shouted a terrible nothing from every pore of his body.

Captain Xavier had firmly forbidden anyone from spending time with Niveus for the remainder of the journey unless the ship's chief security officer was in attendance. And it was this man, a strapping, battle-scarred whale of a sailor—every bit as big as Gorlik—who now stood posted at Niveus' door.

Viktar's mind raced as the evening stretched on. There were many things to make right, and regret plagued him where it should not. He wished he had succumbed to the strangulation before Niveus ever made it to the cottage, and that step—to earnestly wish his own demise—was a narrow leap to his next…his willingness to die for her.

These dark thoughts were not all that were consuming Viktar tonight. He had scarcely spoken to Niveus since Quin's disappearance, and certainly their only time together had been brief, heavenly snatches under miserable conditions.

He longed for her, just to sit with her, to observe the mystifying way she connected with her own existence and mortality with such composure. It made him believe she did not move through this world as others did. On the contrary, the world stepped carefully around *her*.

His finger traced the edge of the scar again. It was both hideous and dear to him. Viktar was not a dreamer—not a woeful romantic tripping after love. The young Prussian was generally quite sensible, but through the thick walls of his tiny cabin, he believed he could feel her presence draw upon him, and he cherished it. Yes, everything about Niveus had captured Viktar so completely that even in his dreams there she was. And lately he heard not one but two heartbeats when he drifted off to sleep.

There was no denying it. Viktar was in love of an incurable sort.

Rolling onto his side, he forced himself to close his eyes. It was critically important that he re-gather his strength, but he only tossed restlessly about. When sleep refused to embrace him, he sat up, lit the lamp by his tiny bunk, and leaned over, dropping his weary head into his hands.

"Think," he whispered. "We land in scarcely two weeks—such little time." Saying nothing more for a while, he finally murmured, "First…"

Pushing himself to his feet, he paced the three steps that took him across his tiny cabin and back. His mind was sharper than it had been in some time, and his legs were beginning to feel familiar to him. No longer did the slow pitch of the boat cause his head to reel as it first had.

"Must keep her alive," he said as though someone else were there with him, listening to his careful plans. "Then…" he whirled again, "get her safely home." He crossed his arms as he paced, tapping his chin with his forefinger. "But…" his jaw hardened, and he softly clenched his teeth, "Malik, Gorlik, money…and my own infirmity."

He halted his pacing long enough to stare at both hands. They still trembled, but barely. Clasping them together, he willed the feebleness from them. He had been left much less the stalwart young man than he had once been, and he was still much thinner than was normal, but he was young, and his body had been given a blessed second chance.

Viktar was swiftly mending, more quickly than he would ever allow Malik to know, and in his heart stirred an unfamiliar fire. It inspired in him a willingness to fight and to sacrifice. Truly…he yearned for the opportunity.

In the days to follow, Viktar avoided Malik at all costs. And there was something new about his being, something that showed a growing determination—a greater certainty to his step. Indeed, the young Prussian was no longer the man his mother would remember.

Before she left, Klarin had given Malik considerable resources to cover her son's needs during their travels, but little of it was being spent on him. Refusing to allow this to dissuade his optimism, Viktar decided firmly his fortune, in coin and character, was to be made, not gifted.

From that day forth, he helped wherever he could on the ship. Some crewmen snorted and turned him away, for they unreasonably connected Quin's disappearance with him. But in short order, he made a few friends. Specifically, and fortunately, the cook took great pity on the floundering young man and set him to assisting in prepping some of the meals. He even grumbled how he would miss the young Prussian when his voyage was done.

"I shall find you again, some day," Viktar promised, "and repay your kindness." The cook gestured with a dull knife to the full bucket of turnips at Viktar's feet and grinned. "You are already about to."

Sitting, knees either side of the tub, Viktar scrubbed the turnips with seawater. When the water became too muddy to continue, he climbed the steep stairs to dump the soiled bucket of water.

Wet and slick, the deck bucked beneath him as he staggered to the railing. When he dropped the empty pail tethered by a cord the twenty or so feet into the ocean, intending to refill it, he did not expect the force with which the water and speed of the ship caught the bucket and was nearly pulled overboard.

Scrambling, with one leg and arm already over, he grasped his elbow around the railing to stay aboard. All the while, he refused to release the bucket. Finally upright on the deck, with legs spread awkwardly wide, he drew the now half-full pail upward.

Laughing, several crewmen pointed at the flailing foreigner, lurching about on the slippery deck with his sloshing pail of seawater. But when he held on, clutching the pail to his chest as though it was a treasure not to be released, one of the seamen slapped him heartily on the back.

"Might be some sea legs beneath you after all." The man laughed again but eased the bucket from Viktar's hands. "Pissing overboard—it's how more men are lost to sea than any other."

When the young Prussian looked bewildered, the sailor explained, "Many a drowned man has been found floating with his trousers undone."

"Thank you. I won't piss overboard," Viktar said with a warm smile.

The sailor nodded, tossed the bucket back overboard, and shanked the rope just as it reached the waves, filling it expertly before hauling up the full pail of salt water.

"*That's* the second way."

"Second way?" Viktar said.

"Second way men are lost overboard."

"Ah," Viktar said agreeably. "Yes, I can see that now."

At the galley stairs, the sailor handed over the bucket and tapped his forehead with two fingers in a friendly salute as he watched Viktar disappear beneath deck.

There was no denying how intensely likable and accepted amidst the crew Viktar was becoming, even with his haunting accent and the peculiar disappearance of Quin still on their minds. That, in itself, was no small feat.

In return for the young man's hard work, the cook fed him very well, giving him choice filets of fish, salted pork, biscuits and stew. He also shared his ration of wine, enjoying the companionship of his blossoming sous chef a great deal.

"I was bit by that land-bug once…years ago. But the sea kept calling, and my Maudie, she couldn't have me gone so much. Fell in love with a butcher, and that, as they say, was that. I've seen it many times." He shook a thick finger at Viktar. "Absence makes the heart grow absent, my boy. Mark my words."

The honest man with arms like barrels smiled whimsically and passed his wine cup to Viktar. "Suppose it's for the best. She'll always be well-fed, which is a gift even God cannot always give us."

Viktar sat with legs dangling on an ale cask and took another strong gulp of the wine, appreciating the fire that settled in his belly.

"I find you exceptionally worthy of true love. As a matter of fact, *I* would love you in an instant." Viktar said it with such benign seriousness and somewhat because of the generous effect of the wine.

But his warm expression, on some depth, grieved beautifully the loss of the cook's true love so much that the cook stopped mid-gulp. Then, both burst into laughter and drank another round.

These past days, the young Prussian could feel his body strengthening, and the sway of the ship bothered him hardly at all anymore. His wounded lung was correcting itself in milestones, and at night he exercised alone in his room, breathing deeply as he balanced first on one leg then the other.

All the while, he skirted his uncle, and this was no easy task, for at first, Malik lurked outside of Niveus' door following Quin's death. But Xavier had ordered the guard to never allow Malik private time alone with her, and before long, he simply ceased to try.

One evening early on, the cook wrapped some of the best scraps of food in a linen cloth and handed them to Viktar. "Go, take these to her. Food feeds the soul with a love that cannot be denied."

"Thank you! Oh, thank you. I've put most of my shares onto her plate all along, the one the captain's boatswain serves her."

The man drew a greasy hand through his beard, a habit that had long ago resulted in a salted, perfectly preserved corkscrew of hair. "Best it comes from you. Now go. I can manage the supper line."

Viktar grasped the linen-wrapped treasure and leapt to his feet. "I'll return for cleanup!"

"Let's hope you don't." The bigger man chuckled heartily.

Shortly, Viktar spoke to Niveus' guard. "I've come with food for her.

"No one is to enter but the boatswain," the guard countered, crossing his arms casually across the expanse of his chest.

"And who clears what she doesn't eat away?" Viktar argued softly.

"I do. Captain's orders."

"And who empties her chamber buckets?"

A pinch of doubt flashed across the guard's flat, square face.

Following swiftly up, Viktar asked, "And will you see to her more intimate needs, if she requires *assistance*?" He waved his hand about, inviting the guard to imagine the forbidding needs of a teenage girl.

Viktar held up the bucket of warm water and towel in his other hand. "I would be more than happy to attend these chores, for I love this woman. I shall be only a moment, and you can observe everything, if you wish."

The guard—a good man, imposing though he was—grunted and gnawed on his enormous lower lip, looking about as though for an answer.

"Very well, but...just this one time." He allowed Viktar entry into Niveus' room that night and for some nights to follow. And no one ever knew...but them.

* * *

Niveus' head snapped about even before the key clinked softly in the lock. She swung her legs over the side of the bed.

"Niveus," Viktar spoke softly as he eased into the room, "I've come with food." He held the folded linen napkin up for her to see before setting it on the table. "And I've brought a clean bucket for..." He glanced away, embarrassed by what he implied.

Hopping lightly to her feet, Niveus said, "We make land in twelve days."

This seemed to confuse Viktar. "Soon...I know, but I think fourteen at least, with the stops. Not to worry. I will care for you.

"My brother is coming for me."

Viktar stepped closer, his voice dropping to a whisper. "How do you know this? I mean, not that it is bad. It's *good*, but…"

He set the pail and towel on the floor and reached for her hand.

* * *

Niveus cared deeply for her family, and Moira too, in the sense of familial love. But with Viktar, there had occurred something entirely new. Never before had she embraced the presence of another as she did him, and now she believed she understood what Risen had suffered when he lost Sylvie. Now she understood what had compelled her to give solace to her brother's loss as long as she had.

She did not pretend to believe she was in love with Viktar, not *yet*, for love was not an easy concept for Niveus, but if Viktar ceased to visit her, she knew her heart would be unhappy for it.

"Can you sit with me for a bit?" she asked, almost happily.

Viktar glanced nervously behind and asked the guard. "A moment? Just while she eats? You can leave the door ajar."

The man shifted his sodden feet and peered down the hall as though someone else approached. Finally, he begrudged, "Five minutes."

"Thank you."

Niveus leaned closer. "Risen is coming, and so is, I believe, my father."

Viktar was at first surprised, then fearful, his brow furrowing.

"What is it? Why do you worry?" She picked at the salted fish and boiled eggs.

"No," he admitted, "that is good, but my mother…and the subjects."

"Yes?"

"If there is war, there will be suffering."

She lay the half-eaten egg aside and reached for him. Touching Viktar, she felt immediately the connection that her heart so recently welcomed. Again, she thought of Risen and Sylvie and was instantly happy for the love her brother had known. Odds were Viktar felt it too, for he flinched when her hand rested on his knee.

"They are important to you," she murmured.

"They are."

"And they are good people, not availing themselves of gain at the expense of others."

"Yes, most of them," he said with honesty.

"There is, however, one who rivals your uncle in malice. He waits for Malik's return."

"Bora Vachir. I know him. He profits in slave trade and has been a colleague of my uncle. They have known each other for a long time."

She sighed. "The tide is shifting. I think it will not be as simple as you hope it might," she cautioned as she flicked a speck of egg white back onto the napkin.

"What do you mean? Can you see what will happen?"

"No," she shook her head softly, almost regretfully. "But I can tell you the thread which weaves its way through the destiny of Malik's domain is a tangled one." She swept her hand gently aside and back. "And it cannot be unraveled."

"I do not understand," Viktar replied. "Unraveled…"

"It must be broken. There is no other way." She drew her attention directly to him, staring hard into his eyes.

The guard cleared his throat from behind them. When Viktar began to say something more, the man stepped into the room and said, not unkindly, "It is time. You must leave, before…" He allowed Viktar to imagine what all their consequences would be if they were discovered.

Viktar gripped tightly onto Niveus' hand as though he might refuse to leave.

Reaching forward, she swept her fingertips across his shoulder and onto his chest, directly over where his wound had been. This simple caress caused Viktar to jump as though shocked by something.

Niveus' lips curled up at the edges, nearly smiling. "Do not worry so much for the destiny of man. All is as it should be. All will *be* as it should be. Tomorrow is a myth—it will never show itself to you. Today is all that there is, and *today*…I am happy that you are here with me."

* * *

Viktar was both thrilled and terrified. He had felt something when she touched him, especially when she touched his shoulder, her hand lingering over his heart. The connection was as strong as ever it had been, but there was even something more to it this time.

He was afraid to put what he believed they shared into words for fear it would somehow lessen it. Instead, with a pure heart, he invited it to be what it would, just as she had said. Niveus wanted to be with him; she *wanted* to be connected to him. He was sure of it.

Later, that night, he considered what a dangerous path it was to allow Niveus to care for him. It complicated many things. But for the first time, he allowed himself to consider a life with her. This was insanity! Malik was determined to possess her, and there was no denying how powerful his uncle was.

She said her brother was coming for her, and her father. But how could they know where she was? He would tell them, *that's* how! When they were home, he would send word and thwart Malik's plans.

The waves slapped hard against the bulkheads of the ship, the sea angrier than it had been. They were well on their way north, and Viktar was consumed with two things as he lay alone in his bed: the fearful urgency at what his uncle was capable of, and another urgency which swept over him as he thought again of the woman he loved, remembering that horrible, wonderful night in La Rochelle when he had held her naked body in his arms.

In the blissful early moments of sleep, he wondered what it would be like to lay with her in *that* way. He had never taken such liberty with a woman before, not that the opportunity hadn't availed itself to him more than a few times. He had simply been of the mind that such a thing must be with someone he truly loved. And now, convinced he was, the happy wolf gnawed at him to be released.

It was late, and he allowed his subconscious to slip even more into this very good, very warm place as he imagined Niveus' arms around his neck, her lips soft against his.... These thoughts brought to his belly an arousal that would not be refused.

He turned onto his side, pulling the blanket up over his bare shoulder, a tender smile tugging at his lips. So happy was he that the sudden, soft rapping on his door was such an affront that he nearly fell off the bed. Naked, he lurched to his feet, wrapping his blanket around himself twice to hide his lust. What emergency could be calling upon him at such a late hour?

"Who is there?" he sighed, his head leaning heavily against the wooden jamb.

When no one answered, he eased open the door and drew in a sharp breath when he saw Niveus standing there, barefoot, an expression of soft expectation on her face.

"How? What?" he began, but she pushed her hand softly against his bare chest, inviting him to return to his bed...

...with her.

CHAPTER TWENTY-ONE

†

Bora Vachir was restless. He lounged slothfully and walked the quiet halls of Malik's castle in his friend's absence. The two were well suited for the company of one another, and their acquaintance was as corrupt as it was old, like long-decayed blood on a rusted blade. But Malik had been gone longer than Vachir cared for, and it was not in his nature to remain fixed for so long in one place, even if it *was* Malik's realm.

To pass the time, and whenever it suited him, he used, and abused, whomever he wished. But cruel as he might be to Malik's subjects, his greater desire had always been to kill. Truly, it was the primary reason he had remained so connected to the Prussian leader, because they had so much in common in this one arena.

The two chose campaigns carefully, picking those that would bring them to the front of opportunity—those that allowed them to feed their lust in a way that eventually became nearly insatiable. And for Bora, that lust had not been fed for some time.

Vachir harrumphed as he shoved the fifteen-year-old slave away. The girl collapsed in a battered heap on the marbled stones at Bora's feet. Even rape was a poor substitute for what he truly craved, and he remained dissatisfied.

Society is becoming too sophisticated, the Turk thought to himself as he arranged his robes. He rubbed his thick beard with his hand, coiling it about his fingers as he watched the slave tearfully gather her things and trip from the room.

His thoughts were not on the girl at all. He was thinking…of war.

Specifically, Bora wanted battle, and he knew he would not have to look far to find it. There was no denying he was a warrior of keen ability. He had eventually become well-known for his excessive cruelty, his greatest namesake being *Impaler Lord*, for he had a great propensity to stake his victims in barbarous displays of harpooned inhumanity, creating cadaver forests where before there had been none.

But his wicked reputation had not gone unnoticed, and he was called upon by the Emperor to align himself more with the civility of God. It was acceptable, he was told, to behead and stack his enemies' heads—another habit of his—but live impalement was considered cruel beyond reasonable suffering, or at least that was the current stand of the Church.

Smiling to himself, Bora calculated what sacrifices would be required for him to campaign once more in the fashion he most craved. Perhaps with Malik's return he could persuade his friend to go with him again to Hungary where they could pillage as they had in their younger days. Hungary was vulnerable right now, and it would make no difference to the King as long as he believed Malik and Bora fought in the name of the Church. Leave the boy, Viktar, in charge.

His bloodlust rose only because of the awful place he allowed his thoughts to go, and he called for a second slave.

Shortly, the girl was shoved through the grand double doors of the hall. She cowered at spear point, head bowed as she approached Bora, sitting on his throne with his groin exposed, stroking himself back to life. The girl let go a single sob as she collapsed on her knees in front of him.

Bora snarled. If he must wait for Malik's return, there would be no slave unsullied before night's fall.

These were Vachir's wicked thoughts as he grasped the girl's head in both hands, heaving her face over his groin. His surprise was complete, however, when in the next instant Viktar's mother interrupted him, slamming into the council room before stalking right up in front of him.

"Where is my son? What news do you have?" Klarin demanded.

Bora ground his teeth, hurled the girl from him, and yanked his robes over his erection, but Klarin did not cower. The slave girl clambered away and ran for the doors.

Klarin ordered, "Answer me, Bora, or I will have you removed from the realm. You know full well that without Malik's finance, you are simply another barbarian, cast to whatever misery will have you."

Vachir despised this woman from every pore of his being. He hated that she ruled a realm nearly as large as Malik's and resented the woman's fearlessness. Females' mouths were useful for one thing, and it was *not* to speak.

Even more, however, Bora despised the ring of truth to her words.

What was truth, anyway, but a lie manifest? Take any lie, any day, wrap it around a blade, and shove it into the heart of another. Then tell him it was now not the truth!

"The brat is in France," Bora spat as he reached for fruit from a nearby tray. He bit into it, the juice running down his beard as his cold stare ran the length of her.

"How do you know this?" she demanded.

Looking about himself with great leisure, he finally spied the note lying crumpled and tossed aside. Pointing at it with the half-eaten fruit, he said, "*There*. Read for yourself."

Truthfully, Bora could not read, something he hid, fearing it might be interpreted as weakness. A scribe had read the note to him, sent when Malik left Crete with the just-finished Damascus sword. It had explained how they were on their way to an audience at the Wintergrave Dynasty, in France, and would be journeying home afterwards. It gave no more details than that.

Klarin passed her fingers over the hand-scrawled words. It was her brother's hand, but there was no mention of Viktar, and the date scribbled in the corner indicated it had been written nearly a month ago.

"How long have you had this?"

He shrugged, taking another bite of the fruit.

Folding the letter carefully, Klarin stabbed at Vachir with it. "My son will rule this realm before long, Vachir. And when he does, you will be cast from it."

Bora's thick lip curled in menacing contempt.

"Mark my words," she threatened. "Be gone now, and your fate will likely draw better. I can see to my brother's realm until their return."

"I will not!" Vachir rose from the throne, casting what remained of the fruit at her feet. It splattered, soiling the hem of her gown.

"Very well. Then your fate will be your own," she spat, disavowing his ill humor. Before he could say anything else, Klarin spun about and stalked from the room, the letter clenched and crumpled in her hand.

No one could anticipate the arrival of those to come in the next few days....

CHAPTER TWENTY-TWO

The castle halls rang empty with Ravan's bootsteps, the echoes falling about him like the ghosts of fallen soldiers he had known. As he tread, several attendants stepped from his path. He could not know they turned their faces away, not because they feared the wrath of their lord but because they grieved for his loss. None could bear the haunting look in his eyes now that Niveus was gone.

Ravan did not see the sad faces as they ducked away. He saw only a child, hair white as snow as she wandered the halls in a world all her own, a frail hand outstretched as her fingers passed softly along these same stone walls. He halted, staggered as Niveus' memory hollowly greeted him. He imagined her pause and peek with one eye over her shoulder at him. Others might not see it, but he could see happiness as much as could be expressed by this child he loved like no other.

I see you there.

He believed he could hear her voice hang in the stagnant air.

I know you love me, she said without words. *Don't worry for me*, she had asked of him in her own way, every day of her life, and yet he could never grant her this singular wish.

It is not possible. You are my child—my daughter. You are Niveus, and I am your father. I shall worry for you from this world to the next...and then beyond.

Ravan faltered.

And I shall see you there.

Her message hung in the emptiness like war-torn flags, so much so that he believed her words could almost be grasped. Holding his hands in front of his face, he stared at them. So much they had seen. So much destiny they had taken upon themselves, but today...they trembled.

No, there was nothing that could equal the despair in Ravan's heart tonight.

Niveus' voice faded, floating to the dark recesses of the castle walls where secrets go, and his hands folded slowly into fists, his body stiffening as he steeled himself and marched on. Finally, he stepped into the great hall of a castle where his children were no more.

Seven years ago, Risen had been taken. The dark mercenary had never believed he could feel such helpless rage as when he chased his son all the way to the wicked edge of the Ottoman Empire. First, he tossed prayers to God, begging him to allow his son to survive long enough for him to reach him. When it seemed for naught, he prayed to the Lord of Darkness, bartering that he would give his eternal soul if Risen's life could only be spared. In the end, neither had answered. It was a crippled child—a girl named Sylvie—who saved his son's life.

Now, Ravan was done with gods and demons. He would deal with them on his final day, when he faced them, but today they served him poorly. Believing hope existed only in the heart of the living, he did what he had done very naturally as a boy. Casting his faith unto himself, he pulled from it a strength only a rare few possessed.

No, there would be no more bartering, and the ones who had taken Niveus had no comprehension of the holy hell that would fall upon them when he found them.

"Tell me everything, as much as you know, and spare not the smallest detail," he asked of his aides and listened intently as their tales unfolded.

He heard the descriptions of the three strange travelers, believed to have taken Niveus, and of the bizarre findings in the Inn. Moulin recounted how Risen had already returned from the coast with word that his sister set sail. He and Velecent, now journeying to *Prussia*, had stopped for scarcely an hour at Wintergrave on their way north.

"Tell father she is there…" Risen told Moulin, "and I will not rest until I've found her."

Ravan could hear his son's voice, clear as though he stood in front of him. And now he was off to Prussia to save her. His mind spun, recounting snippets of comments—the brief moments he had shared with the one called *Malik* while he was in Crete.

'Stay…' the Prussian had demanded of Nicolette.

'You have no idea who I *am*,' he had challenged Ravan openly.

'A daughter…and is she fair as her mother?' he had.

'How *old* did you say she was?' he had wanted to know.

How could I have not seen it? Ravan berated himself. *How could I have allowed this to happen?* And, of course, Risen and Velecent had gone after her.

There was no blame, he told himself, except for his own. He should not have provoked the monster, not enjoyed taunting him as much as he had. It was a fool's folly to allow his guard to have fallen, but the mercenary moved swiftly past self-condemnation to something much more productive, something he understood so much better. His son was chasing an unseen demon, but Ravan *had* seen it—had seen the Prussian, and so had Nicolette.

Ravan knew about fiends such as Malik. He had gone face to face with them even as a young boy, and they had fallen...*all* of them. This quieted his heart. *This* was familiar. He would never again underestimate the capacity of the human heart for evil, but it was a gift of his to be able to *destroy* monsters. And destroying this one, he believed, would be the most gratifying of all.

It was scarcely past midnight when Ravan left Salvatore to a short night's rest and joined Nicolette in their chambers. For years this had been his favorite room of the castle, and for several reasons. It was high in the tower and faced east so he could see not only across the grounds of the castle but across the village—his village, *his* people. He had watched the sun rise eternal from the balcony of this room, and it was here he first held his infant son and conceived and held their newborn daughter.

Tonight, there were no such joyous circumstances to strike a mood of happiness for him, and he was nearly fearful for the grim pall that had come, uninvited, to his sanctuary. The waning moon cast a dim light across the balcony and floor of the darkened room.

No torches were lit, and he made no motion to light them, for Nicolette did not need them. Neither did she speak as Ravan stepped to the edge of the room and watched in stricken silence, powerless to assist his bride.

Ravan had never before observed what Nicolette was about to do. He had never needed to, but one bygone afternoon Moulin had shared with him the how and why of her capacity to find Risen so many years ago. Only once had he spoken of the peculiar ritual in the cottage, while he and Moira watched. Now, Nicolette meant to do the same for Niveus, to discover *exactly* where her daughter was.

She spoke not a word, already having taken from a bedpost a single silken scarf, her favorite. Ravan knew nothing about the details of what was to follow, only that it must be done. He could not know that one of the elements—a bird, dead of its own accord—could in no way be found on such short notice this dark night.

It would have been futile to search the woods for one, and there was no time to wait.

But the other elements were already in place: the mirror, the chalice of wine, the suspended stone, the maps, the blade, the strange book with not a single word written on the pages, and…a single hair from Niveus' comb.

All was ready.

"Nicolette…" Ravan held his hand out toward her but could say nothing more, for his voice caught in his throat by what he saw.

She ignored him entirely, instead drawing two fingers in a slow circle about the circumference of the round, stone slab table situated in the center of the great room. She hummed, something soft beneath her breath, as she methodically paced the perimeter of it.

Suddenly, Moira entered from the bath chamber, dressed in a simple shift of white linen gauze. Crawling directly onto the stone slab table, the handless maiden lay face up and took the mirror, placing first the map upon her belly and then the mirror on top of it.

Ravan felt suddenly out of place and was relieved to have Moulin appear at his elbow. All the while, Nicolette continued to draw the slow circle along the edge of the table, still murmuring softly those words so foreign to everyone else.

It both thrilled and terrified Ravan to see what his bride was capable of— the profound exhibition of her most fundamental need—to discover the whereabouts of her child. He didn't know the meaning of the words, having last heard the peculiarity of such a similar chant on a slave auction platform in the Ottoman Empire, but they seemed somehow familiar to him tonight. It was Nicolette to her very core.

Shifting, he was increasingly at odds with himself, as though his hands were out of place with no good spot for them to be. He fidgeted and bit his lip, something he had not done since he was a child.

A cold gnawing crept into his core and settled ominously across his shoulders, weighing him down as he watched Moira lift the single silken scarf—a gauzy slip that was feather-light and the darkest red, the color of a dying rose. With her only hand, she swept the scarf across herself.

Nicolette reached to assist as together they tied one end of the scarf snugly to Moira's handless arm, just above the stump.

Ravan wanted to call out, to scream something as he watched his wife murmur something to Moira, her voice kind and gentle, like a dying breath.

The maiden nodded, shivering in the damp, cold air. Nicolette then softly unwrapped from Moira's head the beautiful cloth the woman normally wore.

She had given the exquisite garment, finely embroidered with strands of real gold, to Moira, not because she felt the woman needed to hide the awful burn scars or the gaping hole where her eye had once been, but because she had seen Moira try to fashion a lesser cloth in such a way.

Now, with the wrap gone, Moira was a vision of vulnerability, her remaining eye thrown wide and wet as she looked directly up, only at Nicolette's face. Ravan knew, unspeakably, what was to come next before it even occurred. Once the length of scarf was tied and knotted firmly to Moira's handless arm, the two women looped it carefully, securing it once, twice, and a third time...about Moira's neck.

When Moira shortened her grip on the fabric and began to draw it tighter, Ravan blurted, "Wait!" But Moira continued, grasping yet a closer handful of the scarf to draw it even tighter.

With this, Ravan broke his frozen stance and staggered haltingly toward the ritual. "Stop! You can't—"

"*No*," Moulin gasped from beneath his breath and snatched at Ravan's shoulder to stop him. "It cannot be any other way! It must be affected by her free will!"

"*What* must be affected?" Ravan charged, "That she should *die*? You love her, Moulin; I know you do! Can you abide by this?" He tried to sling his shoulder from Moulin's hand. "I won't! I cannot!"

The Swiss pikeman held fast with both hands onto Ravan's arm. By instinct, the mercenary drew his sword and had it in seconds at Moulin's throat as he pushed him against the wall. His gaze, however, remained fixed over his shoulder on the writhing woman upon the table. The two women seemed oblivious of the men grappling in the shadows, and Nicolette's hair hung down and about Moira, hiding the agony on her face.

Moulin reached to place a hand on Ravan's, over the one holding the sword. "We must *trust* them, my lord. Or kill me if you believe I am wrong, for I could not live if Moira dies."

Ravan spat between gritted teeth, "I will go back to Crete. Sayid will know from where Malik hails, or Risen will send word."

"And how long will that take, my lord? Weeks? Months? Do you believe your daughter has that much time?" Moulin pleaded, even as the scarlet noose was drawn tighter. "And if it is too late, can any of us live with that? *Ravan*, it is Niveus."

It was the first time Moulin had called him by name, and Ravan noticed how the pikeman's face was, likewise, twisted in uncertainty, his eyes wide with fear. The mercenary swallowed hard and blinked back the sting of tears.

"I-I don't understand. I..." Ravan's sword slipped and, with his other hand, he clasped Moulin's hand so tightly on his arm that the man flinched. "Tell me what I must do. Please, just tell me..." his voice broke.

"There is nothing to be done." Salvatore's voice spoke in a low timbre, and his hand reached from the darkness to draw the dangling sword from Ravan. "You are amongst friends, and there is naught but love in this room. Let it be as it might."

The Spaniard stepped into the dim light, his face a mask of certainty that perhaps he did not entirely feel. Salvatore looked gravely from Ravan's face to Moulin's and nodded toward the wretched table. "We will suffer this together."

This was no battle. There was no wound Ravan could accept, no weapon to fend away. No, this was pain and sacrifice of a sort which he could scarcely comprehend, and he would have gladly thrown himself on a sword to have it all go away, to have all those he loved safe, happy, and warm until they were old in their own beds. *Why must it be so hard...to simply live?*

Moulin's hand slipped just a bit, and Salvatore reached out for Ravan. It was the only thing that gave the mercenary stability now, and he leaned heavily against his friends, unable to tear his gaze from the dreadful display on the stone table.

Moira writhed, her knuckles white as she sustained her self-strangulation. Her single eye bulged open, and her teeth clamped down hard on her tongue. It was a vulgar, desperate, and beautifully selfless act, and it would not even have been possible except for the courage Nicolette heaped upon her.

With the strange words she whispered, the pale sorceress leaned forward to softly rest her lips on the center of Moira's forehead. With that, Moira's arms trembled, swaying like frail masts in a storm under the ferocity with which she pulled the beloved snare.

Ravan exhaled harshly, not even aware he had been holding his breath through the sacrifice of the tragic woman on the table. A tear stung his cheek and disappeared into his beard as he watched. Eighteen years ago, he had saved Moira's life, and she remained with them ever since. When Niveus was born, she had held his infant daughter, tended her, sheltered and truly loved her as though she were her own child. Ravan abruptly realized he loved Moira, as he did the kind men who stood beside him.

He could watch no further. To do so, he believed he must face a dark sliver of his soul and his own impotence to do something, *anything*, to stop this tragic suicide for Niveus' sake. What parent could choose otherwise? What man could live with the sacrifice?

He closed his eyes. Then, the greatest mercenary in all the land turned his head away as Moira's lips turned an ashen grey, a single line of saliva escaping her tortured mouth to drip obscenely down the side of her face onto the unfeeling stone of the table. Her hand slipped from the scarf, and it loosened enough to allow a single breath—the final exhalation of death—to escape.

Then…she moved no more.

Ravan, eyes clamped tightly shut, heard a dim sob escape Moulin's lips. Then, he heard only the faint scuffling noises as Nicolette cut her own hand, mixed the blood with the wine, chanted the words, adjusted the single hair, moved the map beneath the suspended stone, and executed the ritual to its completion.

After several dreadfully long minutes, there remained a small fingerprint on the map, directly over the little town of Ketrzyn, in a far-off land called Prussia. When there were no more incantations to be said and silence fell like the dreaded voice of an enemy thought long dead, Ravan opened his eyes just in time to witness Nicolette crawl onto the stone slab table.

Moulin maintained his death hold on Ravan's arm, perhaps more for himself now than for the mercenary, and all three men staggered and swayed, helpless and awed as they watched Nicolette draw Moira's thin form onto her lap and press her lips to the ghostly pale lips of the maiden.

"All right, then…" Salvatore mused hoarsely, but Ravan silenced him with a torturous glance.

With one hand pressed firmly over Moira's heart, Nicolette passed her breath slowly into the body and lungs of the dead woman. Then, she simply waited, her black hair surrounding them both like a blanket inviting something good to come of it all.

Then, *she* breathed no more.

Nothing.

Seconds crept by and turned from one to another minute. Still, Nicolette did nothing, not moving at all. Slowly, her porcelain-white flesh began to turn a chalky grey, and Ravan let go a single, agonizing sob.

The two women could be stone, ashen as they both were, simply an extension of the pallid rock upon which they were entwined. Then, when Ravan was certain there was nothing more to come of it; that they had lost not only Moira but Nicolette…Moira stirred.

The fingers of her only hand curled, and she exhaled soft as a bird might fold a wing. In this fashion, her breath entered Nicolette and was then drawn back again.

It was more than the men could bear, and Ravan fell softly to his knees, fearful to interfere lest he halt the mystery of what was happening.

Salvatore crossed himself and murmured, "Dear mother…"

Nicolette's eyes opened at precisely the same moment Moira's did, and she drew her lips away. Then, Moira smiled so tenderly she may as well have just awakened from a deep sleep.

And…

…Nicolette smiled back.

* * *

That night, Ravan studied the maps with his advisors, most particularly the fateful mark where Nicolette had stamped her bloodied fingerprint, just north, in the Gulf of Gdansk of the Baltic Sea.

"It's nearly three hundred and forty leagues," Salvatore announced, tracing his finger from where the Wintergrave Dynasty was marked northeast to the Prussian Empire. He always spoke of miles as leagues. "If we ride sixteen, seventeen leagues a day, it will take us nearly three weeks."

"How will you replace horses?" Moulin wondered.

"I have resources, old friends along the way, but my army will be slower by at least five days." Ravan frowned.

Salvatore nodded grimly. "It's the best we can do, but I agree. We should forge on ahead to discover what evil it is we face."

"Agreed…" Ravan rolled up the map. "Nicolette will follow with the army, and Moulin—you and Moira will manage the realm in my absence. We will find Risen and Velecent first. Then we will deploy a rescue mission of Niveus while awaiting Nicolette's arrival with my forces."

Ravan could not admit that which weighed most heavily upon him—that a rescue of his daughter would depend on her still being alive. He cinched the new Damascus blade at his waist. "I will not leave Prussia until I have cut Malik to his knees. Then he can regret his wickedness at his leisure when I send him to Hell."

Shortly, they were gathered in the courtyard. Ravan checked the cinch one last time before swinging onto his warhorse. He peered above the trees to the east, secretly wishing he could catch up with Risen and Velecent. That would be impossible.

He held Nicolette's chin cupped in his hand as he leaned over to kiss her goodbye. "I will see you soon, my love. We will find her and bring her safely home."

His heart sagged heavily in his chest, for Nicolette had upon her face a look more grim than Ravan believed he had ever seen. She said nothing, only watched as the men spun their horses about and galloped from the courtyard.

Beyond the gates, Salvatore glanced back. "I wish she was coming with us."

Ravan said nothing as they rode northeast, toward the enemy, toward…

…Red Robes.

CHAPTER TWENTY-THREE

Murder is a beautiful thing.

This is what Bora Vachir thought as he ascended the castle stairs, his footsteps echoing in the night. Even so, he had mixed feelings about what he was about to do. This threshold was one he had not crossed before. True, there was much he shared with the ruler of this realm—great debauchery and magnificent deceptions. The two had schemed together on many occasions and shared in the unrighteous spoils of their ill-sought victories. They were indeed brothers of the sword.

But, the liberty Bora intended to take was an uncertain one. No amount of shared battle would ever give to him *blood* rights, for he was not of Malik's clan and never would be. In all truth, the whole notion of lineage was ridiculous to him. He never subscribed to its pull, but neither could he deny the power of it. Too often he had seen empires shift and dynasties rise or fall, all in the name of a few drops of blood.

Ultimately, he believed there simply was no other way to preserve his relationship with Malik and, more specifically, get from him that which he needed. Additionally…he hated the bitch.

Pulling the doors of his bedchamber closed behind him, he went straightaway to his weapons rack, took up his favorite battle sword, and tested the edge with his finger. He scowled. It must be perfect for what he would do tonight.

For nearly an hour, the blade rang hollow as Bora pulled it across the stone, his face twisting in a way that only the truly evil at heart might realize.

Finally, holding the sword up so he could see how the firelight grasped the edge of it, Bora was satisfied, his whole mood elevated for what was to come. He coveted moments like this. It was a seductive addiction to him, and this alone set him apart from an ordinary human soul.

As he strode from the hall with his mind set and his blade keen, his maw broke into a wicked smile, and…he was thinking of Malik not at all.

* * *

Two good men stood watch at Klarin's door.

Both were warriors, both were seasoned, and neither believed their post would be necessary tonight any more than it had been for the last two long weeks. But when Bora Vachir appeared down the stone hallway, his blade loose from its scabbard and abomination in his eyes, they fell immediately into battle stances, swords drawn in swift reply.

There are some things that are perfect, but these things are always rare and usually fleeting—a perfect flower bud, the indigo of a summer sky just before dusk, a newborn fawn. Then there are those rare things that are entirely, perfectly dreadful. These are the things that, try as one might, always seem to escape the list of forgotten memories that the human condition tries to discard. They hook themselves cruelly into the black room of bad memories, no matter how fast the door is locked or how many times the human heart tries to burn the room to the ground.

Bora Vachir hacked the two good men down, leaving them to die, in perfectly awful fashion. Klarin, even inside her room, collected the dreadful memory of it before she ever saw it.

The barbarian crashed through the door, eyes bright with bloodlust, a stupid look of false triumph marking his ugliness like stink marks rot. A brief wash of confusion marked his face when he discovered Klarin standing in the middle of the room, hands folded almost politely in front of her, with her chin held high.

"This is no victory," she said coldly to the beast.

"You're wrong," he snarled. "I will kill you now." And he raised the bloody blade high, lingering as though waiting for her to cower.

Klarin did not cower. Instead, defiant beneath his towering presence, she shook her head in a gesture of near-pity. "Kill me then, you wretched fool, and stop wasting my time. My son will see the end of you."

"He will never know." Bora tightened both hands upon the hilt.

"He *will*."

Bora's contemptible expression narrowed. "How?"

"A mother's son always knows. It is a gift."

Bora hesitated as though trying for an instant to recall his own mother's fate.

"It won't work for you, *beast*," she scoffed, "so you may as well not even look for the woman who spawned you. A son must be pure of heart to know such a thing. You are, therefore, forbidden, for there are scarcely a handful of hearts in all this world as black as yours."

It was exactly as Klarin intended it to be, and all Bora needed to hear.

She closed her eyes as his wicked weapon cleaved air, bone, and a beautiful heart in one heavy turn. Then, she fell with scarcely a sound.

By torchlight, Bora dragged Klarin's body into the woods behind Malik's castle. He had already dug the grave, earlier that afternoon, and he hastily kicked the last of the dirt over her, stepping heavily on where he knew her head would be. After her remains were covered and silence was the only eulogy read for Viktar's mother on this sad night, the unmarked grave collected a fresh skiff of snow.

* * *

Since the first night Niveus came to Viktar's room, she returned there late every night, slipping past Xavier's guard as easily as she used to steal past the castle guards, always returning to her own room before morning's light. Viktar was swept away by her presence, and Niveus was swimming in a river of such beauty, unlike anything she had ever known.

They whispered of beautiful things, scarcely mentioning the danger they were under or the impending end of the sail, when Malik would regain control of Niveus.

Much of the time, they said nothing at all, for there was no need. Theirs was a love rarely pure, and so it did not invite those things that place walls between hearts. They were, figuratively and physically, one.

When they slept, she curled up against his chest, and he held her, feeling her soft breath against his tawny skin. He swore her heart beat in time with his, and it always mystified him how, when he awoke in the morning, she would simply be gone. Not once did he feel or hear her leave.

Most extraordinary, however, was that no longer did he feel her absence, and neither…did *she* feel his.

Tonight, when Viktar awakened abruptly with a feeling of things being not quite right, he was surprised to see her there, sitting instead of lying next to him, the back of two fingers resting lightly on his cheek.

"What?" He pushed sleepily up. "What is it? Are you cold?" He went to pull the blankets more over her, but she stopped him gently.

"You know life is a wondrous thing."

He smiled, but Niveus remained so dreadfully calm he was compelled to ask again, "Yes, of course, but what is it, Niveus?"

"And you know some things are unforeseeable."

"Of course. Only God knows our true destiny."

Her delicate brow furrowed. "Yes, perhaps…but you should also know that I love you and will always love you. That will never be unforeseeable, for you are pure of heart, Viktar."

He smiled brilliantly, believing she spoke, of course, about her feelings toward him. "I love you too, more than life itself. Now come. We must rest to gain our strength, so we might face the rest of our lives together." He reached to draw her nearer to him.

Niveus allowed him to curl around her again, but she insisted on threading her fingers into his and clasping his hand as she rested her cheek on it. Why it made him so sad to have her do such a thing was beyond his comprehension. Eventually his heart quieted, and he slept.

Niveus, however, did not … as Klarin died.

CHAPTER TWENTY-FOUR

The boat made landfall at Ketzryn eight days later, just as Niveus told Viktar it would. All the while, no one knew they had spent those secret hours of the night together. No one knew how they had whispered of escaping, going far away where they would live happily together, in peace, in a mystical land that stretched beyond cruelty or heartache. Mostly, it was Viktar who spoke of these wondrous, sweet dreams. Niveus said very little, only listened. A poetically curious expression lighting her face as her lover spun the future as easily as a child would spin circles on a carefree, sunny day.

Never did she invade upon his fantasy. Not once did she make a move to cast uncertainty onto the beautiful painting he created for them. Truly, to her, there was no moment other than the present. Tomorrow was a myth, a lie, for it was never to be. Eternity was now, and she was truly happy within it, as happy as she might ever be.

Then, the next morning, Xavier came to Niveus' door a last time and turned the key in the lock, sending her in one instant back to the dark realm of reality and...into Malik's waiting hands.

* * *

When Malik dragged Niveus to the livery stable and procured horses and a carriage for the final journey to his realm, Viktar was forbidden to ride in the carriage with her. Away they careened, heading south. Malik was in fine spirits as the carriage charged from the seaside village, and they began their short week's journey to Red Robes.

Niveus cautioned Malik, "Harm Viktar or separate him from me, and you will have me nevermore. Think hard on what I am capable of and what I will refuse to share with you if you do not grant me this one request, for all time."

Malik snorted but begrudgingly allowed her this simple indulgence. It stung him that he could not kill Viktar the moment they made landfall. But it was, to him, incidental, for his nephew was becoming more and more insignificant as they drew nearer to Red Robes. Increasingly taken with his impending future and all the promise Niveus would grant him and his realm, Malik no longer obsessed with the boy's welfare, good or bad.

And so he spared Viktar, even going so far as to allow him a horse to follow along on, although he was forbidden to near the carriage or speak with Niveus. Besides, it would not do to return home and face Klarin—bitch that she was—without her bastard child in tow. Her realm lay next to his, and his sister's resources were significant in their own right, but he simply did not need the aggravation. Malik promised himself, as soon as he was back, Klarin and Viktar would be banished from his realm forever. By then, Niveus would be *his* forever—a rare caged bird—and she would have no further say about it.

It was all so simple, Malik believed. With Niveus at his side, nothing was impossible. Straightaway, word must be sent to the King. The wedding would take place, immediately, perhaps even the day after their return. Yes! The wedding was paramount and, with the blessing of the Emperor, even if Ravan one day found them, there would be nothing that could be done about it. Surely the barbarian could not contest the sanctified blessing of the Empire. Malik even believed he would have Niveus with child by then! And no matter if the Wintergrave Dynasty did object. Bora Vachir would stand by Malik as would a legion of his best soldiers.

* * *

The first night's camp was cold. Snow drifted delicately between the outstretched arms of the forest trees, falling in a queer way. Lingering much too long in the air and with no breeze at all to carry it, it was mystifying and sad, as though the silent flakes were trying to cover, as respectfully as possible…a lie.

Malik and Gorlik sat by the fire, occupied by food and drink. The horses' stamping eventually ceased as they settled in for the night, and Niveus remained locked inside the carriage, the key dangling on the outside lamp-hook.

Viktar was banished from the fire and lay alone in the distance. He bunched the needles of a pine tree beneath him and pulled the saddle blanket over himself. Even so, the night was bitter. But it was not the cold which drove sleep from him; it was because his mind was racing for what he must do. He would suffer the cold as long as necessary, for the moment must be just right.

The fire waned, and Gorlik stoked it one last time to keep the wolves at bay before the two retired, warm beneath their blankets and tucked close to the dying blaze.

Viktar closed his eyes, the saddle blanket now up over his head and chest. His numb fingers were entwined and pressed against his throat for what warmth they might find there, but he did not distress. All was as it should be. She had said it, and so he believed.

The hours marched on, the snow stopped falling, and even the creatures of darkness ceased their calls.

All the while, Viktar waited....

* * *

Are you there?
I am, she replied.
Are you ready?
Yes. It is time.
Wait for me. I am coming for you.

Viktar shifted from beneath the saddle blanket and sat up, willing the frozen rigor from his muscles. Stiffly, he pushed himself silently to his feet and squinted to make out the two men in the distance, sleeping heavily beside a nearly-dead fire. He tiptoed across the hushed blanket of snow toward the carriage.

Overhead, the clouds cleared somewhat, and even without a moon, the stars were brilliant enough that he could pick his way along without raising alarm. Nearby, one of the horses turned its head, curious about the human tiptoeing along, but then seemed agreeable with it all and dropped its head to doze.

Viktar reached the carriage, snagged the key, and carefully released the catch on the door, easing it open. The creak of the old hinge was enough to prompt a snort from Gorlik, but the big man did nothing but turn on his side and continue his slumber. Then, Niveus appeared in the doorway and stepped silently from the rig. She wore, wrapped around her shoulders, a heavy, woolen cape, and on her feet were a pair of plain, familiar slippers. Across her arm lay an additional cloak.

Viktar's face softened. Even in the darkness, she appeared as though she belonged here in the wild—a snow nymph in the woods. She went to hand the cloak to him, but he shook his head in a silent, *no*. He had other things to address first.

Niveus did not attempt to affect the sleep of these men. Indeed, that was something she could not do, for her gifts were only effectual of those with a noble heart. Engaging the thoughts of one as wicked as these could prove a lethal event for her.

So, as she waited, Viktar drew from a chest beneath the carriage seat the Damascus steel sword—the one he was already so intimately acquainted with. He studied the gleam of the weapon's edge for a solemn moment before he turned to face the sleeping men.

Gorlik snored again. Perhaps Malik did as well, but it could not be heard over the snorts and gasps of the larger man. Stepping silently to his uncle's side, Viktar raised the awful blade with both hands high over Malik's head.

It was a bizarre picture, in the queer light of the frosty night, as though the young man was divining death with the awful weapon. Niveus made no move to interfere as Viktar remained as he was and did...nothing.

He must look to someone watching as though he were a frozen spectacle, cast like this forever because of how long he simply stood, foil in hand, suspended above his sleeping uncle. Indeed, had Malik stirred, it would have been the end of him. But he did not.

At long last, Viktar drew his gaze, along with his hatred, away from the one who slumbered at his feet, shifting it to Niveus instead. Wordlessly, her expression told him she believed he was no killer.

But he deserves to die, Viktar thought.
Yes, he does.
I want him to die.
He will.
But I am no murderer.
No, you are not.
Then let the wolves have him.
If that be his destiny.

Viktar looked long at Niveus before silently lowering the Damascus blade. Leaving it lying next to its master, he led Niveus quietly from the encampment, taking the three horses with them.

When they were a safe distance into the woods, he helped Niveus onto one steed and swung onto another, leading the third horse along behind.

He could not know it would be nearly eight hours before Malik and Gorlik would awaken from their too-deep slumber to find themselves with a fine carriage and no horse to draw it.

Viktar trusted his intentions, along with his generous mercy, would be evidenced by the Damascus sword, left on the ground between them.

Because Viktar was pure of heart, he believed the two men would eventually find their way to Malik's realm and things would then be made right. His mother waited for them there, and she would make Malik realized that Niveus must be free to choose her way. Love would conquer hate, and justice would be recognized within the civility of the Holy Roman Empire and the King's law. Viktar even believed that, with Ravan and Nicolette's blessing, he might be permitted to seek a happy life at Niveus' side.

This is what the young man told himself, for it was his nature—the nature of a pure heart—to believe the impossible could be made true. There were few who walked with as much benevolence as Viktar did, and it shone in his beautiful expression.

* * *

Niveus told herself nothing, only held a hand up to the sky as the snow began to fall again, flittering down between the tree branches. She could not see how the flake she captured on the tip of her finger was reflected perfectly in the mirror of her pale eyes.

The horses slowed, moving as though in a land of magic, their muffled steps the only sound in the silent forest. All about them the snow hung softly in a rare, magical way, as though it appeared from nothingness. And it was a fortuitous event, for their tracks would be hidden within the hour.

But this was not what Niveus thought about as she peered at the delicate snowflake, forever capturing the memory of its beauty before it melted away.

The boy she had saved that one night in the village slipped into her thoughts, and she touched the drop of water, which was all that remained of the snowflake, to her lips.

It was still beautiful, like Jori, *exactly* like him. She could taste his young life in the single drop of water, and he was as celebrated as the snowflake had been.

Niveus was immediately glad for the slippers she had chosen to wear instead of her traveling boots, and she wished she had the shawl, not for the warmth it would add beneath her cape but because it was, to her, *significant.*

All the while, she did nothing to manipulate the horse. It simply wandered along just as it was supposed to, knowing exactly where it should go, the reins slack across its withers. They rode a long way that first night and day—over forty miles—to put as great a distance as possible between them and the men they left behind. The land was gently hilly and forested, and they picked their way along, concealed by the wildness about them and lighthearted because of their togetherness.

Viktar would wordlessly point, sharing his joy at seeing a doe standing in the distance with twin fawns at her side. Niveus would gaze overhead, and he would squint to see a pair of hawks circling in a dance high above.

If humanity were never again to affect them, Niveus and Viktar would be as these creatures were—rare in their beauty and destined to live and die in simple majesty.

When they pulled up the next night, Niveus stroked the weary horse on its head, thanking it for carrying her so nobly and for such a long way. Viktar watched her from a short distance, a happy expression lighting the handsomeness of his face.

Shortly, he motioned for her, for he had found a particularly fine pair of sheltered firs with the branches cupped away on one side, creating a perfect little nook for them. It afforded a dry spot out of the wind where they could rest this first night, and Viktar drew the horses in with them so they would have shelter from the wind as well.

Niveus knelt in the secluded alcove of the irregular tree, laying out the saddle blankets next to each other in a specific way, just as her father had taught her to do. This brought Ravan foremost to her thoughts, and by default Nicolette, Risen, and Moira. She didn't worry for them, or even wonder about their state of affairs. She was only happy to have known them.

All is as it should be.

"I want to build a fire, but I'm afraid to," Viktar said.

"They will not see it," Niveus said.

"Perhaps not. We've gone a good, long ways. Even walking they would be, at best, twenty-five miles away from us."

"The woods are too thick and the night too dark. If the fire is out before morning, there would be no smoke in the distance, and they would never know." She briefly stopped her task. "But we won't need one if you prefer not."

He glanced nervously around. "But the wolves. They run in large packs in these woods, and they are fearsome, some of them bigger than a man. " He busied himself stringing the three horses nearby.

"They will not bother us."

Viktar studied her, smiling softly. "How do you do that?"

"Oh, it's easy. If you overlap the edge on the diagonal and then lay a third in the corner, two can share three saddle blankets very easily, especially if we keep our legs close together. My father taught me," Niveus answered, purveying their sleeping arrangement.

"No, not that—though it is lovely." He smiled softly again. "I mean, how are you so certain about such things, like about the fire and the wolves?"

Niveus shrugged. "Some things I see. Some things...I do not."

"I don't know anyone who understands things the way you do. No. It's not *understanding*. It's as though you are connected with...*everything*." He ran his hand along the back of the horse and swept it to the nothingness beyond.

Niveus remained kneeling, her feet tucked beneath her, and lifted both hands, indicating the fir trees. Their boughs reached over and around as though they meant to lift her up in a woodland embrace.

"There is a design. But the course we travel, by the nature of its very being, can be manipulated. It sometimes gives me," she focused intently on him, "insight."

Viktar stared at her as though she were speaking another language.

Slowly tracing one finger along the ground, she drew a circle in the dry, earthen patch of old pine needles, next to the saddle blankets. "Everything is a circle, like this. And all circles have a center. But the center is only another beginning."

She touched her finger into the center of what she had drawn. "It is forever, and we are all within the eternity of it." Next, she swept her fingers gently through the circle and drew some of the pine needles and earth up into her hand. She allowed these to sift and fall through her fingertips, sprinkling back to the ground. "Just because something is changed, or we can no longer see it as we did before, doesn't mean it is no longer there. It only means it exists in another way, for a moment or, perhaps, for a long time." She drew the circle again.

Viktar knelt beside her and peered hard, studying the circle. It was obvious he struggled.

Niveus muddled the circle into oblivion once more. "Look. *Really* look. Not with your eyes but with what you know to be true. Now, do you see?"

He leaned closer, intent upon the scuff of earth and pine needles. "No," he confessed.

"Viktar," she murmured, "look *again*...."

He chewed his lip as he studied the disordered arrangement of needles and earth and sighed heavily. "I just can't see it. It's useless."

She reached out and took his hand, opening his palm flat before pressing her fingertip into the center of it. She traced the circle on his palm.

"Imagine that I draw the circle again, the potential of it, even though I do not. Now, can you see that it is there, but the time for it to be has simply not yet arrived?" She could see an awareness threaten to settle over him and watched how, as it slowly took hold, he lay his other hand down on the earthen spot where the circle had been.

"Yes," he murmured, "I suppose I see it now. Yes! I *do*."

"And..." Niveus encouraged him.

"It is like a promise that can never be broken, but there is no knowing when it will once more be."

She took up his hands in both of hers. "And that is the essence of it. You do not have to know *when*, only that it *will*. Patience does not believe in the concept of time."

He said, "I think I see. But...how can you know so certainly, in the vast expanse of God's plan, that here in these woods, under this tree, that this circle will again be? How can I know without doubt?"

She shook her head. "Time is for always. If you must know when, you have already lost sight of eternity. Don't cast such constraint upon it. It only clouds your vision. Let it be uncertain. Then it will be clearer than you can ever imagine."

When Viktar next glanced down at the earthen, pine-needle bed, there was the circle again, all of its own accord. He stared at it, blinking in amazement. "*That's* how you see, about the wolves, I mean."

Niveus nodded, "Yes," and looked solemnly away. "They do not follow tonight; not us, anyway."

Then, Viktar built a small fire, not for the wolves but because it would warm and light their secluded space in a lovely way. It was strangely homelike and, curled together on the blankets with their cloaks bunched on top of them, they lay with empty bellies and full hearts, holding each other as though they might remain like this for eternity.

As Viktar drifted off to sleep, Niveus noticed his breathing was stronger than it had ever been, his face a vision of peace. He would not notice the sublime happiness on Niveus' face as she lay awake for some time, watching the stars twinkling happily beyond the dying fire.

When she finally slept—an uncommonly normal sleep—she dreamed of a boy with hair white as snow and eyes...the warmest amber she had ever seen.

CHAPTER TWENTY-FIVE

†

Malik and Gorlik walked for two days before reaching a small open patch on a shallow ravine's edge. Gorlik tended a fire while Malik paced wearily back and forth, venting his rage, still bent with fury.

"I'll kill him! The moment I see his face, I will cut it from him and skewer his head for the birds to feast upon his eyes!" He whirled about and kicked senselessly at the frozen dirt.

Gorlik, bent over the moss-wrapped cinder left over from last evening's fire, nodded dumbly. Holding dried tinder across the ash, he blew it gently back to life. They had only two more days of food, but also…two full skins of ale.

All the while, Malik's anger spewed for he was, in his mind, greatly inconvenienced on many fronts. First and foremost, his bride-to-be was taken! Add to that he was now afoot, something he simply could not stomach, for it made him feel terribly common—and *this* insulted him to his core. Never mind he still possessed power, stature, gold, *and* the magnificent sword. Never mind the boy had spared his life. The world had simply tilted wrong to trouble him so thoroughly, and it was, to Malik, very *personal*.

He flopped down, seething, and watched Gorlik lay the dried meat and ale out by the fireside. Snatching up the first skin, he drew long on the spirits, then drew again. His belly gnawed at him from within as though it would consume him, and empty as it was, the ale hit fast and strong.

Shortly, he reclined by the fire, the flask still in hand as he snatched up a piece of meat, chewing angrily before following it with another and then another long drink.

As the spirits took greater effect, Malik's rage ebbed, and for the first time since they had discovered Viktar and Niveus missing, he was somewhat satisfied. The fire crackled confidently, and the night darkened.

He would have his revenge, he told himself, imagining the fashion with which he would exact it. It was only a matter of time; Viktar would be dead, and he would wed Niveus.

He shared his intentions with Gorlik, painting a gruesome picture in graphic detail, and the monster grinned in anticipation, for they both held a fondness for depravity. At just about midnight, the ale was gone, and the fire went untended as both men slept too deeply.

At precisely two in the morning, the big, male wolf wrapped its maw about Gorlik's throat, crushing his trachea completely before yanking it entirely free of the pitiless man. The wolf snapped happily, slinging its jaws upward, releasing the nearly ten inches of free trachea into the air before snapping it up and gulping it down.

Gorlik's hands jerked to the gaping hole where his throat used to be, the two severed carotids spraying dramatically, even in the darkness. Frenzied by the blood bath, the rest of the pack set in on the wretched man. Another large male wolf lunged for and had Gorlik firmly by the genitals while a third, a female, de-gloved his left hand, stripping the skin from the tissue and bone beneath.

His penis and testicles, the next to go, were ripped free of him. Gorlik rolled heavily to his side with his last bit of strength only to have the bulk of the pack gut him as easily as pulling a rotted oyster from a cracked shell.

Malik, who had been asleep on the other side of the fire, had scarcely enough time to stir before the pack was well upon the already half-dead Gorlik. He noticed briefly how horribly the big man's feet trembled. They stuck out and were all that showed from the frenzied throng of wolves.

Rolling away from the awful mauling with a stifled cry, Malik snatched up the Damascus sword and used it to push himself to his knees. Two wolves had already set their red eyes upon him, their jaws dripping with Gorlik's blood, and they snarled, advancing slowly. Malik was left with only one best, bad choice and promptly accepted the unknown, rolling off the edge of the precipice.

The wolves continued to bay as they shredded Gorlik. This is what Malik heard as he fell down, down the steep side of a ravine. The beautiful sword was ripped from his hands as sharp rocks and branches stabbed and slammed at him. Scarcely did he have the chance to blame Viktar, he was so senselessly tossed.

When Malik's body finally found the bottom of the ravine, he was remarkably without serious injury, though thoroughly battered. The Damascus sword was, of course, still intact but now imperfect. Several of the beautiful stones were dislodged and forever gone. It would not affect the purpose of the uncommon weapon, should a tyrant wish to impale a strangled young man with it, but the beauty of it was forever flawed, something that enraged Malik thoroughly.

He had little time to consider the fate of the elegant blade, however, for a cluster of wolves had broken away and were threading their way down the short face of the ravine on one side, their bloodthirsty stares focused intently on their prey.

Nearby, a sturdy, solitary pine tree was his only chance. He grunted and swore as his hands grasped the prickly, sappy branches, and up the tree he shinnied just as the first beast leapt, snagging him by the heel and pulling his boot from his foot. Farther up Malik climbed, nearly fifteen feet above before he was safely out of reach of the circling wolves. The crook of where the tree forked was woefully uncomfortable, not offering an agreeable perch on which to rest, but the Prussian had no choice but to hang there.

Below, the wolves trotted about, howling and snapping at each other in their frustration. Their intended prey would spend a sleepless night in the tree, and upon morning, the wolves would finally leave to find their dens for the day. When Malik eventually crawled down from the tree, battered and terribly thirsty, his mind burned with only one desire—to kill Viktar.

He never returned to check his henchman's fate. Instead, for two days he walked, all the while believing he heard the padding feet of wolves behind him. Eventually he came to a small hamlet farther south. There was no inn to offer him comfort, but the gold belted at his waist had survived and would spend as good as it ever might. Soon, he was provisioned and set off again…with a horse.

* * *

Five days later as they neared Malik's realm, Viktar rode with obvious excitement. He sat tall, his eyes shining with hope.

"We're nearly there! And I don't want you to worry. When my uncle arrives, all will be set right. I have a plan, and my mother will temper his anger. She's always been the best at that." He talked almost too fast in his growing optimism.

Niveus' horse slowed.

"Viktar…" She breathed his name as though it were a beautiful spell.

"Hurry!" he exclaimed, urging his horse along faster. "It isn't long now!"

"Viktar," she repeated softly as her horse halted entirely.

He was a short distance away before he noticed she had stopped. Turning his horse about, he jogged the gelding back.

"What is it, my love? You shouldn't have trepidation. I—"

"Do you remember...back on the ship?"

He blushed. "The ship? Why, yes, of course I do. But...but none of that matters! We are almost home."

"That night when you awoke, and I was there with you; I told you that I loved you," she said softly.

He drew himself up, circling cautiously around her so that he could take her hand in his. "Of course, as do I...but..." His voice trailed off.

The foreboding in the air was heavy and sifted down about them both like spent blossoms from an overripe tree.

"And you remember we agreed some things are unforeseeable, but all is as it should be...like the circle we drew." Niveus' lips became so pale they appeared as though frostbitten. They always did that when she struggled to explain unbelievable things to another.

"Niveus," he said a bit impatiently, "you are speaking in riddles again, but we don't have time right now. I need to—"

"She is gone," Niveus said straightaway, for she knew no other way to say it.

Deafening silence drew them apart, and she murmured again, "She is no longer with us, Viktar."

For a long, dreadful moment, he only stared at her, and it hurt Niveus' heart. The confusion on his face was so awful, but he said nothing as though daring not to confirm what she had shared.

Niveus' next thought was of how the first notice of tragic news was also the very pinnacle of the years of pain yet to be suffered. She had seen it many times before. It was when a mother fell to the floor. It was when an old man sobbed, cradling his dead bride of seventy years. It was the piercing tip of true despair.

Sadly, if the sufferer could just be without the tragic news for even a second longer, it might somehow be better. But that narrow haven is a myth— a nasty lie.

As it always was—and was for Viktar now—honesty waited patiently outside the grievous door, waited for the suffering one to open it enough to strike the deception to the ground. The pain that remained was called *Truth*.

"*Gone*? Home, you mean? Very well, but if that is so, we shall ride on to my mother's realm instead and...and...."

Niveus sat unblinking, unmoving, absorbing all of his confusion with sorrowful compassion.

"And…" he choked as disbelief threaded itself into every pore, soon to be replaced by rage.

"Her life here is done," she murmured.

"*What?*" he demanded harshly, but Niveus did not flinch. "What are you saying? That she is *dead?*" He yanked his hand free of hers. "Are you telling me my mother has *died?*" His voice rang through the winter trees in frozen disbelief, and the few birds that sang fell silent.

The sad regret of Niveus' mute gaze struck Viktar merciless and hard, but even so, he refused to allow the awful messenger across the threshold of the door.

"You lie!" he spat. "How do you believe you can manifest such a thing as wicked as this? You…you are a *witch*! As your mother is, and…and you *lie* to me!"

His words were born of agony, but there was still something to them that moved Niveus' heart in a way she had never experienced before. She looked away, into the darkening trees, at the ghost of a snow-white deer, which only she could see. The creature named *Outcast* circled there, capturing her in its lonely stare. Niveus knew that, starving and with the wide, red eyes of truth, the deer was herself.

Viktar's horse shied away, and he yanked the reins too harshly, causing it to rear up on its hind legs. Ignoring the upright beast, he yelled at her, "Why? Why do you say such things? As though you know! How dare you? How *dare* you!"

Niveus drew her gaze from the hallowed trees, away from the white deer, and looked upon his anguished face. She allowed him to say what unkindness he was compelled to so that he might endure the first wave of pain. Unsure why humans required this pardon, she only knew that they must, as a way-station perhaps, on their way to acceptance.

It was at exactly moments like this she did not comprehend humanity— did not understand the human heart's inability to allow destiny, in all its tragedy, to simply be.

She slipped from her horse, dropped the reins to the ground, and approached Viktar. His horse backed away, but as she extended a hand it halted, its head hung low as though it felt regret for what its rider now suffered.

Sliding her hand onto Viktar's thigh, Niveus reached with her other toward his face, asking only to touch him. He looked at her as though he had never seen her before.

"Come to me, now," she said.

Tears threatened as he grit his teeth, his whole being contorted in misery. "You *lie*," he whispered again.

"I do not," she said softly.

There was no blame to be cast. There was no anger to be heaped upon an innocent, and Viktar's expression jumped from anger to sorrow and back again.

Finally...truth slipped through the door.

Sliding from his horse, Viktar wrapped his arms about Niveus as though he could squeeze the last awful moments away. She rested her head against his chest, allowing his sorrow to crash openly upon her. His lips brushed against her hair as he asked the questions no one would ever be able to answer.

"How? Why?"

Niveus simply held on to him. It seemed the entire forest stopped its song in silent respect until, finally, he held her at arm's length. "She is dead," his voice croaked.

Niveus nodded solemnly.

"Bora Vachir killed her," he said.

She didn't need to reply. The truth would have its way, but she asked, "What is now the worst that can happen?"

"The worst? The worst is he *killed* her, cruelly, mercilessly!"

"No, *now*...this moment, as you hold me. What is the worst?" she asked again.

"That she...she..." He stumbled as though his mind searched for the details of her fall but could not say outright what horror he imagined.

Niveus knew where his thoughts journeyed. She knew he was considering the torturous moments of her execution and touched his cheek, directing his face toward hers. "Not her death, Viktar, for she has gone beyond. It is as it should be."

"But I...I can't..." As he faced life for the first time without the person who had given him his, he confessed, "You exhaust me, Niveus. I simply cannot."

"It is not about you now. It is about her."

She held onto him, could feel how his grief ran deep and bottomless, and her instinct was to turn away, but she did not. And it drew something from Niveus, as though a transfusion of healing were being pulled from her. It was altruism of the purest form.

"I can take it away," she murmured, her lips brushing against his chest.

Viktar pushed away enough to see her face. His was a mask of confusion.

"The pain," she explained, "I can take it from you for eternity...if you wish."

He looked at her as though she asked that he disavow sunlight for the rest of time.

"Why would I do that? The pain is now part of who I am and...part of her."

This was very curious to Niveus. She studied his sad face. "Yes, of course it is. Why would you?" Immediately, she comprehended why this man spoke to her heart like no other. Viktar was not like the others. He was meant...for her.

As he helped her back onto her horse, she noticed his demeanor was changed; something about the set to his jaw that was more serious.

"There is much to be set right. I would like for you to be by my side as it is," he said in a low voice.

"I shall be. I promise."

Setting off at a much slower pace, he murmured over his shoulder, "I'm glad to have heard it from you first. And, I'm sorry. It was unkind of me to hurt you with the things I said."

She wondered curiously about this power he believed he had—an ability to "hurt" her—for there existed no one who possessed the power to truly hurt Niveus. Perhaps others confounded the notion of hurt with confusion, for on that count, humanity *confused* her a great deal.

The day waned as they wove their way through the tangled forest, and by evening, two unlikely riders approached the massive gates to Malik's castle.

CHAPTER TWENTY-SIX

†

The question of Niveus' whereabouts was no longer vague, for Nicolette and Moira had exacted that information with the ritual, at the near cost of their lives, and placed her near the southeast coast of the Baltic Sea. She was evidently taken by ship, but Ravan already knew who had her. He was convinced it was *Malik*.

Ravan recalled how Sayid had described Malik—his *patron*—as Prussian. And this had been how the man had announced himself, had it not? *Prussian, but of Arabic lineage?* Those had been his exact words, but while visiting the Wintergrave Dynasty, he had claimed to be Lord Vedlund of Poland.

There remained the possibility that Malik had not lied outright, for lords frequently had more than one name and title, something that annoyed Ravan a great deal. He thought it a ridiculous hobby how some nobility seemed bent on collecting as many titles as possible. Preferring to collect other things, Ravan intended that the sword he carried—the new Damascus blade—would collect its first stain of blood before long.

Ravan and Salvatore headed northeast. As it so happened, the King of Poland was visiting the German states, following the amicable finish to the Gollub War, to enjoy an extended stay in Luxembourg at the grand castle of Vianden.

Conveniently, King Wladyslaw and the Count of Vianden both agreed on short notice to meet with the unlikely travelers. Ravan peered upward as they approached Vianden Castle.

The structure stood huge and gothic, perched on an immense, rock base, and granted a spectacular view of the river to the north and east. At over three hundred meters high, the fortress towered over everything else in the realm; even grander, Ravan thought, than the castle Adorno had built—the one Nicolette had taken and renamed the Wintergrave Dynasty.

The horses shook their heads in grateful reprieve as Ravan and Salvatore left them to the stablehand's care. Walking through the castle's grand entry doors, Ravan heard a herald announce their arrival, accompanied in fine fashion by trumpets.

Salvatore quipped, "Why haven't you had those for me when I come to visit you?"

Ravan ignored him as they entered the long hall. In the distance, the king sat upon a guest throne, guards in several rows on all sides.

To the monarch's left, on a lesser throne, sat the Count of Vianden—obviously younger than the king and of a brooding, intelligent countenance. He was known for—and carried the demeanor of—one possessed by a quick wit, when he allowed it to escape.

Ravan closed the distance between them in long strides, took a brief knee, and rested comfortably with his hands clasped behind his back. He nodded politely, waiting for the king to speak first. Even at ease, his presence was, without dispute, formidable, and his reputation was not only widely-known, it was well-respected.

"Lord Wintergrave, it is such a pleasure to finally meet." The king looked him up and down.

"Your highness. Thank you for seeing me on short notice."

"So it is you who put the great Duval asunder, rose from the dead, and wed the despot's bride. And I only hear of good things that come from your realm."

What the king knew of Ravan's history surprised the mercenary in no small measure, but he had no time to reply as the monarch continued.

"I gather you have not requested an audience for overdue salutations. And because I am a man of business first, I encourage you to explain straightaway why you are here."

The king, nearly thirty years Ravan's senior, was anything but frail. He sat tall and regal, and studied the mercenary from beneath a thatch of white eyebrows, rubbing his chin thoughtfully as he spoke.

This monarch held great power, ruled one of the largest realms in Europe, and had united the Kingdom of Poland and the Duchy of Lithuania with abject precision. And the count, with whom he was obviously good friends, was also a man of great power, one of the mightiest lords between France and Poland.

Ravan answered easily. "No, your highness. I've come to ask about one of your own. Lord Vedlund, or…*Malik,* as he might be better known."

At this, the king frowned, and the count smirked.

"*Malik*," the king repeated. "Now there's a name! Might I ask, do you enquire of him as friend...or *foe*?"

The king's suspicion was obvious, but Ravan did not hesitate. "He is my sworn enemy, for he has abducted my daughter. I intend to have his head before I am done."

"*Do* you, now?" The king seemed mildly surprised. "A daughter, you say? Taken by Malik?" He grunted, brushing the possibility aside with a sweep of his hand. "Not likely. The man has killed four wives; he is sterile as a eunuch. No heir will ever spring from his loins, so it seems a long way to travel to steal a girl he has no use for—no more than he would of a common whore."

The man's quick judgment set Ravan aback, but he was swift to reply. "I have little insight into what inspired the Prussian to take my daughter; and his motives, known or not, will follow him to his grave. All I seek is my daughter's safe return home."

"I do," Salvatore interrupted, stepped forward, and bowed with a great flourish. "I have insight into what might inspire the tyrant."

Ravan regarded his friend with dismay.

"And you are...?" the king began.

"Capitan Salvatore Fidalgo, at your service." Salvatore, enchanting brown eyes sparkling, spread both arms wide so that all in the room might feast upon the entirety of him.

To that, the king sat more upright, an expression of sincere curiosity sweeping across his face. Ravan was thoroughly surprised when the king blurted out, "I know your father, Captain Fidalgo!"

The Spaniard smiled broadly. "No surprise, your highness. Many know the great shipbuilder Fidalgo. But I pray you know only the good *rumors* of his son, for I swear that none of the scandalous truths are to be believed."

The king laughed heartily. "I wish to speak to you of ships! I've yet to successfully chase one of yours down."

"Over ale, I would be happy to ply you with tales taller than the good count's castle. But first..." Salvatore became more serious, "your grace, if you would allow me to speak as a man, not as father of the abducted child."

The king gave him the go ahead, and Salvatore cleared his throat.

"The girl is exceedingly...*unusual*." Salvatore glanced sideways to see how Ravan received his appraisal of Niveus. Ravan only studied the floor in front of his feet, and Salvatore pressed on. "Her mother could steal a sailor from the seas. I swear it, true as my blood runs red." A crimson blush creased the tops of his ears as Ravan shot him a growing look of surprise.

Salvatore added hurriedly, "And the girl, though perhaps not cut of the siren's identical cloth, can compel a man in other ways, on a much...deeper level."

When this seemed to gather the attention of not only the king, but all the other men present, Salvatore finished hastily, "A righteous man would covet this girl. I've no doubt an unrighteous one would not hesitate to abscond with her, given the opportunity."

"A beauty of the most enviable sort, is she? And with talents besides?" The count chuckled lasciviously.

"No, my lord. U-mm...no, not in *that* way, though her beauty is certainly uncommon. It is more of an attraction that cannot be defined." Salvatore shrugged as though unable to explain further. "You have only to meet her once to understand. She is like a rare, dying bird."

The king frowned. "So, the tyrant has your daughter. And make no mistake; Malik *is* a tyrant, with a host of tyrants at his disposal. But I must inquire, how do you intend to negotiate the girl's release? His forces are some of the most formidable in Prussia. He is, after all, a Teutonic Knight and member of the Hanseatic League. He has been a vexation to me for years; the bastard digs in like a pitted viper!"

The king's expression became cold, and he leaned forward in his chair.

"I signed a truce with him not four months ago, but make no mistake, I will have Thorn under my flag before I die. For now, at least, the treaty will hold him to my demands."

Salvatore asked, "Demands?"

"Yes. As I mentioned, he has killed another wife. I care not, except it destabilizes the region. So I've commanded that he groom his nephew as heir apparent. The boy is of sound mind, and his mother is reasonable—lady to a significant realm of her own. I *will* have stability on my borders, and my demands will secure it."

Ravan took a slow, deep breath. So *that* was the rub. Malik's realm sat precariously on the edge of Prussia...in Thorn, and the king had ordered Malik to establish Viktar as heir to secure the Prussian-Polish boundary. That explained the obvious animosity Malik held toward his nephew in Crete.

The king droned on, "By God, Malik will do as I command or it will be his head on the block." Then, as though reminded of the real reason for Ravan's presence, he swept his hand about in the air and added, "So, as is plainly apparent, the girl is of no strategic importance to Malik."

Ravan shifted restlessly. This king was no enemy, and harsh as the words might seem, he spoke the truth.

There was no way any of them could know what Malik had observed of Niveus that dark night as she bent over a dying young man.

The count spoke up. "Please. You've obviously ridden long. Avail yourself of the castle, join us for supper, and we will talk more. There will be time enough to negotiate the ransom of the girl."

The king nodded appreciably and clapped his hands together. "Yes! Wine first! Then we will talk; I wish to hear tales of how you were the undoing of the Duval!" He set his scrutiny again upon Ravan.

"It is an old story, your highness, and one that I'm sure would bore you." Ravan struggled to hide the impatience in his voice. Gracious as the king's gesture was, he only wished to gain what information he could and be gone. He was cautious, however, for he knew he must not insult Wladyslaw.

Eying Ravan respectfully, the king said, "I do wish you success on your journey. But great as your army might be, and noble as they might be trained, they will be no match for Malik's, and France is stretched thin, certainly too thin to fight on your behalf just for the sake of a girl."

"I ask not for your favor, nor for your sword. I ask for information. How great are his numbers? How many archers? Is his battle heart forged of blood or of stone?"

The king thought for a long moment, finally considering Ravan's passion. "So, you wish to topple the viper, do you? Well, I can tell you Malik is a man of small character wielding great power. He rules with an iron fist, but even so, sometimes blood speaks to him in a way perhaps it should not. There is a reason why his realm is called Red Robes, but his troops are weary. I have been at war with him for nearly three years, and they, if not *he*, have welcomed the truce." He glanced appreciably at the count. "Even great warriors need relief from battle at times."

Paying very close attention as the king described the might of Malik's forces in greater detail, Ravan finally said, "Thank you, your highness. You have helped greatly. We would gladly stay the night and be off at first light."

The count climbed to his feet and joined the conversation after a long, studious silence. "Perhaps I can assist you in your endeavor. I have four, maybe five hundred men I can release to your command, but my motivation must be clear. I am not so much concerned with the girl as I am bringing the tyrant down."

"Then we share a common goal."

"But...I would need *security*. If you fail...half your realm is mine."

Ravan's expression darkened. "The tyrant *will* fall, with or without your forces. Then the realm can fall rightfully to the nephew. I've no interest in war-confiscated land, though your generosity is duly noted."

"You misunderstand my intentions," the count countered. "I have no desire to engage my own realm in a campaign. I already hold ready access to the North Sea and have better ways to entertain myself."

He glanced briefly at the king. "Like his highness, I only desire *stability*, for Luxembourg and the lands around it. So, even though your dispute is personal, your success would benefit me as well as his highness. Then, let the nephew takes control of Red Robes...*if* you win."

"It seems reasonable," Salvatore said. "It would feel good to have his troops, with yours, at our backs."

"You have already dispatched arms?" the count asked, obviously surprised.

"My army follows, but will be at least four days behind me," Ravan explained.

The king smiled. "Lord Ravan, you would be wise to seize the gesture, for there is one thing Malik does very well. He surrounds himself with opportunity and with those who can contribute to it. Why else would he always have at his side the Mongol, *Bora Vachir*?"

To that, Ravan's eyes widened and the glimpse of a rare, bitter smile tugged at the corner of his mouth.

"You don't say..."

CHAPTER TWENTY-SEVEN

✝

Bora snored, having dulled his boredom with too much wine...again. Sagging heavily on Malik's throne chair, he snorted, scarcely stirring when a horn echoed from a distant castle tower. When the horn sounded again, signaling someone was approaching the realm, he blinked, dragging himself heavily from his slumber.

He squinted, believing it had been a dream, but when the horn sounded a final time, he wiped the half-dried spittle from his cheek and sat bolt upright. It must be Malik! Home at last.

He shouted to the guards posted just outside the door, "More wine! And whores! Bring them! And stoke the fires! The lord returns!"

Just then, a scout burst into the great hall and dashed up to Bora, dropping to one knee with his head bowed. "My Lord, two riders approach."

"Yes!" Bora slammed meaty fists down on the armrests, believing it was Malik returned with Gorlik. He had completely forgotten about Viktar.

"'Tis the boy," the scout added without delay.

"What do you mean? What *boy*?" Bora snarled as though fault lay with the messenger.

The scout cringed. "Our lord's nephew, sir—Viktar. And he travels with a woman and...a riderless horse."

There were some talents Vachir had great affinity for. His battle strategies were not terrible, he was a formidable warrior, and remorse would never weaken his nature.

But deciphering possibilities was no great talent of his, and his mind twisted as he tried to figure the circumstances of Viktar's return without Malik. Surely it was just that the boy was home a day or so early and bringing word of his uncle's great journey. Yes, that must be it. He considered it inconsequential that there was...a *girl*.

However, what Bora *did* possess in droves was an uncommon, undying suspicion. Consequently, before long he peered from the tower, squinting into the dimming light at the three horses advancing in the gray distance.

By the time Viktar and Niveus rode across the portcullis and into the great yard of the castle, Bora had returned to the throne room and was seated regally to await their arrival.

* * *

"This way, my lord," a guard motioned for Viktar to follow. "Lord Vachir awaits the honor of your presence, you *and* the lady."

"Why is Bora in the throne room?" Viktar paused.

When the sentry only shook his head and stared at the floor, Viktar stepped swiftly past and strode ahead of him, finally flinging open the double doors of the great hall. Bora sat up stiffly and glared down his thick nose as the young man came to a halt in front of him.

"Why do you sit on the throne?" Viktar demanded of Bora.

The Mongol's hand gripped the arm of the ornate chair, and his glare darkened. "I am in your Lord's service in his absence. Speaking of which, where is your uncle? And who is the wench you travel with?"

He peered over Viktar's shoulder to the girl lingering at the door.

Viktar ignored the questions. "My mother sent word. She came here to await my return. It is she who should be sitting here in charge in my uncle's absence. Tell me, Bora, where *is* she?"

Viktar, of course, had never received any such correspondence, but he knew immediately that the terrible disclosure Niveus had shared was true. His mother no longer walked amongst the living. So, scarcely able to contain his growing rage, he bluffed Bora magnificently.

Bora shrugged. "What should I know or care of your mother's whereabouts? I am not the bitch's nursemaid. And...who is the wench you travel with?" His focus returned to somewhere down the hall.

Viktar took a step toward Bora. "You are no longer welcome here. By the king's appointment, I am heir to the realm and shall assume rule until my uncle returns. I command you, step down."

"I will not!" Bora spat as his hand crossed his waist, settling onto the hilt of his scimitar. "On the contrary, I command *you* to leave while you still have legs to stand upon."

Rising from the throne, his full height towering above Viktar, he began to unsheathe his sword.

Viktar flinched, not because Bora raised the sword but because behind him the stomp of heavy boots indicated the first-in-rank of Malik's infantry were filing into the great room, lining the hall on either side. They were terribly efficient, their armor clanking in unison as they were immediately in place, spears forward and at the ready.

Most curious was what they did this in response to the threat on *Viktar's* life, for Malik was lord, woeful as he was. And in his absence, blood ruled, even in a land as miserable as Red Robes.

Bora's lip raised in a terrible snarl. This was certainly a regrettable turn of events. It was likely dawning on him that killing Klarin was one thing, but Viktar was indisputably, by the king's command, in charge.

What Bora could not know was that the soldiers lining the hall were uncertain at best. Yes, Red Robes had suffered because of Malik's insistence on an alliance with Bora Vachir, but Viktar was a fresh piece of the puzzle—good or bad—and as of yet, untested.

It was an uncertain future for the people of this realm, and that translated to shifty glances shared between the soldiers. All became quiet enough that a sigh could be heard, but the echoes of silence were only a sweet premonition of the woman who would enter next.

Vachir squinted hatefully from beneath a thick brow, and the edge of his lip curled even more as he struggled to identify the peculiar woman who walked slowly, as though she floated, down the long hall.

Viktar did not look back, only landed a dead stare on Vachir. "It would appear my uncle's troops have tired of your *temporary* rule. Raise that blade and you will fall to their numbers as a pig to wolves."

"I would have you dead first," Bora snarled.

To that, the forward charges stepped even nearer, lances dropped toward Bora, having made a decision. Viktar would rule in Malik's absence, just as the king of Poland commanded.

Niveus stepped up to Viktar's side, and it was not Viktar, his stern words, or the troops that Bora was focused on—it was the girl.

"Who *are* you?" The Mongol indulged himself in his first thorough appraisal of Niveus.

She stared at him, blinking slowly as she glimpsed something no one else could see. She knew in an instant who Bora Vachir was and what he meant to her father, rather what Ravan meant to *him*.

Viktar began to speak, but Niveus drew him to silence with a gentle sweep of her hand. She could not see how her eyes had gone so darkly red that they were nearly black. Still, she spoke not a word.

"I would know who you are before I relinquish the realm!" Bora commanded and took a step toward Niveus.

When she held her ground, Viktar stepped in front of her. "She is my guest and under the shelter of this realm. You, however, no longer are." He pointed to the door. "Be gone before nightfall, Bora, or be gone forever. You are not welcome here."

It was evident that Bora's rage was scarcely contained. Viktar knew the barbarian could strike him down—could likely strike Niveus down as well—but then the horde would be upon him. That would surely be his final stand, and it was, perhaps, not as Bora would imagine his death to be. Viktar was gambling mightily that the tyrant's will to live would surpass his need to kill.

It was a narrow gamble, but then Bora re-sheathed his sword, his stare still locked firmly on Niveus. "I know not of which coven you hail, *witch*, but I will know. And when Malik returns," he said, swinging his focus to Viktar, "you will both burn. I swear it on your *mother's* grave."

Viktar watched as Bora stormed angrily from the room, waited until the doors slammed closed, and turned to Niveus. "What was that about? Tell me, what does this man know of your family?"

Niveus looked to where the brute had disappeared and murmured, "The Mongol barbarian carries an old fear—his *only* fear—an obsession that has vexed him for many years. It was destiny undone, but…there will be time enough for that to correct itself."

Viktar's surprise was complete when Niveus added, "Bora Vachir nearly fell on a battlefield…to my father's hand."

That evening, Viktar stood, crushed with grief, in the hallowed alcove where he last said goodbye to his mother. He imagined her reading his letters, the ones that spoke of such hopeful optimism. Niveus crept silently up behind him and waited, just as she had done so many times for Risen.

Eventually, Viktar allowed Niveus to draw him from the castle to a remote thicket in the eastern woods, and together they knelt at the edge of a sodden, shallow grave. "I cannot leave her here," Viktar murmured sadly, his hand resting on the frozen soil that blanketed his mother.

Niveus murmured kindly, "She is not here."

"But her body. It pains me that it should rest in such a spot, in such a way. I fear she will have no peace." He motioned about the black woods, made blacker by the torches they held. "I want to take her home."

"As you wish, but we cannot move her, not yet. Malik returns, and we must leave at once." She nodded toward the west.

Viktar sighed and hung his head. "I know now that I must destroy him.

There is no other way, for when he returns to Red Robes, it will once more fall under his command—a terrible burden for the people to bear. And their needs are greater than my own."

He pushed himself upright and brushed the soil from his hands Taking her hand he led her from the forest, speaking in hushed tones along the way. "I must fortify an army. I know you are exhausted; we both need rest, fresh horses, and provisions. But tonight we will ride to my mother's..." his voice caught, "*my* realm. There we will be safe, at least for now."

His step carried a new purpose, and with Malik as a clear enemy, for a greater reason, his resolve only seemed to bolster more as they reached the edge of the sad, little woods.

"Once home, I will assemble forces and see that you are returned safely to your father's dynasty. Then, I will return to Red Robes, dethrone my uncle, and bring compassion to this forsaken realm, once and for all."

He cast one last look back over his shoulder, toward where his mother's shallow grave was being heaped upon by a new layer of snow. "Then...I will bring her home."

"I wish to remain with you."

This jarred Viktar to a halt, for scarcely had Niveus ever made her wishes so known to him. "Niveus, your family, your *home*..."

She glanced about the dark woods in a familiar way. "I have never understood why my happiness has always been such a concern for my family. *I* control my state of being—not them." She frowned. "But they worry for me. If I stay with you, it would give me happiness, and that would matter to them."

Viktar dared smile and reached for her, kissing her cool lips. "We shall see, but I cannot allow you to come to harm, no matter what."

Side by side, they returned to the castle and, nearing exhaustion, drew up their plans to escape. Scarcely an hour later, they left for Klarin's realm, for safety and to prepare...for war.

* * *

After leaving the small village, Malik rode like a wraith bent on one thing—finding Niveus. True, his spite for Viktar gave him great fortitude, and the thoughts of how he would eventually destroy his nephew crept at intervals into his black heart. But Niveus had a much greater hold on his being, and it was a perfect poison, one he could not help but swallow in draughts. Consequently, he brutally flogged the horse and ran on.

Reaching a farmer's homestead, Malik spent the last of his gold on two more horses, both of them drafts, and ran them beyond hard. Again, he beat them when they slowed, changing to the other only when the one he rode could carry him no more.

Late the next day, when the beast he rode fell once more to the jog, Malik, near exhaustion himself, could scarcely raise his arm to beat the animal. Cresting a small hill, the sad horse stumbled and fell, rolling down the incline and casting Malik from him. Lying with its chest heaving, the horse sprayed blood with each breath from its nostrils, a cruel crimson across the virgin snow.

The other horse lacked the good fortune to escape from Malik, for he had tied it with a long rope to his waist, just in case. But the horse bolted a short distance before coming to a stop, and for a few stunned minutes, Malik just lay, the air stricken from him. What he did not see was that he now missed an ear, sheared off on the rocks with his fall and the subsequent dragging.

Finally, he pulled himself to his feet. A short distance away lay a felled tree. He crawled upon it, mounted the second horse, and with the rope tied himself onto the beast. Then, onward he journeyed, all the while gaining ground.

By evening, he left the now-ruined beast behind at another small homestead and commanded the family's only service horse, this time simply taking it. In this fashion, Malik advanced upon Red Robes, riding night and day, nearly nonstop. In his delirium he had visions—strange, black and white apparitions of him wedding a porcelain statue with burning eyes.

A day later, scarcely able to sit astride the horse, for he swayed terribly from side to side, Malik finally staggered into his realm. As he broke the last tree line and halted, what should he see but a vision galloping toward him across the fields from his castle. The vision was…Bora Vachir.

* * *

Niveus and Viktar rode side by side up to the drawbridge to leave Red Robes' castle. But when the heavy, wooden door of the outer gatehouse was thrown open, there on the other side stood an earless, despot-ruler, barely able to sit his horse, and…Bora Vachir.

A small battalion of Malik's men, assembled at the gates to wish Niveus and Viktar farewell, did what they were supremely trained to do. As ancient fears turned the tide in an unfortunate way, they cast their allegiance against Viktar, allying themselves once more with the ruler of the realm—Malik.

Niveus and Viktar were going nowhere, for the dreaded overlord was returned.

"Put him in the dungeons!" Malik screamed, stabbing a finger at Viktar, his words slurring as he was untied and drawn from the ruined horse. "And take her to the keep! Lock her inside, and bring the key straightaway to me!"

His eyes swung wide and glazed, for Malik was more desperate than he had ever been and had no better idea how to force Niveus' obedience. He needed time to recover and think.

Later, as Malik rested upon a silken bed, Aya fed him water and meat. For the first time, he did not leer at the Syrian woman as she tended his needs. Instead, he was distracted and slapped her small hand away when Bora entered.

The Mongol, pacing the floor of his bedroom, ranted, "What do you mean, the dungeons? Your nephew is not fit for the dungeons! Kill him, I say, or let me at the whelp! I will flay the hide from him and hang him for all to see what happens when the true lord of this realm is disrespected!"

"There will be enough time for that," Malik growled. What he did not say was that he feared Niveus' response to killing Viktar would be that she would somehow *disappear*. As much as he hated to admit it, he knew the boy had an unreasonable hold on her.

But, he wondered, *could not the hold be broken?*

First things first—he must marry Niveus without delay. Then he would have all the time he needed to capture Niveus' heart and soul. And he would keep Viktar in chains forever if that's what it took to remove her unreasonable attachment to him. Let him rot in the dungeons!

And Klarin was dead! That was a nagging detail he was grateful Bora had taken care of in his absence. How resourceful of him!

Things were looking up. The boy's imprisonment would render him impotent in managing his sister's realm, and once weakened by their leaders' absence, Malik intended to swoop in and claim it all as his own. No one would be the wiser if they never saw Viktar alive!

"Bread and water for him. No light, and not even a pot to piss in. But…it is my wish that he live," Malik said with finality.

Bora countered, "Then the white witch, let me at her! She disrespects me with her silence, so I will rape and burn her! When I light a pyre beneath her feet, we shall see if the mute bitch does not speak, and you can watch!" The brute's intentions were real, for he had done just such things before.

Malik, however, surprised Bora, for he turned on him in such a fashion as he had never done before. Off the bed he leapt, staggering, upending the pitcher of wine on the stand. Snatching up the Damascus sword, he struggled to extract it from its scabbard and backed his comrade nearly across the room, whipping the ruined blade back and forth in front of Bora's face.

"Speak of Niveus in such a way again, *ever*, and I will cut the tongue from your mouth and feed it to you! Do you *hear* me?" He stopped, the sword inches from Bora's face.

The Mongol's face showed no fear, only confusion. He shrugged, smiled a wicked smile, and gently pushed the tip of the blade aside with two gloved fingers.

"Ah, so the witch has a spell on you. There can be no other reasonable excuse for your obsession with her. Certainly there are others of much greater beauty. Very well. I will not touch her...not yet."

"She is not a witch!" Malik spat and turned his back to Vachir. "Not in the fashion you believe."

"Enlighten me..." Bora mused.

Moving to his balcony, Malik opened the double doors and stepped into the night, the snow falling in fat flakes around him. Resting his hands on the balcony rail, he looked out over Red Robes and then up at the darkened tower where Niveus was being held. He sighed heavily.

"The girl has a...a *gift*. With her touch she can draw a human from the precipice of death." He reached for the key, hanging about his neck on a cord, to make certain it was still there.

"It is not true," Bora countered.

"You know nothing, for I have seen it, several times over. She lays her hand upon those who suffer, and...they live."

Bora's face ran a gauntlet of possibility. "But...that is *good*! She can heal, when your greatest warriors might otherwise fall!"

Malik spun on Bora, his face contorted maniacally. "It is not for anyone else! It is for *me!*" He stabbed at his chest and wailed, "Me alone! Don't you see? She is to be my bride, for I simply cannot live without her."

Bora flopped into a chair. "You would hold this advantage for only yourself? After as long as we have fought and as much as we have seen together?" He said it in an unsavory way as though Niveus was a whore to be shared. And that is exactly how Malik took it.

"Silence! She is not something to be *used*—some tincture to spread upon whatever ails you!" Without closing the balcony doors, he staggered inside. "She is given to me by the gods, and I will be greater than I have ever been!"

He pointed a trembling finger at his comrade. "Touch her at your peril, Bora. I will kill you myself if you even look dishonorably upon Niveus."

Bora's mouth broke into a slow, wicked scowl, his malaligned teeth enormous, as though they would crush all good intent.

"And where did you find this...this *gift*? Perhaps she has a sister?" He laughed. "Certainly she didn't simply fall into your lap or between your loins because she could not resist what sways there? We both know better than that!"

Ordinarily, this would have drawn Malik to a rage, but tonight it only drew him silent as he stared again over his shoulder into the blackening night. He murmured, "She is the daughter of a sworn enemy, a man I had intended to spite. The gods sent me to her for revenge, or so I thought. But when I found her, when I found Niveus and saw what she was, I knew...*knew* the gods' true intent."

Bora harrumphed and pushed himself heavily from the chair.

"I tell you, the witch has a spell cast upon you. A good night's rest, a full belly, and a whore beneath you will cure this lunacy. Then we will decide what is and isn't to be done with your prisoners."

When Malik only continued to stare at the black outside, Bora moved toward the chamber door. "Well, do what you will with the witch. But I will hold you to your word. We campaign again before the month's end."

The barbarian released the heavy latch but paused, casting an amused glance over his shoulder.

"Malik...who did you say this man was—the one you had such great intention to spite—the father of this *witch*?"

Malik dragged himself from his dark scrutiny, scarcely able to whisper the name. "*Ravan....*"

To that, the color drained from Bora's face and he staggered.

The entire realm, if it listened close enough, would have heard all complacency fall from the Mongol's shoulders and crash to the floor.

CHAPTER TWENTY-EIGHT

†

Niveus stood near the floor to ceiling windows of the castle's keep. Thrown ajar, they allowed a cold wind to lift the gossamer layers of Niveus' gown, the same gown she had worn for many days, ever since Quin drowned. Snow settled about her, disappearing against the white of her skin, attaching its heavy flakes to her eyelashes and hair.

All the while, as the hours crept by, she scarcely moved.

Behind her, new gowns made of the finest satin and velvet hung on racks for her pleasure or disposal. Next to them on a grand chest lay a remarkable assortment of fine jewels, exquisite as could be bought. And across the room behind her, a bed—luxurious as could be—lay undisturbed.

A fire died in its cradle on the farthest wall, but Niveus gave it not an ounce of attention, ignoring it as much as the stack of wood nearby. Neither were the candles lit nor the food and wine consumed.

Most astonishing, however, was the wedding gown—yard upon yard of velvet and fur, fit for a winter queen, and of the deepest blue as to be nearly black. It hung in the dressing alcove, an ominous premonition of Malik's cruel great ambition.

Curiously, none of the surprising disregard was piteous intention on the part of the peculiar girl. Luxury heaped high as a mountain could gather no attention as Niveus gazed with enormous, crystalline eyes beyond, into the snowy, white darkness. All of her being was occupied by the belly of the wicked castle—for there lay Viktar in chains—and by the forest beyond the edge of the realm—for there ... lay her *brother*.

* * *

Aya slept, as always, in a small alcove quartered off with silken drapes.

Her accommodations were lavish, just in case her master chose to visit her unannounced, a habit he occasionally indulged, for it delighted him to add surprise to the other elements of degradation he heaped upon his favorite slave girl.

But Malik had not summoned Aya nor visited her velvet prison since his return. Although considerably relieved because of it, this confused her a great deal, and because there was little else expected of her, she slept as she normally did—a bitter sleep tucked between the finest linens gold could buy.

Tonight, however, something drew the small, brown girl from her slumber. She snapped awake and just lay for a bit, taken with a voice she was sure she heard whisper to her from within her cloistered chamber.

"Who is there?" she asked.

After no response, and when the whisper came again, she rolled over and sat up, her bare legs dangling over the side of the bed. Reaching for the coal pot, she blew gently while holding a fire stick against the ember. Shortly, the dry kindling sliver burst into a small flame, and she lit the bedside candle. Looking about her small chamber, she saw no one there. But then, again, the voice called.

This time, it did not whisper to her. It commanded gently, *Come to me if you are kind of heart and fearless of spirit.*

Aya thought to herself that she was neither of those things. This was no surprise, for the cruelly abused often believe of themselves the character flaws that belonged instead to their abusers. But neither did she lay down again; only sat for a very long time, listening to the darkness. The voice came again, clear as though its speaker sat beside her. *Come to me if you are kind of heart and fearless of spirit.*

This time, Aya rose and drew a robe over herself, donned her slippers, and murmured aloud, "It is nothing but a dream come to disturb me." All the same, she stole into the chilly castle hall and stood there, clutching her robes tightly around her as she looked about in the empty silence.

The voice came no more, but something else drew her now. Aya reached her hand in front of her as though she felt a thread pull, and began to step, one foot in front of the other. Through the castle halls she wandered, across a barren battlement to the castle's keep and the tower steps that rose in a forbidding spiral upward.

Up, up Aya climbed. The wind moaned lonely through the window slots, but all she heard was the echoed memory of the voice's summoning. Pausing to rest four times, she finally stepped, breathless, onto the top floor. A single guard slept too deeply before a single locked door.

Aya hesitated, hands clenching. She turned abruptly about, but stopped, her foot suspended over the first step down.

I am here. Please stay, for it is you I seek.

The voice, rather the *thought*, came from behind the locked door. Aya turned slowly about and crept forward in the darkness, one tiny step after another. She hesitated in front of the somnolent guard, unsure, but when he did not stir, she passed, standing directly in front of the door. Then, saying nothing, she rested a small hand on the rough, wood-plank surface that separated her from whatever beckoned from the other side.

* * *

Niveus rested the palm of her hand on the door, and a soft smile crept across her lips. She murmured…"Hello, Aya."

CHAPTER TWENTY-NINE

†

Viktar hung suspended by his wrists in the cold, isolated dungeon, deep within the castle. His shoulders ached as though a dozen fire pokers seared into them, and overcome with exhaustion, his head bobbed. Each time he dozed off, the chains and the pain in his joints jerked him cruelly awake, and he scrambled to gather his feet beneath him, pushing himself with great effort back to standing.

Worst of all was the burning that had laid claim to his mouth and throat. It raged, sucking in its scorching wake the lifeblood of his body, for he thirsted as he never had before. The small of his back ached terribly, worse than any beating he had ever endured by Gorlik, as his kidneys begged to be hydrated, and his hands and feet were numb.

With a groan, his head bobbed. It would not be long before he sagged a last time and his lungs, caged between a flailed rib-cage, breathed no more.

But two voices from down the hall roused him, the first soft and foreign, the other carrying a deep, begrudging cruelty. In his stupor, he whispered between cracked lips, *"Niveus...?"*

* * *

"He is my master's nephew. Traitor though he is, you mustn't allow him to die," Aya argued gently.

"I have my orders. He will not die, not on my watch. But, you are the lord's whore. Why are you here pestering me about it?" The guard shifted his bulk, leaning heavily on his spear as though happy to be entertained from the boredom of a dying man.

Aya appealed with both hands out, smiling softly. "I know Lord Viktar. I grew quite fond of him before Lord Malik and he traveled to Crete."

The guard scowled suspiciously as he examined the exotic woman, so out of place in the belly of the dungeons where, except for the torchlight, there was no light at all. He leered. "That right? Did Lord Malik watch his nephew have his way with you? Is that how you grew so fond of him?"

Blushing, she looked away and lied, "'Tis true. He had me many times, before a cast of others, and I crave to look upon his face again, for he is beautiful. Please...please allow me to see him this last time."

The man shifted, summoning as much rare intelligence as possible to champion a self-serving cause for himself. "Well, he's not so pretty as you might remember, and what do I get for it all?" His leer widened, and he licked his lips. "I know! I would have you! Yes, I would swive the lord's bitch myself, here, bent over in a cell!"

Aya gazed up at him from beneath dark lashes, her brown eyes dancing in lovely expectation. "Yes...that can certainly be arranged." She allowed her robe to fall invitingly from her shoulder to expose the greater part of it and her left breast. As the brute stepped toward her, she covered herself again. "But *first*, I would see the lord's nephew."

The man grasped at his crotch, pushing his already growing erection away as he glanced urgently behind her, back up the stairs.

Aya urged, "There is no one here, sir—no one but you, me, and the prisoner. Our lord will never know. Now...let me see him."

The guard fumbled through his keys as he led her to the last cell. Looking nervously about, he warned her, "Five minutes. That is all."

"Ten, a cup of water, and unchain his hands." Aya stood tiny and defiant in front of the cell door.

The guard wavered. "Water, but he remains shackled, and I watch."

"Then you shall see...but not touch," Aya said firmly and pulled her robe more tightly about her throat, closing the door of sweet possibility.

The man shifted from foot to foot like a spoiled child, but finally plunged a ladle into a barrel of water. Handing it and the shackles key over, he grumbled, "Ten minutes and your precious privacy. Tell him to grease you well, for after he is done, you will have a true man split you open." He let go a rude guffaw and allowed her into the cell, locking her inside.

* * *

Viktar squinted, offended by the meager light of the single torch Aya held in one hand. "Who..." his voice caught miserably in his parched throat, "who are you?"

"*Shhh*," she held her finger to her lips. "We haven't much time."

First slipping the torch into a wall cradle, she held the ladle to Viktar's lips, allowing the infusion of precious water to run down his throat, and it seemed to him much too swiftly gone. Next, Aya released the manacles.

Dropping to his knees, he asked hoarsely, "Niveus—do you know where she is?"

Aya knelt close enough to whisper. "She sent me, but we haven't long. The guard will return in ten minutes."

Viktar peered into the darkened hall beyond the dungeon door, his mind racing with possibilities. But before a single one could solidify itself in his head, Aya said, "Niveus told me what you should do…"

* * *

Ten minutes later, the guard returned, squinting into the dimly lit cell. Viktar appeared to be securing his trousers, and Aya remained kneeling, half disrobed.

Hand on the hilt of his sword, the guard commanded, "Chain him up; back in chains or you stay with him."

With his lips pressed grimly together, Viktar said nothing as he stepped obediently to beneath the chains. Raising both arms, he submitted as Aya stretched to secure the first manacle about his wrist.

Viktar could not see how his muscles flexed as she fumbled with the key. His gaze cast sharply from beneath lowered lashes, and he studied the guard as Aya moved to the other side.

Seeming to struggle with the second manacle, Aya finally turned to the guard, holding the key out. "I cannot affix it. The set appears jammed."

The guard scarcely hesitated before unlocking the cell and coming to her aid. "Give it to me," he snorted, taking the key from her before lifting both hands to secure the other side.

Blindingly, Viktar's hand was loosed from the other side, for Aya had not truly locked it in. What he did not anticipate was how quickly the guard would have the key in the lockset of his other wrist.

Now dangling by his left wrist, he grasped the guard by the hair with his free hand and swung both legs upward, locking them around the guard's thick neck.

As the big man swung about, arms up and clawing at Viktar's legs, Aya pulled from beneath her sash a slender, double-edged blade and clutched it with both hands, arms extended stiffly in front of her, eyes wide in terror.

"Now!" Viktar exclaimed between grunts.

The guard drove against him like a battering-ram, but Viktar held firm with his legs, his free hand keeping his head from crashing against the stone wall. "Aya, *now*!"

The slave girl broke free of her trance and, stepping near, slid the delicate blade between the ribs, in the guard's left armpit, just above his armored chest-plate.

When the guard faltered, she stabbed again, just as she had once seen Malik do to an unfortunate soldier. Malik had smugly crooned as he let his victim fall from the blade, "You have to find the *window* of opportunity when it would seem your enemy is too strong for you."

Aya buried the short, slender blade three more times through the opportune window, collapsing the guard's lung and dissecting the aorta. Staggering backward, she watched, terrified, as Viktar held his legs firmly grasped about the dying man's neck. When the guard thrashed no more, only then did Viktar let go, allowing the near-dead guard to collapse to the floor.

"Aya…Aya, hurry. The key." His still-manacled wrist stretched above him. He grimaced, his free hand going to his wrenched left shoulder.

It was a long moment before the small woman was able to draw her gaze from her own bloodied hand and the blade she still clutched.

"Aya…" Viktar encouraged softly.

Dropping the knife, she scurried to gather up the key, fallen to the side in the skirmish. Handing it to Viktar, she allowed him to release himself. In one swift movement, he had the lockset free. Once loose, he went straight to Aya, pulling her robes back up to cover her still half-naked body, and wrapped his arms around her shoulders. She trembled.

"Shhh…Aya, you have done a good thing. I promise you this."

Still, she stared at her bloodied hands.

"Aya…" he said softly. Holding her at arm's length, he gently lifted her chin and looked into her stricken eyes. "You will be all right. I will change things, for you and for others. But first, where is she? I must release Niveus."

"No, you cannot."

"I must find her. Just tell me where Malik has her."

Aya shook her head. "You *cannot*. The door is locked and Lord Malik sleeps with the key about his neck."

"Then I will have his head and recover the key." Viktar covered Aya's hands gently with his own. "Go now. Wash your hands, burn your robes. Feign nothing but ignorance of what has happened here. You are a warrior now, the most dreaded kind."

When her expression turned to confusion, he smiled. "You are a wolf...disguised as a lamb. Malik will never know it is you who freed me and started the fire."

Aya's brief smile faded. "You cannot save her, Viktar. Not like this," she insisted again. "But Niveus told me what to you should do. She said you must go to the forest, south and west. There you will find the strength to free her."

"I don't understand." Viktar grasped her gently by the shoulders again. "What could Niveus possibly wish for me to find there?"

"She said you must go to the highest forest hill, for at the peak of it lies *Risen*." Viktar's surprise was complete when Aya added, "Lady Niveus said to find her brother first or...you will surely die."

CHAPTER THIRTY

†

Risen and Velecent camped on a small hilltop, well hidden within the lush forest that covered the western margin of Malik's realm. They had stopped at towns four more times to exchange spent horses for fresh ones. One of the beasts had sorely tested Risen's patience, but the steed beneath him now was solid and willing, and he was grateful for that.

As night fell, the two wordlessly made camp, each having, by now, become implicitly familiar with the routine of the other. Lean and drawn from the long, hard trek, both their faces held a sharpness of grim anticipation for what was to come. They were two warriors facing an empire for the sake of one extraordinary girl, and both believed, beyond anything, that their lives were well worth the sacrifice.

Risen tossed a small armload of deadwood onto the fledgling fire with great care, so that the smoke would not be too obvious, and watched his friend from the corner of his eye. Velecent was skinning the two rabbits Risen had taken late that afternoon.

"Supper!" Velecent said optimistically, holding the carcasses up for Ravan to see. "And they're fat ones!"

The sandy-haired warrior, one of Ravan's dearest, old friends, paused from spitting the rabbits on the edge of the happy flame. He had known Risen since the young man could barely crawl.

Velecent cleared his throat. "You're a good shot, you know. Nearly sharp as your father."

When Risen said nothing, he added, "He would be proud of you. You know that."

He said it not as flattery, but as a simple observation.

Risen, head still down, murmured, "Yes, well, let us pray my aim is as accurate as his when it really counts."

"M-mm, yes. I suppose it is unlikely we'll ride away from all of this with our sweet Niveus and no objection from whatever beast has taken her." He gestured the direction they still must ride.

"No, I suppose we both know it is not to be." Risen was unusually somber as he set about clearing a small space to lay his blanket.

"And she is here?" Velecent glanced to the east, to where they would find Malik's castle by the end of the next day.

"She is."

Dropping wearily onto his blanket, Risen sat with legs crisscrossed, his head drooping with more than fatigue. The dark hair that swept across his eyes concealed the burden that showed there, and he wearily dragged a bridle across his lap so he might check the bindings. A rein had broken loose at the bit that afternoon, and he fumbled with the old leather, pulling *Monster-Killer* from his boot to cut away the rotted lacing.

He manipulated the blade perfectly for it was very familiar. It was, in fact, the one his father had helped him fashion as a boy—the one Sylvie had killed a monster with. Ever since, he could not hold the blade without thinking of her, and his sad face softened with bittersweet memories.

And never could he think of her without his thoughts wandering far away, to a happier time when he had held her in his arms. It had been a charmed love, pure as they were young. He paused, the knife dangling in one hand.

Some said he should forget. People who did not understand told him time would mend the hole in his heart and that another would find him—that *true* love was yet to be discovered.

This only confused Risen, for they were *wrong*. Love was not missing, never had been. All he had to do was search, and there it was, burning within his heart bright as the day they were married. It seemed the only one who understood was *Niveus*.

He tossed the bridle aside. There was nothing more to be done. He loved Sylvie, and more than anything, he believed love was patient. Now, all that was required of a patient man with a broken heart was to wait.

As he re-sheathed his blade, he breathed in deeply and worked to quiet his mind. Tomorrow he would meet an enemy he intended to destroy and, perhaps, die trying. He tried not to think about it. The potential for loss was more than he cared to consider and, so much like his father, his concern was never for himself. It was for Velecent and Niveus.

He closed his eyes again, and there she was—the only one who could help him through this. His face softened. Nicolette's blood that had given him this gift, that with certainty and clarity he could sense the presence of the one who gave him strength. And Niveus had helped him refine it.

He sighed. All would be as it should be, for there she was...*Sylvie*.

Risen stretched out on his makeshift bed. Again, he regarded the man who sat across the small fire from him. He wanted more than anything to tell Velecent they would be successful. He wanted to tell him they had sacrificed nobly, that they would save Niveus and would all live to feel the sun on their faces again, but it was something he simply could not do. The man deserved honesty, and so, Risen said nothing.

Velecent turned the spit, slow-roasting the meal they would share and, without looking up, said, "You realize I would be here even if you were not."

Risen raised his head on his elbow. "What do you mean?"

"If you weren't here. Even if you did not exist, *I* would be here." Velecent stabbed with his finger toward the cold ground.

Pushing himself up, Risen crossed his arms across one bent knee, and tipped his head to the side. As Velecent looked gravely across the dancing flames at him, threads of gray hair shone silver in the firelight, and Risen's heart warmed. It was no surprise this great man had stood by Ravan for so many years. They were cut of the same cloth in many ways, perhaps as brothers might be.

As though reading his thoughts, Velecent said, "Even if you had never been born, because it is important to your father, I would be here. But more than that..." He took a deep breath. "I would be here for *her*. I would stand alone, against them...for Niveus."

It was more than Risen could have asked, and it lightened his heart a great deal to hear him say such a thing. Overwhelmed by the warrior's valor, Risen swallowed deeply and dropped his head again, this time to hide the emotion that threatened.

Stupid, he thought to himself, *how a blade's cut cannot pull such a thing from a man's eye, but let a good man say something so selfless, and tears can no more be denied than the next beat of a heart.*

Silence fell comfortably between the two, and the men ate to their fill. With bellies full, they slept head to head as snow blanketed them. Risen dreamed of Sylvie, and beside her...Niveus held her hand.

The next morning, as the two seasoned warriors broke camp in silence, Risen's head jerked up abruptly. In the distance, over the trees, a cluster of the forest birds squawked, exclaiming their excitement over something they were not ordinarily accustomed to seeing.

Velecent heard it at the same time and paused from saddling his horse and held a single finger to his lips, tossing his head in the direction of the chatter.

Risen nodded in the direction of the sound, and the men wordlessly mounted their horses and separated, one sweeping to the right, the other widely to the left. Riding with bow and arrow at the ready, Risen squinted into the early morning shadows of the forest. As he eased his horse forward, one slow step at a time, he finally glimpsed what all the grousing was about.

A single rider rode, leaning forward and at a swift jog. He handled the horse with the poise of an accomplished equestrian and pushed it as though driven with a grave purpose, west.

Risen whistled—the soft call of a woodland thrush—and the call was returned from beyond the solitary rider, off to the other side. Simultaneously, Velecent and Risen looped about and swung in so that when the man turned in surprise, he found them nearly directly behind him, bows raised.

The first thing Risen noticed was how uncommon the stranger was. Young, perhaps not much older than himself, he had light brown hair and tan skin. And his eyes were like none he had seen—almost gold, like late summer grass. He also appeared travel-worn, too thin, and with a bleak determination about him.

Risen began to greet the lone traveler, but before the words were even from his mouth, the young man blurted out, "Are you *Risen*? Niveus said you would be here."

Velecent and Risen looked at each other, and Risen said, "You know where my sister is? Take me to her, now. You will be greatly rewarded."

"I will, but there is no reward that could give peace to my soul other than Niveus' safe release, for I am in love with her."

To that, Risen pulled his horse up short. "*What*...did you say?" His next, unreasonable thought was that there were two of his sister in this universe and this man was obviously in love with the other.

"What did you say?" Velecent echoed.

"I love her. And would fall on my sword if it would set her free."

"Free?" Risen pressed him. "Who has imprisoned her? Is she harmed?"

Viktar spoke with grave honesty. "She is safe, for now. But the ruler who has taken her intends to wed her, and his intentions—for Niveus and the people of this realm—are only nefarious."

Risen snarled. "That is not possible! She would never agree to such a thing. I know my sister. Niveus would die first!"

Viktar's tortured face betrayed his misery. "Perhaps you are right...except that Niveus is changed. You see, your sister is also in love and, against my wishes, has agreed to my uncle's terms only if I am allowed to live."

It was as much as Risen could endure. With a sudden cry, he lunged from his horse, grabbing the stranger and bowling him over the other side, off of his horse. Both men hit the ground hard, but Risen landed on top and had several blows delivered in quick order.

"You left her at a tyrant's mercy! To save your own skin!" Straddling the stranger, Risen shook him hard by both shoulders. As it became obvious the young Prussian would not defend himself, Risen shook him once more for last measure.

Viktar sputtered through a broken lip, "She sees things. You know she does, and she said we would not survive without your help. I am torn, but I *believe* her, and that is why I allowed her to send me away…to find you."

"Let him up," Velecent said gruffly.

"But he left her behind!" Risen raised his fist again.

"Yes…I did, at her request." Viktar's eyes flashed in challenge.

Risen struggled for a long moment to cast disbelief from the labyrinth of impossibility. "You say…you say Niveus—*my* sister—loves you?"

Viktar nodded. "As I love her, and I grieve much more the miles between us than any beating you could ever give me."

"Careful what you wish for." Risen snorted and shoved, allowing him to hit the ground hard. Then, stepping off of him, he reached to pull him to his feet. It surprised him that the stranger was nearly exactly as tall as he was, and he asked, "So, was it you? Were you there, at Wintergrave…when this man took her?"

"I was. And it was my *uncle*. We first met your father in Crete. You…are so much like him." Viktar looked down and brushed the dirt from his hands.

"And you allowed your uncle to take Niveus." Risen's fists clenched again.

Viktar let go a long sigh. Then, he pulled his coat open and his tunic aside enough to expose the wicked scar. "At my uncle's hand, unbeknownst to me, he did this to draw her out. I would rather have died than have her fall to his awful deceit. But then…" He only shrugged and closed the jacket, leaving Risen and Velecent to imagine the first moments of the two lovers together.

But it was Niveus! She would never…. Risen caught himself, surprised at how suddenly he thought again of Sylvie. Others said it could not be, said he was far too young. He swallowed thickly and appraised the stranger with the strange, Slavic accent. "She loves you."

"Yes, and we desperately need your help."

"Tell me of the tyrant who took her," Risen said.

"His army is weakened by war with Poland, but stronger than most."

"*Shit....*" Velecent tossed the stranger's reins to him. "We just couldn't be fortunate enough to have Niveus' captor be a lone madman."

Viktar shook his head. "Malik has power, enough to demand a truce with the King of Poland."

"What is your name?"

"Viktar, son of Klarin."

"And that matters because—"

"Because my mother is dead. But her realm—*my* realm—is significant. It lies three hard days' journey north of here. Ride *with* me. I will gather my army and we will return, together, to destroy my uncle once and for all."

Risen snorted, glared at Velecent, and swung onto his horse. "It would be good to have an army. Very well. Go, ride with him and bring them. I will go on ahead."

"You cannot!" Velecent pulled his horse hard about. "We will gather the army, together. *Then* return for Niveus."

"No. I cannot. *I* know where she is, and now I shall meet the one who has taken her. He will answer to me." Risen peered east. "And if he will not negotiate her release, then in six days, we will gather outside his gates and wage war."

There was no disputing him, for Ravan's son would have it no other way. In the end, Velecent and Viktar rode on to his realm while Risen rode alone...into the maw of Red Robes.

CHAPTER THIRTY-ONE

✝

Another army, of three hundred fifty men, swelled across France and northeast, following scarcely three days behind Ravan. It was not all of his forces, but it was his most elite, trained by his own hand. *This* army knew advanced tactics with the blade, were exceedingly trained in hand combat, and at least a hundred were supremely accomplished with the longbow.

More than that, however...Nicolette led them.

When she passed through Luxembourg, it didn't surprise her at all that the Count of Vianden, after making her husband's acquaintance, asked for an audience with her. The soldiers set up camp outside the walls.

"Buy from the villagers to keep our supplies stocked. Pay them well and treat them respectfully," Nicolette instructed her second-in-command.

"Of course, my lady," the battle-hardened warrior—one of Ravan's most trusted—acknowledged.

A castle sentry met Nicolette as she stepped from her horse. He fidgeted as though uncertain where to cast his gaze, finally settling it on his feet. "Please, my lady, our lord expects you, and King Wladyslaw is here as well. They request an audience with the lady of the Wintergrave Dynasty."

Then he flourished with a hat that was absurdly large for his head. Nicolette said nothing as she followed the man through the splendid castle corridors to the great hall where Count Vianden and King Wladyslaw waited.

* * *

When word that Ravan's bride approached Vianden, the count's curiosity grew. He recalled Salvatore's description of the "...beauty that could steal a sailor's heart from the sea," and imagination of the "beauty" had occupied most of his thoughts, especially because she commanded such an army.

The good count was without a bride and prone to appreciation of lovely women, though he would never consider overstepping a boundary. This was Ravan Wintergrave's wife. But, as a matter of consequence, he was so preoccupied with his ruminations of Nicolette that he jumped when the tall doors swung open.

Nothing could prepare him for what entered the great hall—a creature of such supreme composure in the way she moved. And she was beautiful, but also something else, like an exquisite piece of glass, a fractured, *very* sharp piece of glass.

Even at a distance, the count could see that her eyes were greener than he had ever seen—the color of emeralds. As she approached the two men in a peculiarly deliberate fashion—not at all as though she had just ridden over two hundred miles—her robes and long, black hair swirled about her.

Count Vianden chuckled nervously and said in a low voice to the king, "We finally meet the mother of the absconded girl. Let us see if she is as Salvatore claims, and if her daughter is indeed worthy of war."

The king cast a wry expression his way but said nothing as Nicolette halted, studying them in turn. Curiously, she was not captivated by men of great power in the way others were. Scarcely even curious about the two men, she was neither enthralled nor intimidated, and this was perhaps how her demeanor was perceived.

The count spoke first, sitting somewhat straighter in his chair as he drew his short beard to a neat point with his hand. "My lady, you do not wish to take a knee before the king?"

Nicolette's stare fixed on the count as she dropped briefly to one knee. "If he cannot endure without it, allow me to accommodate ritual."

Then as though she did not notice their surprise, she said flatly, "And now that we've satisfied convention, can you tell me how many days my husband is ahead of me and whether or not you have pledged soldiers to his forces?"

The count, nearly slack-jawed, only stared at Nicolette. So engrossed was he by the uncommon creature that he did not notice how the king, who likewise stared, declined to answer her question, his toe tapping nervously—unusual for the seasoned monarch.

Nicolette, expression unchanged, lifted her hand palm up and extended it gracefully toward the king as though she would receive something from him. Briefly closing her eyes, she lifted her chin, breathed in deeply, and exhaled.

When her eyes opened, she said, "Well then...so it has been three days."

The count was about to say something else when the king spoke for the first time. "Anyone might have told you that."

Nicolette allowed her hand to drop limply to her side. "Yes, they might have."

The king frowned. "But they did not."

"And thank you…for your gracious hospitality and generous contribution of arms to my husband." Nicolette spread both arms, tucked her chin, and bowed again.

It was the count's turn to be surprised when the king jumped up, swiftly descending the four steps to stand in front of Nicolette. The guards on either side of the throne immediately stepped forward, lances drawn, but he waved them aside, focused only on Nicolette.

"My lady, your husband is a noble man and worthy of our assistance."

Nicolette's voice carried mild surprise. "Of course, your highness. It is why I chose him, above all others, to stand by me."

The king's demeanor brightened even more. "Rumor has it that you finalized your *choice* on your wedding night with Adorno de Bourbon; that you slew him with your own hand."

She swept a hand casually to one side. "People do enjoy rumors, don't they? I find that rumors are best cast aside, buried, perhaps, in lieu of…good choices."

"Is it a good choice that your husband wages battle for the sake of one girl?" The count interjected as he also stepped down from his chair.

Nicolette met the dynamic ruler halfway, halting only after he did. "Who is to say that a single drop of rain does not carry with it more importance than an entire empire?"

Count Vianden felt a strange excitement take hold of the back of his neck. It ran down his spine and settled into the core of his belly in a thrilling way, and he inched even closer to Nicolette. "You speak riddles."

Nicolette said, "Consider for a moment how that drop might extinguish the spark that would start a whole nation on fire, burning it to the ground— would you then spare it?"

Both men fell silent, casting worried glances at each other. Finally, the king asked, "And Niveus is that drop?"

Nicolette became very serious. "Niveus…

…is *more*."

* * *

The next morning, Nicolette continued northeast with nearly eight hundred troops following her.

From the battlement of the castle, King Wladyslaw and Count Vianden watched as she crossed the river and headed toward Thorn.

"That was most unexpected and…most agreeable," the king admitted.

"I envy Lord Ravan, envy him very much," the count confessed as he watched the mercenary's bride disappear into the dense forest.

"Why, my dear friend! You could have any lady in the land!" The king slapped him jovially between the shoulder blades.

"Any but the one I now desire above all others." The count allowed a bittersweet smile and sighed. "I shall dream of that woman forevermore, for the Spaniard spoke the truth. And…" he rested his elbows on the battlement ledge, "if his appraisal of the girl is half as accurate as it was of her mother, I should have sent twice the army, for I am now greatly curious…of Niveus."

CHAPTER THIRTY-TWO

Malik's pale eyes betrayed *everything* as he waited for his bride, the grim crease of a smile foretelling his grand anticipation. Now, and forever, she would finally be his! And when Niveus stepped up the path to the sanctuary, so overcome was he at his great providence that he nearly staggered.

But Bora Vachir supported him by the arm and chuckled, "Steady yourself, my lord, and be patient! You'll have her in your bed soon enough!"

Several maidens, one of them Aya, walked on either side of Niveus, and behind her stepped four soldiers abreast, swords drawn. Malik had ordered it this way, in case she faltered, but it proved unnecessary. She walked as she always did, with such a slow deliberation, steady as the arc of the moon.

Finally, everyone was gathered outside the church doors for the solemnization of vows. As the priest droned, Niveus tipped her face upward, regarding the lonely arbor of barren tree branches, the winter long having taken their leafy robes from them. As though in reply, snow began to silently fall. Drifting mournfully downward, the downy flakes attached to Niveus' eyelashes and adorned the velvety softness of her midnight-blue gown. Through all of it, she scarcely moved, even breathing so shallow that she appeared as though frozen on the steps of the church.

The priest asked those few things that required of him before they would enter the church for the wedding mass. "Do you agree to marry this man?"

The small crowd seemed to inhale at once, collectively holding their breaths. One of the guards, sword still drawn, glanced nervously at his counterparts.

Niveus regarded none of them as she continued to look at the falling blanket of snow. "Yes," she murmured and said no more.

Malik nearly leapt in his excitement. It was official, and tomorrow would hold such wondrous opportunity for him and all of Red Robes!

Now, he would have power like never before!

He forced the iron ring onto Niveus' finger. Even then, she did not look at him, only allowed her hand to fall limply back to her side.

Malik's heart lurched. She was so...so *beautiful!* Yes! Why had he not seen it before, when he had smashed her face with his fist? Her hair, braided into many silver strands, was wound about perfectly, some of it as a wedding crown, others hanging long down her back. And her skin, in the icy cold of the day, looked as perfect as...as a winter's *queen*! Yes! She was now his queen!

All the words were spoken, and the etiquette was followed explicitly. God had been implored, disgrace vanquished, and all that was left to do was consummate the deed.

Niveus did not tremble as the moment arrived.

"I proclaim you now, by the grace of God, husband and wife." The priest folded his hands solemnly and bowed his head.

No cheers erupted from the small audience. No sighs of relief. Only the wind moaned its cold, lonely lament across the frozen land.

Malik turned to Niveus and stroked her cheek. "You know how much I love you," he murmured to his bride.

A single muted sob escaped someone's lips distantly in the small crowd.

Finally, Malik drew his hand from her and stepped back, addressing the crowd. "It is done!" He clapped both hands together. "A mass! Then we celebrate! Long live Red Robes!"

"Long live Red Robes!" a solitary, innocent child, standing next to his noble father, called back....

* * *

Malik shut his chamber door and rested his forehead against it, savoring this moment greatly. Viktar was vanquished, apparently disappeared into the night as the coward that he was—this was what the guards told him—and Klarin was long dead and still rotting in the woods nearby.

Additionally, Niveus had offered no resistance, and they were now married before every god that might object. No lightning bolt had sprung from the clouds, no mouth had uttered objection, and presently she stood in her wedding gown before his open balcony doors.

"Undress," he commanded, his head still resting against the door.

When he heard nothing in reply, he turned to find her still looking out the open balcony doors.

"I said…close the doors, Niveus, and *undress*."

"I love you," she murmured in a voice so low Malik could not hear. She whispered it to the gentle wind, inviting it to carry her words across the miles to the one they were intended for—for Viktar.

Malik was across the room in several long strides. Grasping Niveus by the shoulder, he dragged her away from the doors, thrust her toward the bed, and kicked the doors closed with a crash.

Staggering, she turned to face her attacker as he clawed at her gown, ruining the beautiful material, slinging her about like a dog's plaything. Ripping the bodice, he tore the garment from her body and stomped upon the remnants. Then, he shoved her, naked, onto the bed.

But this time, as Malik's intentions became clear, Niveus did not go to the safe place she went before. *This* time, as Malik towered over her, she did not escape to that haven of sanctity. No, for tonight she was stronger than she had ever been before, stronger because…she was in love.

Niveus kept her stare fixed fast on the monster, fixed on his eyes. And he saw that she knew his heart; knew that she beheld the filth of his small soul. It only enraged him.

"Part your legs," he demanded harshly as he struggled to loosen his trousers.

She did not

"Part your legs!" he screamed as he yanked feverishly on his penis.

She did not.

"Submit to your husband and ruler!" he insisted and grasped her by the ankles, flinging her legs apart before casting himself heavily on top of her.

Not a word did Niveus utter as the Prussian grunted, plunging himself into her. Not a cry escaped her lips as the man humped, rutting over her like a mongrel beast. Scarcely did she even blink as he grimaced and groaned, willing his climax be released. But…also…not once did he look her in the eye.

He finally moaned—an acrid, simpering sound—and sunk his teeth into Niveus' shoulder. Still, she did not move as the marital rape was finally fulfilled. Malik rolled heavily from her and drew a robe over his nakedness.

Only modestly satisfied, he grumbled, "Well, now, that should spring an heir from your womb!"

As she grasped the coverlet, drawing it slowly across her nakedness, Niveus' eyes shone with the faintest hint of happy distraction, so faint that he almost…*almost* didn't notice.

"What? You find it improbable?"

"No. Not improbable, my lord." She swung her long, thin legs from the side of the massive bed. The bloody bite showed starkly red against her pale skin, and she drew the coverlet over her shoulder, obscuring the weeping wound. "I find it *impossible*."

Malik interpreted her reply as a consequence of rumors—rumors of his infertility. "It is different now!" he insisted. "The gods have finally given me a woman worthy of delivering an heir to me. You *will* bear me a son."

Niveus faced him. "It is impossible, because a child already lives within me."

Malik's face contorted in confusion, dismay, then rage as wretched awareness settled into him like crooked bones in an old man. "*No...*" was all he could whisper. Then he screamed, "No!"

Niveus voice carried with it a strength Malik had never before observed. "Cast yourself upon me to exhaustion, Malik, but it is only futility, for a child will be born before autumn's end, and it will be... *Viktar's* son."

Malik raised both hands slowly, his clenched fists hanging above his head in mute rage. He trembled and swayed, finally screaming, "Nooo!" and plunged himself at Niveus, grasping her by the wrist and dragging her across the room. Flinging the balcony doors wide, he shoved her, still wrapped in only the coverlet, to the balcony's edge.

"Viktar will never have this child! I won't allow it!" He twisted her about, wrapping his hands around her neck.

"Do you hear me, Niveus? *Never*!"

The coverlet fell from her shoulders onto the thick blanket of snow as he bent her naked body backward over the railing. She gulped, her hands clutching his wrists, eyes shut tight as her body swayed, teetering between the snowy balcony and five-story fall to the courtyard below.

Malik raged. "I will kill him! I will track him down and kill him! Your bastard child will never have a father!"

Just when it seemed he would hurl her from the balcony, there came an urgent pounding on the bedroom chamber door.

"Leave me!" Malik screamed over his shoulder.

"Open the door!" Bora Vachir insisted from the other side, and he pounded again. "Open the door, Malik! There is someone here to see you!"

"It is my wedding night, and I will not be disturbed!" Malik released Niveus, and she crumbled onto the snowy balcony, gasping raggedly.

"You will want to take this visitor," Bora's voice warned in such a way that he could not be denied.

"I will kill you myself if it is anything other than *Hell* at my gates!"

"Open the door…"

"Stay where you are." Malik shot a murderous look at his bride and stomped to his bedroom door. Unlatching it, he flung it open to discover Bora Vachir leaning with his arm up against the jamb, head hanging on his elbow.

"Who *is* it?" Malik demanded.

Bora raised his head. "He claims to be…

…Ravan's *son*."

* * *

It was late when Malik stormed into the assembly hall. Gathered about were his most trusted advisors, captains, and guards. In actuality, he trusted none of them except Bora. And that was whom he set immediately upon.

"Where is he?"

Bora did not answer.

Instead, an advisor, the one foremost and center, dipped his bald, wart-speckled head. "He waits in the reception hall."

"Why is he not in my dungeons? He claims to be my enemy and I see no army outside my gates. I would have him as my prisoner!"

"My lord, you mustn't say that! If he is indeed the Lord Wintergrave's son, as he claims, his father most assuredly knows that he is here and will come for him."

"You don't know that!" Malik challenged.

The advisor, his shoulders bent forward like a crane, dipped his head again. "My lord, it is simply unreasonable to assume otherwise. We have only recently obtained a truce with the King of Poland. Your army needs time to recover. If you invite another conflict, it could prove—"

Malik would hear none of it. "He claims to be Ravan's son?"

Bora scowled. "How should we know who the bastard really is? Likely he has heard of your good fortune and only wishes to attach himself to it."

"So you believe I should pay him off?" Malik mused.

"No. I believe you should kill him."

This surprised Malik greatly, that Bora should so swiftly go in *that* direction. He considered his most trusted ally for only a moment before exclaiming, "Bring him to me! I would speak to the man myself!"

Bora snorted and left the room.

* * *

Risen stood between two guards and waited. All the while, he studied his surroundings. Obvious wealth, meticulously outfitted troops, and...a blanketing air of discontent in the subjects' eyes were evident everywhere.

His father had coached him well, had taught him what it meant to step into a viper's lair. He waited, right arm crossed over with his hand resting lightly on his sword, and sighed. Even the air here hung heavily with unspoken regret. Red Robes was, indeed, forsaken.

Finally, when it appeared his only recourse would be to kill the guards and press on, the door swung open and a Mongol warrior entered.

Bora Vachir circled the stranger, his lip curled. Risen knew the look, had first seen it as a boy of only twelve. It was an expression of cruelty, of one who enjoyed hurting those who were weak and helpless. But *he* was not one of those.

In less than a moment, Risen had the Mongol appraised—the blood of others yet to be washed from his blade, the arrogance of his stance, the constant shifting of his eyes. No, this was no noble warrior. This was a murderer, but it didn't matter. Risen was his father's son and no longer a boy of twelve. He would gut this monster if need be.

"Our lord has agreed to speak with you," Bora Vachir announced, his stare now fixed on the young man.

"You have my sister, and I intend to see her. If seeing your lord is requisite, so be it."

When the air of complacency fell from Bora's expression, Risen could not know that it was because he so resembled the only man who had ever forced the Mongol to cower in fear. He was unaware of how Bora wondered if Ravan was, in actuality, already dead, and his ghost had risen—come to finish that which he had not before—for Risen looked that much like his father.

Vachir motioned to the guards. When one of them pushed forward as though he would escort his captive forcibly from the room, Risen set the man back in his steps with only a stern look. Then, he followed the Mongol of his own accord to the throne room.

Vachir was noticeably silent as the guards marched alongside Risen, escorting him to front and center of Malik. "You have my sister. I wish to see her," Risen said. He knew straightaway, when he saw Malik, that this was the man who had taken Niveus from her home. *This*...was the viper.

Malik appeared surprised and shifted nervously on the throne.

"Your...*sister*? *Why* would I hold your sister? My subjects are free to come and go as they please. Go. Look about the town and see if she is there."

"I did not say you held her, although I know that you do. My sister is not in your village. Niveus is here, in your castle, and I will see her now."

* * *

How did he know she was here? There is no way he could have known!

Malik blurted stupidly and spread his arms wide. "*Niveus*? Oh! Why, yes! She is my bride—lady of the realm!"

Risen's hand went again to his sword. "I demand to see her, and if what you say is true, you are now my family and owe me at least that courtesy."

"So you say…" Malik's pasted-on smile dropped away. "And if I do not?"

"If you do not, my father will be here with an army, and your realm will fall. And he will kill you, Malik, if I do not first. So consider carefully your words, for it would be a fitting death, one you will beg to have finished."

Malik could no longer contain himself and leapt to his feet!

"How dare you speak to me in such a way! Come to my house and threaten me!" He motioned with one hand, and the guards dipped their lances toward Risen. Bora unsheathed his terrible blade as well.

"Let me see my sister." Risen insisted and ignored the guards, his intent remaining fixed firmly on Malik.

Just when it seemed an impasse had been reached and a fight would be the only recourse, the hall door opened with a heavy *clunk* behind Risen. He turned in time to see Niveus, followed by a small, dark woman, step solemnly into the room. "Niveus…" he cried softly and stepped toward her.

As they approached each other, they were stopped—Niveus by guards, and Risen by Vachir's scimitar blade.

Risen began to unsheathe his own sword, but Niveus called out, "No!" and both men halted. "He is my brother. Hurt him at your peril," she called to Malik.

"You can hurt no one, my dear! Not even to save *yourself*!" Malik scoffed and waved the threat aside. "I know that about you now. But look who has come to see you! Your long-lost brother!"

He laughed and stepped past Risen to join his wife, taking her roughly by the arm and jerking her close.

Risen spoke only to his sister. "Have you been hurt?"

"Yes, but I am recovered."

"Did he force you to leave?"

"No."

Risen was surprised at her answer, but he knew Niveus, knew her well enough to know that although she was always truthful, *yes* could mean *no*.

"And you are his wife?"

"Yes."

"Of your free will?"

"Yes and no."

Risen sorted out the details nearly immediately. For whatever reason, the tyrant had taken her and forced her to marry. Why she had gone willingly was still unclear, but he was sure it had to do with the young Prussian they had discovered in the forest—the one who was at this very moment returning with an army.

"Release her. Allow her to decide her own fate. If she chooses to stay, I will give her my assent and leave," Risen said.

"I will not! It is not her decision to make!" Malik protested.

Bora Vachir spoke for the first time since they had entered the hall.

"A *tournament*."

His announcement drew everyone to silence, and they all turned in surprise to regard the Mongol. Only Niveus staggered a step forward and cried softly, "*No.*"

There were looks of confusion about the hall. Surely the advisors and soldiers wondered at the bizarre sequence of events. Was this not the brother of their new lady? And if the blood was bad, he was but a single man. Why not banish him—bind him and send his horse beyond the edge of the realm. He certainly had not the power to object!

What they could not know was the burning hatred Malik still held for Ravan, and the grievous need for atonement Bora Vachir required for his cowardice of many years before. Both men would be greatly gratified by killing this man. Both wanted it, like the perfect poison to kill a dying thirst.

Malik repeated with growing enthusiasm, "A tournament! Yes! That is a splendid idea!"

Risen did not hear his sister's repeated soft cry, only looked about in confusion as Bora stabbed his blade tip first into the air then at him.

"At first light. You...and I, to the death. If you live, she goes free. If you die...she stays forever."

Niveus' staggered against Malik's hold. "I do not consent to this barter."

"Silence!" Malik spat at her and took his turn at complicating things. "Yes! A tournament, to the death!" He drew the damaged Damascus blade and stepped away, pointing it with finality at Niveus, his eyes locked on Risen. "A tournament, three days hence, or she dies...tonight."

It had been a long while since Risen had stomached such rage as he did at that moment. Five years to be exact. "I will fight," Risen said firmly.

Niveus tried once more to reach her brother, but guards grasped her by either arm. "*No*. Risen—"

"Then it is done!" Malik lowered his blade! "Tonight we feast! In three days, a tournament!"

* * *

Risen was cast to the dungeons to wait out the three days. It was Malik's intention to have him weakened for the tournament.

The first night had nearly passed, Risen thought, but was not sure, for there was no light to mark the passing hours. At least he was not chained, and he sat with his head resting heavily on his knees, his arms around bent legs. The only sound that disturbed him was the squeaking and scurrying of rats.

Just as he nearly dozed, the cell door creaked open, and a single torch lit the shadows. He squinted, uncertain who called on him. Then he saw. It was the slave woman—the one who entered the hall that first day. And behind her…was Niveus.

He was on his feet and covered the small distance of the cell in an instant, wrapping his sister in an embrace he intended never to break.

"Oh, are you hurt? Has he hurt you?" He nearly cried tears of relief just to be close to her again.

"I am not." Niveus appeared so small and frail in the arms of the warrior and pushed both hands at his chest so she could look up into his face.

"Why have you not escaped? Taken yourself into the night as you have done so often before, at *home*?" he asked.

"She cannot," Aya explained. "Malik guards every gate with a legion. It is too much for her."

Niveus brushed it aside. "You mustn't fight Bora Vachir. Leave at once, and do not come back."

"I cannot! I will not leave without you, and if we flee together, it will be war between the realms. Countless will die, and you know this land already suffers gravely under Malik's rule."

"Countless will die either way. We cannot control what is to come," Niveus replied.

"*I can.* I will destroy the barbarian in the tournament and hold Malik to his word. Then, if he breaks his vow, Viktar and Velecent will have soon arrived. They can hold the front until Father joins them."

Niveus did not appear at all surprised that Risen knew about Viktar.

"War will have its way, but…" She looked across the black vacancy of the cell as though she saw what was to be playing out on the stone walls. Her hand slipped from his and she whispered, "I cannot lose you, brother. Aya can help you past the gates."

Risen was overwhelmed by her need to protect him at all costs. It had always been this way, but this was not five years before. He no longer sat balanced upon the precipice of eternal despair.

He tried to smile but failed. "I am no longer a boy, Niveus. A few days in a dungeon will not be my demise, and we have the grace of at least that much time. No…" he said with finality, "I will not leave you with Malik. You will go with me or…I die here."

For the first time in all his life, Risen saw tears well in his sister's eyes. It so alarmed him that he looked hastily about as though he might find something in the cell with which to abate her sorrow. He was more confused than he had ever been.

"Why do you cry? I am my father's son! I can kill this man; he is *nothing*, and I've fought worse! Tell me you believe this of me. Tell me!"

Niveus only dropped her sorrowful gaze and wrapped her arms once more about her brother. Then…she just held him.

He sighed and kissed the top of her head. "It is the right thing to do, for us, Niveus. For the people of this realm. You have taught me so often that destiny will have its way. You know it is not my place to deny it now."

Niveus said nothing more. Then, they knelt together on the dungeon floor so that they might spend some time together. Such a strange little group they were, so different from one another, yet so connected. Aya revealed a small basket of food and fresh water, and Risen ate, greatly fortified by it.

Now, there was nothing to be said or done except wait…two more days.

CHAPTER THIRTY-THREE

They were nearing the heart of the beast; Ravan knew it, for they had already crossed the invisible boundary of Red Robes late yesterday. Today, he believed he could feel the air become more thin and acrid, the way it always seemed as he approached an enemy. Curious—that always lifted once the monster was dead.

Onward they pressed, slipping into the wolf's lair like the last thread of smoke from a dying fire. No one was better at moving unseen than Ravan, and he would reach Malik's door, veritably undiscovered, within two days' ride at most.

Cresting a small ridge, which afforded them a clear but sheltered line of sight along a tree-lined valley, Ravan and Salvatore rode in silence. It was Ravan's horse that first noticed something in the great distance, its head shooting high, ears swept forward in keen interest.

This was not Ravan's familiar battle steed, for that one, exhausted, had been long replaced. So the mercenary slid from the animal and swiftly clasped his hand gently across the horse's nose, just above the nostrils, to keep it from trumpeting a greeting to those distant others it believed it smelled, saw, or heard.

Salvatore did the same, edging up closer to his friend as he did. "Horse?"

Ravan nodded, all the while studying the distant tree line. Nothing. But horses were not to be ignored, and finally, there within the cover of the trees, they saw him, a single rider jogging along, nearly concealed by the woods.

The man wore light battle leathers and had an official crest on the saddle blanket. He posted his horse almost noiselessly, balancing over the withers of the beast as he searched left and right.

Abruptly, the rider turned back, tracking deeper and in the other direction, back into the woods.

Once the horse was gone, Ravan released pressure on his mount's nose and motioned with two fingers, indicating they had discovered an outrider. Still, for a long moment, he said nothing, finally murmuring under his breath, "Army scout."

He and Salvatore turned back to investigate, and scarcely two hours later saw what they expected...well, not exactly what they expected....

A small band of men rode swiftly through the forest, south. But as they neared and stepped from the forest onto the edge of a clear meadow, Ravan's surprise grew, for behind them, line after line of a mounted battalion drew into the clearing, followed by a foot army. As the wave moved remarkably silent into the meadow, Ravan counted—one, two, nearly three hundred soldiers.

He and Salvatore pushed back down the small, thickly-wooded hillside to where their horses were tied. Then, swinging onto their horses, they too moved swiftly and silently through the woods, down along a narrow, dry creek bed at a trajectory parallel to but hidden from the army and scout. All the while, they remained downwind from the advancing troops.

Finally, when they were far enough ahead, Ravan leapt from his horse, tossed the reins to Salvatore, and left him and the two horses down a small hollow as he scurried up a small knoll to a sufficient vantage point. Dropping to his belly, he inched, hidden from view, up over the knoll. Here he could study them more closely and, more importantly, the leader of the force.

What he saw surprised him even more. The infantry moved efficiently and insidiously, like an ant swarm—obviously well-organized. Their weapons were held at casual readiness, and the foot soldiers wore light chainmaille, affording them mobility without excessive fatigue. Ravan frowned. The troops were well conditioned, for they kept pace with the horses without obvious distress, and the animals were also clearly fit, moving easily off the leg aids of their riders.

All of this was instantly clear to Ravan, as he was skilled at noticing details such as these. It was these details that could determine failure or success in battle, and failure, to him, was never an option. He took a deep breath. This army was a worthy opponent, crafted from discipline and cunning, and could take on an army twice their size with success if the other was less so. He had seen it happen many times.

Lastly, Ravan studied the leader. The man rode in front, not behind captains for additional protection. He also wore battle leathers and full armor and sat tall upon a striking grey horse. Ravan drew a sudden sharp breath. Blinking, he stared again.

It was seldom the mercenary could be taken by surprise, but today he was, for the strange leader was young, keenly unusual, and...*familiar*. It was *Viktar*, Malik's nephew.

And alongside him rode...

...Velecent.

* * *

It was Wednesday, and the morning broke with sun for the first time in many days, glistening happily across the blanket of yesterday's late-winter snow—the only happiness to be found in the icy realm. Before long, those who had been invited and were expected to be present, would file in, somber faces flush with regretful anticipation as they found their seats. This would not be the first time Malik had drawn up a tournament. Generally, it involved some poor soul accused of a victimless crime.

The man...or woman, would inevitably fall to whatever warrior was pitted against them. Then Malik would claim victory for the realm, a feast would be held for those of notable importance, and Red Robes would sag once more beneath the coagulating mantle of blood that was its namesake.

None of the guests would be notified as to what today's battle entailed, only that the outcome would set Red Robes along a new path—a new destiny. This was the only thing that made the event stand out as unusual.

Groundskeepers raked and shoveled, clearing away the arena so the combatants would have adequate footing for the tournament. It would not do to have one fall too quickly, Malik warned. *What sport would there be in that?*

And because this tournament decided the trajectory of his marriage—of course, he had no qualms about the outcome—there was no element of ceremony left unaddressed. Banners flew, vendors provided blankets for the patrons' knees, and canopies were erected in case the weather did not hold.

Before long, preparations were complete and the guests were seated, only half filling the steep stands of the open arena.

* * *

Inside the castle, Bora Vachir made final preparations for the battle, his aides helping him adjust his battle leathers. There was to be no armor today, for armor obscured blood. But that would simply not do for Bora. He wore a single plate under his uniform, over his heart.

Ravan's son, on the other hand, would be stripped to only his tunic. Bora knew he not appear at too great an advantage to the audience.

Malik entered the room in high spirits. "Leave!" he commanded the attendants.

Bora, ordinarily at ease, was nervous. He adjusted and readjusted his bracers and paced the floor like a cat amongst dogs. "I have been ready to fight for over an hour. The constant delays wear on my nature!"

Ignoring him, Malik motioned for someone else to enter.

The mage was bent like a vulture and with about as many sparse hairs on his head. Spidery thin, he wore a long, velvet-trimmed robe, and his hands were clasped and obscured by the generous sleeves. His face was a mask of impropriety—his happy sneer exposing a nearly toothless mouth—and he moved to the table with what seemed, to Bora, like too much deliberation.

With considerable display, the sorcerer withdrew and wielded for all to see that which he hid in his sleeve, a small ceramic urn. Placing the urn on the table, he loosened the lid, revealing what appeared to be water.

Bora could not summate the purpose for the visit and growled, resuming his pacing, "I am not thirsty."

"Your weapon," the twisted little man crooned and extended a branchlike arm, slowly unfurling one knotted twig of a finger after another.

Malik fairly burst with anticipation. "It is poison! Don't you see? It will destroy Ravan's son! Do it! Do as he says, and the victory will be yours for the taking!"

Bora would not be immediately convinced, taking it first as an insult. "You doubt I can fell the mongrel? You believe Ravan's son could land victorious against a warrior such as I?"

Easily prone to indignation, Bora's hackles rose with the very thought of it. But he became more serious when the smirk fell from Malik's face.

"Defeat is not an option. True, you are my most trusted warrior, but provisions must be in place, for...*security's* sake. Niveus is a jewel I cannot risk losing her."

"Your blade," the mage wheedled again, his queerly opaque eyes suggesting he was also gratified by the prospect of the unseemly advantage.

Bora wavered but finally drew the twin scimitars from the rack, holding the blades so he could more closely inspect the razor edges. "What does it do, this poison?"

The mage drew his parched tongue across decaying gums and spoke as though of his favorite child. "'Tis an adder's venom, most deadly, though your foe will not feel its sting at first. But take care you do not cut yourself.

Even the slightest nick will slow a man sure as spring will have its thaw."

The wicked little man wheezed a barking cough. "Fifteen minutes and Wintergrave's son will first appear to tire from the fray. Then his breath will come only with great effort and he will be unable to lift his weapon. For you, it would be easy to sustain the drama, but even if you stepped aside, he would simply succumb to the paralytic."

Bora was inclined to refuse, but doubt is stickier than valor, and so he gave in, allowing the fiend to paint the edge of both blades. Then, carefully, he deposited them in their scabbards and followed Malik as they made their way to the arena.

* * *

Niveus appeared to be sleeping as she sat on the edge of the bed, her hands lying softly in her lap. She had been like this for nearly two hours, not moving, for the moment was near at hand.

She had not returned to Malik's room since her wedding night. After her announcement, he had been so enraged that he was, for now, unwilling to summon her. "I will rip the child from your womb once your heathen brother is dead!" were the last words she heard him say before he locked her once more in the tower's keep.

Niveus' eyes opened just before a soft rap came upon the door. A key toggled the lock, and in stepped Aya, a somber look upon her face.

"Niveus, it is time."

* * *

Risen's muscles ached. It was damp and icy-cold in the cell, and he had been still for too long. At intervals, he had pushed himself to standing, testing the strength that remained in his legs, and swung his arms, willing warmth back into them.

Now, as the hour drew near, he knelt, head bowed and prayed. In the unforgiving, hollow darkness of the cell, he summoned first that which might give him strength today. *Let my arm be true, let my legs not falter, and allow my blade to obey,* he murmured.

His prayer was for fortitude, for Risen had no fear. No, fear was not even a shadow of a whisper upon Ravan's son this day. In fact, the minutes could not pass swiftly enough, for today he wanted, more than anything, to face Bora Vachir and...to strike the barbarian to the ground.

Then he prayed again.

For those who have suffered beneath the Mongol's cowl of cruelty, I will avenge you. For those who have fallen beneath his tyranny, I will give you peace. And, if you have naught better of which to occupy yourself, Satan, today I send a monster to your gates.

As Risen's soul aligned itself for the task at hand and his heart found courage and peace, he was surprised to find that his thoughts wandered to another time and place, long ago. He was no longer a young warrior sitting in a cell...he was a boy—eleven years old—playing in a forest not far from his home. And a girl, not much older than he and with the face of an angel, was stepping from behind a tree, dressed in boy's clothes and with such a look of triumphant happiness on her face.

He was nearly unable to breathe; she was so *beautiful*. And when Sylvie smiled at him, it broke his heart more perfectly than he believed possible.

Now, sitting weary and cold in the cell—his head a heavy weight in his hands and waiting to fight Bora Vachir—he smiled softly and whispered...

... *Sylvie, I love you.*

CHAPTER THIRTY-FOUR

Bora Vachir stepped into the arena amid trumpets and the forced applause of the home front. Slowly unsheathing both swords, he held them high above his head and turned slowly so that all might behold and fear his great presence. He wore a scalp-helmet, horned and set with glass fragments so that it would cast glare upon his opponent. His battle leathers creaked with newness and polish, and his beard was so greased with pig fat that it shone in the sunlight.

He told himself to be calm and to remember how badly he wanted this. He had dreamed of this moment ever since that day on the battlefield, never expecting to have such an opportunity. For Bora, today's battle represented the supreme slaughter—not the killing of Ravan through his only son, but the swallowing of the last ounce of cowardice the Mongol believed he carried in the dirty recesses of his being. Finally he would be rid of his great nemesis, purging it from himself at last.

The barbarian let go a roar and pumped his weapons repeatedly to the sky, imploring the throng to stand behind him. His eyes, gleaming with the gluttonous anticipation of an ill-fated victory, eventually found Malik in the stands, and he saluted his lord.

Malik sat in his finest robes as though he were a king, a scepter balanced in his right hand. With it he gestured toward Vachir as though he would knight him, and the Mongol bent a knee, head reverently bowed. It was all pomp for, truthfully, there was nothing and no one Bora hailed other than himself.

As Vachir raised his head, his attention became fixed not on Malik but on the one who sat at his side. Dressed in a gown as white as she was, Niveus appeared carved from winter itself. She stared hard and fast...at Bora, her eyes burning red as any blood he had ever spilled.

His grinning smirk faded ever so much.

The white witch had vexed him from the first moment he saw her, and briefly he wondered at what it might take to kill her, of course without Malik knowing. He blinked. She did not, and it unnerved him—unnerved him so much that he scarcely noticed the murmurs from the crowd for the dark warrior who entered the stadium behind him.

* * *

Risen, shackled at the wrists and ankles, stepped from the black shadows and blinked in the bright sunlight of midday. Guards were posted on either side, spears at the ready, and the one behind him shoved him farther into the arena. Obligatory jeers and slurs erupted from the modest crowd as the shackles were removed. He didn't notice these at all. Instead he squinted, scanning the audience left and right until he saw the fiend who postured from across the expanse of the grounds. Scarcely giving him an ounce of his attention, Risen narrowed his gaze and saw…her.

Niveus rose slowly to her feet, one hand lifting slowly as she extended it first palm down and then palm up toward her brother. A glimpse of a smile tugged at the corner of Risen's mouth, and he swallowed heavily.

Malik would have none of it and motioned with his scepter. Guards moved up and to either side of her, forcing her back to sitting.

The heckling faded as, lifting his hand, Risen took the first two fingers and touched them gently, patiently, first over his heart and then to his lips, all the while looking only upon her face.

There was a stricken murmur from the crowd, as though a wretched, undeserving beast had, for the first time, witnessed a compassionate hand.

Bora began to distantly circle, and Risen pulled his attention from his sister to face him, his intense expression of love replaced by something altogether different. He reached without looking and retrieved from a guard a blade, *his* blade—the one he had fashioned for himself after years of careful tutelage by his father.

This sword was as familiar to the warrior as his own hand, and as the sharp glare of the bright, blue day abated and his vision became clearer, he swung the weapon, elegantly and in several sweeping arcs, left and right. It was poetic, what he did, and the crowd was immediately mesmerized, for as the handsome young stranger manipulated the sword in a series of familiar but complex maneuvers, it was a dance—a beautiful, deadly dance.

Risen could not see the cold-set expression on his face. He could not see the tempered clench of his jaw or the fierce determination that lay in his eyes, certain as a rising sun. And Bora did not advance upon him. No, it was Ravan's son who stepped first…toward the Mongol barbarian.

As the young warrior neared the Mongol, his wits sharpened and his focus became keenly in tune with this battle of the most vital sort. In his veins ran his father's blood, and he knew how to gauge this enemy. Most critically, he knew Bora was no amateur.

He studied Vachir, noticed the machination of his methods as the man schlepped his twin blades to shoulder height. Even so, he knew that what the Mongol lacked in finesse and valor would be made up for in brute strength. Above all, Risen knew the heart of this one, had heard from Aya and Niveus of the man's insatiable thirst for blood. No, he would not underestimate this foe.

Risen was awake, more awake than he had been in a long time. This was a good moment, for the world would be a better place rid of Bora Vachir, and Niveus would be free. He breathed in deeply of the chill air. He could feel the wind whip through his beard, could feel it on the back of his hands, wakening every pore to his destiny, requesting from his heart the steady beat that would feed him for battle, and it was *good*.

For the second time since stepping into the arena, a smile tugged at his lips, begged to be released, for only once had Risen ever wished to destroy a man as greatly as he wished to destroy *this* one. He would call upon everything his father had ever taught him—every year, day, hour, and minute that Ravan had schooled his son to be what he was—a champion and, more importantly, a survivor.

He swung his sword again, more firmly now, and the blade arced and spun, appearing to take on a life of its own.

Bora roared and hurled himself at Risen, crisscrossing the sickle blades back and forth. But the air between would have none of the younger man, and Risen feinted easily, stepped left, and took the sharp initiative, counter striking in the midst of his attack. Swiftly binding Vachir's right arm in such a way that he could not swing across with his left scimitar, Risen swung his free fist, smashing the Mongol's nose even flatter than it already was.

Vachir, momentarily dazed by the blow, staggered backward, and the moment would have been a gravely tactical one for Risen, except that a dog—*Malik's* dog—bolted from a darkened passage and streaked across the grounds. As Risen raised his sword to land a blow on the Mongol, the beastly hound grasped and sunk its teeth into Risen's calf, dragging his attention from the fight.

Bora collected himself, rallied, and raised a blade, swinging it down toward Risen.

With a heavy groan, Risen thrust the flat of his blade, intercepting Bora's strike, and spun the Mongol's weapon to the dirt, feinted, and with his back to Vachir, launched an elbow, catching Bora again across the bridge of his nose. This time, the bigger man stumbled, blood gushing down his chin and neck. All the while, the hound thrashed, its jaws firmly locked on Risen's leg.

Risen drew a sharp breath, but the only cry to be heard was *Malik's* when Risen, leaning backward, blindly swung his blade in a sweeping arc, double-fisted, behind his neck and back. After the sword completed its arc, all that had hold of Risen's leg was Kobal's head, for the decapitated body of Malik's dog fell away.

Malik pounded with both fists on the railing as the crowd leapt to their feet, cheering. When the mongrel's jaws loosened and fell from Risen's calf, he spitted the skull between the eyes and raised the head, jaws frothy red, and flung it at Bora Vachir. Then, he motioned with two fingers, inviting the Mongol to be the next to suffer such a fate.

Circling again, Bora kicked the killer hound's head away as he broke the measure of the fight.

Risen countered with a tempo that caused the Mongolian to fall back, bewilderment mixed with rage on his face. All the while, Risen's forte defended the critical line between his body and the vicious scimitar.

Three, four, five, blows, fell on the Mongol, and all the while Bora was scarcely able to engage Risen's blade. Cut on both forearms, his shoulder, and across his abdomen—the Mongol was now struggling to wield the scimitar.

Spinning in desperation, Bora whipped out recklessly at Risen's head, but the younger deftly bent at the waist, ducked and skirted the blade, stepping behind his foe so that he was able to drag his own sword across the Mongol's hamstring, half-severing it.

Vachir, his face contorted as a demon, howled and staggered about, his one leg hobbled from the wound.

Wrapping his lead finger around his weapon's ricasso, Risen aimed, willing the tip to do its bidding, and thrust. Through Bora's battle leathers the weapon cut, chest center, and...*deflected* off the plate armor hidden beneath.

When Risen's blade glanced away, his dismay was only briefly evident, but enough that the Mongol gained a moment's advantage.

Sacrificing his hand, Bora grasped at Risen's blade, pawing it away, and hacked wildly, willing his blade to touch Ravan's son.

In the ensuing melee, Bora was finally shoved away, but only after barely cutting Risen across the back of his hand.

Bora's maniacal expression brightened as though the victory, absurdly, was already his. He backed away, held his scimitar across the flat with both hands in a measured guard pose—one meant only to defend.

The crowd uttered calls of foul as confusion spread across the coliseum.

Risen halted, uncertain. Why did the baboon smirk like a crazed lunatic? Bora was three limbs injured, a weapon down, and winded. Risen was scarcely winded and, except for a mild cut on the hand, unharmed.

As he moved on Bora, two more hounds lunged from the barracks. It was frustratingly poor sport, and Risen snarled—not that he must engage the beasts, but that it drew him for what he burned to do; to sink his blade in the Mongol's throat, for no armor would prevent that killing blow, and he would *not* miss.

Stepping aside so that the hounds drove more in together, Risen swung, de-legged the front of one beast, and followed through, low and up, catching the other in the throat. Leaving this one dead, and the other thrashing about on only its back legs, Risen turned again to Bora…

…and coughed.

His sword dipped, barely, not even an inch, and he paused.

Bora stabbed at thin air, still afraid to close the gap, and gasped a harsh, barking laugh. The crowd booed and hissed at him.

Risen halted, blinking thickly, and coughed again. He was vaguely aware of the Mongol's increasing laughter as he tried unsuccessfully to lift his blade. Instead, it slipped from his hand and dropped to the frozen ground with a soft thud.

Then…he fell.

* * *

Bora advanced on Risen, who now languished on his knees, head dropped heavily to his chest. A true coward, Vachir kicked Risen in the chest, shoving the younger man onto his back. When Ravan's son made no effort to rise, Bora raised his weapon high and plunged it downward. But his aim was poor, and instead of striking Risen in the heart, he stabbed him in the right chest, collapsing his lung.

Risen flinched, his feet lifting off the ground, but remained unmoving—helpless upon his back. Bora howled fiendishly, the bloodlust surging through his veins, but before he could lift and swing again, a rare voice broke the stunned silence of the crowd and shot across the vacant, cruel air.

"Stop!"

All turned to see Niveus running out the gate and across the frozen earth.

Bora hesitated but then reset his weapon as though he would ignore her. By then, however, she was near enough that her repeated command stayed his strike.

"Stop!" Niveus cried and fell to her brother's side

Guards swept in, prepared to drag the girl away, but Malik roared, "Leave her!" He rose in his seat, the epitome of delirious excitement. "Leave them alone and...*watch*!"

Confused murmurs ripped a second time through the crowd, and heads whipped left and right, looking for accountability.

Bora, wrapped in his own slow-witted perplexity, challenged Malik, "But he is dead! Mine to kill!"

Malik shrieked to everyone present, "See for yourselves your queen—my bride! Behold, one and all, as she denies death to those of my choosing!"

The crowd waited as though suspended in time, to observe what strange wonder Niveus might perform.

CHAPTER THIRTY-FIVE

†

All he saw was the blue of the sky, bluer than he had ever seen. Then, Niveus' face obscured everything as she bent over him, her hair hanging about them like a sterling veil, hiding them from everything else. It gave his great joy that she was so close, but her expression—it was so worried, so...sad.

He coughed and tried to speak. *"Niveus..."*

It was all that he could say, and even the enshrouding canopy of silver seemed to fade until all that was left was darkness.

"Risen," he heard someone whisper and felt a firm hand upon his chest. "Come to me...*now*."

* * *

Ravan's son could make nothing out, for he was engulfed in total darkness, without pain or wound. It was curious, this blank, black space, but he could feel his feet beneath him as he turned slowly about, could feel that he moved, but still nothing, until....

Distantly, a warm beam of light shone, soft as a moonlit kiss. The ray was of an uncertain, happy type—the kind that moved in threads when sunlight dared dance upon water or...her hair.

The light did not call for him, but it spoke in his mind as surely as though it had.

"I am here. Come to me now."

Just when he almost took a step toward it, he felt a hand land softly upon his shoulder and turned about to see Niveus gazing up at him, eyes gently pleading.

"Wait. *Please*...I can save you."

As a sudden, profound realization crept from his feet upward, finally sweeping like a hurricane across his heart, Risen looked longingly over his shoulder once more at the gentle beams of light. They danced in the distance, like the perfect promise of a bright summer's day.

"Risen, don't leave," he heard Niveus whisper again. "You can't. I...I *love* you." Her voice broke like a thin branch beneath the cruel weight of snow.

He took both her hands in his and brought them to his lips, kissing them softly. "But, Niveus, *she* is there."

A tear slipped down Niveus' cheek. "But you don't have to leave, not yet. I can help you. You can stay here until...until...."

He brushed his thumb against her cheek and smiled, sad and sweet.

This time, when he glanced at the meadow, there *she* was, the light illuminating the long ringlets of her hair in such a beautiful way. But it was not her hair, nor even her face that he noticed. It was the eternal kindness of her eyes. They were exactly as he remembered them.

Sylvie, from the great distance, lifted a hand, reaching, toward Risen.

He pulled his gaze away and looked again at Niveus, brushing a tear from her cheek. "You know I love you. But you also know I want nothing more than to be with *her*. I've been trapped, separated from happiness. But now...I am free."

* * *

She knew.

For the first time ever, Niveus understood what had kept her brother sitting upon the ledge for so long, those many years ago—when Sylvie died. It had been one thing to sit near him, to carry the weight of his sorrow when he no longer could, but she had never understood completely the origin of his pain.

Now...she did.

Risen kissed her softly on the cheek, his beautiful face alive with splendid anticipation. Niveus could not recall ever seeing him so alive. He looked down, toward her belly. "And I have a *nephew*." Then his happy smile became more serious. "And you love Viktar."

I do.

She did not say the words, only thought them. But her brother heard them clear as though she had spoken, and it gave him great joy. Risen pulled her close, arms around her shoulders so his lips were close to her ear.

"Then…you understand."

He sighed, his breath soft and warm on her skin. "I love you, Niveus, and I would never have found my way if not for you. *Thank you*."

As he turned from her, he was finally free. The years of suffering sorrow slid from his shoulders and fell with a crash at her feet, and his pain became…*hers*.

Opening the fingers of her hand, she let Risen slip from her.

Then, Niveus watched as her brother stepped from this world to the next. In the distant glow of light, she saw him take Sylvie into his arms and drop his lips to hers. And she saw Sylvie…kiss him back.

The dancing beam retreated, fading, taking both of them with it until…

…Risen was gone.

* * *

A girl, pale as the coldest winter sky, knelt on the frozen earth, her arms around a young warrior. Only one of them breathed. Only one heart beat.

The frosty wind blew across Niveus' face, and strands of her hair lifted and fell in cold compliance, screening prying eyes from the sad affair.

She gazed only at him. He was beautiful, hair black as a midnight wish, long, thick lashes resting so softly on his cheeks, the corner of his lips barely turned up as though he had a wondrous secret to share. At first, she believed her brother had shed a tear, for one lay glistening like a translucent pearl on his cheek. Then, she realized…it was her own.

The audience sat unmoving, fixed on the tragic scene, grim expectation in their hearts. Not a word was spoken, not a sound uttered, until the peculiar girl—Red Robes' queen—lifted her chin, turned her face to the sky, and broke the still with a single cry, mournful as a dying dove.

* * *

Nicolette's horse halted, and behind her, so did an army of eight hundred. They had been pushing toward Prussia with a drive very near desperation for some time and were scarcely a day's ride away.

"My lady, what is it?" the captain at her flank asked with some urgency.

She said nothing, only peered overhead at the bare entanglement of tree limbs and the crystal blue sky beyond. Suddenly, from seemingly nowhere, a pair of doves took flight, swept across the blue expanse, and in a slowly widening circle, flew up and up, until they disappeared.

All the while, the army waited with silent, bewildered respect.

Still, Nicolette only looked up, as though watching something very dear to her...*leave.*

Finally, she dropped her head, her grief-stricken face as foreboding as a first winter's snow. She swallowed, said nothing, and...the horse moved on.

CHAPTER THIRTY-SIX

†

A sweeping confusion shoved Malik's victorious optimism aside. Ravan's son did not move, not at all....

But why? Why was there no resurrection, no marveling in awe-stricken wonder by the crowd? The guards dragged Niveus from her brother's side, her head dropped in defeat, silk-slippered toes dragging across the frozen ground.

"Bring her to me!" Malik ordered but was interrupted when trumpets sounded from the battlements. *Confound the sentries! This is no time for distraction!* Before anything, he must discover why Niveus failed. He could not risk, no...would not accept that she would not perform!

The trumpets sounded again—this time, not three, not four, but five long blasts. That was finally enough to draw Malik from his own egocentricity, for it meant only one thing—an *invasion*.

As though mocking his dawning awareness, the gates on the far side of the arena crashed open and a rider, horse lathered and heaving, charged up to in front of Malik before skidding to a halt. The beast, sides raked and bloody from the rider's spurs, dropped its head in grateful reprieve.

"An army, my Lord! Half a day's ride out," the rider shouted.

"Who? How many?"

Malik grasped the gilded railing in front of him and leaned forward, his face twisting in outrage.

"At least three hundred, your grace; a third mounted, the rest cavalry. And...and it is your kin, my lord." The man cleared his throat.

"My kin?" Malik's astonishment was complete. It was not possible! Klarin was dead, buried by Bora's own hand in a shallow grave!

"Yes, my lord. 'Tis Lord Viktar who leads, with three commanders at his side."

It was as though the ghost of the dead warrior who still lay on the battlefield struck Malik, for he pitched forward, nearly falling over the railing. Only the quick reflexes of a nearby guard grasping him by his arm prevented it.

Malik's greatest disbelief was that Viktar had not only escaped to his mother's realm, but also returned so swiftly with a show of force. But why? Surely he could not believe Niveus would go with him…or know anything about the unborn child!

Malik shook the guard's hand free of his elbow. All of it was of no consequence! Niveus was *his* now, by law if nothing else, and no one but he would ever know of the bastard child, for he intended to kill it!

What Malik neglected to consider, as these thoughts assaulted him in maniacal sequence, was *who* the three commanders were who rode at Viktar's side. There was no way he could know that they were Velecent, Salvatore, and…

…*Ravan.*

He slammed his fist on the railing and screamed, "My council! Assemble them at once!" His face darkened with malice. "But first…bring *Niveus* to me."

* * *

Dismissing his servants, Malik paced his room like a tormented beast. Stalking and frenzied, he whirled about only when the walls forbade he advance farther. All the while, he tore at his beard, drawing what was left to a malevolent point as he spoke aloud his vexations.

Curiously, it was not so much the threat of the advancing army as it was his tenuous hold on Niveus that unhinged him most. His agitation had such a firm grasp on him that he did not hear his ghost-bride slip into the room behind him.

Finally catching a glimpse of her from the corner of his eye—a phantom lingering in the shadows—he set upon her, his voice rising to an awful wail. "He died! You could have saved him, but you let him die!"

Utterly composed, Niveus circled away, her ruined slippers padding deliberately on the stone floor. Filth-streaked tears were already dried, marring the porcelain of her face like ashen veins.

"I could not save him," she said, her composure strangely cold.

"Lies! You saved Viktar! I watched—*saw* it. His injury was more mortal than your brother's!" Malik slashed at the air with both fists.

Niveus stepped nearer. "What does it matter, my lord, for I have rethought my destiny. Viktar abandoned me; you are my husband. One can only deny the gods' wishes for so long."

Malik stared in mute disbelief.

She smiled—a peculiar smile. "I've decided...I wish to stay with you and bring my child forth as your son. Otherwise, he will be a bastard, and...what is the purpose in that?"

Now she faced him, hands raised in appeal. "It is the only reasonable path and would yield stability, and an heir, to your...*our* realm."

Stepping aside enough that Malik could not see her face, she murmured, "I love my brother, but I fear he was an obstacle. Now, with him dead, no one else knows of my whereabouts, and...no one needs to know."

Malik dropped his hands limply to his sides. "Yes! That is the all of it! And as it should be! You are my wife—queen of a very powerful domain. It is me you should serve, and no one else!"

What Malik neglected to disclose was that Viktar's army was fast approaching and that he intended to destroy every last one of them. Before this chapter was ended, he would burn Viktar alive, an example of what would happen if he were ever again challenged. And with that, evidence of his nephew's existence would be erased forever. He would fortify Red Robes by annexing Klarin's estate, and perhaps invade Poland next year.

"I understand you are going to battle," Niveus murmured as though reading his thoughts, her back to Malik.

Sidling up behind her, he planted meaty fists heavily on her shoulders, and dropped his lips to her neck. "It is only a distraction, my love. Nothing to concern yourself with. But I shall be engaged for a short while, a few days at best."

He allowed his tongue to taste the salt of her tear-stained cheek.

"I wish you to stay safe in the castle, until it is finished. You will be guarded, but I will not lock the door. You are free to move about, with escort, of course."

He allowed his tongue to run from her ear down the delicate slope of her jaw, and went to kiss her neck.

She leaned away. "My lord, I ask for my brother's body, for I wish to prepare it for eternal rest."

Malik gritted his teeth and shook his head in stubborn agreement. "Of course; how insensitive of me. You must be grieving, and I have neglected your needs. Forgive me, my love."

He clapped his hands together, calling for his attendants.

"Take her to her room. Bring her brother's body, and see to it she has whatever she requires to...to dispose of him." He dragged a finger softly down the length of her arm. "We will resume our lives when all of this *misfortune* has been put aside."

Shortly, Malik strode into his conference chambers. His commanders were already engaged in heated debate, all of them speaking back and forth across a long table at once. Bora Vachir, battle-beaten, limping, and wearing his armor *outside* of his tunic, led the assembly, strategizing their preemptive strike in great detail.

They finally decided that Red Robes would intercept the invaders northwest of the castle grounds, in the greatest expanse of the peasants' fields. Their attack would spring in two waves. The first would be infantry with pike, a sacrificial battalion to take the wind from them. Then a following surge of mounted soldiers with melee weapons—their best warriors—would deal the killing blow. On such short notice, Bora was certain it was the best strategy, for even as fatigued as their forces were from the three-year war with Poland, they still had the raw numbers to defeat Viktar's army.

Malik listened, but didn't hear. His thoughts were occupied, instead, with his bride. Knowing Red Robes carried the greater advantage, his complacency was, as always, more abundant than lies in a whore's bed. Besides, with Vachir at the helm, he had no doubt they would roll a blanket of death over his nephew like a boot over an insect.

Malik had fought alongside Bora Vachir enough to know what to expect. The campaign would be swift and pitiless; bodies would sway, spitted and twitching, like the long arm of a stalled timepiece, and Red Robes would live up to its namesake once again.

Even as the final particulars were drawn up, the infantry were already readying themselves so that they might be in position before nightfall. Bora said he anticipated the enemy would strike at first light, which was to their own advantage, for the rising sun would be in Viktar's eyes if the weather held and the battle was a prolonged one.

Malik's one proviso was that Viktar was not to be killed. *He* wished to gut and then burn his nephew...himself.

* * *

"You are weak! To indulge her so!" Bora Vachir opposed Malik's decision to grant Niveus' wish, to allow her brother's body to be brought to her room.

"I will allow her this final concession," Malik snorted. "Give her the corpse. What do I care, for tomorrow I will drag it to the wolves."

He laughed, a maniacal burst that ended as swiftly as it began. One by one his enemies were falling—Klarin, Risen, and tomorrow…Viktar.

* * *

Two men carried Risen's body up the steep, winding staircase. Up, up they went until they reached the highest tower and…Niveus' room. After they laid the corpse on the stone table, as though it were a funeral slab, Aya, carrying Risen's bloodied battle sword across both palms as though it were a sacrifice, reached up and laid it gently upon his unmoving chest.

"Leave," Niveus commanded everyone, even Aya.

"I would build the fire first," insisted a guard, a stocky fellow with thinning hair, thick hands, and kind eyes. Over the last several weeks, this particular guard had come to revere the sorrowful girl who had appeared so mysteriously in Malik's realm.

"No," Niveus murmured. "It is not necessary."

He lingered in the doorway, but finally backed away and closed the door. She knew the man would stand watch for the rest of the night, for her sake alone; not just because Malik had issued the order.

At last, Niveus was left alone with her brother. She appeared as though she were a solitary angel standing vigil over some strange, tragic wake.

Opening the balcony doors, she first invited the wintry night to join them, and with the sky so clear, it was a bitter, beautiful cold that swept in. The stars twinkled bright against the velvety, black blanket of sky, and beyond, a moon peeked, barely above the treetops as though to say, *Wait. I am here, I am coming to you.*

Niveus did not light the fire, nor did she light the candles, for the starlight and gently rising moon were all the light she required for what she must do. Circling the table, she reached, removing the battle blade from where it rest on Risen's chest, and cast it aside. It was no longer part of what defined her brother.

She murmured, soft words that her brother had not heard before, words only her mother would know. Next, she drew a hand towel through the basin of warm water Aya had left, and swept it gently across his wounds, cleaning the blood from the dog's vicious bite and the saber cut on his hand. As she washed the blood and grime from Risen's face, she paused, considering how kind and beautiful he was, especially as he appeared only to be sleeping.

But this was an eternal sleep, not to be denied, and so she pressed on.

In Risen's boot lay his knife—*Monster-Killer*. Niveus knew this was where he kept it and retrieved it. Slicing at the heavy lacings, she cut and pulled the battle leathers from his body, depositing them in a small heap onto the bed. They, like the sword, were forevermore inconsequential.

Now that her brother lay in only his tunic, trousers, and boots, she tipped her head to the side. When they were only children, this was how he always dressed. She recalled how often he had appeared at her door, trying to coax her from her eternal realm of solitude. She had never joined him, and eventually, he no longer asked.

Even so, he had always peeked in on her before leaving, "just because" he had said. "I'm going to the woods again. Are you sure you don't want to come with me?" he would ask. She would look at him with eyes pink as a blushing sunrise; he never once told her how beautiful he thought they were, when others believed them ugly. He had never needed to.

Niveus passed the damp rag one last time over his brow and across his cold lips. Then, when everything was in place just as it should be, she crawled onto the stone table and lay down beside her brother, her cool fingers laced into his cold ones.

Finally, laying her head gently above her brother's silent heart, Niveus gazed out the open doors at the night sky. She appeared as unmoving as he, and they remained like this for the rest of the night.

When morning was but a whisper against the final, blue hour, Niveus lifted her head, moved to the door, and lay her hand against the wood. Outside, the guard with the kind eyes was taken softly by a notion that he must descend the stairs—that something of grave importance awaited him there.

When he was gone, Niveus…

…lit the room on fire.

CHAPTER THIRTY-SEVEN

"We will hold the front with a hundred—our best warriors. You…" Ravan pointed at Velecent, Salvatore, and Viktar, "…will be amongst them."

"I cannot ask you to stand the front. My army is outnumbered by nearly double." Viktar shook his head.

"I fight for my daughter, but we, *all* of us, fight for the oppressed people of this cursed realm." Salvatore and Velecent nodded quiet agreement as Ravan explained further. "Our archers will have already moved to either side, along the tree line." He motioned with two fingers into the distance.

A growing optimism captured Viktar's face, made bright by a nearly full moon's light. He nodded as Ravan continued, scratching their strategy into the frosty earth with a twig.

"Malik will advance north and west, up along the greatest stretch of fallow ground…here." Ravan stabbed the stick at the ground.

"How do you know this?" Viktar asked.

Velecent bumped him gently, shoulder to shoulder, as the two men crouched side by side. "If he says it is so, it is so."

Salvatore grinned, his white teeth brilliant even in the darkness. "He said he would hurt me if I tried to kiss his wife again. I fairly well believe he would…and *could*."

Ravan shot him a wry look before going on. "We've allowed their scouts to discover our position on purpose. Not only do they believe they know the size of our army but also the direction of our attack."

Leaning in, Velecent agreed heartily. "Yes! Complacency is a fool's conviction. We've added to our numbers one third again because our enemy suffers that thought."

"So we're now four hundred to their six hundred?" Salvatore could not help but point out the obvious.

Ravan pressed on. "At first light, just before we engage their front line, the archers will fire, felling a share of them before drawing some into the trees. Once they've exhausted themselves, those who remain will join us for a charge onto the battlefield."

"But that leaves nearly one hundred of our men unaccounted for," Salvatore pointed out.

Ravan's jaw muscles tightened. "Two hours before daylight, those hundred will split and move to a position past the archers, nearly to the river. They will stand firm until they see our archers move onto the field. By then, Malik will have deployed a second wave, his stronger rush. It is then that these one hundred will drive lateral from the flanks and draw them back on themselves. It will give us more time to reduce their numbers on the front and simultaneously close the window of retreat." He snapped the twig and tossed it to the ground.

Viktar's face brightened. "It is good. We are outnumbered, but my uncle will not anticipate such a strategy."

"And what of Bora Vachir?" Salvatore asked.

"You know of him?" Viktar's expression was suddenly more serious.

"We've heard something of him." Ravan scowled, recalling the Polish king's description of the Mongol.

Viktar shrugged. "The man is truly evil, fights with a blood-lust like no other. But he does not have this…" He gently thumped his chest with his fist, over his heart. "Vachir believes he holds the greater army, so he will advance first, try to meet us early and capture the element of control."

"Good." Ravan nodded from one to the next. "That is exactly what we want him to do. Now, talk to our men. Don't speak of the size of Malik's army to them—this strategy will help pull the battle more even."

"And is there another strategy, to possibly pull it *more*?" Salvatore wondered.

Ravan considered them all, huddled about him, possessing such beautiful conviction and ready to sacrifice for the greater cause.

He was suddenly stricken with the inexplicable notion that he—possibly the most solitary creature ever—had gathered about himself men worthy to be called friends.

And these were friends worth dying for. Even if Risen and Niveus were not part of it all, he would fight and, if need be, die for any of them. The sudden, stabbing memory of another long-gone friend—a giant—pulled at him, and a whimsical smile tugged at his lips.

Ravan pushed himself to his feet. Tomorrow, he would stand with these men as though he were once more facing battle alongside LanCoste.

His jaw hardened. "We *lead*. We step forward first and fight with the heart of one who has everything to gain by a good death. That is how we herald that fearlessness to our warriors. *That*...is how you slay titans."

* * *

Dawn threatened, the pinpoint treetops running black and jagged as a wild hog's back along the horizon. Ravan blinked to clear his vision from staring so long at the wide, seemingly endless expanse of field. A single bird chirped, the first brave voice of dawn.

Two things gathered the mercenary's attention straight up. First, in the distance, a slow movement of hunched-over soldiers—Malik's first assault—pressed into the field. Second, and more gravely, just above the tree line, a barely visible thread of grey-white smoke snaked upward like a serpent, marking just about where the castle...and his son and daughter...would be.

* * *

As the darkness lifted, the open field that stretched in front of Malik roiled with a shadowy fog like steam lifting from a hot cup of broth. It was difficult to tell where the earth ended and the air began.

He took a deep breath and exhaled. That's when he noticed it—a ghost legion appearing on the far end of the great expanse, not stepping from woods but just as though suddenly there.

Malik blinked again, not at all certain the shadow-army was real, but when Bora Vachir pulled the visor down on his helmet, he followed in kind. The slots in his face-shield brought his distance sight into greater focus, and he drew in a sharp breath at what he saw.

There, in the forefront of the distant army, rode his nephew, his battle tunic a resplendent black against the polished bronze of his chainmaille. He could not know that this was because Ravan had insisted it be so. "...black, so your enemy does not see you bleed."

Bora Vachir, still suffering from the thrashing Risen had given him, sat his horse heavily.

Malik heard him yell, "It is a good day to kill!" and watched the Mongol lope cautiously along in front of his troops, rallying them for the first strike. His own horse stepped in place, champing at the bit.

His attention was drawn back to across the field.

He watched intently as Viktar circled, battle-sword raised high above his head in an attempt to rally his troops. What he failed to notice were the three men who rode beside him.

As the black curtain of hatred blotted everything else from Malik's sight, he scarcely heard Bora Vachir's battle cry, scarcely noticed the surge of warriors gallop past him and across the field. All he wanted, all he was driven to do, was to smite only *one*—cruelly, mortally, and to the very core of his being. He vowed that he would hold Viktar's still-beating heart in his hands before this battle was through, and then he would burn it and send it to hell.

With a fiendish yell, Malik sank his spurs into the ribs of his steed and charged the field.

* * *

Dawn was upon them, but there would be no blinding sunlight this morning. It was overcast, densely foggy, and bitterly cold. Viktar held his hand up, signaling for his men to hold as, in the distance, the greater half of Malik's army, nearly three hundred in the first wave, ran—swords and pike staffs held high—across the frozen expanse.

He could hear Bora Vachir scream a bloody howl as the barbarian charged with sword raised high. And he saw the horde surge after him. It was a terrifying thing to behold as Malik's forces advanced, nearly two hundred on foot followed by at least that many mounted.

Viktar glanced sideways, saw Ravan hold an arm out, hand held down. It was awe-inspiring, how the mercenary motioned and called, "Steady! Steady, men!" as he thundered up and down the ranks. Viktar was amazed at how composed he seemed. Viktar could scarcely keep his seat as his horse leapt, stopped, and leapt again.

Still, Malik's army rushed their charge, and the earth began to tremble beneath them.

Finally, just about when Viktar believed Ravan had been wrong and they were destined for slaughter, about half way across the field...something happened.

Men and horses randomly fell, as though gravity were suddenly too much for them to endure. Beasts tripped over their fallen comrades, men and horses' necks snapped alike. Some ran headlong into those in front of them who had stopped too fast. Chaos ensued until someone amidst the maelstrom circled, gesturing frantically toward the woods.

Viktar watched as Bora Vachir sawed on the reins of his steed, dragging it to a sliding stop. That was when he first noticed an arrow. It streamed past Bora's helmet so near that he was certain the Mongol must have heard the whistle of the fletching through the frozen air.

"The woods!" Bora screamed. "Archers in the woods!" He motioned with his drawn blade at the forest, stabbing in the direction he intended his army to attack.

Still, Viktar held his ground, waiting for Ravan's signal. For the next few moments, Malik's army only mulled about, uncertain whether to charge farther down the field or engage the unseen archers from either side of them. There was only one thing for certain—if they stayed put, their advantage would be swiftly whittled away.

As planned, by the time a group of the enemy broke off either side to ferret out the archers, it left a much more loosely committed core. Viktar watched as his tyrant uncle tried to rally his men with shouted promises of accolades and immortal fame. Bora, meanwhile was demanding a tighter formation for those men who remained on the field.

They were almost, but not quite, organized. *That*...was when Ravan's arm fell.

* * *

"Now!" Ravan charged and sent his steed lunging forward.

Velecent and Salvatore bolted right behind him.

Viktar's horse, ears pinned, leapt forward of its own accord as its rider let go a battle cry of his own.

Then, like one great, living beast, Klarin's army followed, surging forward to meet Malik's on the battlefield.

When they plowed into Malik's forces, it was something akin to a tsunami-wave crashing against a cliff. The two hordes became an instant mass of jumbled flesh, horses kicking and screaming, men dodging, thrusting and swinging their weapons and crying out as they fell or were felled.

Viktar's army fought brilliantly. Even though they were not Ravan's legion, these men were courageous and willing, greatly inspired by those who led them, just as Ravan said it would be. And they listened, following orders as Ravan told them to surge, hold, fall back, or break to one side.

On the battle raged, but it seemed to Viktar only moments before Malik's second, stronger infantry appeared on the rear line of the skirmish, prepared to deal much more damage to the fiercely defiant but still outnumbered challengers.

His heart fell as he watched Malik's second wave of men, dressed in the red tunics of the Red Robe's realm, surge fresh upon the field.

But then, just as Ravan said it would be, another swell of men appeared from the woods flanking the enemy from either side.

These men wore Viktar's black, and they ran with spears and swords lifted high in willful defiance, their howls dreadful in the thin air, just as Ravan had instructed they be. Like hungry wolves, they attacked and flayed at the haunch of the foe.

This turned half of the second wave about, and as Malik's men circled back on themselves, it added yet another element of confusion to the madness.

Now, it became each man's fortune or fate to fight for himself and live...or die.

* * *

Ravan drew his blade from yet another, allowing the soldier to fall aside. Forever scanning the fray, he searched for those enemies who might deal the greatest damage, focusing next on them. As he maneuvered deeper into the battle, he did what he did best, dropping the opposition one by one, like icebergs calving from a glacier.

Then, he saw...

Salvatore, unhorsed and on foot, valiantly held two men at bay. He swung his battle sword—the one that had belonged to his father—as though he were defending the wind's right to roll across the sea. Backward the Spaniard moved, parrying, deflecting, stepping over one, two, three bodies as though over the coiled ropes on the decks of his beloved White Witch.

One of his attackers fell to his blade, but then, as Salvatore staggered backward over yet another fallen soldier, *this* corpse was not yet undone. Ravan watched in horror as an arm came abruptly to life, snaked out, and snatched at Salvatore's boot....

"No!" Ravan called as he saw his friend go down, saw a nearby barbarian lift a wicked blade with both hands and lean from his horse to stab downward. With another cry, Ravan plunged his horse forward, crashing into and driving the barbarian, and his horse, clean off their feet and away from Salvatore.

Ravan's horse stumbled, and he was thrown from his mount, hitting the ground hard. A stabbing pain ripped through his left shoulder, and he moved to shove himself up off the ground only to discover the shoulder broken and his arm useless. With a groan he twisted about and used his sword to push himself up.

Then, stumbling to his friend's side, he abandoned his attack, dropped to one knee, and laid a hand on the Spaniard's chest.

Salvatore still breathed, but his eyes were closed, and...he did not move.

From the corner of his eye, Ravan caught a sudden movement. The Mongol barbarian approached, limping, a wickedly curved blade—the one that had impaled Salvatore—raised with both hands.

Ducking and lifting his sword in short reply, Ravan met the Mongol's scimitar with a deafening crash of metal against metal. The Mongol's blade snapped with a dull crack, the bulk of it broken away by the mercenary's remarkable sword and the strength and brilliance with which Ravan wielded it...single-handed.

The Mongol fell away, but not before Ravan pushed to near standing. He roared, and with another reaching, sideways blow, he swept the Damascus sword and severed the Mongol's arm.

Then, with as much deliberation as he had ever possessed, Ravan stepped up to his full height, his left arm dangling, worthless, and stood face to face...with *Bora Vachir.*

* * *

Bora stared first at his left arm, rather what was left of it. It was severed clean at the elbow. Then he stared at his right hand, still clutching the broken hilt of the scimitar blade—*his* blade. How easily this warrior had destroyed it! But how? His was a *mighty* sword—had decapitated many!

Thinking the blade suddenly defective, Vachir dropped what was left of the worthless weapon and pulled from his scabbard the other scimitar, raising it against the dark warrior who was just then rising from the muck.

The second notion to capture the Mongol's attention was of his worthless leg, for his hamstring was now completely severed. He hobbled backwards as the old wound—the one Risen had given him—tormented him. At last, he found his balance on his good leg, and turned to confront his enemy. One arm or not, he would have blood!

But then, sweeping the grime from his eyes...Bora faltered.

How casually *this* one swung his blade—how different *this* one made battle appear—so effortless and almost...*familiar.* His frown turned to dismay as the Mongol watched his foe pull loose his helmet and drop it to the ground.

No! What an evil trick this is!

Bora was immediately taken with the warrior's eyes, for they were a bottomless ebony, and he had seen them before.

Bora believed this man could see everything that he was made of and, more significantly, what he was *not*.

Ravan's expression twisted as though in mild confusion, and his voice rumbled—a throaty baritone. "*You*...have I not seen you before?" His grip tightened on the Damascus blade as dawning slowly settled about him. "Yes...I believe we have met before," the dark mercenary murmured as though to himself and swung the magnificent blade in a lazy loop with his only good hand.

The weapon seemed alive, as though it moved of its own will. Vachir's mouth dropped open, but no words escaped, for mute disbelief had a stranglehold about his throat.

He stumbled backwards, haunted by the wraith that had stepped from his past and come for him. "*Wait...*" he croaked and held both hands up in front of him.

How can it be? How can Ravan be here? Bora begged, "No...*please...*"

Ravan tipped his head casually to one side. "You...*you* are Bora Vachir."

"No," Bora gasped and tripped, falling hard to the frozen earth, his scimitar blade clattering from his hand. Holding both arms—what was left of them—plaintively up in front of his face, he screamed, "Wait!"

As he kicked away, he snatched up the shield of another fallen soldier, wrenching it from the grip of the not-quite-dead man to hold in front of himself. He wielded it in feeble resistance as he pleaded again, "*Stop!*"

With one crushing blow, Ravan knocked the shield from Bora Vachir's hand. Then, planting a boot on the writhing Mongol's chest, he lifted his right arm so that his elbow was crooked above his shoulder, his first two fingers directing the implicit accuracy of the path the Damascus sword would, *should* travel.

The blade hovered as though alive, begging to be released.

Grasping Ravan's boot with his hand and the stump of his other arm, Bora writhed and sputtered beneath the weight of his captor and gasped, "I-I have your *son*! Risen is my captive. If you do not free me, I will kill—"

Ravan stomped, choking the Mongol to silence.

"If you have my son...it will not be for long."

Then...Ravan's blade fell.

* * *

Velecent took up watch near Salvatore, fighting any who came near him in a valiant effort to keep his dying friend safe from further harm. It was all he could manage until shortly, Ravan was at his side, and the two men fought, back-to-back, in the center of the battlefield.

Meanwhile, distantly, Viktar was occupied of his own defenses and tiring. His troops were still outnumbered, and Malik's army, ruthlessly trained, seemed entirely unwilling to give up the fight. Victory would come at no easy cost, but Viktar told himself he would be the last to stand if it came to it.

He felled one, but was swiftly attacked by another, and another. Swinging hard, he was nearly upended by the brute force with which his blade connected. Desperately, with both hands and cutting himself in the process, he ran his sword up to the fuller of his opponent's blade, all the way to hilt. Swinging it about, he deftly captured the weapon, thrusting it point down into the ground. Then, Viktar brought his knee up hard, into the temple of his hunched-over foe.

As Viktar pivoted away, slipping his blade into the unfortunate man's back, he said another silent prayer—his thirteenth of the battle. *Peace be with you brother. If not here…then beyond.*

It broke the young Prussian's heart to see the carnage, the waste of all that need not be. He believed no creature craved annihilation as much as mankind, and it seemed the earth itself only thirsted for more blood. Sadly, man was all too willing to oblige it.

He pulled his sword from between the man's shoulder blades and lifted his weary head. Winded and with blood dripping from his hand, Viktar finally grasped the innate need to destroy. He did not embrace it but, unmistakably, he understood it, for just then, Viktar saw…*him.*

CHAPTER THIRTY-EIGHT

✝

Malik was at first unsure. *No.* This could not be! He blinked again. There, fifteen paces away, stood a man battle-worn and bleeding, but with the determination of a warrior in his eye. But it *was* Viktar.

Malik dragged his helmet from his head.

Viktar…did the same. "Where *is* she?"

Malik narrowed his line of sight on the man who had dared love Niveus, whose child lay within her. It seemed suddenly hard to draw a breath, and he rubbed a grimy gauntlet across his face.

Hatred—father of all evil, infant of all infected souls—stirred at the very center of Malik's heart. It raged, grabbing him by the belly and throat, clawing its way over his tongue and out his mouth.

Then, he roared—a pitiless, monstrous bellow. Retrieving a long pike from the field, he lunged.

Viktar feinted the wicked staff but received a glancing blow across his brow. He tripped, falling hard backward, and rolled heavily onto all fours, the air knocked briefly from him.

Malik had followed through too far on his charge, and was only just collecting himself by the time his nephew had clambered to his feet.

They circled one another.

"She doesn't even remember you. She pledges her love to me!" Malik spat.

"Say it all you wish. It will never make it true," Viktar replied easily, eyes never leaving those of the monster.

It was all that was needed to provoke Malik into another attack, but this time Viktar, younger and more agile, effectively parried the blow, sending his uncle careening past, and the fight ensued.

As wielding the heavier weapon took its toll on Malik, he panted heavily, setting himself up again. But his greater vulnerability came with his careless desperation, for hopelessness walked hand-in-hand with his hatred.

Spinning the staff about, Malik stabbed, retreated, and stabbed again. Viktar countered each blow, chips of wood flying as his blade deflected the spear.

Groaning, Malik swung the spear with arms outstretched, side-swiping across Viktar's head, but the younger man dodged, leaning and arcing backward. The spear passed scarcely an inch above Viktar's face.

As Malik staggered by, he could not know to what extraordinary degree Viktar pulled every thread of his being to counter him. Swinging, reaching with one arm, the younger landed a glancing blow.

At first, Malik believed himself barely wounded. The blow came beneath his chainmaille, through his lacings under his shoulder, and along his ribs and the inside of his arm—a smarting burn that pulsed, tugging in a queer way at his throat. It was not until he felt something running sticky and warm down his side that the wound confirmed otherwise.

Both men paused, noticing the steady drip-drip from Malik's fingertips onto the frosty, boot-scuffed earth. Malik lifted his bloodied hand and peered through red fingers as though through Hell's prison, drawing his stunned gaze beyond to that of his nephew.

"Uncle...it's finished. Lay your sword down and take a knee." Viktar remained unmoving, sword at ease. When Malik only stared blindly, he added, "Let not your hatred of me necessitate the fall of even one more man. Call off the battle."

The moment hung suspended as the battle raged on about them—the two men standing face-to-face, the benevolent grace of the one opposite the baleful abomination of the other.

Malik began to tremble, not as yet from the injury, but from something else, something altogether toxic. His face contorted with rage born of bitter realization, for he wanted something he could not even comprehend.

The tyrant ruler of Red Robes—cruel diviner of anything he had ever desired—all at once wanted more than anything what *Viktar* had. But he had not an inkling of what that even was, for Malik could not recognize *compassion*.

He flung the blood from his fingertips, despising his nephew for his own confusion, hatred spewing from his mouth in one long, loathsome roar as he lifted clenched fists.

Everything, however, was just then deafened by something else, something extraordinary...and growing.

* * *

Time was forced to a standstill; men of both sides stopped their fighting, arms still suspended, shields up, blades dripping. The peculiar, paralyzed battlefield was made even more bizarre by the slowly increasing rumble that caused the ground to quiver beneath them as though it would suddenly open its throat wide and swallow them up.

All could not help but turn to the west and observe, galloping from the dense thicket of woods, a sorceress with hair black as pitch. Her robes swept about her like great wings. It appeared so curious that a single rider, extraordinary though she was, could cause the earth to tremble so.

Everything was soon made apparent, however, when from the mist behind her, an army over eight hundred strong emerged like a rising black wall.

As Nicolette and her force advanced, the battle turned. With the crushing wave of greater strength, some of Malik's men fought to their deaths while others ran to the trees. All, however, eventually took a knee.

More curious, however, was that Malik was abruptly gone. Having snatched up a riderless horse, he had fled, back toward the castle.

Viktar lunged after him, but there was not another horse nearby to catch and give chase. Looking furtively about, he called to an approaching horse and was taken totally by surprise when the rider—a woman on a grey horse—ignored him and charged past.

* * *

The pounding of the horse's hooves made it feel as though his brain sagged in his skull, and his tongue felt numb and too thick for his mouth. Malik's altogether state of wretchedness was made even more woeful by the vortex of black and grey smoke shooting up from Red Robes' castle.

"Burn the bridge!" he screamed to a confused lot of his men as he galloped across the canal to the village. Yanking weakly at the horse's reins, he finally dragged it to a standstill. "*Why* is my castle on fire?"

"'Tis your bride!" a soldier exclaimed. "Her room—it caught fire!"

For a long moment, all Malik could do was stare dully at the bleak inferno that his kingdom was swiftly becoming. But more horrible was the thought of losing Niveus, or more accurately, losing what Niveus could *do* for him.

The distant thunder of a galloping horse drew Malik's attention behind him. He twisted about to look over his shoulder. There, across the field, came Nicolette, soaring as though flying, only now she was not as she appeared in a

Mediterranean garden behind a bladesmith's cottage in Crete. Today, Malik was nearly crippled by the presence of her, for he scarcely recognized her. He had never seen Nicolette as death come to call.

He pointed and screamed at his men, "Kill her! Kill her!"

Then he galloped his horse toward the castle. Shortly, he stormed across the drawbridge and through the portcullis into the open courtyard, which was awash with smoke and falling cinder.

"Where is she? Where is she!" he demanded of the first servant he saw.

"The sanctuary, my lord! She is safe—secured in the sanctuary!" The terrified man held his arms over his head so that falling ash would not light his hair afire.

Everywhere, servants and staff were dashing, some already ablaze, others ridiculously carrying what few relics and riches they could from the calamity. It was truly remarkable how swiftly the blaze appeared bent on destroying everything. Even stone and mortar fell in chunks around them like heaven's holy blitz. Any who lingered would surely be entombed before long.

Malik swayed. The muddy, red streak running down the horse's foreleg was a grave indication of just how wounded he really was. He blinked, the epic failure about him now only a blur. No matter. All Malik needed was to reach Niveus. Then everything would be made right. He just had to make it to the sanctuary….

* * *

As the battle swiftly played out to its close, Ravan worked to extricate himself from it all. Nicolette, however, had already seen the one to be destroyed and charged on…after Malik.

She halted the horse on the near side of the bridge. It spanned nearly thirty meters across the Vistula canal, linking the mainland to the primary village and Malik's castle. And, the bridge was on fire.

The grey gelding she rode reared, unwilling to approach the flames even under the calming touch of her hand. The heavy timbers were swiftly becoming a curtain of blazing pitch, right about the center of the structure, and it would not be long before the arcing joists gave way and the bridge fell into the icy, slush-flow of the canal.

From the far side of the wall of fire along the embankment, guards held their position and foolishly taunted the strange maiden. Their lord had returned victorious from battle, or so they believed, and surely only because he had seen the smoke from the inferno.

But there was still killing to be done, and the death of the niggling woman on the other side of the bridge was now their happy task. The men were of good spirit for, having been left to tend the final front, they had escaped the greater risk of battle. Now their boring morning was just becoming very interesting.

"Come here, bitch!" one guard motioned through the blaze.

"Yeah, get up here! We'll douse the flames, just for you!" another called and grabbed himself by the crotch, squatting and yanking.

Their jests halted, however, when Nicolette stepped down from the horse and freed it. Away it galloped, along the frozen river's edge.

Then, Risen's mother...walked onto the bridge

* * *

The dark, torched emeralds that were Nicolette's eyes were the first thing to change. The color drained from them like water from a funnel as she stepped slowly, deliberately, toward the blaze. As she walked, her chin dropped and she peered at them from beneath her brow, her arms lifting, fingertips meeting in front of her.

Drawing nearer and nearer to the fiery curtain, the lapping flames distorted her image, and the heat lifted her hair and skirts about her in a tempestuous veil.

She appeared as though she were rising from a blazing netherworld; and one by one, the guards fell mute, their jaws dropping nearly in unison. They had never seen one such as this, had not noticed when she was farther away how pale she was, like...like *Niveus*.

The witch's lips were moving, but at first no sound was uttered. Then, an unfamiliar language ushered from her. All the color was leached from her eyes; instead, orbs of crystal, clear as any diamond ever cut, shone brightly. And the words—those unintelligible strings of syllables—were more urgent than before.

Still, the men did not move, for between them and the witch remained the sheltering wall of fire.

Nicolette's hands parted, arms extended to either side, level with her shoulders, and her chin snapped upward, toward the sky. The men took one simultaneous step backward as she abruptly clapped her hands together, in front of her.

As her hands struck, a loud, crashing boom and gust of wind, not unlike a lightning strike, separated the thickening wall of fire.

All of the men stepped back, one of them tripping and somersaulting down the short embankment behind him.

Nicolette, crystal gaze set on the rest, stepped unscathed onto and over the charred remains of the bridge. Behind her, the smoldering timbers finally gave way, tumbling out of view just short of her step, but she moved as though not even noticing.

Back, back the men scrambled, all except a small handful. These few struggled to load their crossbows, but not before Nicolette, fingers bent queerly like so many claws, shoved her hands, one and then the other, toward them.

Down several of the men went, hurled backward off the embankment to join their compatriots. Those few who remained standing swung their bows wildly about, trying in vain to center their aim on the mysterious woman who had removed nearly every ounce of courage from them in less than a minute.

Two more sweeps of her arm, head tipped and face still turned blankly to the sky, and the remaining men were unhinged as though a gale had leveled them. Down they went, and were not seen to rise as the witch's eyes returned to green and she walked through them...and beyond.

* * *

Malik slid from the horse and limped across the flat stone steps, through the grotto, past the very spot where he had killed his wives, and up to the cloistered, stone façade of the sanctuary. In truth, he had never spent much time here other than the beheadings.

Two guards kept a nervous watch of the door. One offered right away, "She is safe, my lord, sheltered within."

Leaving a trail of blood droplets, Malik lurched and stumbled into the sanctuary.

* * *

The room was cold, and the few candles that burned on short stubs made the space seem even more morose.

Niveus edged closer to the altar and lifted her chin. Her gown, the same one she had worn to the terrible tournament, was stained with her brother's blood, and her face was smudged with ash.

Her eyes, however, were the most sublime rose they had ever been. Risen...would have thought them perfect.

She had not been dragged from the burning tower. No, she had slowly descended the spiraling steps of her own volition, not looking back as her brother's funeral pyre grew to a blazing elegy high above.

It was not until she stepped onto the ground floor that anyone even noticed her. Then, of course, she was whisked away to the sanctuary, *for her safety*.

Now, it was not the altar that drew Niveus' attention. It was the jagged cut, colored glass that was framed beyond. Even gray as the day was, the light came through it in a beautiful way, casting a rainbow of color upon the white flesh of her hands as she held them out, turning them slowly over. One of the colors was more beautiful than the rest, golden as the purest honey, amber as...Viktar's eyes.

As though consideration of the beauty was no longer allowed, Niveus turned about and let free a long breath. Casting her gaze down, she stared long at the blade—*Risen's* blade—*Monster-Killer* that lay in her hands. Then, she slipped it behind her as...

...Malik stumbled through the door.

* * *

Ravan and Viktar came to the bridge just as Nicolette crossed, just as the smoldering timbers fell behind her. They watched as the bridge crashed, crackling and sizzling, sending up a wall of ashen steam from the river. When the scorched haze cleared, she was gone, lost in the chaos of the whipped soldiers and blazing castle. And they were left behind...with no way to know where she had gone.

* * *

The enchantress moved swiftly and with single-minded intent, seeking only that which drew her—seeking *Niveus*. As Nicolette moved across the burning courtyard of the castle, she scarcely noticed the vile form of another moving within a darkened archway's shadows.

Raising a crooked staff above his head, the mage stepped from the dark, lips curled back in a toothless snarl. He smoldered from cinders, which had attached to his robes, and began to spout a chant and stab his staff at the dark witch come to call.

Nicolette paused, fixing a slow, hypnotic stare on the mage. Darkness swept her heart as she realized instantly *who* this was—knew without doubt what treachery the man had dispensed upon her son.

In the next instant, she cast one hand up and toward the sorcerer. Back the wicked man flew, his feeble carcass smashing against stone. Writhing about, he raised an arm over his head and shrieked as the wall behind him caved down, burying him alive.

Never to consider him again, Nicolette…walked on.

CHAPTER THIRTY-NINE

"Niveus…*wife*…I am injured," Malik gasped and dropped to his knees.

She remained unmoving, saying nothing, staring beyond him to the cloistered, shadowy archway of the entrance.

He groaned and reached a bloody hand toward her. "*Help* me, Niveus. I shall die if you do not."

Still, Niveus only stared, and her gaze was so exacting that Malik was forced to glance over his shoulder. Nothing…until he heard the soft *thud, thud* that was the unmistakable sound of bodies crumpling to the ground.

"*No…*" he whimpered as the black witch moved from the shadowed alcove of the door into the dimly-lit room. He kicked, scrambling like a bloody rat, but there was nowhere to go.

"No!" he cried again, hand raised and trembling as Nicolette's scrutiny fixed upon him.

Malik could not have recognized this figure as the woman he had so obscenely rutted for on a Mediterranean island. She raised one hand toward him, two fingers pointed, and dipped her head.

"Stop!"

Nicolette's head jerked harshly at the sound of her daughter's voice.

Niveus raised a hand limply. "No…Mother. He is my husband—mine to minister to. The choice is mine, not yours."

Malik jerked his head from Nicolette toward Niveus and back. He shrieked, clutching with one hand at his side while pointing with the other at his bride.

"She speaks the truth! She is my wife, lady of this realm and salvation of my soul!"

Nicolette considered her daughter, their eyes locked upon each other for a staggering, long moment.

"I *must* do this," Niveus said.

Casting her attention upon the vile creature that lay at her feet, Nicolette nodded…and backed away.

Niveus moved away from the altar, knelt beside her husband, and took him into her arms….

* * *

Niveus, unlike most, treasured the dark. In her silent way, she rejoiced in all the beauty of the night, for she knew it was those hours in between that offered the shedding of the bright cloak of judgment and discrimination. All the confusion that stirred of daylight was stripped away by the velvet blanket of the other hours.

But this was not a dark like that….

Never had Niveus invited her soul to step into a space such as this. To do so, she knew, would mean her death. And for the first time, she *feared* it—not her own death but the separation from someone she loved and…the loss of their unborn child.

Then, without hesitation, Niveus allowed herself to slip into that infernal beyond.

All about her was a black, sticky malignancy, devoid of any sense of beauty or compassion. She walked, looking for the pinpoint of light that would mark the wounded, reached for a hand that was not there.

"Here…I am *here*," she heard the creature croak.

She could not see it, neither could she sense a form…*yet*. There were only the twisting claws grasping at her ankles. When she stepped easily away from them, the form rose up—a lurching, splintered pillar—and towered directly in front of her.

Its horrid mouth opened, and shards of those things that comprised the beast fell from it like rotted teeth. Hatred, lust, arrogance, cruelty, vulgarity— on and on the aspects of evil poured from it until only a wretched, withered sound fell from it, begging…

"*Heal me.*"

"I will not."

"But…but you are mine! And you came…you are *here,* to do as I demand." Confusion wrapped about the miserable form, and it jerked bizarrely in place as though taken by a seizure.

"You do not belong in the world of the living," Niveus said, though not unkindly.

"You can't!" the monster shrieked. "You must obey me; I command it!"

It tried to lift what would be an arm, but the bulk of it broke away and fell to solid ground, shattering into a thousand quivering shards.

"Go," Niveus said softly and lifted a tender hand, pointing.

The creature scarcely twisted about, only enough to see, a short distance away, the sucking cavern that was opening up from apparently nothing. Within it shone a dim light, not of a good sort.

"I will not!" the creature shrieked again and lunged for her but was met by an unseen wall, for Niveus held a hand up, touching the monster's chest with only the tip of her finger.

"*Wha*...what—" the wretched beast began, its mouth opening and dropping so that its face became a long, gaping void with nothing more remaining but the hole and its eyes. These gruesome orbits stared at her finger, fixed so firmly on its chest, and snatched at it trying to rid itself of her hold.

"Go," Niveus repeated softly and pushed gently, as though releasing something.

There were no screams. There was only the mute gurgling of a beast as its feet were pulled from beneath it, and it was dragged to the edge of the sucking cavern and beyond.

Niveus watched until the abyss closed in on itself and disappeared, leaving a shimmering, oily slick in its wake. Then...

...she collapsed.

* * *

Malik, face drawn and mouth open in an eternal, silent scream, no longer stirred. From his chest protruded *Monster-Killer*.

Nicolette already had her daughter's limp body in her arms, for Niveus had not breathed once during the entire ordeal. She hastily took the pallid face of her daughter in both hands and lifted her lips to her own.

One, two, three breaths and Nicolette murmured, "*Reapinon, furnay, avaron.*" Another breath and...Niveus sucked in a long, tortured gulp of air. Then, she drew another, and another.

Nicolette smoothed her daughter's silken locks as the ashen grey of her lips faded and her eyes opened. "You're back," she murmured softly and stroked Niveus' cheek.

"Mother..." Niveus let go a sob.

A sad smile crossed Nicolette's lips. "*Shhh*...I have you. It is done."

Niveus' eyes filled with tears, and she reached up, wrapping her arms around her mother's neck, and let go another soft cry.

"Mother, he...he is gone."

Nicolette nodded. The grief they shared was not for the monster that lay dead on the stones beside them. Their sorrow was for another—a young man of light and beauty. She brushed a kiss against the cheek of the extraordinary girl. "It is as he wished. As...it should be."

Then, Risen's mother bowed her head...and wept.

* * *

Ravan and Viktar crossed the channel by boat and threaded their way through the strangely vacant village. A smoky haze distorted the tiny cottages, giving it an otherworldly effect while, in the near distance, the castle blazed like a mountainous furnace. At startling intervals, some of the stones became so hot they exploded, like cannon drums echoing the fall of a dying giant.

The two men were not even certain where to look and were just rounding a bend leading to the castle when Nicolette seemed to just appear from within the mantle of smoke...with Niveus. Mother and daughter clutched onto each other, both staggering as they limped along.

Seeing one another, the four battered souls just stopped, still fifty meters apart.

Viktar blinked, unbelieving, then dropped his sword and sprinted the distance to Niveus. Swinging her into his arms, he kissed her as though it were his last and promised, "My love, I will never again let you go."

* * *

Ravan staggered, not from his wounds but from the terrible weight of unknowing that balanced so precariously upon his shoulders. He swayed again with the uncertainty of it all. Here was the door, that final, last moment when he would *not* know, and on the other side...was truth.

He looked only at his love—at Nicolette's face, at her eyes...into her soul. And in that one instant...he *knew*. Risen was gone.

Then, despair snatched up the greatest warrior to ever live...

...and dashed him to his knees.

* * *

Salvatore lay unconscious, his normally brown skin a worrisome gray. Velecent knelt beside him, holding pressure on the wound. The good man had already lost so much blood, and Velecent grimly clenched his jaw. There was nothing to be done, and it would not be long now.

Beyond the sad scene, the castle's last wall fell with a mighty crash, finally succumbing to the maniacal demands of the fire. When Velecent's attention was drawn to the sound of it, he blinked, disbelieving at first as four friends appeared from the fog, limping over the small knoll. Velecent moved aside as Nicolette knelt at Salvatore's side.

They all watched as she drew the Spaniard's head onto her lap and murmured softly, "I have come, but the courage to stay...or leave, must come from within you."

Nicolette dropped her head and whispered more words—the kind only she and Niveus would understand. Then, her right hand went over Salvatore's chest, to where a wicked blade had severed his chainmaille and left a gaping, mortal wound.

With her other hand, she cradled Salvatore's head. Leaning near his face, she breathed a soft breath over one eye and then the other.

Finally, she brushed her lips to his....

* * *

For a long moment, there was nothing. The wind blew soft and mournful, a whisper of regret for those fallen, a sigh of hope for those who lived. For Salvatore, there was only a melancholy warmth, until...Nicolette stood beside him.

In the distance, an ocean more beautiful than any he had ever seen glistened, its tiny wave-caplets sparkling like jewels in the glorious light of a flawless, setting sun. Ships, more magnificent than even he could imagine, swept across the water as though engaged in a dance.

Salvatore could scarcely draw himself from the splendor of it all, except for the one who considered it alongside him.

"It is perfect," he breathed.

"It is."

He turned to her, his eyes dancing, his smile faultless. "You know what else is perfect, yes?"

She said nothing, only reached a hand up to touch his cheek.

The Spaniard smiled. "Your kiss. It could...any day...draw me from God's greatest sea."

Then…his lips brushed hers.

* * *

Salvatore's eyes flitted open. He peered blurrily left then right before seeming to notice Nicolette's lips upon his. The two remained like this, the kiss unbroken until…he closed his eyes again and lifted a hand to cradle it gently behind her head.

Nicolette abruptly broke the kiss.

The Spaniard coughed and sputtered, letting his hand fall limply to his side, then searched for and found Ravan's gaze. He shrugged sheepishly.

"*She* started it…"

But the weak smile vanished the moment Salvatore saw Ravan's eyes. He knew…knew unmistakably that one of their own—one of their best—was lost.

"Aaagh…" Salvatore grit his teeth, his vision blurring with grief, and he drew his arm across his eyes to hide his pain. He believed his own life was too small a victory and would have given it up that very moment if it would spare his friend what he suffered now.

CHAPTER FORTY

"I had him," Niveus said in a small voice. "His hand—it...it was in mine."

Ravan, cradling his worthless arm, only watched his feet, surprised that they even stepped one in front of the other as he walked with his daughter in the moonlight. Onward they crept through the simpering, ashen ruins of the fallen castle.

"Where?" Ravan finally found the strength to ask, and Niveus nodded to where the tower had been.

When they stopped, Ravan slipped his hand around his daughter's and swallowed, looking about himself for a long time. But no amount of time would ever raise his son from the smoldering grave.

"*She*—Sylvie—was there...with him," he said hoarsely.

Niveus only nodded.

"I'm glad you were with him too, to tell him..." Ravan collected himself with great difficulty, "...*goodbye*."

With nothing more to be said, Ravan knelt and took up a handful of still-warm ash.

* * *

As Ravan rode Alerion slowly through the village of Wintergrave, people—*his* people—stood in their doorways and leaned from their open shutters, their gazes inevitably falling to the ground. It was too painful to look upon the face of their grieving lord. They also mourned the loss of a son, *their* son, for that was who Risen was—beloved child of the realm.

Ravan, Nicolette, Salvatore, and Velecent approached the castle grounds, and the guards opened the gates wide for them, their faces etched with sorrow as they rode past. It was as though the entire realm breathed a sigh of despair, so great was their loss.

Sliding from Alerion's back, Ravan handed the reins to Leon. All the old stable master could manage was a nod before he led the stallion back to its familiar stall. For the second time, the great horse lost its master.

That evening, Ravan stood beside Nicolette as together they cast the ashes of their son across Sylvie's grave. An early spring rain began to gently fall—warm, soft tears for the beautiful one who walked here no more.

Later, Ravan looked wearily out upon the dusk that settled over his realm with a sad, comforting familiarity. He would never again see his son gallop Alerion across this land, waving to him from afar.

With a heavy heart, he turned from the window and laid Risen's blade on his bedside stand, beside his own. Peeling from his battle leathers, tunic, and trousers, he crawled beneath the blankets next to his beloved Nicolette. The dark mercenary believed he had never been so exhausted and was reminded of a day not unlike this one, years ago, when he had buried a brother—his *twin*. D'ata had looked so much like…

…Risen.

Ravan sighed heavily, as though he had held his breath his entire lifetime, and closed his eyes. He felt Nicolette stir beside him, felt her brush a gentle kiss against his cheek. Then, before sleep claimed him, she reached for him and drew his hand…onto her belly.

That night, he would dream of twins—a boy and a girl, both with raven-black hair and eyes…like his. The following November…

…he would hold them.

CHAPTER FORTY-ONE

†

Salvatore was finally ready to return home, back to the warm seas of the Mediterranean. His smile shone bright as it ever had as he and Ravan stepped onto the *White Witch*, and that night, they set sail together....

* * *

Days later, Ravan walked through a tiny, picturesque village, snaking his way along the narrow streets until he found a familiar little cottage on a dead-end street. He rapped on the door with his knuckles until a familiar face answered.

"Yes?"

The man's expression jumped from recognition to surprise to even greater surprise when from behind Ravan stepped a girl, meek and with eyes full of wonder, a crescent scar upon her cheek. She was bent with humility, still not able to grasp her new great fortune—that Niveus' father had liberated her. It would take time for her to familiarize herself with her brother, his family, her *freedom*. But today there was an excitement to her step that had not been there for a great long time.

Sayid froze, his stare fixed on the thin woman in the simple gown, peering meekly from behind Ravan's arm. Today, she wore no jewelry; no rouge reddened her lips; no kohl darkened her eyes. She was...*beautiful*.

"*Aya*..." was all Sayid could muster before choking on his words.

"Sayid!" she cried, tears running down her cheeks as she hurried to hug her brother for the first time in many years.

Behind them, Luchina held her hands to her mouth, tears welling and streaming down her face. Sayid held his sister at arm's length, inspecting the length of her before settling his gaze on Ravan.

"Thank you. *Thank* you...forever."

Sayid surprised Ravan when he moved to wrap his arms about him, but the mercenary allowed the simple gesture. Patting Sayid gently with one hand, for his shoulder was still mending, he held in his other a box about the size of a large melon, draped with canvas.

"You are welcome, my friend. A promise is a promise." Ravan gently pushed the Syrian away. "Here, for you to do with as you please." He pulled the canvas aside so that Sayid could see the nearly square wooden box.

"I-I'm not sure what to..." Sayid began, clearly confused. But then his voice trailed off. He glanced from the box to Ravan and back. "Is that...is *that—*"

"It is the head of Bora Vachir. Malik's general was your sister's captor. Neither will ever harm another. Aya's freedom is complete." Ravan said it with such casual authority that Sayid was left momentarily speechless.

Aya nodded, confirming that what Ravan said was true.

"I want it thrown away, somewhere no one will ever discover it," she said softly.

Sayid agreed. "Yes. Yes, as it pleases my sister. Let it and our memory of it vanish forever."

Ravan tipped his head. "As you wish."

Sayid, Luchina, and Aya bustled into the house, of course inviting Ravan and Salvatore to stay for as long as they wished.

"One moment. I'll be in shortly," Ravan said as everyone else filed in. Once they were inside, he pulled *Pig-Killer* from his boot and frowned, searching overhead.

There it was, the blood mark he had left on the door jamb so many months ago. *A promise is a promise.* He smiled a bitter smile and reached to chisel the mark away.

Then, Ravan dropped the blade into his boot and went inside. He and Salvatore spent a very pleasant evening with the Syrian family. They all drank sweet wine and talked about magnificent swords, ships, and friends.

Later, about the middle of the moonlit night, Ravan waded chest deep into the warm Mediterranean waters. Then, the sea-creatures that fed upon the girl—the one Gorlik dumped into that same harbor—feasted upon a dead Mongol's head.

EPILOGUE

Viktar was surprised and delighted when Niveus asked to remain in Red Robes, because, "…we belong here, for *them*." She swept with her hand, indicating the many vacant, abused faces that were left behind with the scorched legacy of the forsaken realm.

Klarin's landholdings, now Viktar's, became an extension of Red Robes, and the unified realm became a welcome ally to the King of Poland before the end of the year.

In Thorn, a splendid new castle began to rise from the ashes of the old—elegant and strong against the stunning backdrop of the Vistula River. More incredible than the castle, however, was the compassion the new lord and lady held toward all in their realm.

Peace had come at last, and the people murmured in awe about the strange visitor—the girl—who would sometimes visit when a suffering moment was too much to bear.

Per Viktar's request, Klarin was exhumed from her cruel slumber, and a proper burial was held for her—a lovely spot by the meadow so she could watch the new foals romp—something she had always loved.

There were two weddings late that spring. At the first, all of Wintergrave rejoiced as Moulin married Moira. The following month, Ravan gave his daughter's hand to a young man he was greatly pleased to call "son." And amongst the fragility of life, it was a time of great happiness for all.

That summer, Niveus planted wild peonies and roses—all of them red—about the grounds of Red Robes. Curiously, they required much attention as it seemed a number of rescued, orphaned deer nibbled away at them at their leisure. And it was not long before the villagers began to do the same, planting the red beauties along paths and in window boxes each spring in honor of their beloved Lady.

Before long, everyone forgot why the realm had first been labeled *Red Robes*. They believed it was, and always *had* been, for the beauty their lady—the one with the rose-colored eyes—had brought to their land.

And, as though the Earth agreed, the seasons became kinder, bringing a beautiful bounty, including…a boy with amber eyes and hair white as snow.

THE END

Also by Sharon Cramer...

The WINTERGRAVE CHRONICLES

The Execution
(Book One)

RISEN
(Book Two)

The Cerulean Star: LIBERTY

Marlow and the Monster

The Cougar Cub Tales

About the Author

Sharon Cramer is the author and illustrator of the award-winning, three picture book series, *Cougar Cub Tales*. She is also the author and illustrator of the Book of the Year Finalist, children's picture book, *Marlow and the Monster*, and is currently working on a new young adult series called *The Cerulean Star*.

Sharon's first novel, *THE EXECUTION*, is the first book of the *Wintergrave Chronicles,* followed by *RISEN* and *NIVEUS*.

Cramer lived throughout the United States before coming to Washington State. Long settled in the Pacific Northwest, she says she will stay, "...because I love how beautiful it is, and the crazy weather patterns lend themselves to creative writing."

It is in Spokane Valley, Washington that she lives and writes. She is married and has three grown sons.

You can connect with the author at...

www.SharonCramerBooks.com